CAUGHT IN A WEB

Joseph Lewis

Black Rose Writing | Texas

The final approval for this literary material is granted by the author.

First printing

This is a work of fiction. Names, characters, businesses, places, events and incidents are either the products of the author's imagination or used in a fictitious manner. Any resemblance to actual persons, living or dead, or actual events is purely coincidental.

ISBN: 978-1-68433-024-9
PUBLISHED BY BLACK ROSE WRITING
www.blackrosewriting.com

Printed in the United States of America
Suggested Retail Price (SRP) $20.95

Caught in a Web is printed in Minion Pro

To Elizabeth "Betty" Kriska
1941 – 2017
My Sister; My Friend; and My "Second Mother."
Love you always!

ACKNOWLEDGEMENTS

Anytime a writer comes up with an idea for a story and puts words on a page, there are any number of people who helped behind the scenes in order to bring the story to publication. I want to thank Jamie Graff, Brandon Gates and Earl Coffey for their expertise in drugs, gangs, police and FBI procedure; James Dahlke for sharing his forensic science work with me; Jay Cooke for his IT expertise; Sharon King for patience in answering all my medical questions; Steve Murkowski for his help with and knowledge of owls; and the folks at Sage and Sweetgrass, Robert Johnson and various personnel at the Navajo Museum for taking the time to answer my questions about Navajo culture, tradition and language. I want to thank Theresa Storke for her patience, coaching and superb editing skills. Lastly and most of all, I want to thank Reagan Rothe, Dave King and the folks at Black Rose Writing for giving *Caught in a Web* a home.

CAUGHT IN A WEB

CHAPTER ONE

"You've gotten shots before, right?"

The young blond boy licked his lips and nodded. He wanted to back out, leave and go home, but he didn't know how he could do that. He was only thirteen and he was alone with three high school kids.

"You'll be fine," the high school kid with the tat on his forearm said. "I've done this tons of times."

The blond boy lost it a little as the fat high school kid tied the rubber hose on his upper arm.

"I don't want to. I want to go home."

The blond boy hated that he cried in front of the two older boys, but he couldn't help it.

The two high school boys looked at each other, and then at the third boy standing in the corner, who shook his head once. He had longish hair and was in charge, but stayed in the shadows.

"It's no big deal, kid. You'll be fine." To reassure him, Tat Boy added, "Really."

The boy struggled to get out of the chair, but the fat boy held him down and tightened the restraints on his arms.

"Don't get all weird on us. We paid you fifty bucks and all you have to do is get this vitamin shot."

The younger boy struggled against the restraints, but was too weak. He cried harder.

"You need to hold still because I don't want to miss your vein," Tat Boy said.

"No! Please don't. I want to go home! Please!" he sobbed, his voice rising in pitch.

Ignoring him, Tat Boy held the syringe and said, "Okay, here we go. Hold still now."

The needle punctured the young boy's arm, found the big vein and the syringe was depressed. The milky liquid flew through the small boy's body. He sagged into the chair, his eyes blinked and rolled back into his head. His mouth opened and closed, and then stayed open. His head lolled from one side to the other before tilting backward.

Fat Boy released his grip on the small boy's shoulders as Tat Boy pulled out the needle and loosened the rubber tube.

"The kid pissed in his pants," Fat Boy said. "Jesus! Why do they always piss and shit their pants?"

Tat Boy watched the younger kid anxiously, hoping the mix was correct.

It wasn't.

The younger boy began to shake and convulse. He puked onto his shirt and in his lap. His hands clenched and unclenched. Veins stuck out in his neck and his feet tapped the floor. His head fell to the side. He was gone.

"Fuck!"

The two boys looked over at the third boy for guidance, but didn't receive any.

Fat Boy said, "Put his sweatshirt back on and let's get him out of here."

Tat Boy stared at the little kid feeling something like remorse, but he wasn't sure. He was sad, maybe. At least he thought he was.

"Let's go, let's go! Before he shits his pants!" Fat Boy said. "I don't want shit in my car. It's bad enough he pissed on himself."

Angrily, Tat Boy wiped down the needle and syringe so his fingerprints weren't on it, and did the same with the rubber tube. He set them on the floor and helped the Fat Boy put the red sweatshirt back on the little kid. He didn't understand why the kid needed the sweatshirt since he was dead, but he figured it was maybe the thing to do.

Together, Fat Boy and Tat Boy carried the kid out to the car and laid him down on the plastic tarp in the trunk. Fat Boy rolled him onto his side, snatched the fifty dollar bill out of the little kid's pocket and stuffed it into his own. Fat Boy rolled him over onto his back.

"It's fucking cold! I want to get this over with," Fat Boy said with a shiver.

"Where are we going to take him?"

"I know a place in an alley not far from here."

Tat Boy ran back into the building. He used a paper towel to pick up the syringe and tube, and put them in the trunk with the dead kid. Fat Boy slammed the trunk shut and jumped in the car on the driver's side.

Before he got in the car on the passenger side, Tat Boy watched the third boy, the one with the longish hair, walk out to his car, get in and drive off without saying anything.

Hardly fair, Tat Boy thought.

He got in the car. He and Fat Boy drove off with yet another dead kid in the trunk.

CHAPTER TWO

Graff hated late night or early morning phone calls. They were almost always bad. Actually, no *almost* about it. They were all bad.

His wife, Kelly, was already sitting up in bed by the time Jamie answered his cell.

"What do you have?"

"Another body. A boy who looks like a middle school kid."

"Cause of death?"

Patrol Sargent Todd Collins hesitated, not wanting to say anything, but he did anyway.

"The ME hasn't confirmed it so it isn't definite, but it looks like another OD."

Graff shut his eyes, rubbed his face and shook his head tiredly. So far, three high school kids and now a middle school kid.

"Where are you?"

"Alley behind Causeway." As if he needed to explain further said, "The hardware store on Sunset near the hair place. Empire."

As soon as Collins told him they were behind Causeway, he knew where they were. He knew his city. He knew his county.

Graff looked at the alarm clock and saw that it was a couple of hours before he was going to get up. It was his day off. Rather, it was supposed to be his day off.

"Be there in thirty," and he ended the call.

"Bad?" Kelly asked.

"Bad."

Graff didn't like to bring his work home with him. His home, his life with Kelly and his son, Garrett, was his sanctuary, his island, and he didn't want to poison it with his work. But Kelly was his best and closest friend, besides Jeremy Evans and Jeff Limbach, and as hard as he tried not to, he ended up sharing bits and pieces with her. Just bits and pieces. Not the whole story because he felt the whole story was too much. Kelly had disagreed, arguing that bits and pieces were worse because it left her imagination to fill in the rest.

Like the summer a year ago and that mess with Brett and the boys in Chicago. Like what had happened to George and Jeremy in Arizona. CNN and the local news filled in some of it, but Jamie had never told her what had taken place in that warehouse in Chicago. He never told her about the fire fight and how Gary Fitzpatrick ended up getting shot, or how little Mikey Erickson was so beaten up and how he started stuttering, or how Brett ended up in the hospital with a gunshot wound, or how George ended up with so many scars or why he was given both an open and a concealed carry for the large knife she often saw on his hip.

Jamie laid back down, his face buried in Kelly's breasts.

"We don't have time for this. You have to go catch bad guys."

"The bad guys can wait."

"Get going, big guy. You jump in the shower and brush your teeth. I'll make you an egg sandwich and some coffee."

"Friggin' A," Graff said. "I hate these calls."

"You hate any calls that wake you up before you're ready to get up." She kissed the back of his head and said, "Get going, big guy."

He sat up and said, "Crap," but he crawled out of bed, both arms above his head as he stretched on his way to the bathroom.

CHAPTER THREE

George turned off the alarm before it went off just like he did each morning. He never needed an alarm, but set it anyway as a precaution. Careful that way. And because it was Saturday, he didn't bother to reset it for his fifteen-year-old brother, Billy, who would sleep in longer. Maybe a lot longer, since he and Randy didn't have basketball practice that morning.

He rolled over onto his back, scratched an armpit and put both hands under his head and stared at the ceiling, listening to the comforting sound of Billy breathing slowly and steadily. Even though they shared a queen-sized bed, Billy's version of sharing was to curl up against George and tuck his feet under George's legs. It didn't matter if George rolled away, because like magnet to metal, Billy always found him.

George took his right hand from behind his head and placed it on Billy's bare shoulder. Billy's arm was out of the covers, and with the window slightly open, Billy's shoulder was cold. George pulled the covers up to Billy's neck.

He was a full-blooded Navajo, one of the *Dine'* who grew up in Northeastern Arizona on the Navajo Indian Reservation, or as it was referred to among the more traditional Navajo, *Diné Bikéyah* which meant, Navajoland. He was a member of *'Azee'tsoh dine'e* or The Big Medicine People Clan, fitting because before George had come to live with Jeremy and the twins, Billy and Randy, he was being groomed to follow in his grandfather's footsteps.

But that had changed when his family, including his grandfather and grandmother, were murdered. Shot where they had stood, huddled together in the dirt driveway in front of the small four room ranch house, their *hogan*. His mother. His little brother, Robert, and his little sister, Mary. All murdered because of him. His brother, William, only younger by a year and a few months than George, was shot while he tended the sheep and died alone on the side of a hill.

He thought about them and every now and then, privately wept for them. He couldn't help it.

He loved his new family and his new life in Wisconsin. He loved his adoptive father, Jeremy. He loved his twin brothers, who like him, were also fifteen-years-old. And he loved the McGovern brothers, fifteen-year-old Brett and fourteen-year-old Bobby. Both looked like Tom Brady minus the cleft chin. They called Jeremy "Dad" and were treated by Jeremy as his sons, just like Randy, Billy and him. And he loved Brian, or Kaz to most everyone. Jeremy treated him just like he was one of the family, too.

Brothers. Friends. Inseparable.

They lived out in the country on twenty acres of land given to Jeremy by his best friend, Jeff Limbach. Jeff and his son, thirteen-year-old Danny, lived in a big house of their own down a path through the woods a little over a hundred yards or so away. And it was in Jeff's stable that George had kept his stallion, Nochero, along with the roan and the pinto he had brought with him from Arizona.

Carefully so as not to disturb Billy, George got up out of bed and tucked the covers around him.

He bent down, scratched Jasmine and Jasper behind their ears and tiptoed across the hall to the bathroom. Jasmine followed as far as the hallway and waited for George, while Jasper never moved.

George relieved himself, washed and dried his hands and he looked at the scars on his legs and his arms, and using the mirror, the scars on his back. Some of the scars from the 127 stitches had faded, but others were still visible and would be a reminder forever. A sad reminder of the summer of death.

He traced the long raised scar up high on his left leg near his groin with his forefinger and did the same to the scar on his left arm, and on his right leg just below his butt. Each morning, each night, the same inspection. Those three scars bothered him. More so did the two additional scars, one on his upper left arm and one on his outer left thigh. Both were actually indentations where chunks of skin had been blown away. He didn't like the look of them and while guys in the locker room would usually stare at them and at his other scars, none of the guys had ever asked.

Neither George nor Jeremy had told them what had happened up on the mesa that morning, so no one other than George or Jeremy knew how George got those two particular wounds.

He pursed his lips, shook his head and went back into the bedroom and dressed into shorts, a long-sleeved Under Armour t-shirt, heavy, thick socks and his Gore-Tex reflective running suit. He dressed quickly and quietly. He picked up his shoes, gloves and hat, bent down to pet the puppy, Jasper, one more time and left the room and quietly shut the door to a crack behind him with Jasmine following him. The big dog, Momma, was parked where she always parked each night, in the hallway facing the top of the stairs.

George tiptoed across the hall to Randy's room. Each morning, George would find Randy in his usual position with one knee up, arms thrown out to the side and his head off the pillow. George smiled, entered the room and covered Randy up, who mumbled something unintelligible, rolled onto his side and continued sleeping. George gently squeezed Randy's covered shoulder, but was certain that Randy wouldn't even know he had entered the bedroom.

George had performed this ritual every morning since he had moved in with the twins and Randy had never remembered it upon waking.

The table lamp on Jeremy's nightstand was on and Jeremy was sitting up in bed.

Following his near daily morning routine, George stopped at Jeremy's bedroom doorway, stuck his head in and softly said, "Father?"

"Good morning, George."

Jeremy was a thirty-something high school counselor and a former social studies teacher and head boys' basketball coach. He had thought of himself as permanently single, but that had changed ever since he had met Victoria McGovern.

He had wrestled with that relationship. He liked her a lot. He thought it was love, but wasn't quite sure. Yet. But he supposed it was only a matter of time and he didn't mind that. Not at all.

A lot like giving up on the idea of becoming a priest.

Jeremy gave up on it because celibacy was a bit too much to deal with even though he was never promiscuous. His interest in the priesthood stemmed from the mysticism, the meditation and prayer life, but he had eventually decided he could still practice that part of the religious life while being single.

And as much as he had considered the priesthood, there was a part of him—a large part of him—that wanted a child, a son. So he entered the foster care system. Randy, at the age of twelve, had run away from an abusive home and was placed with Jeremy and adopted almost a year later.

When a picture and story on the foster care system and adoption featuring Jeremy and Randy appeared in the *Milwaukee Sentinel*, Billy spotted it, read the article and confronted his parents. Billy hadn't known he had been adopted. A war began in the Schroeder household that ended in Robert's and Monica's divorce. Billy had blamed his mother and eventually, she moved out of the home. Billy ended up spending as much time with Jeremy and Randy as he did with his father.

One September afternoon, Billy came home from school and found his father in the hallway with two chocolate chip cookies in his clenched hand, dead from a massive heart attack. Monica lost a brief legal battle for Billy, and Billy had moved in with Jeremy and Randy and eventually, Jeremy adopted him too. Out of respect for his former adopted father, Billy kept his last name, Schroeder.

Every morning, Jeremy would wake up, read the Bible and pray, meditate and think. Think about his single life drifting away, happily so, because he was drawn closer and closer to Victoria. Not sure why, he still wasn't sure of his relationship with her. Not really. So he, and she, decided to take it slowly.

On most mornings, George stopped in to talk with Jeremy. It was their time together. And after, George would go off for a run and finish as the sun rose. When it did, George would say his prayers facing east just as the more traditional Navajo did. At some point during the day or early evening, he would go out into the yard to practice with the knife he had received from his grandfather when he had turned twelve during a coming of age ceremony high up on an Arizona mesa. The same mesa where George received those two additional scars. Where, more importantly, it all came to an end.

His knife was a gift from his grandfather and one of the only remaining links to his previous life. It was eight inches of razor sharp steel, tied to an elk bone with leather, extending the length to a full twelve inches. It fit George's hand perfectly and though he wasn't technically ambidextrous, he could use either hand efficiently and expertly. He had shown that ability three times, and three very bad men found themselves on the receiving end of the knife's blade.

The knife routine George went through looked to Jeremy like a sort of martial arts, like Tai Chi or Kung Fu. Both the knife exercises and the prayers were taught to him and overseen by his grandfather.

George entered Jeremy's room and lay down on the bed and faced Jeremy, while Jasmine lay down on George's side of the bed.

"You're going to run? It's really cold out."

George smiled and shoved his long black hair behind his ear to keep it from falling in his eyes. He wore his hair long like the more traditional Navajo and it extended past his shoulders. He had dark copper-colored skin and his eyes, the color of his long hair, saw everything and missed nothing. He had a straight nose and had a noble, handsome appearance. Just four months into his freshman year of high school, he was receiving phone calls and texts from girls, just as Randy and Billy were.

"I like running. I'll be fine once I get going."

Jeremy reached over and grasped George's hand and said, "I don't know anyone as disciplined as you."

"Brett."

"Well, yes. He's about as disciplined as you are."

"Father, Brett and I were talking."

George had always called him *Father* because he felt *Dad* wasn't respectful enough, and Jeremy smiled at the thought. It was just one of the endearing things Jeremy loved about George.

"Detective Graff invited us to go ice fishing up north."

Jeremy nodded and said, "Yes, he mentioned that he was going to ask you guys and Gavin."

George hesitated and said, "We would like to go, but we don't want Randy or Billy or Bobby to feel left out."

Jeremy smiled and said, "Randy has never expressed any interest in any kind of fishing. Billy tried it once and hated it, so I know he wouldn't like ice fishing. I don't know about Bobby."

Even though Bobby was younger than Brett by a year and a couple of months, the two of them were very close. Especially close since they had moved with their mother from Indianapolis to Waukesha in order to give each of them a fresh start.

"Brett doesn't think Bobby would want to go."

"But you're worried that if you and Brett and Gavin go and because they didn't get invited, they'd feel left out."

"Yes."

"So, what do you think you're going to do?"

George thought for a minute and said, "I think we will ask them if it's okay."

Jeremy smiled and said, "You know it's okay if you and Brett have lives independent of the twins and Bobby."

George rolled over onto his back and put both hands under his head and stared at the ceiling.

It occurred to Jeremy once again how much George and the twins had grown. George probably wouldn't get much taller than he was right now and probably would not be as tall as the twins, or the McGovern boys for that matter. He probably wouldn't even be as tall as Brian. But all of them had grown, gotten bigger and filled out. Matured too quickly than their years. Lost the childhood that most kids had, thanks to the summer of death.

"What are you thinking?"

George said, "Sometimes I think of my grandfather and my family."

"I know, George."

George turned his head towards Jeremy and said, "It's not that I don't like living with you and Billy and Randy or when Brett and Bobby and Brian are with us. And if you and Mrs. McGovern decide to marry, I would like that." He paused and sighed, "I miss my family and grandfather sometimes."

"When you lose someone, you always miss them. Just like I miss my dad and mom. Just like Billy misses his father. Just like Brian misses his brother."

George didn't respond and didn't look at Jeremy. Instead, he stared at the ceiling.

Jeremy reached over and ran his fingers through George's hair.

Needing to change the subject, George said, "Brett is worried about Billy and Randy and Brian."

"Why?"

"Tucker, Sweeney and Goldfarb were suspended from the basketball team last night. Coach Harrison told Brett he would be the starting point guard and

Billy would start at forward. Randy and Brian are being brought up from the junior varsity team."

Jeremy and the head coach, Tommy Harrison, were not only colleagues, but friends. Harrison had phoned Jeremy about the three seniors getting busted at a party and his enforcing the athletic code that called for a four game suspension.

Jeremy said, "Brett plays quite a bit already and he's ready to start. Billy already had playing time and he's done well. I don't know how much Randy or Brian will play, but both boys are athletes and they're smart. Once they settle down, they'll be okay."

"Brett is worried that they might freeze up."

Jeremy thought about that. Randy was a nervous one. Brian and Billy, not so much. Of the three, Billy was a natural athlete who was good at whatever he did. But in the end, Jeremy decided that none of the boys would freeze. They might get nervous before a game, but that happened to any kid. He saw that in his own players when he had coached.

"What's the plan?"

George shrugged and said, "Brett hasn't decided yet."

Jeremy playfully grabbed at George's nose and said, "You and Brett will think of something."

George smiled at him and said, "I am going to go running."

"Is anyone going with you?"

George nodded and said, "I'm picking up Brett and Brian and we're running back here."

"I'll have breakfast ready for you."

"Thank you, Father."

"Do you know what everyone's plans are for the day?"

George said, "They want to go to the Y and play basketball. Brett wants to work with them."

Jeremy thought for a moment and said, "I could take them to school. It might be a little quieter and without distractions. I can always do some work for an hour or two." He said, "What are you going to do?"

"The horses need work." He hesitated. He finally asked, "Would it be alright if Caitlyn came over?"

They had met running on the cross country team. She was about the same height as George with short blond hair, bright blue eyes, a dimple when she smiled and a sprinkle of freckles on her nose and under her eyes. Cute and friendly and reserved like George. Jeremy liked her and had liked her older sister who had graduated a couple of years earlier. She had two younger brothers, one in seventh grade and the other in fifth.

"Just be careful and smart, okay? Make good choices." This last statement added because Jeremy knew that George was experienced when it came to girls. At fifteen-years-old, far too young to be that experienced.

"I will, Father." He smiled and said, "She is not Rebecca and that was a long time ago."

"I know, but I worry. I know you and Rebecca . . . were close."

"She is my oldest friend, Father. I loved her and we made a commitment to each other."

"A little young, though."

"I have not been . . . *with* any girl since Rebecca. Since I left Navajoland. Billy and Randy have not either."

Jeremy felt himself blush as he said, "I just don't want you guys growing up too quickly. You need to become friends first. You need to get to know each other and that takes time. Mostly, it has to be love, George."

"I loved Rebecca, Father."

Jeremy sighed and said, "I know, George."

He embraced Jeremy and kissed his cheek.

"I will be careful, Father."

"I love you, George."

"I know, Father. I love you too." He kissed Jeremy's cheek again and said again, "I will be careful."

CHAPTER FOUR

Graff drove around to the back of the strip mall, spotted flashing blues mixed with flashing reds and a small huddle of cops with little clouds of breath coming out of their mouths as they spoke to one another. They stood around stamping their feet to keep them from freezing and turning into cement blocks.

He rolled to a stop just outside the yellow tape and decided to leave his squad car running to keep it warm. He grabbed his traveler cup of hot coffee and got out, shutting the door behind him with a metallic clunk that didn't echo in the dark night. It was that cold.

He spotted the ME, turned up his collar with his free hand and hunched his shoulders as he walked in that direction.

"Ike," he said with a nod.

Mike Eisenhower, whom everyone called, *Ike*, was in his sixties and bald except for a fringe of snow white hair that ran around the sides and back of his head like a misplaced halo. He was short and a little stooped, but his mind was clear and sharp.

"I will never understand the attraction, Jamie. I don't get it."

"What do we have?"

The older man shook his head and said, "A middle school kid, maybe eleven or twelve. On his back, head to the side in a puddle of frozen puke with snot frozen to his face. That's what we have. What the hell is the attraction of drugs when it ends like this?"

"Cause of death?" Graff caught the old man's frown and corrected himself. "Tentative cause of death?"

"OD. Some sort. Not sure what, though."

"Time of death?"

The old man shrugged and said, "The kid is frozen stiff. I'd say four or five hours ago at least, but because of this damn cold, I can't pinpoint it for you until I get him back to the office."

"Do you have a guess as to what drug it was?"

He shook his head and said, "I'll do a tox screen and be able to tell you for sure."

Eisenhower's office was in the basement of Waukesha Memorial Hospital, a five or ten minute drive away.

Graff squatted down next to the boy. Blond. Skinny. Wearing only a red hooded sweatshirt. No hat, no gloves, no boots. A pair of Jordan's on his feet. His upper lip and cheek coated in icy snot. The pavement under his head was frosted in yellowish or brownish puke, depending upon how the light hit it. The boy's eyes and mouth were partially open. A lovely picture of another dead kid added to the collection of dead kid pictures Jamie had stored away in his head. Not that he had wanted to hold onto any of them. Ever. No fucking way!

"Thanks, Ike. You have my number," Graff said as he strolled toward the huddle of cops.

He recognized most of them and said, "Guys, anyone catch any radio chatter on missing kids? Kids who didn't show up after dinner or who might have snuck out at night?"

They stamped their feet and shook their heads and muttered, "No."

"Okay. I need all the dumpsters checked for anything that might fit the crime. Look for anything out of the ordinary, anything that doesn't quite fit. I'll need pictures of boot or shoe marks and any tire treads. Again, look on the ground for anything that might fit with the crime, anything out of the ordinary. Later this morning, I'll need some of you to canvas the neighborhoods in a three or four block radius from here. Ike said the kid might be a middle school kid, eleven or twelve-years-old. I'm guessing unless this is a dump site, he'd live close by because he isn't exactly dressed for a long hike. Not in this weather, anyway."

As he walked away, he said, "Whoever decides to canvas the neighborhood can go home. Start about eight in the morning. That will give you a couple of hours sleep."

Jamie poured the coffee out of his traveler cup onto the frozen pavement, no longer thirsty and sure as hell not hungry.

CHAPTER FIVE

There were eight boys with their shirts off and dripping with sweat because Brett had been putting them through their paces for the better part of two hours. He'd bark orders, point and yell, "Freeze!" and the boys did just that. He'd point out possibilities and correct mistakes. But as much as he'd bark, he was lavish with his praise.

Tommy Harrison had wandered in from somewhere in the building and sat down on the floor next to Jeremy and watched. He'd nod, smile, and nod some more.

"Suspending Tucker, Sweeney and Goldfarb might be the best thing that ever happened," he said without taking his eyes off the court.

Jeremy tried to suppress his smile but was unsuccessful. He had coached Sweeney's older brother, or rather, cut him from the team when he was a senior. One was as much a drinker and partier as the other. Goldfarb was an idiot and a follower. Tucker was a good kid who had made a poor choice. Of the three, Tucker was the best athlete.

"Who's the big dude roaming the baseline?" Harrison asked. "He's what, six one . . . two?"

Another example of how much the boys had grown in a year and a few months, Jeremy thought. Bobby was an inch or so taller than Brett, but both had gotten taller, and Brett had filled out from weight training and a proper diet.

"That's Gavin Hemauer, but the boys call him, Big Gav. He and Brett's brother, Bobby, and the little guy out on top, Mikey Erickson, are eighth graders at Butler. You'll get them next year."

"For a big guy, he has the ball skills of a guard."

Jeremy nodded and said, "He was a point guard before he moved here. Still works at it."

Harrison watched them for a moment or two. Bobby sunk three long three-pointers from the top and side of the key and Gavin tore down two rebounds after missed shots, one by Randy and one by Brian Kazmarick. He blocked Randy's shot, snatched the ball out of the air and tipped it to Mike, who quickly found Bobby open for a jump shot.

"What's Brett's brother's name?"

"Bobby."

"Does he ever miss?"

Jeremy laughed and said, "Not often."

Harrison watched some more and said, "Brett is fearless. He steps out on the court and everyone forgets he's a freshman. I saw it on the football field. Hell, Putrell couldn't keep him or Schroeder out of the lineup. He made some big time plays. It didn't matter how big the runner or end was, Brett took him on. And damn, is he quick."

"He's tough all right. And quick. I don't know if you know this, but he holds records for the hundred meter and two hundred meter in Indiana in his age group. National times."

But what Jeremy liked most about Brett was that he was loyal and protective and kind. He cared about others, more so than most kids his age. Under that tough exterior, he was a gentle kid. And smart."

"How did he get the scar on his shoulder?"

Jeremy hesitated, unwilling to say much because he didn't know if Brett would want him to.

"I think if you pull him aside when you're alone with him, he'll tell you or at least tell you as much as he wants you to know."

Jeremy knew that if it weren't for Brett, Mikey Erickson and Stephen Bailey and those other kids wouldn't have made it out of that warehouse in Chicago the summer before last.

"I know he was in Chicago. In that place."

Jeremy nodded and said, "For almost two years."

"That explains why he plays pissed off."

Jeremy thought it over and said, "He's learned to channel his anger, just like Mikey and Stephen, but they still struggle. Even Randy struggles and it's been over three years."

"Ya think? Shit, I can't imagine what those kids went through."

Jeremy knew exactly what took place because he had been counseling the boys. He also knew there were other boys who didn't make it out alive.

Brett brought the guys in for a quick huddle, stepped away and yelled to Jeremy, "Dad, can we play for another half hour, maybe forty-five minutes?"

"I'm okay with it. Just don't kill them off."

Brett grinned, turned back to the others and said, "We're good, right?"

None of the boys answered him.

"He calls you, 'Dad.'" It was a statement, not a question. Harrison had noticed it before.

Jeremy shrugged it off and said, "He and Bobby are sons to me."

"I didn't know there was an open gym."

Sweeney and Goldfarb had wandered in and watched Brett and the other guys play four on four half court.

"It's not. The boys wanted to shoot around some, that's all," Jeremy said.

Doug Sweeney was a flabby six foot senior with dirty blond hair. Beer and sugar were his two main food groups. Jerry Goldfarb never looked directly at anyone, especially adults. He stood six two and was rail thin and dark-haired with a face full of pimples. He had small beady eyes that flit everywhere.

"Who did you bring up to take our place?" Sweeney asked.

Harrison nodded at the floor, but otherwise didn't say anything.

"Kazmarick sucks. He won't help us," Sweeney said. "And Evans isn't that good. His brother isn't much either."

Jeremy bit his tongue.

"They'll be fine," Harrison said.

"We'll be back after four games and they'll go back to JV."

"They will be given an opportunity to stay on varsity, but that doesn't concern you."

"I'm captain," Sweeney suggested.

"Not anymore."

"What do you mean?" Sweeney spit.

"A captain is a leader, someone I can count on. You stopped being a leader the minute you stepped foot into that party, didn't leave when you saw what was going on and when you blew positive on the breathalyzer."

"Are you saying I'm not captain anymore?"

He wanted to say, 'Duh!' but instead said, "That's what I'm saying,"

Harrison said.

"That's bullshit! Who's captain? That piss ant McGovern? He's a fuckin' freshman."

Harrison turned, squinted at him and said, "Who is captain doesn't concern you. And one more word, you won't be on the team."

"Maybe we'll quit, right Jerry?"

Goldfarb said nothing.

"Whatever," Harrison answered.

"Come on, Jerry. It stinks in here." He turned around and walked away. Jerry Goldfarb, his head hung low and with his hands shoved into his pockets, followed at Sweeney's heels.

"And don't let the door hit ya where the good Lord split ya," Harrison mumbled as they passed through the door out of earshot.

CHAPTER SIX

"Sit your ass back down on that couch! You're not going anywhere!"

Gary Adair was seething. More than that, he and his wife, Pam, were scared. He tried to calm himself down by shutting his eyes and breathing deeply.

"Zak, we found this in your bedroom. I want to know where you got it."

Zak folded his arms and glared at his parents. He had already stonewalled them for an hour and he could keep it up the rest of the afternoon and all night if he had to. There was no way in hell he was going to talk to them. He had threatened to leave, but in all honesty, he had nowhere to go. At least, nowhere he could go.

"Zak, your mom and I want to help you. This isn't like you. You're an athlete. You're a good student. You're popular." Gary stopped and shook his head. As much as he was angry, he was utterly disappointed. Destroyed.

"Zak, we love you," Pam pleaded with him. "Please help us understand."

Zak looked away. He couldn't bear to look at either his mom or dad. He loved them too much and he knew how much he had hurt them. Somehow, he had to come up with something that would give him an out.

His dad composed himself, though his hands shook as he held out the three baggies of weed, the pipe, and the sheet of paper containing cartoon characters in small squares.

"Your mom did your laundry and she folded your underwear. When she went to put it away, she found the pot and your pipe. Your mom checked your sock drawer and found LSD."

Zak glared first at his mom, then at his dad and said, "I told you I can do my own laundry."

Ignoring him and with his voice shaking, Gary said, "She was putting away your laundry when she found this."

"You searched my room! It's my room! My room!"

"It's our house!" his father shouted. "You live in our house. We put the food on the table and clothes on your back. You drive a car that we paid for, so we make the rules! Our house, our rules!"

"Zak, please," Pam pleaded. "Where did you get this and how can we help you?"

"It's not mine, okay? It's not mine."

"Well good! That's a relief! So when your mom and I take you to the hospital for a urine and blood test, everything should come back negative."

Zak's tongue flicked over his lips, his eyes wide. Every instinct told him to get up and run. Somewhere. Anywhere.

He ran a hand through his hair and over his face and said, "I . . . I don't need a drug screen. That stuff isn't mine."

"Then you don't have anything to worry about. We'll go to the hospital, they run the tests and we come back home," Gary said, though he wasn't buying any of it.

"We don't need to do that. God! Didn't you hear me? It's not mine."

"Tell us where you got it. If it isn't yours, tell us who this stuff belongs to," Gary said.

"I'm not going to the hospital! I'm not taking any tests! I have rights! You can't make me!"

Gary and Pam exchanged a look and Pam sank back in her chair. This was going nowhere.

"You're seventeen-years-old. You're a minor and we're your parents. You don't have any rights as far as we're concerned. Especially after finding this in your room."

Zak began to cry. He was caught and he knew it and he knew that his parents knew. Worse, he was scared because if anyone found out, he was screwed.

"Zak, we love you. You know that don't you?" Pam asked.

"Tell us about this stuff. How long have you been using? How did you start? Why? Where did you get this?" Gary knew he had asked too many questions, but he needed to know the answers.

Zak sobbed. "I can't tell you anything, all right? I can't say anything. If I do, I'm a narc, and if they find out . . ." his voice trailed off.

Gary stared at his son determined to do something. There had to be a way to tell someone without getting Zak in trouble.

"Zak, how can we help you?" Pam asked.

"That's what I'm trying to tell you! You can't! No one can! If you tell anyone, I'm . . . screwed!"

Gary and Pam stared at their son and then at each other.

Gary stood up and said, "We don't go to the police directly. If we do, we do it anonymously. You give us the names of the kids who gave you this stuff. We can use the tip line. There's no way to trace it to us."

"You don't get it. These guys are smart. If you say anything to anybody and if it gets back to them that I was the narc, *they will kill me!*"

"They won't kill you," Gary said. His son wasn't given to drama, but still.

"Oh my God! Dad, you don't understand!"

Pam was worried before, but now she was flat out scared. She bit her lip and stared at Gary.

"Who is your counselor?" Gary asked.

"Beatleman? She doesn't know shit!"

"What about Mr. Evans? We could go to him. You ran cross country with George."

"We can't say anything to anyone! We can't tell anyone at school!"

Gary spoke in a quiet voice. "Zak, you have to trust us. Okay? We love you and we'll take care of you. We have to tell someone."

Zak sobbed. He rocked back and forth in the chair. Other than that, he said nothing.

Gary sat back down and stared at his son.

Zak, their only child, was a handsome, bright boy. He ran cross country and track for three years since his freshman year. He had a wide circle of friends, all good kids. Happy, laughing, bright futures- all of them. He couldn't understand what had happened. Mostly, he couldn't understand why. Why his son, their only child, would use this shit when he had so much to look forward to.

There had to be a way to help Zak. There just had to be.

CHAPTER SEVEN

George had mixed feelings. On one hand, he had wanted to share the day with Caitlyn doing something he loved to do, hoping that she might grow to love it as much as he did. Or more accurately, as much as Rebecca did. On the other hand, Caitlyn had never been on a horse and was more than likely a little cold. Probably uncomfortably cold, and it wasn't fair to expect her to love riding and working horses as much as he or Rebecca did, being it was her first time out and freezing while doing it.

He found his feelings about Caitlyn peculiar. All through eighth grade and the first few months of ninth grade, he tried not to show too much interest in any particular girl, treating each of them equally and only as friends. But his feelings for Caitlyn were different. They weren't like the feelings he had for Rebecca. Maybe wouldn't ever be. But he liked her and liked the growing friendship he had with her.

George felt like he could talk with her and laugh with her easier, maybe more naturally, than he could with any other girl. Perhaps it was because Caitlyn was a cousin of his friend, Sean Drummond.

Sean and Caitlyn even looked alike. They had the same blond hair, the same blue eyes, and were the same height. They even smiled the same. The two of them were more like brother and sister than cousins.

The feelings he had had about Rebecca were different. The first time he and Rebecca had kissed several weeks shy of his twelfth birthday, he had felt a special feeling. At the time, he couldn't identify it and was dumbfounded. After all, he and Rebecca went through elementary school together and had been friends for many years. They had rode horses, watched over and worked their families' flocks of sheep, camped and innocently shared blankets with each other, and skinny-dipped in a pond in the foothills of the Chuska Mountains.

It was during that first real kiss that he felt the stirrings of a first love. Not only did they kiss, but laying down on a blanket, their hands touched and fondled and explored the never- before- traveled, the undiscovered areas of each other's bodies. It was on that first late afternoon under a beautiful cloudless blue sky, nestled among the pinon pine, when that raging river in both of them broke open and gushed forth for the first time.

Their first real encounter under blankets on the bank of the small pond did nothing to quiet their passion or quench their thirst for each other. Both were only twelve, but both felt the *need* to return to the blanket and lay together naked save for the leather and turquoise necklace George wore around his neck.

It had been a year and a half since George had last tasted from that well and just as any boy might, he had longed to drink from it again. But he also had a strong sense of right and wrong. He had given his word to his father that he wouldn't. At least not yet.

Caitlyn Watkins was cute and athletic. In cross country, she was the top female on the team, just as George was the top male on the team. Unusual since they were only freshmen. The only race either of them had lost was at the state meet when George had finished third to two seniors, while Caitlyn finished sixth. Their coach, Phil Voight, salivated for spring when they'd be out for track.

Caitlyn had been on dates with a few boys, though they were mostly group dates. She was even asked to homecoming, but that relationship, if you could call it that, ended a week later when she told the boy that she just wanted to be friends. Teenage code for "not interested." Many of her group dates included her cousin and his friends, and Sean's friends included George, Randy and Billy.

And Brian.

Even before his twin brother, Brad, had died, she had had a crush on Brian. Most of the other girls tripped and fell all over themselves chasing Brad, who was more outgoing and more daring. Brian was guarded and more reserved, like George. Like she was. There was something about the two boys. Similar, but different.

She had never pictured herself sitting on a horse, but there she was. Though the roan was gentle and tame, it was big to Caitlyn and she wasn't sure what she was doing. She gripped the reins or the horn on the saddle and hoped she wouldn't embarrass herself by falling off.

To Caitlyn, George looked every bit like the cowboy he was. Or rather, an Indian, or more politically correct these days, a Native American. Tall in the saddle on top of the biggest blackest stallion she had ever seen. The horse, Nochero, looked like a monster, but George rode him as if he were a knight coming home from victory in a far off land.

Every so often, George would stop and her horse would pull up next to him, and he'd point at ice cycles hanging from pine trees or the way the sun would shine through trees just right so that the dusting of snow and ice on the ground would shimmer and shine. It was sweet and gentle and Caitlyn liked that about him. There was a genuineness George had that other boys didn't.

And he'd smile. A most dazzling smile. His teeth as white as the dusting of snow on the ground and on tree limbs, set against the dark bronze of his skin. The same smile he wore whenever they would glance at each other. His long black hair hanging long and low on his shoulders and back. Not particularly tall. Not particularly broad. But even she sensed his strength when she watched him run in cross country and that afternoon when he helped her up in the saddle.

What intrigued Caitlyn most was the dual nature of the boy: George's quiet, reserved nature and his intensity, yet he was quick to smile and was easy to talk to, though he'd mostly listen. When he did speak, she liked his soft western drawl. Similar to Brett's and Bobby's slight southern accent, but at the same time, different. She enjoyed listening to the three of them.

She and George had gotten to know each other through Sean, but more so through cross country. They would talk and laugh and cheer each other on. He would sit next to her on the bus to and from their meets.

She had wanted to ask him about the scars she had seen on his back and arms and legs, but was too embarrassed to do so. She had started to ask him on several occasions, but would stop herself. It was none of her business, but the mystery was intriguing, as was the story of why and how he had come to live in Wisconsin, in Waukesha, and to live with Jeremy, the twins and every now and then, Brett and Bobby.

"Are you cold?"

"I'm okay," Caitlyn lied. She would tough it out, just as she did each and every time she raced. Just as she ignored the stitch in her side as she'd run up a steep hill, she ignored the bone-chilling cold that knifed through her.

"Your nose and your cheeks are red," George said with a frown, concerned that she might be uncomfortable.

She smiled at him and joked, "That happens when it's cold out."

The two of them led the other four horses and the three dogs along the path through the woods. At times, the big dog, Momma, would run ahead with Jasmine and Jasper at her sides. George explained that all of them had needed the exercise having been cooped up all winter. The stable was heated and cozy and clean, but the horses, like the dogs and like people, needed to get out and move. So they galloped and cantered and trotted. Mostly, they walked their horses along the trail through the woods taking their time, talking quietly and laughing a lot.

"Just around that bend is the stable," George said.

"That's good, because my face is frozen."

George made a clicking noise and Nochero took off on a trot and as he did, so did Caitlyn's roan and the four horses behind her. Momma and the pups were already up ahead, knowing where they were headed. Caitlyn found herself laughing all the way to the stable as she bounced around in the saddle, almost falling off, but hanging on for dear life.

George swung himself off Nochero and caught the roan by the bridle and the horn on the saddle. He reached up and plucked Caitlyn off the horse and into his arms. They briefly clung to each other. George held her gently, but tightly.

Caitlyn kissed him on the cheek. It was friendly and light and innocuous. She blushed, as did he.

After an awkward silence, she said, "Thank you. That was fun."

"I had the feeling you did not like it all that much."

Caitlyn smiled at the formalness of his speech.

"It is okay if you did not. We won't do that again, if you do not want to."

She smiled again, blushed, and said, "I wouldn't mind doing it again."

George didn't respond, but stepped away from her to take the saddle and blanket off the roan and led it by the reins to the stall. He undid the bridle, hung it over the fence and took a brush and ran it over the smallish horse. He cleaned the snow and ice off the horse's hooves.

He led Nochero to the next stall and followed the same routine as he had done with the roan.

"Um . . . what's happening to your horse?" Caitlyn asked.

George looked up at her, at Nochero and said, "Danny's mare is in heat and that excites him." And indeed, Nochero was excited. "He's showing off."

"Just like most boys," Caitlyn laughed.

George shrugged and said, "It is natural among all animals."

"That's gross."

She watched him work and said, "Can I help?"

George hesitated. If one didn't know much about horses or hadn't spent much time around horses, like any animal, they could be dangerous.

"Come here and I'll show you how to use a brush."

He gave her the brush, but put his hand on hers and guided it over the horse. He cautioned her, "Never go behind a horse. They can be skittish, especially if the horse doesn't know you."

She nodded.

While she brushed, George cleaned Nochero's hooves.

When they had groomed each of the horses, George fed them apples and oats and filled their troughs with fresh water.

That done, he stood back with his hands on his hips and surveyed his work. Satisfied, he nodded. Jasmine stepped up to him, begged for attention and he obliged by squatting down and scratching her behind her ears.

"Do you think I could shower and change my clothes? I smell like horse."

George laughed and said, "A good smell."

Caitlyn laughed and said, "Maybe if my name was Annie Oakley."

CHAPTER EIGHT

Sheriff Detectives Pat O'Connor and Paul Eiselmann squatted down next to the body. Two sheriff deputies stood behind them and the ME and his assistant from the city stood by with a gurney and body bag. The scene was Waukesha County jurisdiction because they were not quite four miles out of the city on Highway 59. O'Connor and Eiselmann were assigned to it because it looked like drugs, just like the bodies of the kids found in the city.

The boy's dirty blond hair was matted with frost or snow or both. He wore a gray hoodie with AE printed on the front. His jeans had fashionable holes on the left thigh and right knee. He wore black vans and low cut Reebok socks. Not dressed for a night or morning outside in a Midwestern December.

O'Connor was lanky with shoulder-length brown hair and a hawkish face. He was the department's undercover guy, considered by some to be quirky, considered by most to be an expert when it came to drugs and gangs. Like any city, drugs and gangs went hand in hand. As tall and lanky as O'Connor was, Eiselmann was the opposite. He was short and compact. He was O'Connor's control and didn't work undercover because he'd stand out with his dark red hair and freckles. Both were life-long friends who had known each other since grade school.

Eiselmann looked back over his shoulder towards the road. "Maybe twenty, thirty yards?"

O'Connor nodded and said, "He was dumped. Some puke and snot on his face, but none on the ground."

"I'm calling Graff. He caught a body this morning behind Causeway on Sunset. Another kid."

"Some similarities from what I heard. They ID'd the kid this morning. He was a seventh grader at Horning Middle. This kid might be a little older, but not much."

"Be interesting to know if they knew each another."

O'Connor nodded and said, "Another kid from Horning? Same party, maybe?"

Eiselmann stood up, stretched and stepped away, pulling out his phone as he did. He had Graff on speed-dial.

"Jamie, it's Paul. We have a scene like the one you had this morning, only out on 59 towards Genesee. You might want to come take a look."

"On my way."

"Hey, can you bring the file on your kid?"

"The same age?"

Eiselmann nodded and said, "Could be."

"I'll bring what I've got."

CHAPTER NINE

She had forgotten her clean underwear and her shirt and her jeans, which was really stupid of her. They were in her duffle in the room across the hall, which she had found out was George's and Billy's room.

Caitlyn finished showering and dried off with a soft fresh blue towel that matched the color of the bathroom. For a house full of boys, the bathroom like the rest of the house, was spotless. George had given her a brief tour of the upstairs, showing her the bedrooms and telling her who slept where and showed her the bedroom he shared with Billy across the hall from the bathroom she used. He showered in a bathroom at the end of the hall near the two spare rooms.

She considered wrapping herself in a towel and making the quick sprint across the hall to retrieve her clothes. She listened for any noise on the other side of her door, but heard nothing. She thought that either George was incredibly quiet or still in the bathroom at the end of the hallway where the guest rooms were.

Caitlyn took the bottle of lotion off the counter, wrapped herself up in the towel and stuck her head into the hallway while hiding the rest of her behind the bathroom door. Still no sound.

She took a deep breath and on tip-toes, ran to the bedroom and opened the door and found George standing in front of an open drawer of his dresser, similarly covered with a towel, though his was around his waist.

He turned around, smiled and said, "Hi."

She blushed, started to explain herself, but only said, "Hi."

They stared at each other, both rooted to the spot where they stood.

He saw the bottle of lotion in her hand and said, "As long as you're here, would you put some lotion on my back?"

It took her a second or two to consider that body lotion was a lot like suntan lotion and if they were on a date at the beach, putting suntan lotion was roughly the same as putting body lotion on his back, so she said, "Sure." She added, "If you'll do the same for me."

George smiled and said, "Sure."

He turned around so that his back was to her, pulled his long hair over his shoulder, and she stepped forward, tucking the towel tighter around her neck and back.

She squirted a little on his shoulders and he flinched.

"Cold?"

"A little."

She breathed into her hands and gently spread the lotion around on his back, her fingers light, but lingering on the long scar on his shoulder.

"How did you get this . . . all these scars?" and as soon as the question was asked, she regretted it and said, "I'm sorry. It's none of my business."

She felt him relax and he said, "There is much you don't know about me."

"You don't have to tell me. I'm sorry."

"No, it's okay. We are . . . friends."

"But, you don't have to."

He paused, thinking of the best way to start, and he couldn't help sighing a little, worrying what she might think of him. "We were in a hotel near an amusement park in Missouri. Randy, Billy, Danny Limbach and me. There was a boy with us, Patrick. He was one of the boys saved from that place in Chicago."

"Where Brett and Mike and Stephen were?"

"Yes, the same place."

George paused considering just how much to share without going into all the gory details.

"There was a man who wanted to kill this boy . . . Patrick. One night, he showed up and began shooting into our room. No one was hurt, but it was dangerous. I had my knife and I waited until he ran out of ammunition. I jumped through the window to stop him."

Caitlyn pulled her hand away from him and gasped.

"It was the only way I could stop him from hurting my brothers. If I hadn't done that, I think Randy would have been killed. He was too exposed."

She touched the long scar on his shoulder, tracing it with her fingertips and did the same to the smaller ones on his back.

"You got these cuts when you went through the window?"

George nodded and almost in a whisper, "And when I slipped on the broken glass on the balcony. I was covered in glass."

"What was the man doing when you crashed through the window?"

"I took him by surprise and he was standing with his gun in one hand and the ammunition clip in the other."

"What did you do?"

George hesitated, unwilling to say it out loud, hoping she would understand.

"I did not have a choice, Caitlyn. I had to stop him from killing my brothers."

"You killed him?" she whispered.

George nodded and said, "I did not have a choice."

He remained with his back to her, not wanting to face her, hoping she wouldn't turn and run and never speak to him again.

"You've never told this to anyone before, have you?"

"To the FBI and the police."

"Not even Brett?"

"Yes, Brett, Bobby and Gavin know. Mikey and Stephen know. And Brian and Sean."

"My cousin, Sean, knows? He never told me."

"I asked him . . . them, not to tell anyone." And he also didn't want anyone to know about the man sent to kill him and the twins, or the man who had come to kill them at the cabin in Arkansas, or the men in Arizona. Far too much killing and even though he had done so in order to protect his brothers and his father, he felt ashamed and embarrassed. It wasn't the Navajo way.

She frowned, because she and Sean shared secrets. But she also knew that if Sean gave his word to someone, he would never betray it.

Caitlyn squirted more lotion and gently coated his back.

"My turn."

George tightened the towel around his waist and took the lotion from her.

"You don't have any scars on your stomach or chest," Caitlyn said.

"I have scars on my legs."

"How high up do they go?"

"Very high."

He finished and she turned around, holding the towel loosely in front of her, but still covering herself. They were inches apart. He could smell her warm sweet breath and he was sure she could smell his.

"Can I see the scars?"

"If I showed you, you'd see more than just my scars."

She stared at him and whispered, "That might be awkward."

He smiled at her.

She blushed and said, "A boy showing off, I suppose."

George smiled and said, "Only when there is a pretty girl."

Caitlyn stepped forward and kissed him on the cheek.

Not sure what to say or do, George said, "I like you a lot."

She smiled and said, "I better get dressed."

Disappointed and uncomfortable in more ways than one, George said, "Okay."

She kissed him again and said, "I want to be friends."

He said, "I understand." But he didn't at all.

"I'll get my clothes and change in the bathroom."

Before she left the room, George said, "Caitlyn, I am sorry. About everything. Riding horses in the cold. I am sorry."

Caitlyn came back over to him, kissed his cheek and it seemed to George that she was struggling with what she wanted to say.

"I had fun horseback riding. I just didn't like the cold. I want to be friends, George."

She reached out and held his face and as she did, pressed herself against him and kissed him, and turned and left the room, shutting the door behind her.

George did not attempt to stop her and didn't say anything to make her turn around. He listened as she shut the bathroom door across the hall.

CHAPTER TEN

The three cops sat in a booth near the front window in a George Webb. Graff had already finished off a greasy cheeseburger and was taking his time munching on French fries and sipping a Diet Dr. Pepper. O'Connor also had a cheeseburger, but hadn't taken more than two bites. His fries were mostly untouched, but he did drink his Coke. Eiselmann was a power eater, but his meal only consisted of tomato soup and a toasted cheese sandwich with a mug of hot tea. He had explained that Sarah Bailey had invited him over for dinner.

After Graff ate a couple more French fries, he said, "Pat, you're the expert. What do you think?"

O'Connor wiped his mouth off with a paper napkin, sipped his Coke and said, "I," and he stopped. He had a habit of starting and stopping and both Graff and Eiselmann were used to it. "I haven't seen the tox screens on these two kids yet. But what I saw on our kid and what I saw in the picture of your kid . . . the one from this morning, I think we're dealing with heroin. Same as the other kids. Only this stuff is different. A mix of something. I think. Maybe."

"Why wouldn't it be just heroin?" Eiselmann asked.

"Because an OD on heroin doesn't have the effect we saw on our kid or Graff's kid. Not quite, anyway. Different."

"Where would it come from? Who would be running it?" Graff asked.

"Obvious answer would be MS-13. The Salvadorians own the drug business in and around Milwaukee, including Waukesha. They run shit up from Chicago, up I-43 into Kenosha and Racine, all the way up to Green Bay and Door County," Eiselmann said.

O'Connor shook his head, "I don't think so."

"Why?" Graff said.

"We have three high school kids and two middle school kids. I don't know much about the two kids today, but the others had nothing. No previous drug involvement. They didn't hang around any of the shits I know. They didn't have records of any kind. They don't fit the profile. So, how did they get heroin? Why did they even think of using heroin? From what I know in the reports, these kids didn't hang with one another. We don't even know if they knew one another."

The three men picked at their food, finished off their drinks and got refills.

"What do we have?" Graff asked looking out the cold wintery late afternoon.

"Shit if I know," Eiselmann muttered. "If it's not MS-13, we have another player or players. We'll have a mess on our hands if the 13 finds out someone is working their territory.

O'Connor thought it over and asked, "The schools the kids were from. What were the high schools again?"

Graff wiped his hands off on a napkin, opened up the manila folder and leafed through the pages.

"Two of the high school kids were from South. A sophomore and a junior. They might have known one another, but South is a big school. I have a buddy who's the athletic director there. Dan Domach. I can check with him. The other high school kid was a junior from West. My middle school kid was from Horning. Horning feeds South and it's only about eight hundred kids. I'm meeting with the principal, Mark Wegner, later today. Your kid was a seventh grader at Central. Most of those kids feed West, but some feed North."

"Would Mikey or Stephen know him . . . them? The one from Horning? I know they go to Butler now, but maybe they knew him from when they went to Horning. Maybe Brett or the twins or George knew the high school kids."

"I can check with Mikey and Stephen and see what they know," Eiselmann said. "I'm taking them to a movie tonight."

"Are you and Stephen's mom going to get married?" Graff asked.

O'Connor smiled knowingly.

"I haven't asked Sarah . . . officially, that is. But we've talked about it. I have to make sure Stephen is okay with it."

"It's been, what, a year and a half?" Graff asked.

"Ever since the summer from hell."

"A lot of shit that summer," Graff said. "Bad stuff."

"Well, at least now all the boys are safe," Eiselmann said.

"I'll ask the twins and George and Brett, but I doubt they knew the high school kids," Graff said. "They boys roll with a tight group. Not a lot of outsiders."

O'Connor shook his head and stared out the window.

"What?" Graff asked.

"Don't know yet." He shook his head, sipped his Coke and said, "Don't know yet."

Graff glanced at Eiselmann, who shrugged his shoulders and sipped his soup.

"If you can, have them keep their eyes and ears open. Not do or say anything, just listen and watch."

Graff and Eiselmann exchanged a look, but O'Connor didn't catch it. Deep in thought, he was staring out the window.

CHAPTER ELEVEN

There was more noise in the Evan's kitchen than Caitlyn was used to.

The boys had trooped in single file and each greeted Caitlin with "Hi, Cat" except for Brett and Jeremy who said, "Hi, Caitlyn." This was followed by laughter and everyone carrying on multiple conversations at the same time. She was stunned at the noise, but fascinated as well.

"So, how many times did you fall off?" Billy asked dryly.

"None, although I came close when we were riding back to the barn," she answered elbowing George in the ribs.

"You did fine," he said with a blush.

"Pretty cold?" Jeremy asked.

"I froze!" she answered with a laugh. "I couldn't feel my face until after I showered."

Brian sat across the kitchen table from them and glanced at Caitlyn every so often and when he did, he'd blush. Brett, George and Jeremy noticed, but didn't say anything, though they wondered.

"You made fry bread!" Randy said, grabbing a piece off the plate. To Caitlyn, he said, "Did you try this?"

"Yeah, it's good."

Brett debated whether or not to snag a piece before it disappeared, but decided instead to grab an orange from the refrigerator.

"You guys just ate!" Jeremy said with a laugh.

"We're growing!" Billy countered.

"You're bottomless pits!"

Billy and Randy sat down at the table next to Danny and Brian and talked basketball, while Brett, peeling an orange, worked with Bobby on his math homework. Bobby had wanted to finish it before heading to Danny's for the night.

"Look closely at your problem setup."

Bobby frowned at the sheet of paper in front of him and said, "I don't see anything."

Brett leaned over him, his chin resting on Bobby's shoulder, cheek to cheek and said, "Look at the first set."

Bobby started to object and said, "Oh man! That was stupid."

Brett laughed and said, "You rush sometimes. Just slow down."

Bobby reworked the problem under Brett's supervision and when he finished, Brett said, "Okay, do this one just to make sure." He quickly wrote down a problem and Bobby flew through it.

"Yup. Just remember to go slower and don't rush. The setup is the important part."

Bobby nodded, did the four that were left and put his homework away, as he half-listened in on Danny explaining to Caitlyn, Brian and George what they were going to do that evening.

"The idea is to come up with at least one or two really good songs. That's our goal."

"We have six so far," Randy said. "Some, Danny and I wrote. Some Bobby and Danny wrote."

Billy asked, "What are the chances of someone like Tim McGraw or somebody actually recording one?"

"Honestly? Slim to none." Danny leaned forward and said, "First of all, there are so many talented writers in Nashville. Writers who artists already look for. We're unknown and we're not in Nashville, so anyone actually listening to one of our songs is a longshot."

"But no one will listen if you don't try," Jeremy said.

"That's what dad told me," Danny said. "So, Randy, Bobby, Sean and I will see what we can come up with."

He paused only to take a swallow or two from his glass of ice water and said, "The second thing to remember is that there are tiers of performers in Nashville. You have one tier, artists like Kenny Chesney, Tim McGraw, Blake Shelton, Jason Aldean and Luke Bryan. A bunch more, but singers like that. It would be great to get one of our songs recorded by one of them, but like I said, the chances are slim to none. Then you have a second tier and even a third tier and then there are singers just starting out. We might have better luck with them. The big names seek out certain writers and if you look at their album credits, you'll see some of the same names. Those names are the writers we're competing with."

"Next weekend, we record demo tracks with Chris and Troy," Randy said. "G-Man will do the recording using the studio equipment at Danny's."

"Who's G-Man?" Caitlyn asked.

"Garrett Forstadt," Randy, Billy and Bobby answered in unison.

"Are Chris and Troy as good as you are?" George said.

"Both can sing really well," Randy said.

"Are you forming a group?" Jeremy asked with a smile.

The boys grinned back at him and Randy said, "We're starting one, yeah."

"The thing about Chris and Troy, they're rockers, so they won't let us get too country," Danny said.

"I wouldn't let that happen anyway," Randy offered. "I hate twangy stuff."

"Chris is the drummer for the jazz band and Troy plays cello and bass for the orchestra," Danny said. "Sean will play keyboards with Bobby, and Bobby will play guitar with Randy and me."

"Who's the lead singer?" Billy asked.

Randy said, "Depends on the song and who writes it."

"Mostly, the type of song," Danny said. "You don't want too many lead singers because the band won't have an identity and listeners can get confused and not know who the group is."

"But what's cool is that all of us can sing," Randy said.

"How will you get your songs to someone like Tim McGraw?" Brian asked.

"A couple of years ago, I was on the Letterman Show. I'm still in contact with Paul Shaffer."

"Wait . . . the band guy?" Brian said.

"Yeah. I was on the show a couple of times and he and I text back and forth. He said he'd listen to them and if they're good, he'll put in a good word for us. My dad's literary lawyer said he'd contact Tim McGraw's manager for us."

"Wait, how did you get on the Letterman Show?" Caitlyn asked.

Danny laughed, and his eyes lit up.

"I made a YouTube video singing Reo Speedwagon's song, *Roll with the*

Changes. I played guitar, piano and organ. Paul Shaffer saw it and they had me on."

"That's so cool," Caitlyn said. "I never knew that!"

Danny blushed.

Randy rescued him by saying, "We have to come up with really good songs or nothing happens."

"Can I ask you a question?" Brian asked Danny.

"Yeah, sure."

"I've heard you sing and I know you play like a hundred different instruments. You're really good. So, how come you never tried out for *American Idol* or *The Voice*?"

Danny shook his head. "Randy and Bobby sing better than I do."

"I like your voice," George said.

"If the song is kind of bluesy, I sound pretty good. But honestly, Randy and Bobby sing better than I do."

Randy blushed and said, "Gees, Danny, I don't know about that."

"But secondly, let's say I won *Idol* or *Voice*. I'd be a solo artist and I'd have to form a band anyway. I'm not interested in being a solo act. I'd rather be a part of a band and these guys are my friends. Lastly, because of my age, I'd end up being a novelty act. Acts fade all the time. I don't want to be in a high school garage band that cranks their amps up to ten, play nothing but power chords and cover everyone else's songs. That doesn't interest me. I want to establish us as singers and songwriters. That way, we have credibility."

"It's cool that you have it all thought out," Brett said.

Danny smiled, and his face lit up. "It's my dream. It's always been my dream."

As Danny spoke, it was hard to understand that he was closer to Bobby's age than he was to Brett's, George's or the twins'. Having an eidetic memory helped, but he was also gifted, not only musically, but academically. He had skipped a grade and could have skipped two, but his parents refused the school's recommendation citing social adjustment reasons.

He looked like his mother except for his blue eyes. His hair was a matter of debate. Depending upon the light or how the sun hit it, his hair was either blond or light brown or red.

"Are you like the leader of the group?" Brian asked.

"Yes!" Randy and Bobby said in unison.

Danny smiled and said, "I like to think that we'd all have a say in any of the decisions."

"But you know music better than any of us," Randy said.

"And there might be a time when someone will have to make a decision from time to time, don't you think?" Jeremy said.

Randy and Bobby laughed and pointed at Danny.

Danny shrugged nonchalantly. "Well, none of it matters unless we come up with a couple of songs that are really good."

"Are you guys spending the night?" Jeremy asked.

"Yeah, Randy, Sean and me," Bobby said.

"What time is church tomorrow?" Brett asked.

"Nine-fifteen," Jeremy answered.

Brett turned to Bobby and said, "You'll need to be back here by eight-thirty. Earlier if you shower and stuff. And text me."

Bobby smiled at him. He loved his older brother. Ever since Brett's rescue, the two of them had grown almost inseparable. "Sure. What are you going to do tonight?"

"Thinking about going to a movie," Billy said.

Bobby frowned.

"We can go next weekend after we record," Randy said.

"Hey, guys, before you leave, George and I have something to ask you," Brett said.

He looked over at George and said, "Jamie Graff asked George and Gavin and me to go ice fishing. Is that okay with you?"

"I don't care," Randy said.

"Me, neither," Bobby echoed.

"Fishing has to be the world's most boring sport ever, right up there with bowling," Billy said. "And fishing on a frozen lake freezing your butt off sounds like way too much fun for me."

"Ice fishing is fun," Brian said.

"You've gone ice fishing?" Brett asked.

"My dad used to take Brad and me. I like it."

Billy reached around Randy and put the back of his hand on Brian's forehead and said, "He has a fever. He's burning up and delirious."

The boys and Caitlyn laughed.

"If Jamie says okay, would you want to go with us?" Brett asked.

Brian shrugged and said, "I'd go. I'd have to ask my parents, but I don't think they'd care."

Brett pulled out his cell and his fingers flew over the keypad.

"Gotta go," Randy said. "Dad, we're going to take one of the four wheelers."

"Just be careful and behave yourselves. No racing," he added pointing a finger at them.

Randy and Bobby got up to leave, gave hugs and kisses to Jeremy and Bobby hugged Brett who said, "Don't forget, by 8:30. And text me."

"I will, promise."

"Love you," Brett said.

"Love you too."

They left the house as Sean's dad pulled up in the driveway. Sean got out of the car carrying a small drawstring bag and with a wave hopped on the back of Danny's four wheeler. Danny and Sean led Randy and Bobby to his house using the path through the woods.

Dr. Drummond was an orthodontist, tall and slender and built like the jogger he was. He had the same blond hair and bright blue eyes as his son and evidently the gene must have been a strong one because Caitlyn, his niece, had the same slender build along with the same color of eyes and hair.

He knocked on the door, opened it and said, "Hello?"

"Come on in, Dave," Jeremy said.

He stamped his feet on the rug in the little hallway off the kitchen and walked in.

"It's cold out there."

"I don't think we should ever have to go outside unless the temperature doubles my age," Jeremy said.

He laughed and said, "I can agree with that."

"Can I get you anything? Coffee?"

"No, thank you. I am Caitlyn's taxi." He turned to his niece and said, "So, how many times did you fall off?"

Everyone laughed and Caitlyn said, "Why does everyone think I fell off?"

"Well, did you?" Dave Drummond asked with a laugh, nudging Brian.

"*Nooo,*" she answered with a laugh.

"She rides well," George said.

Brian glanced at Caitlyn, looked away and blushed.

It occurred to George and Brett that Brian liked her more than as a friend. And maybe, Caitlyn felt something for Brian.

They chit-chatted a little and Dave said, "Ready to head home, Little Lady?"

"Yes. I'm not ready to go out in the cold again, though."

George stood up and went to the front closet and retrieved Caitlyn's jacket, cap and gloves and brought them into the kitchen. Like a gentleman, he helped her into her jacket.

"I'll walk out with you."

He grabbed a heavy sweatshirt out of the little hallway off the kitchen and followed Caitlyn and her uncle to the car.

Dave got in and shut the door, but before Caitlyn did, she turned around and said, "I had fun today."

George smiled and blushed. He figured she was just being polite, but said, "I'm glad you did."

She kissed him on the cheek and said, "Really."

She got in the car, buckled up and waved as they drove around the driveway circle and back out to the county highway.

George looked on with his hands shoved into his jeans pockets, long after the taillights had disappeared, then walked back into the house.

CHAPTER TWELVE

Jeremy sat in his office on his soft plush couch facing the warm fire in the fireplace. The soft pop and crackle soothed him as he read the newest Baldacci paperback. He alternated between using his Kindle and reading a paperback, but there was just something about turning a real page, something about the smell of a paperback that a Kindle couldn't compete with.

Brett wandered in from the family room, disregarded Jeremy's solitude and his book and stretched out on the couch using Jeremy's thigh as a pillow.

Jeremy put his book down and held Brett's hand. "Aren't you cold, Little Man?"

Brett wore a blue Under Armour t-shirt, navy blue Nike sweatpants and black low cut athletic socks.

"Nah, I'm good."

He watched the fire, content with the silence and Jeremy's company.

"What's all the racket in the family room?"

Brett laughed and said, "George and Billy want to take a nap and are fighting over who gets the couch." He looked up at Jeremy with a grin and said, "George will win."

"What's Brian doing?"

"He's asleep in the recliner. He sat down and was out."

Jeremy finger-combed Brett's hair, pushing his short bangs off his forehead. His and Bobby's hair was cut much like Randy's and Billy's, and was much shorter than when Jeremy had first met them.

"What's on your mind, little man?"

Brett smiled up at him. "I was thinking."

"Oh, that's dangerous. I hope it didn't hurt too much."

Brett ignored him and said, "I really like football."

"You're really good at it. You're tough and you're fast and it's rare that a freshman makes the all-conference team, and both you and Billy earned that."

"Second team," Brett said dismissively.

"Still, to be recognized as a freshman is rare."

"And I really like basketball," Brett said.

"Well, you're good at that, too. I like the way you take control and run the team. You have great court vision. You can pass and shoot, but I think your real strength is defense."

As if Brett hadn't heard him, he said, "But my best sport is track. I went online and I think this spring, I can make state in the one hundred and two hundred."

Jeremy nodded and waited for him to continue.

"So, I was thinking," Brett said looking up at him. "If I get hurt in football, it could screw up my basketball and track."

"You could also get hurt in basketball or track."

"Yeah, but the odds are greater in football. I return punts and kickoffs. I play free safety and next year, Randy and Billy and I could end up in the backfield. Randy and Billy are thicker than I am. We're all pretty strong, but I'm smaller. Statistically, the chances of me getting hurt are greater in football than in basketball or track."

"So, what are you saying?" Jeremy asked, gently rubbing Brett's cheek with his thumb.

"I think my chances of getting a college scholarship for track are greater than getting a scholarship for football or basketball."

"Do you like playing football?"

"Yes, but that's not the point."

"Brett, you could step off a curb and break your foot. You could fall down the stairs and tear an ACL."

"But I'm careful that way. I can't play football carefully because I'd be thinking too much. Football is about pre-snap reads and reacting or forcing the action."

"So, what are you saying?" Jeremy repeated.

"I just wonder if I should concentrate on basketball and track and not play football."

Jeremy pursed his lips, thought it over, but didn't say anything.

"What do you think?"

Jeremy didn't answer right away, but ran his fingers through Brett's hair while Brett waited.

"Let's say you sat out of football. Both Randy and Billy play and like most everyone figures, they'll start. Randy at quarterback and Billy at one of the running backs. How would you feel?"

"I think I'd go frigging nuts," Brett said with a little laugh.

"Would that be worth it to you?"

Brett shrugged.

"There have been a number of college guys, even pro guys who played football or basketball, or football and track. Yes, there is always the chance for injury in anything you do, but you can't live your life afraid."

"So, you think I should keep playing football?"

"Brett, I'll never tell you what to do, just like I won't tell Randy or Billy or George what to do. It's your life, not mine. You're the one who has to be happy with any decision you make."

Brett smiled at him and said, "I knew you were going to say that."

Jeremy hugged him and kissed his forehead.

"I would like to do some races this summer, you know, like I used to, before . . ." he stopped not wanting to go there. "I looked up the Badger State Games and I think both George and I should run. But if it's okay with you, I'd like to also run in Hershey. I think George would too."

"Hershey, Pennsylvania?"

Brett nodded. "I ran it before and it's fun. There's an amusement park there."

Jeremy remembered the last amusement park he tried to take the kids to and the outcome wasn't all that amusing.

"Have you spoken to your mom about this?"

"I wanted to ask you first."

Jeremy nodded and said, "Why don't you make a list of all the possible races and places you'd like to go to, talk it over with George and even Bobby, because I think he's going to be almost as fast as you, and your mom and I will talk about it. Okay?"

"I think Billy wants to go to a couple of camps. Even Randy. Bobby and I wouldn't mind going to a basketball camp."

Jeremy smiled and said, "They've talked to me about it already."

Brett nodded and stared at the fire, but held Jeremy's hand. After a time, he said without looking up at him, "Can I ask you a question?"

"Always."

"You're my dad. You're Bobby's dad."

Jeremy felt himself blush, but he couldn't help smiling. "And you and Bobby are my sons, just as much as Billy and Randy and George are. Even Brian."

Brett nodded and said, "I love them . . . all of them. I love Brian."

"Me too."

He turned and looked up at Jeremy and said, "So, I was thinking. Let's just say if by some chance . . . if you and mom don't marry or if mom starts dating some other guy and ends up marrying him. Would you still be Bobby's and my dad?"

Jeremy smiled down at him and kissed his forehead and gave him an Eskimo.

"I doubt that will happen, little man. Honestly. But if by some chance that happens, you'll have three men in your life who care about you and love you very much."

"Three?" Brett asked. "You're including Tom?"

"He is your biological father."

Brett shook his head and said, "He's nothing to me."

Jeremy knew better than to argue the point. He'd never win, and he'd never dissuade the boy.

"Do you promise that no matter what, even if mom marries someone else, you'll be Bobby's and my dad? Promise?"

Jeremy hugged him fiercely and Brett hugged him back. They held onto each other and kissed each other's cheek.

"Brett, you and Bobby mean as much to me as Randy and Billy and George and Brian. I mean that and that will never change." They hugged each other again, exchanged kisses and Jeremy repeated, "Ever."

Brett nodded and wiped his eyes on his t-shirt.

"If I take a nap, can you wake me up at five-thirty? We're going to the movie and it starts at six-forty-five."

"Which theater?"

"The Marcus on Bluemound."

And not waiting for an answer, Brett curled up on the couch using Jeremy's leg as his pillow. Still holding onto Jeremy's hand, he shut his eyes and was out. Jeremy took the blanket off the back of the couch and with one hand, covered Brett with it.

Jeremy alternately watched Brett sleep and watched the fire, happy with his life and his growing family.

CHAPTER THIRTEEN

Sitting on the floor in the hallway near the doorway with his knees drawn up to his chest, Brian heard most of the conversation between Jeremy and Brett. He hadn't intended to eavesdrop, but he didn't want to butt in either. Still, he found he couldn't leave.

He never worried about getting hurt in soccer. It had never occurred to him. Sure, there was a sprained ankle and a bruised knee here or there and sometimes his hip pointer bothered him. Sometimes even his hamstring bothered him, but all of that was expected. Eventually they went away. Never did he ever think of quitting. He liked soccer too much, probably better than basketball, but he liked both.

Twice, he heard Jeremy say that he was as important as Randy and Billy, George and Brett and Bobby. Twice, he heard Jeremy say that he was part of their family. Well, not actually a part of the family, but kind of. And he had heard Jeremy and Brett say that they loved him.

Ever since Brad had died, his parents had changed. In the year and a half since, he never had a conversation with his mom or dad like Brett had with Jeremy and that was unusual, because he and his brother always talked to his parents. Little things, big things, mostly everything.

But all that changed the night Brad was shot and killed along with so many others. Part of the summer of death. Ever since that summer, his parents sat around the house like extras in *The Walking Dead*.

Quietly, slowly, Brian stood up and walked back to the family room.

George was covered with a light blanket and asleep on the couch with his dog, Jasmine, on the floor beside him. Billy was covered with a blanket and asleep on the floor next to the couch.

Jasper, with his tail wagging, looked up at him from the floor next to the recliner. Brian knelt down and scratched the dog behind the ears and in return, Jasper licked Brian's face. He hugged the dog and Jasper responded by snuffling into his neck.

Brian stood up and sat down in the recliner and patted the chair, signaling to Jasper to join him. The dog jumped up and nestled in Brian's lap as Brian curled up and fell back to sleep.

CHAPTER FOURTEEN

There were a couple of friends, but mostly, there were kids he only saw in the hallways or in one or two classes. The ones he attended, anyway. He knew them by face, but not necessarily by name. His real friends, if he actually had any real friends, weren't there.

The party was billed as an island party with beer and rum, so what the hell- he didn't really care who was there or who wasn't.

His girlfriend got invited and asked him if he wanted to go. He said sure, only because he hoped to get laid or maybe get a blow job. If he was lucky, both. He wasn't super good-looking, but he looked okay. Not a jock or one of the popular guys, but above average maybe. A couple of pimples here and there, but he had nice teeth and hair. But she liked the tat on his forearm and liked what he had to give her every so often, so all was good as far as he was concerned. She was plain, but she had nice boobs and she put out. He'd ride that horse, pun intended, as long as he could or until he got tired of her, whichever came first.

His cell buzzed so he pulled it out of his back pocket to see who the caller was.

It was him.

The boy downed what was left of his beer in three gulps and it tasted bitter. He considered whether the beer actually tasted bitter or if the man on the other end of the line made it taste bitter.

The boy walked out into the backyard unnoticed, pushed the green button and said, "Yeah?"

"We can't have any more deaths. The cops are looking hard."

The boy swallowed uncomfortably and said, "They were accidents."

"We can't have any more accidents. We won't have any customers and those we do have might get nervous and talk."

The boy's mouth went dry. "We're looking for the right mix. The little shits took too much. Same with the high school guys. That's not my fault."

"What I'm saying is, if there are any more accidents and if the cops find a leak, you guys are screwed."

Boldly, if not recklessly he said, "You mean, *we*, don't you?"

"Is that a threat?"

The boy didn't answer, but he wasn't about to back down either. He knew enough to bring everyone down if someone tried to put it all on him. Maybe the man knew, maybe not. But no way was he going to go down alone.

"I-I think we have it about right. There shouldn't be any more . . . accidents."

"For your sake, there had better not be."

"We're testing it again later tonight."

"Where did you find him . . . or her?"

"Him. One of my regulars."

"When can we begin distribution?"

The boy hesitated at first, but answered, "Next week."

The call ended.

He didn't feel much like going back into the party, but the girl was in there along with the promise of getting laid or a blow job, so back in he went. He could always prime the pump with some rum and some beer and maybe with a few of the goodies he brought with him. Might end up making some money.

CHAPTER FIFTEEN

"Did you mind that I didn't go to the movie with the guys?" Brian asked quietly.

Jeremy shook his head, smiled and slipped his arm around Brian's shoulder and said, "Not at all. A little surprised, but I don't mind a bit."

Brian shrugged and said, "I can go see it with Randy and Sean and Bobby and Danny."

Skyfall was about half the way through. They had decided to watch it because both Jeremy and Brian liked action adventures. They shared a big bowl of popcorn that sat on Brian's lap. Brian had a large glass of iced green tea and Jeremy sipped a Diet Coke.

What surprised Jeremy was that when he had seated himself in his favorite spot on the couch in front of the fire and the large screen TV above the mantel, Brian sat down right next to him. *Right* next to him. Up against him and actually leaning on him.

Brian had longish dark wavy hair and greenish, hazel eyes. He was broad-shouldered with thick, strong legs and a thin flat waist. He stood about the same size as Bobby and a little taller than Brett. He was quiet and reserved like Brett and George, a little more like Randy, who was a bit more talkative. His twin, Brad, was more outgoing like Billy and Bobby. Both Brad and Brian were intelligent and more than that, confident.

"How long have you liked Caitlyn?"

Brian had a handful of popcorn that stopped midway between bowl and mouth. He set his hand back down, but held onto the popcorn. He turned six or seven different shades of red and didn't say anything.

Jeremy smiled and ruffled his hair a little. "I could tell by the way you looked at her."

Brian blushed deep crimson and said, "Did George or anyone else notice?"

Jeremy laughed and said, "Probably. George doesn't miss anything. Brett doesn't either."

Brian sighed and bit the inside of his mouth.

"I've known her like forever. Sean and Caitlyn and I always hung around together."

"So why didn't you ever ask her out?"

Brian blushed a little more, if that was even possible. He shrugged, but didn't answer. Jeremy let the silence pass without comment, because he knew Brian well enough to know that eventually, he'd circle around and answer him in his own way. A lot like George that way.

"Can I ask you a question?" Brian asked.

"Sure, anything."

"You don't have to answer if you don't want to."

"Bri, you can always ask me anything and you'll always get an honest answer. That's one of the rules in this house. If we can't be honest with one another, we can't trust one another. And if we can't trust one another, we can't have any kind of relationship." He finished by giving him a little hug.

Brian nodded and said, "Randy was your first son and Billy was your second. George and Brett and Bobby came this last summer after . . . everything."

Jeremy nodded.

"Do you have a favorite?" Brian turned to look at him, to study his eyes as much as he wanted to hear his words. "I mean, is there one you like more than the other?"

Jeremy smiled at him, shaking his head, and kissed his forehead before answering. "No, I don't have any favorites. As hard as it might seem, I love them all and you, the same."

Jeremy experienced a strange sense of *déjà vu* having had the same conversation with George shortly after meeting him.

"Brian, love is like a candle. You take a candle and light it and no matter how many other candles you light from it, you never lose the light from that first candle. In fact, you can light a hundred candles and the only thing that happens is that the room becomes brighter. And that describes love."

Brian's face clouded over, but he said nothing.

"Bri, love is magical in that the more you give away, the more you have."

Brian nodded, started to say something, but stopped.

"You're a lot like Randy and George and Brett. You guys are thoughtful and deep. You have playful sides, but generally, you guys are quiet. Billy and Bobby are a little more outgoing."

"Like Brad . . . was."

"Yes, that's the way I remember him. What I like about our family is that even though each of you are a little different from one another, you're all similar to one another. I like being a dad to you guys. Even you, Brian. I know you have your own mom and dad, but I like it when you come over."

"Everybody liked Brad."

"Well, I happen to like you." Jeremy hugged him and kissed the side of his head. He waited a little and said, "Brian, what are you really asking me?"

He watched a tear or two trickle down the side of Brian's face that Brian didn't bother to brush off. It occurred to him that Brian probably would have held it together and not cried at all if the boys were present, because he was a little self-conscious, maybe proud that way.

"I think my parents liked Brad more than me."

Jeremy's heart sunk. "Why do you think that?"

Brian shrugged and wept, but never answered. Jeremy let him, but didn't let go of his shoulders.

"Brian, your parents love you very much."

Brian said nothing.

"What you and they are experiencing is grief. They lost a son and parents should never outlive their own children. I can't imagine losing one of my sons. And you not only lost a brother, you lost a friend."

Again, Jeremy experienced *déjà vu* thinking about being alone with George up on the Mesa facing those three men. He thought about facing the man in the cabin, tied up to a chair with duct tape across his mouth, unable to come to Billy's aid when the man pinched his nose shut. Billy had only passed out, but Jeremy thought Billy had died. All of what had happened during the summer of death.

"Brian, your parents are in pain."

Brian struggled. Each sentence came out as a sob. "They. Still. Have. Me. It's like I don't exist. I was on the varsity soccer team. A freshman. I started every game. I played the whole game, every game. Do you know how many games my parents came to? None. My dad came to the soccer banquet, but left. Sean and his parents took me home."

Jeremy was aware of what had happened. He had tried getting Brian's parents some help and they had seemed receptive to it, but had never followed through.

Back when he was in eighth grade, shortly after the summer had ended, Brian began spending at least one night a week, usually on the weekends, with him and the boys. It was Billy, Brett and George who had looked after Brian the most, but each of the boys accepted him as one of the family.

"Sometimes I wonder if it was me instead of Brad . . ." but he couldn't finish the thought.

Jeremy held him, whispered to him and Brian wept, but eventually quieted down. He never raised his head from Jeremy's chest.

Finally, Jeremy kissed the top of Brian's head and held his face so that the two could look each other in the eye.

"Brian, I know you're hurting as much as your parents. You lost your brother. I can't imagine what you're going through. It's a lot like George losing his whole family. Like Billy losing his dad. But I want you to know that I love you like a son. The boys and I love you just as if you were a part of our family. I mean that."

Brian nodded.

"As long as your parents give you permission and know where you are, you're welcome here anytime for as long as you like. You'll always be welcome here. Always." As if he needed to remind the boy, Jeremy said, "I love you Brian."

Brian nodded again. He hugged Jeremy and didn't let go.

CHAPTER SIXTEEN

"It was kind of slow," Billy said as he stood up and stretched. "I liked it okay, I guess."

"I liked it," Brett said.

The boys followed the herd of people up the aisle towards the exit and dropped their empty bucket of popcorn and mostly empty soda and water containers into the large trash bag held by the theater attendants waiting to clean up. They were high school kids and looked familiar to the boys, but only to smile at and nod to.

"What did you think?" Billy asked George.

George made a face and said, "It was okay. I like movies about spies. Cop movies, too."

Billy laughed, and Brett smiled and said, "I can see you doing stuff like that."

George smiled and followed the two boys out into the red-carpeted hallway. They moved to the side and zipped up. None of them had a hat, but Brett had a scarf and both George and Billy wore hooded sweatshirts under their coats. They slipped the hoods over their head.

Billy pulled out his phone, read the text and said, "Kaz said he and dad are on the way. They're picking us up and we're going for pizza."

They trudged out of the warm theater and their breath was sucked from them by the cold air. Instinctively, they hunched their shoulders and huddled together near the corner of the building against the wall, looking for Jeremy's car. The theater goers dispersed to their cars quickly, chased by the icy wind.

"McGovern, you're a fucking pussy!"

Doug Sweeney stood in front of them. Another kid, one that usually hung around with Sweeney stood a little to the side and behind him.

"I should kick your ass just because you need it."

"I'm kinda busy, Doug. Your mom wanted me to fuck her tonight, but I'm not looking forward to it. She's old and wrinkly and kind of ugly like you. The good part is that when she gives me a blow job, I don't have to worry about her biting my dick because she's missing most of her teeth."

Sweeney clenched his bare fists, glared and said, "You little fucker!"

He took one step towards Brett, but George stepped in between them.

"What are you going to do, Indian Boy?"

It happened so quickly, that none of the boys could actually describe what took place next. As he reached out to push George aside, George grabbed Sweeney's hand and bent it awkwardly behind him and to the side at an improbable angle. Using Sweeney's forward momentum, George used his foot to trip Sweeney, throwing him face first into the brick wall.

Still hanging onto his hand, George moved up alongside of Sweeney and whispered, "You will leave my brothers, my family and my friends alone. Do you understand me?"

Stunned for just a moment, Sweeney yelled, "Fuck!"

Hanging onto his hand and bending, almost breaking his arm, George lowered Sweeney to the sidewalk, scraping his face against the brick wall leaving a bloody trail.

"You're breaking my fucking hand, you mother . . ."

George torqued his hand just enough to stop him, except for Sweeney yelling, "Jesus! Jesus!"

George squatted down and repeated, "You will leave my brothers, my family and my friends alone. Do you understand me?"

"You're breaking . . ."

"Do you understand me?"

"Yes! Jesus! You're breaking my arm!"

Still holding onto Sweeney's hand, George lifted him off the sidewalk, pushed him around the side of the theater and sent him headlong into wet, slushy and dirty snow. Sweeney stayed down long enough to test his hand and his arm. He got to his hands and knees and shakily stood up. Blood and snot dripped from Sweeney's nose and blood dripped from a cut above his eye and from a scrape on his cheek.

George stood in front of him calmly and relaxed, his hands out to the side, feet spread slightly for balance and quickness. He pointed at Sweeney's friend, who lifted both hands as if he were being robbed, shook his head and took two steps backwards.

"You fucker!"

"What's going on, boys?"

Sheriff Detective Paul Eiselmann appeared next to George. Stephan Bailey and Mike Erickson stood with Brett and Billy, though both of the older boys positioned themselves slightly in front of the two younger ones.

"That fuckin' Indian tried to break my arm!"

"Is it broken? Because if George meant to break it, I'm sure he would have."

Sweeney glared at him, wiped at his nose, his hand coming up bloody.

"He assaulted me! I want him arrested!"

Billy and Brett started to object, but Eiselmann held up his hand and said, "You're what, about a foot taller and maybe fifty or sixty pounds heavier? That might be tough for you to explain. I'm a deputy sheriff, so maybe I should call Jamie Graff and he and I can investigate this further. I'm off duty, so I don't really want to." He pointed at the bank and ATM across the street and the traffic camera at the corner and said, "However, if I investigated what happened, I might wonder about some things. Such as, I might wonder what those cameras might show. I might wonder who the aggressor was. I might wonder who actually started . . . whatever happened here tonight, and I bet those cameras would show me quite a bit."

Billy said, pointing at Sweeney. "He tried to go after Brett, but George stopped him."

Eiselmann nodded and said, "Seems like we have some witnesses who would be willing to make a statement and statements are important if an investigation is going to be thorough. And if Jamie or I do an investigation, you can be certain that we're going to be thorough."

He saw Sweeney's eyes flit from side to side. The boy licked his lips, all the fight and bluster suddenly out of him.

"Maybe all of us want to walk away from this," Eiselmann suggested. "Maybe walking away might be the thing to do. It's cold and late and I think everyone might want to go home."

The other boy, who remained as far from Sweeney as he could, said, "Let's go, Doug."

Sweeney took one more look at George, wiped at his nose, pointed and said, "This isn't over, Indian Boy. You and me."

"Did I just hear you threaten George? Did you really just threaten him in front of me? *Really?*"

Sweeney shut his mouth and his friend took a step away from him.

"See, now if something was to happen to George or Brett or Billy or anyone else for that matter, I would have to investigate and because I have a very good memory, I would remember that threat, now wouldn't I?"

"But you're a sheriff," Sweeney said not hiding the doubt in his voice.

Eiselmann moved so quickly that in three steps, he stood nose to bloody nose with Sweeney.

"I'm law enforcement and I work closely with the police department. I smell alcohol on your breath and I know you're not of age. You want to play junior lawyer and tough guy, I'll play along. Let's see how far that gets you."

Sweeney took a step backward, turned and walked away. His friend hesitated, but followed keeping a safe distance from him.

Eiselmann watched the two boys and after he made sure they were actually leaving, he turned around to George and said, "What was that all about?"

"Sweeney threatened Brett and wanted to fight him. George stopped him," Billy answered for them.

He nodded and said, "It's cold and getting late. Is someone coming to pick you guys up or do you need a ride?"

"Dad's coming to get us," Brett answered.

Eiselmann nodded and said, "Okay. Be safe and smart. I think this is over, but you never know."

The boys nodded, and Billy said, "We will."

Eiselmann nodded one more time and said, "Okay." To Mike and Stephen, he said, "Let's go home, boys."

They left the three boys on the sidewalk to wait for Jeremy and Brian.

The three of them sat in a beefed up nondescript muscle car across and down the street from the theater. They had watched the confrontation and the outcome.

"Who is the red-haired dude?"

Angel Benevides, a seventeen-year-old junior at North High School, knew each of the boys. Privately he cheered for George, because he couldn't stand Sweeney. He had not wanted to come along, but was ordered to by his older brother, Manuel, who used to go to North before he was expelled for selling drugs in one of the restrooms. Manuel hadn't been back since, but probably had more money than all of the teachers and administrators at North combined.

"He's five-oh, Dude. Sheriff," Angel answered.

Manuel drove, while Angel sat in the back with three handguns and two Fallout 10 Mm machine guns with two fully loaded clips each hidden under a blanket. Angel had no intention of touching any weapon. Ever.

The short, slightly built, dark-skinned guy sat in the passenger seat next to Manuel. Angel had never seen him before and from what he saw, didn't care to know him or ever see him again. He knew he wouldn't be that lucky. His brother would see to it. Other than that one question about the red-haired dude, Ricardo Fuentes had remained silent, thoughtful and almost brooding. Angel had no idea how old he was. Somewhere between twenty and forty, he couldn't tell.

"How connected is this George Tokay?"

"Very," Angel said. He didn't like Fuentes. He didn't much like his older brother either, for that matter. Unfortunately, family was family and MS-13 wasn't fussy about giving orders. Or killing.

Fuentes froze Angel with a stare. He glanced back out on the street.

"How *very* is very?"

"His dad is a counselor at North. They're friends with a police detective, that red-haired dude and this other skinny, long-haired dude. They're all friends," Angel said in hopes that Fuentes and Manuel would back off.

They watched as a Ford Expedition pulled up and the three boys jump in.

"Keep a distance, but follow them."

Angel sighed and said, "I know where they live."

Fuentes turned around and scowled at Angel and said, "I don't give a fuck what you know or don't. We're going to follow them, and you can keep your mouth shut until I ask you a question."

Angel glanced at his older brother who shook his head once in warning. He sighed again, wishing he was anywhere else.

Keeping two cars between them, they followed the Expedition to *Mia's Italian Restaurant* on Clinton Street. Jeremy and three of the boys got out and hustled inside. Angel knew each of them and he was pretty sure they knew him, so he sunk low in the back seat as his brother parked across and down the street.

He watched George get out of the backseat on the street side, stop at the back of the vehicle and turn and stare in their direction before he went inside with the others.

"Did he make us?" Manuel asked.

No one answered, but Angel hoped he did.

CHAPTER EIGHTEEN

They had fed and watered the horses, cleaned out the stalls and put down fresh hay. George had decided to try to mate Nochero with Danny's horse, Star, so he led Star out of the stable and gave the reins to Brian to hold. He led Nochero to her and with a little help from George and Billy, Nochero mounted Star until he was sated.

Brett didn't want to help, and he didn't want to watch the two horses or listen to the noises the horses made. He left the stable, braved the cold night air and wandered around outside until Billy called him back in.

Not wanting to leave the stable, the four boys sprawled out on bales of hay. George lay on his back with his hands under his head and a piece of straw in his mouth, with Brett leaning up against him with his head half on George's shoulder and the other half on his chest, facing Billy and Brian. Jasmine had her head on George's stomach and Jasper had his head on Brian's thigh, content with Brian scratching him behind his ear.

Nochero roamed the small stable and stood in front of Brian, staring at him.

"Uhh, George? What's he want?"

George lifted his head, smiled and said, "He wants you to pet him."

"How do you pet a horse?"

As George sat up, Brett shifted to his side and propped his head up on his hand, using his elbow to give him a bit of height so he could watch.

"Under his head, run your hand down his neck slowly."

Brian scratched Jasper one more time, stood up and faced the big black stallion.

"Okay, Horse, I've never done this before."

He stepped to the side and followed George's instructions, marveling at how smooth Nochero's skin was. The big horse shifted and using his head and neck, pulled Brian towards him.

"Woah, Big Guy. George, what's he doing?"

"He's giving you a hug."

"Seriously?"

"Besides me, he's only done that to one other person."

"Who?" Billy asked.

"Rebecca."

"Oh," Billy said.

"How come he wanted to hug Brian?" Brett asked. He wasn't envious, just curious.

George's answer was interesting, but didn't quite answer Brett's question. He said, "My grandfather told me that a horse chooses the rider. The rider doesn't choose the horse."

"Hmmm," Brett said.

Brian stepped away from Nochero and with each step Brian took, Nochero blocked his way.

"What's he doing now?"

"He wants you to ride him."

"Seriously?"

"Yes."

"Don't I need a saddle and stuff?"

George chuckled and said, "Jump up on his back. Nochero will walk around the stable a little."

Brian looked at the horse and then at George doubting this whole thing.

"How do I get up there?"

"Jump, White Boy! Jump!" Billy laughed.

Brian flipped him off, tried once, twice and failed both times and the boys laughed, including Brian. Nochero stood by patiently.

"I can't get up there."

Billy jumped down from the hay, stepped around to the side, bent down and used his hands to help Brian up.

"One, two, up . . ." and Billy easily lifted Brian up onto Nochero's back.

He straddled the horse and said, "What do I hang onto?"

"His neck."

Brian looked down at the floor and considered what it would feel like if he fell, hoping that he'd land on his feet and not on his head. Slowly, Nochero walked around the stable in a slow circle. He stopped at the far end and did a side step, actually walking sideways.

"Gees!" Brian said, holding the stallion's neck tighter.

"He's showing off," George said.

"Yeah, well . . ."

"George, how did you do that? I mean, with Sweeney?" Billy asked.

"Do what with Sweeney?" Brian asked as Nochero resumed walking normally in a slow, small circle.

"He tried to pick a fight with Brett and ended up with half his face stuck on the brick wall," Billy answered with a laugh. "It happened so fast, but it was really cool."

Brian glanced at George, but George, unreadable, betrayed nothing.

"Where did you learn to fight like that?" Billy asked.

George shrugged and said, "I'm not sure. It just happened."

"I would have liked to have punched him," Brett said.

"You're in season and you can't afford to get hurt or get suspended from the team. He'll come after you again, so you have to be smart," George said, placing his hand on Brett's shoulder.

"Sweeney's a tool," Brian declared.

Nochero stopped in front of the bale of hay Billy sat on and didn't move. When Brian didn't get off, Nochero swung his head around, flicked his tail and nickered.

Brian got the hint and swung his leg over and hopped down. Like before, he tried to get around the horse, but Nochero blocked his path.

"What?"

"He wants another hug," George said.

Brian stepped under his head, stroked the horse's soft and muscular neck and embraced him. Nochero used his head to hold him tight. At last, Brian released the horse and the two separated, Brian to his perch on the bale of hay next to Billy and Nochero to his corral next to Star.

Billy playfully grabbed him from behind and put him in a loose headlock. Brian fought back, but because Billy was behind him, Brian was at a disadvantage.

"You smell like horse and you're a weenie. Say, 'Uncle!'"

"Aunt!"

"Say, 'Uncle!'"

"You're an old lady," Brian said with a laugh.

Billy let him go and the two boys settled in, content with the soft noises from the animals, the warmth of the stable and the comfort of best friends, brothers.

Brian scratched Jasper behind the ear and said, "Why didn't you defend me? Huh? Why didn't you bite him?"

Jasper licked Brian's face as George said, "Jasper knows better. Billy wouldn't taste very good."

"I am sweet and delicious," Billy laughed. "Just ask my many girlfriends."

"In your wet dreams," Brian said with a laugh.

"Guys, dad said we need to make a list of any camps and stuff we want to go to this summer. George, Bobby and I want to run in the Badger State Games and in Hershey, and Bobby and I want to go to a basketball camp."

"I'd like to go to a football camp and a basketball camp," Billy said as he nipped Brian's left ear playfully. "Randy wants to go to a quarterback camp and a basketball camp."

"What about you, Brian? What do you want to do?" Brett asked.

"Me?"

"Yeah. Dad said make a list of all the camps and stuff for everyone."

Brian said, "Well, okay, I guess. I'm going to the Schwan's Cup with my travel team for sure." He flicked on his phone, chose the calendar app and said, "It's in mid-July and it goes from Thursday through Sunday." He looked up excitedly and said, "There are teams from all over the world. We exchange pins and collect them. It's really cool. But the best part is that there are college coaches watching us. Because Mario is on our team, he's sure to have a bunch of coaches watching. And if they're watching him, they're watching us . . . me." To be safe, he added, "Hopefully."

Brett checked his calendar, smiled and nodded. "So, are you interested in going to a basketball camp?"

The excitement left Brian's eyes as quickly as it arrived. Whereas his eyes danced as he talked about the soccer, all the joy had vanished in an eye-blink.

"I don't think my parents can afford to send me to a basketball camp."

Billy put a hand on Brian's shoulder and slipped his arm across Brian's chest and held him.

"I think dad is planning on sending you with us. Billy, Randy, Bobby and me. I think Gav's mom is going to send Gav to the same camp. There's one that fits in between your soccer tourney and the end of July and beginning of August. So, don't worry about it."

"It doesn't seem right."

Jasper, with his dog's antenna up and sensing a subtle shift in Brian's emotions and body language, raised his head and licked Brian's hand and cheek before settling down. He rested his head in Brian's lap.

"Let dad worry about that, Bri. It'll be fine," Billy said.

"So, did you know who was following us?"

Billy and Brian took off on the four wheeler with Brian driving. Brett offered to walk back to the house with George. Jasper and Jasmine walked in front of them, but to the side and close by. Their ears and eyes alert.

"No. The driver looked familiar, but I don't think I saw him before. The guy in the passenger seat, I never saw before. He was older. Mid-twenties, I think. Maybe a little older. There was someone in the back seat who tried very hard not to be noticed."

"When did you spot them?"

"When we came out of the theater. They were parked down the street with the motor running. At first, I thought they were going to pick up someone. When no one went over to the car, I wondered."

"It wasn't Sweeney," Brett said matter-of-factly.

"No, it wasn't Sweeney."

"Hmmm," Brett said.

"How did you know?"

Brett smiled at his friend, his brother and said, "I saw you glancing behind us. When we got to the pizza place, I watched you stare them down."

"Did Father notice?"

"No. Dad and Bri were hustling into the restaurant. Billy was behind them."

George and Brett walked a short distance in silence and Brett said, "Is Brian going to be okay?"

George thought for a minute and said, "He has Father. He has us. He will be okay."

"He likes Caitlyn," Brett said with a glance in George's direction.

"I know." What he didn't say was that he thought Caitlyn liked Brian.

Brett glanced at him again, but chose to say nothing. George had lost Rebecca to Billy and now possibly, Caitlyn to Brian.

They stood in the circular drive at the side of the house. The two dogs stood on the front stoop waiting for them.

George looked up at the stars, but they were hidden by clouds. He had only lived in Wisconsin a short time, but like his beloved *Diné Bikéyah*, he could tell the weather just as his grandfather had taught him. It would snow while they slept and he'd have to do some shoveling in the morning before church.

"I can hear my grandfather telling me that a girl's heart chooses the heart of a boy."

"And a boy's heart doesn't have any say? Doesn't seem fair, does it?"

George didn't answer him, but looked off in the distance towards the end of the driveway to the road beyond. No one was there and no one was coming, but he couldn't bear to look at Brett.

Brett knew George was hurting, but he also knew that George wouldn't say anything to him or to anyone else for that matter, that he didn't want to say. George would choose the time as well as his words and to whom he'd say them. So Brett said nothing and didn't push George with any other questions or commentary. Rather, the two boys stood in silence feeling the cold seep into their bodies, the wispy plumes of their breath rising in the frigid night air.

CHAPTER TWENTY

"Fuck!" The fat boy yelled, throwing the syringe against the brick wall. "Why can't we get it right?"

Tat Boy was as worried about another death as he was about the syringe with his prints. He'd have to remember to pick it up before they left.

"Let's get him outta here," Fat Boy said. "Fuck!"

"Calm down. It's over and done. We almost had it right. He didn't puke, and he lasted longer than the others, so we know we need to lessen the dose." He tried to sound confident, but he wasn't. He still had to make the phone call to the man since the long-haired boy wasn't with them.

The two boys struggled getting the dead kid's sweatshirt on.

"Oh my God! He shit his pants already!" Fat Boy slipped his face up to his eyes inside his Badger sweatshirt.

Tat Boy tried holding his breath, but couldn't hold it long enough, so he breathed through his mouth. That didn't work either.

"We have to move fast. Go get the plastic from the trunk. We'll wrap him in it."

Fat Boy took off on a run, tripped going up the stairs and sliced his hand on a screw that had been sticking out of the rusty, broken railing, ripping open the palm of his hand. "Jesus, Fuck! Fuck!"

He grabbed at his hand, a flap of skin hung like a kite in the wind, blood flowing freely, dripping onto the steps as he gathered himself up and stumbled up the stairs. One step from the top, he tripped again, leaving a bloody handprint on the landing. He picked himself up, pushed himself out the broken and dented metal door to this car, pulled open the driver's side door with his good hand and popped the trunk. He raced around to the back of the car and pulled out the clear plastic tarp and ran back to the rundown building.

Not thinking, he pulled open the door with his bloody hand, yelled, "Fuck!" and ran inside, stumbling down the stairs.

"Oh my God! He stinks! He's going to fuck up my car."

"Put the plastic down on the floor."

The two boys stretched out the tarp on the dirty cement floor and pulled the dead boy unceremoniously onto it. They rolled him over and over until he was completely wrapped in it like a cheap oversized cigar. Fat Boy grabbed his feet as best he could, trying without success, to ignore his throbbing, bloody hand. Tat Boy grabbed the dead body by the head and shoulders.

Both stumbled and swore as they carried the plastic wrapped dead body up the stairs and out to the car where they threw the body into the trunk. Fat Boy jumped in behind the wheel and Tat Boy jumped in on the passenger side. Fat Boy backed up a little too quickly and too recklessly and knocked over a large green recycling bin and a large black garbage container that had been sitting side by side across the street, sending both onto the sidewalk spewing garbage as they rolled.

Tires squealed, and the car zigzagged up the street, catching both dry pavement and patches of ice. As the car sailed through a stop sign and on down the street, Tat Boy had the vague feeling that he had forgotten to do something. He spied the bloody hand on Fat Boy and the vague feeling grew into panic. And he had yet to make the call to the man.

CHAPTER TWENTY-ONE

"Are you sure this is the right thing to do?"

It was the third time Pam had asked that question in the last two hours and it evoked the same response from Gary each time: a bewildered, if not frustrated and anxious look along with a shoulder shrug. If he were a lost puppy, he might have tilted his head and whimpered.

"What if Zak is right? What if these people try to kill him?"

Gary glanced up at his wife, but quickly looked back down at the document he was finishing up. It detailed all the information Zak had given them: names of dealers he had bought from, names of users that he knew of and as many dates and places where drugs were sold as he could remember.

Zak had sobbed. He was petrified, expressing the belief that as soon as the dealers put it all together, it would lead back to him. And if that happened, he would be dead.

Zak was their only child. He was a good kid. A great kid. Happy. Successful. Popular. Gary and Pam didn't deserve such a great son.

Gary put both hands to his face and wept. He was long, long past angry. Instead of pointing his finger at Zak and his friends, he was pointing it right back at himself. He felt, *he knew*, that he was a failure as a father.

Pam embraced him from behind, holding him and resting her cheek on his head not knowing what else to do. He with his thoughts and she with her thoughts, but both heading down the same path.

As parents, were they that horrible? How could this happen in *their* home to *their* son? How was it possible? How could they have not noticed? What could they have done differently?

Gary scrolled down the sheet and looked at the names of the kids Zak identified as using and he couldn't believe the number of names nor the names of the kids themselves, many of which he knew. Not all of them, but far more than half.

Good kids. Athletes. Smart kids. Kids who had been over at their house. Kids whose families were upstanding, part and parcel of the fabric of the Waukesha community. Teachers' kids. Parents who were attached to city hall. Parents who coached. Doctors. Lawyers. Real Estate Agents. Insurance Salesmen. Parents who were wealthy and some who struggled to pay their bills. How was it possible that all of these kids could be involved in this? Selling drugs in the school bathrooms, in the school parking lot before and after school, in the cafeteria at lunch, in locker rooms, in the hallways between classes and in classrooms while kids were being taught by teachers who were unaware of the transactions taking place.

And not just marijuana. Adderall. Heroin. Cocaine. LSD. Other narcotics neither Gary nor Pam recognized by name.

He composed himself, dried his eyes and sighed as much as in hope as he did in despair.

"Pam, this is the only way we can get help for our son. We can't just close our eyes to this. There are lives at stake beyond Zak."

"Will he suspect Zak? I mean, is there any way this might come back on him?"

Gary shook his head. "I'll wait until he's in church and then I'll put it on his windshield. I'll wait until no one is around and I'll leave as soon as I know he has it."

"But what happens if someone else sees it and gets curious? What happens if someone else takes it?"

Gary stood up and embraced Pam, holding on tightly. "We have to do this, Pam. For Zak and the other kids. It's the best we can do. It's the only thing we can do."

CHAPTER TWENTY-TWO

It was late, but the street light was bright outside his window, shining off what was left of the snow and ice.

Jamie sat in the dark in the living room in his favorite faux leather brown recliner, the manila file folder closed on his lap. His feet were up and he stared out the window at the cold, dark landscape. Garrett had long gone to bed as had Kelly, though Jamie doubted she was asleep. She complained that she didn't sleep well if Jamie wasn't bumping up against her.

He opened the file one more time and reread the autopsy report.

Heroin mixed with fentanyl.

When Jamie received it, Ike told him that fentanyl is an extremely powerful synthetic painkiller, part of a drug group that includes opioids such as oxycodone, methadone and codeine. Over the past twenty years, it has emerged as a legitimate pain medication for cancer patients and in veterinary use for quickly anesthetizing large animals. But that was under the care of a physician or veterinarian. Improperly used, it caused death by shutting down the respiratory system.

Jamie did a Google search and found out that the Center for Disease Control and Prevention described it as "approximately 80 to 100 times more potent than morphine and roughly 40 to 50 times more potent than pharmaceutical grade – which is 100 percent pure – heroin."

Jamie reached for his phone, speed-dialed O'Connor and said, "You up?"

"Am now." In actuality, he had been up because he had been unable to fall asleep.

"A quick question. What do you know about fentanyl?"

O'Connor yawned, checked his watch, thought for a moment and answered, "Among hypes, it's mixed with heroin to heighten the experience. Problem is, the user is playing with two powerful downers that can slow, even stop, the respiratory system. Used together, they'll stop your heart. Not as fast as a bullet, but a lot more painful."

"If I'm a user and I want to find fentanyl, where would I get it?"

O'Connor didn't have to think very long before he said, "It has its legitimate purposes. Cancer treatment and vets use it for horses and cows, so you'd have to be connected to someone prescribing it. You can always get it from Mexico, even Canada. But both of us know the street has its own sources. If you want anything bad enough, you can find a way and someone to get it for you. Hell, a tech-savvy kid who knows where to look can get it off the internet, no questions asked."

"Yeah, but how would high school and middle school kids get it?"

O'Connor sighed. Jamie pictured him in his apartment sitting alone in the dark and unable to sleep.

"So that's what our bad boy is? A heroin and fentanyl point?"

"Looks like it. All of the vics . . . the boys had it in their systems along with heroin. The only difference was the amount of each. The earlier boys had greater amounts of fentanyl than the more recent boys. But it was there." Graff thought for a minute and asked, "What did you call it? A point?"

"Those who don't know shit call it a cocktail. Street guys would laugh at you. The scientific name, if you want to use that, would be a druggist fold. On the street, a kid would call it a bundle. It's no more than a one by two inch square of a piece of paper with the powder folded inside. That's why it's so easily passed between the buyer and the dealer. It can go down as a handshake. Maybe stick it in a folder or binder. It wouldn't be recognized in school because a teacher might think a kid is passing a note."

Maybe in disbelief or disgust, O'Connor wasn't sure, Graff asked, "How does a kid get started on something like this, Pat? I don't get it."

O'Connor sighed.

"What happens is a kid experiments with Oxy or Roxy. But that's expensive. It can run you a buck a mil. And it's not like somebody is running around with a big bag of pills. A kid might steal from grandma's bottle and sell it. A kid gets hooked. They look for something cheaper, faster and someone introduces them to heroin. That's equally addicting, but the high wears off and you end up needing more or a different kind of high, so now the bundle is mixed with fentanyl."

"What does a point or bundle or whatever cost?"

"In our area where the supply is less than Milwaukee, Racine or Kenosha, maybe twenty or thirty bucks. In urban areas like Milwaukee, it goes for ten to twenty bucks. You know I-94 and I-43 are the drug and gun highways from Chicago to Sturgeon Bay. At Green Bay, they use highway 41 to get it up north. Remember Earl Coffey? They're up to their asses in this shit."

"Hell, when I was in school, my buddies and I would grab some beer and sit out in a field somewhere," Graff said with a humorless laugh.

"Kids are still drinking, Jamie. It's just that they're looking for something bigger and badder."

Jamie liked O'Connor a lot. Good mind. Great investigator. More of a *do-it-by-myself* kind of guy. He was never afraid of getting his hands dirty and never worried about how long it took to get the job done as long as the job got done. And he always got results.

"Can you and Paul do some checking to see where kids might be getting fentanyl?"

"I'll do some digging and get back to you."

"Hey, Pat?"

"Yeah?"

"Get some sleep. This could be a tough nut to crack."

"Aren't they all?"

Jamie ended the call, closed the file and ran his hand through his hair and over his face. He pushed himself out of his chair, walked down the hallway and looked in on Garrett and wondered for the millionth time what kind of boy he'd grow up to be. Privately, he hoped he'd grow to be like Randy or George or Brett. Maybe a combination of the three.

He sat on the edge of his small bed and brushed his cheek with his thumb. Dark complexion with black wavy hair and dark eyes like his dad, but with Kelly's sunny disposition and sense of humor. A softness that Jamie hoped he'd never, ever, lose.

"Don't wake him," Kelly said from the doorway.

Jamie bent down, kissed Garrett's forehead and whispered, "I love you."

He joined Kelly at the doorway, their arms around each other as they watched their sleeping son, wondering what he was dreaming, if he was dreaming.

Of course he was dreaming. Innocent dreams. Happy dreams filled with sunshine and laughter.

All little kids dreamed. It was only when they got older that they sometimes stopped dreaming for one reason or the other. Sad. Really sad.

CHAPTER TWENTY-THREE

"She's a hundred year-old lady, Boyd. She told us she was half asleep."

"Yeah, but only half asleep. She saw and heard something."

The two patrol officers caught the call from dispatch and arrived in separate cars. Wes Hodder was young, skinny and fit and had only been on the force for a year and a half. Boyd Fortune was graying, but middle-aged with a bit of a paunch. Neither could point a finger on how or when, but the two cops hit it off. Fortune saw himself as a mentor and viewed Hodder as a kind of son he never had.

Fortune sipped coffee and conducted the interview while Hodder listened in and ate two sugar cookies.

She had told them that she woke up because of some noise. At first, she thought it was a dream or maybe her cat that had knocked something off a counter. She got up, went to the front window of her small apartment that overlooked the old abandoned building and peeked out of the corner of her window. She said she saw two boys, maybe high school aged, carrying what looked like a carpet roll wrapped in plastic out to the trunk of a car. She thought that was strange because the building had been abandoned ever since forever or as she put it, "Since Moses was in diapers."

After the interview, Fortune led Hodder back to the street where they retrieved large Maglites from their squad cars and as they approached the entrance to the rundown building, each re-holstered their revolvers.

"I'll lead. Chances are there's no one in there."

Hodder placed a hand on Fortune's shoulder and said, "We might have something here after all." His light caught blood on the door handle.

Fortune thought for only a second and said, "Call it in and I'm going to call Graff."

Graff was there in under seven minutes, leaving Fortune to consider for the hundredth time if he ever slept. Fortune and Hodder had waited inside Fortune's squad car with the motor running, heat on and lights off. Graff rolled up and both men got out.

"What do you have, Boyd?"

He pointed at the door and said, "Wes caught a smear of blood on the door handle. We didn't enter because we thought the crime scene guys would get all weird on us."

"Crime scene guys are weird anyway." He turned to Hodder and said, "Wes, go around and cover the back. Don't enter. Just prevent anyone from leaving if we spook someone. As you get into position, look for any footprints, anything that seems out of place and anything that doesn't fit. I want you to look for syringes, used condoms, garbage like McDonald's crap. Stuff like that. Boyd and I are going to go in just to take a quick peek before CSI gets here."

On the drive over, Jamie thought about contacting Pete Kelliher and Summer Storm at FBI to see if they could spring Skip Dahlke free, but that would take too much time and not knowing exactly what they had, decided it might not be worth it to have him fly in. He thought about calling O'Connor, but decided to wait until he knew what they had for sure.

"Boyd, we need to watch where we step. If there are footprints or anymore blood, we back out and let the science guys take it."

Graff did a slow three-sixty to study the rundown neighborhood. A crumbling, low rent three-story apartment building stood stoop-shouldered across the street. It housed mostly folks on welfare, some immigrants and the elderly. The building he and Fortune stood in front of was one of a bunch that, because of the recession, was closed and abandoned. It, like the others, had a *For Sale* sign on it, but the sign, too, was weathered and old and no one had shown interest. And both buildings had the look, feel and smell of a crack house. At the very least, it might be a home to the desperate, those who had no home and who lived on whatever scraps the streets could give them.

The area was east of the city. Three blocks to the west was the YMCA. Seven blocks to the northeast was Carroll College. Graff had a hunch that the two high school boys weren't carrying a carpet roll. The thought that college kids might be involved flew through Graff's mind but didn't take root. College kids wouldn't have the access to middle school kids that high school kids might have, unless they were involved coaching in a rec league or some such thing. He'd have someone check it out nevertheless.

He also knew that the chances were pretty high that they'd find another dead body at some point in the morning, if not sooner.

Lastly, he looked at the ground where they had walked and where they stood. No noticeable footprints other than their own. Not surprising since the driveway was made up of broken pavement, potholes and gravel with little ice or snow covering it.

"Okay, ready?"

Fortune nodded and radioed to Hodder, "We're going in."

CHAPTER TWENTY-FOUR

"When you think about it, we have the best family," Billy declared.

The boys sat in the hot tub as low in the water as possible because the air was freezing. Their nude bodies were a tangle of feet and while the tub was rather small, the boys were politely keeping away from each other except for feet and legs.

"I mean, how many other families have best friends living with each other in the same house? The only guys we're missing are Big Gav and Sean."

"And Danny, G-Man, Mikey and Stephen," Brett said.

"Yeah, well Danny only lives a hundred yards away, but it's still pretty cool, huh?"

"I don't actually live with you guys," Brian suggested.

"But Kaz, it's like you live here," Billy said with a smile. "I like it when you come over."

Brian shrugged.

"Oh, hey, I forgot to tell you," Brett said giving Brian a shove. "Jamie Graff said you can come ice fishing with us."

"Are you sure? I mean, it's okay if I don't go."

Brett broke the unwritten rule of nude hot tubbing when he reached over with one arm and hugged Brian, but Kaz didn't mind.

"We want you to go."

The timer went off and they did a quick *nose goes* to see who would get out and reset it. George was too slow, so he got up, faked tripping and fell on Billy, got himself up and fell on Brian and Brett on purpose.

"Hurry up before we get cold," Billy said.

"And you have your bare butt in my lap," Brian said.

"He's a little horny after being with Caitlyn this afternoon, so he'll take whatever he can get," Brett laughed.

George took his time getting himself up, taking a long step onto the wooden deck and making a show of stretching and yawning.

"Damn, George, aren't you cold?" Brian asked.

"Of course he is," Billy laughed. "Can't you see that his dick and balls shrunk?"

"They didn't shrink," Brett said. "They've always been that small."

George cranked the timer for another twenty minutes, faked tripping back into the tub, falling on top of Brett and then Brian. He ended up laying crossways on Billy's lap.

"Whose feet are these?" Brian asked.

"Mine," Billy said.

"They're huge."

"They're not so big. Only size ten and a half. What size are yours?"

"Ten." Brian turned to Brett and said, "What size are yours?"

"Ten. Bobby and I can wear each other's shoes. Yours, too."

"What size are yours?" Brian asked George.

George lifted a bare foot and leg out of the water and said, "Nine."

"Small feet match his small dick," Billy laughed, which caused George to try to dunk Billy. They only succeeded in splashing a lot of water.

"You two are gross," Brian said.

"Nah, he doesn't have anything I want," Billy said, "unless I'm really hard up."

"It's too small," Brett said causing George to splash him.

Billy asked Kaz, "How come you never asked Cat out?"

Brian blushed, wiped hot tub water over his face to warm it up, glanced at George, but didn't answer.

"You're kinda homely, but she's cute. You and she and Sean hang out a lot. It's not like you don't like her."

Brian knew everyone was looking at him and expecting a response. He said the only thing he could think of. "I don't know."

"I think she likes you," George said.

Brian blushed and said, "We're just friends. Besides, you two are talking to each other or seeing each other or something."

George said nothing.

"I wouldn't do that to you."

George smiled at him and said, "It would be okay . . . I think."

"You don't like her?" Billy asked George.

"I do, but I think we're just friends."

"*I won't* do that to you," Brian said.

In part to rescue Brian and George, Brett said, "Hey, Jamie wanted me to ask you guys if you know anything about guys doing pot or heroin and stuff."

"How would we know anything about that?" Billy asked as he held George's hair up in the air trying to get it to freeze. "None of the guys we hang out with do that. None of us even drink."

"That's what I said, but I told him I'd ask you guys anyway."

"The only time Randy smoked a joint and drank was when those two guys picked him up and made him," Billy said. "Now, he doesn't even like to take medicine if he can help it."

"I don't either," Brett said.

Billy laughed and said, "Look! I froze George's hair." And he did. It stuck straight up in the air. "And if your dick keeps poking out of the water, you're going to freeze that too."

"You're like a two year old," George said with a laugh as he sat back up in his seat. He did however, stretch his legs out so his feet rested on Brian's thighs.

"What stuff did they make you do?" Brian asked Brett as he held onto George's toes just to make sure they didn't accidently end up in his crotch.

Brett shrugged and said, "The assholes never used needles on us. The pervert doctors came once a month and gave us checkups and sometimes gave us shots. They were *supposed* to keep us healthy so perverts could keep doing shit to us. Sometimes they'd make us smoke pot or do lines of coke. Sometimes they'd bring whiskey or beer and we'd have to drink that with them."

"What was it like?" Billy asked. "Smoking pot or doing coke . . . what did you feel like?"

Brett was silent for quite a while before he answered. He didn't really like talking about that part of his life. It brought back too many ugly memories.

Brian let go of George's toes with his left hand and reached over and placed his hand on Brett's thigh. Brett smiled sadly at him.

"Pot makes you drowsy. Like you don't give a shit, like you don't care. The best part was that when I was high, I didn't care what they did to me. Or what I had to do to them. Coke made me really jumpy, kind of nervous. I hated it."

"Weren't you afraid of getting hooked?" Billy asked.

Brett shook his head and said, "We never did it that much. We were more afraid of the shit they made us take each morning to keep control of us. They gave us a pill and it made us feel like zombies. The doctor at the hospital told us that we could have gotten hooked really easily."

"They gave you Viagra, right?" Billy asked.

Brett nodded. "That was good and bad. It actually helped because of the number of perverts we'd end up with. The bad part was we got used to it. I mean, I had a hard on twenty-four seven. It never went down. Even now, every night when I get ready for bed, I get a boner. There are times during the day. I can't help it."

Trying to keep it light, Billy said, "Well the good thing is it's so small, no one really notices."

"You wish," Brett laughed. "Bobby and I are Italian, so ours is double the size of yours."

Changing the subject, Brian said, "I don't like using the restrooms at school."

"Why?" George asked.

"Sometimes the guys in there smoke and stuff. Sometimes when I go in they stop talking and pretend to wash their hands, but they watch you pee and stuff."

"What guys?" George asked.

Brian shrugged. "I don't know who they are. Juniors and seniors mostly. Sometimes a freshman or sophomore." He shrugged again. "I don't know their names. They smell like ashtrays."

"I make an excuse to visit dad and I use the faculty restroom around the corner from his office," Billy said.

"I only go if I can't hold it," Brian said.

Brett thought it over, looked at George, Billy and Kaz and said, "So we agree we don't know anyone who does any of that, right?"

He looked from one to the other and each shook their head.

"Listen. Nobody does any hero shit," he said looking directly at George, who merely looked back at him without expression. "But if one of us sees anything or suspects anything, tell me and I'll tell Jamie. Agreed?"

The guys nodded. Even George, but Brett didn't necessarily believe him.

CHAPTER TWENTY-FIVE

Once Jamie saw what they had, he called in the crime techs or as they were commonly called among the detectives on the force, *the Science Guys*. He got O'Connor out of bed, though he didn't actually think O'Connor was in bed. Hell, Jamie didn't know if O'Connor owned a bed.

One of the science guys, Walter Spence, found Jamie, Wes Hodder and Boyd Fortune leaning against Fortune's squad car sipping lukewarm crappy coffee that one of the patrol cops scrounged around for them.

"Tastes like shit," Hodder complained.

"But it's warm shit," Fortune said.

"What do we have, Walt?" Jamie asked.

"We have a full hand print on the landing coming up from the basement. We have a syringe with prints on it. We have substance in the syringe and DNA on the needle. Whoever sat in that chair in the basement shit and pissed his pants. There's trace on the chair and on the floor."

"Along with a wonderful smell," Fortune added.

Spence nodded and said, "Yes, that too."

"Where's O'Connor?" Jamie asked.

"Right here," Pat said as he walked over to the group.

Jamie handed him a paper cup of coffee, but O'Connor waved it away. Instead, Spence took it from him without it being offered.

"It's amateur hour down there. Anything but professional."

"How can you tell?" Jamie asked.

O'Connor said, "Nothing was cleaned up. Blood would have been wiped up. The syringe would have been picked up along with the rubber tie."

"We have prints on the rubber tie," Spence added. "This place was used more than once. I'm betting we pick up DNA from several individuals."

Jamie made a leap and asked, "Can we tie the other boys to this place?

Their DNA?"

O'Connor shrugged and looked at Spence.

"That's not for me to say. For sure, that is."

"But if you had to guess?" Jamie asked.

Unwilling to commit verbally, Spence nodded.

Immediately, O'Connor walked away from the little group, stood in the street and scanned the area in both directions thinking that if the building was used before, maybe whoever used it would come back again and maybe, might come back before the night was over.

CHAPTER TWENTY-SIX

Tat Boy ditched Fat Boy and jumped in his car to head back to the building to clean up. Or rather, take care of anything that might have his prints on it. Driving slowly, he approached the building and spied two squad cars, but their lights weren't flashing. He didn't see anyone on the street or near the building, but the two cop cars made him nervous. Hell, a lot more than nervous. Scared shitless. It was all he could do to stop himself from staring, but he managed to prevent himself from doing so. He had almost panicked and sped past, but instead slowed down giving whomever might be looking the impression that he was just a cautious driver.

He drove two blocks and rounded a corner and in the middle of the block, pulled to a stop on the dark street and sat with the engine off. He wasn't a worrier like Fat Boy, but he knew there was blood and he knew there was a syringe and he knew there was the rubber strap and the devil himself knew what else was down there. The night was cold, but Tat Boy found was sweating.

He shut his eyes and pictured the basement as best he could, but in his mind, he kept coming back to the syringe and the rubber strap with his prints. Fortunately, he had never been busted for anything, so his prints wouldn't necessarily match with anything the cops might have. The trick was, he decided, that he couldn't ever do anything that might get him busted, because they would have his prints and they'd match and, *oh fuck*! He didn't want to go there. He also believed that if Fat Boy got caught, all bets were off because he'd roll and sing and swear off on everyone.

Shit!

He waited and wondered how he could get in there and clean up. Maybe somehow get in through the back door to the basement, grab what he could, wipe down the rest and get the hell out. If he couldn't and if they found his prints, he'd be screwed. If they found the blood and pieced it together with the gash on Fat Boy's hand, it would come back on him.

Tat Boy had decided when the first kid died that he wasn't about to go down alone. No way in hell! Maybe he could make a deal in exchange for telling the cops all he knew. Maybe.

After thirty minutes or so, Tat Boy started up his car, pulled out of his parking spot and eased into a driveway across the street. As far as he was concerned, he was a kid on his way home from working the late shift. There was nothing that would link him to the basement . . . yet.

He pulled around the corner and stepped on the brake when he saw all the flashing lights and the cars parked up and down the street and a couple of official looking trucks in the driveway. *When did they show up? Oh fuck!*

The hairs on the back of his neck stood up.

Tat Boy had a choice to make: drive right past the building just as he had planned to do or turn around and go back around the block to get away.

He inched forward until a cop stepped out into the street and waved him back.

Thankfully, the decision was made for him and that brought him a modicum of relief.

Neatly, almost expertly, Tat Boy did a three point turn. He even added a wave goodbye. But once he turned the corner and was out of sight, he stepped on the gas and got the hell out of there.

And he had yet to call the man. But maybe before he did, he'd make a different call and tie up a loose end.

He'd have to think about that.

CHAPTER TWENTY-SEVEN

"Billy, your feet are cold," George said quietly, his eyes shut, preparing himself to sleep. He had the feeling that Billy wasn't ready just yet.

Billy laughed and said, "Yeah, but your legs are warm," and he laughed again as he snuggled closer.

They were not in their normal spoon position. Rather, Billy lay on his back but up against George, while George draped an arm over Billy's chest and one leg thrown over Billy's. Both boys liked to sleep with the window open, so they snuggled close to each other.

"And your feet are a helluva lot bigger than you think."

"I'm a growing boy."

George found himself smiling. He loved his brothers and like Billy, believed that his was the best family. Sleeping like this reminded him of his first family and how his youngest brother, Robert, would sleep up against him. Remembering Robert made him wistful, but it didn't shake the joy he felt with Billy or for that matter, with Brett or Brian or with Randy and Bobby. No matter who he slept with and on this night like most nights it was Billy, he and whomever could lay together like this. It wasn't even close to being sexual, but it certainly was love. There was joy and a kind of freedom in just being with each other.

He squeezed him a little tighter. Billy turned his head slightly, smiled and held onto George's arm.

"It was a navy blue Camaro. Two door. Although it didn't look like a normal Camaro. I think they had it tricked out." Billy didn't really know cars and he added with a laugh, "I think they call it tricked out. That's what they say on cop shows. Anyway, to be sure I did a Google search when we were eating pizza."

George pretended not to know what Billy was talking about and said,

"What was?"

Billy turned over on his side, smiled at George and said, "The car that followed us from the theater to the pizza place."

George couldn't hide his surprise.

Billy smiled again, very proud of his achievement. "I did exactly what you've been telling me to do and what your grandfather taught you to do. I watched, and I listened. When we came out of the movie, I scanned the street in both directions. I saw them across the street. Even during your Sweeney beat down, I watched them. That's when I suspected they might be watching us. No one went to their car and they never turned it off and they never went to the movie. When dad picked us up, I kept track of them using dad's side mirror. I think that's when Brett noticed. He was watching you watch them."

George nodded approvingly and as he did so, remembered that his grandfather would often do the same to him when he had done something his grandfather was proud of.

"Pretty good, huh?"

George smiled and said, "Yes, very good."

"But I didn't recognize who was in it. But I was thinking. The guy riding shotgun looked familiar, but I can't place him."

"There was someone in the backseat."

"Yeah, I know, but I couldn't tell who it was."

George nodded.

"When are you going to tell dad?"

George remained silent and his face was noncommittal.

"So you're not going to tell dad."

George shook his head and said, "Nothing to tell him. Yet."

Billy smiled and said, "I kinda figured."

"Can I ask you a question?" Billy asked. Without waiting for an answer Billy asked, "What's your biggest regret? The one thing you could change if you could?"

George was used to Billy's penchant for rapid fire change of directions in conversation, but this threw him a little. He didn't answer right away, but pursed his lips in thought.

"I know for Brett it was not telling anyone what his uncle did to him that day by the river. He blames himself because he ended up getting abducted and

Bobby ended up getting . . . you know, molested by his uncle. Randy said his biggest regret was running away and getting into the car with those two perverts who ended up molesting him. He was lucky to get away." Billy shivered at the thought. "Bobby told me his biggest regret was not telling anyone about his uncle or that he knew that Brett was still alive. He feels really guilty about that."

Billy sighed, rolled onto his back and stared up at the ceiling, but turned his head and stared at George.

"I have two regrets. The first is that I wasn't nicer to my mom and dad." He shrugged and said, "I was pissed that they never told me I was adopted. It shouldn't have been that big a deal, but for some reason I was pissed that they never told me. I grew up thinking I was their son. I was, but you know what I mean. Mom moved away, and Dad ended up lonely and I think he died of a broken heart. I know that doctor said it was a heart attack, but I think it was a broken heart and I caused it."

"I don't think you caused your parent's divorce and I don't think you caused your father's death. I know Father doesn't think so."

"I can't help feeling like I did," Billy said with a shrug.

Even though Jeremy and Randy had talked it over with him and even though Jeff Limbach talked it over with him, Billy still felt responsible for both the divorce and his father's death.

"What is your second regret?"

Billy swallowed, blinked and said, "That I took Rebecca away from you."

George smiled sadly and whispered, "You didn't take Rebecca from me."

"I did and I'm sorry. I love her. I really do. And I miss her. I think about her all the time, but I'm sorry."

As best he could without falling out of bed, George rolled over onto his back and said, "It was my fault, not yours."

Billy asked, "How was it your fault?"

George shook his head, but didn't answer.

Billy rolled to his side to face George and repeated, "How was it your fault?"

George turned his head. He frowned and turned on his side to face Billy.

"I had you go with Rebecca to keep you safe. I needed to keep you safe."

"I don't understand," Billy whispered.

"Originally, my plan was to have you and father go with me up on the mesa to face those men. I thought you could keep father safe while I faced them."

Billy's eyes widened, and his mouth formed a perfect o.

"But Fuentes showed up at the cabin. You and the others were taped up and couldn't move. I watched him grab Danny between the legs. Danny was in so much pain. And he pinched your nose shut and you couldn't breathe because he had duct tape over your mouth. I didn't know you had only passed out and I was afraid that he had killed you. I knew it was only a matter of time before he killed you and the others."

"So?" Billy asked, not understanding at all.

"After I killed Fuentes, I knew you could not go up on the mesa with father and me, because you would have been in danger. I had to keep you safe."

"But I could have helped you," Billy whispered.

George shook his head and said, "No, Billy. I needed to keep you safe. I love you and Rebecca. I needed to keep you both safe, so I made sure you and she would be together. I knew there was a possibility that you and she would end up loving each other. I hoped it would not happen." This last, George whispered and ended with a shrug.

George gripped Billy's shoulder and said, "I knew Charles would take Randy and Danny and Uncle Jeff to the high country. That is where he always hunted. I knew this, and I also knew that Rebecca would take you to the pond. It is where she and I spent our happiest times."

"But you loved her, George. Why me? Why not Randy?"

George smiled and said, "Randy needed to be with Danny and with Uncle Jeff."

"But," Billy said shaking his head.

"I love both you and Rebecca. I needed to have you together. That way both of you would be safe and neither of you would worry, because you would be . . . busy. You would keep each other busy."

Billy nodded. Until the shooting began early that morning, he had barely thought of George or his dad. All he thought about was Rebecca and what he and she did with each other. He and Rebecca had spent more time unclothed than they did clothed. It was his first taste of love and his first taste of sex. Just thinking about her now and what they had done alone with each other for a day and a night under the desert sky with nothing but one blanket to share made him excited and aroused.

Pushing those thoughts away, Billy said, "But," not at all comprehending the enormity of George's decision.

George smiled at him. "My best friends. Two of the people I love most in this world."

"But George, you loved her, and she loved you."

Remembering what he had told Brett earlier that evening, he repeated, "Remember what my grandfather said, 'A horse chooses the rider. The rider doesn't choose the horse.' Like a horse chooses the rider, a girl's heart chooses the heart of a boy."

Billy thought about that for a little while and rolled onto his back. He turned his head towards George and said, "That last night in the desert when it was Randy and Danny, Rebecca and her brother, Charles, and you and I . . ." he didn't finish.

"Yes?"

"She left my blanket and joined you on the little hill."

"Yes."

"And you and she . . ."

George nodded. "Yes."

"But she came back to me."

George smiled, nodded and said, "She came back to you."

"Didn't that hurt?"

A couple of tears rolled down George's face, he smiled. He kissed Billy's cheek and said, "Yes."

Billy began to weep and said, "George, I never meant to hurt you. I would never hurt you. That's my regret. I took Rebecca from you."

The two boys embraced and clung fiercely to each other. George kissed Billy's cheek and said, "The heart of a girl chooses the heart of a boy. Rebecca chose you. She loves you and you love her."

"I do love Rebecca, but I love you, George."

"I know you do, Billy."

The boys dried their eyes on the sheet and Billy rolled back onto his back. George pressed the flat of his hand on Billy's chest and said, "Your heart is a wild animal."

Billy turned his head slightly. "I can't help thinking about Rebecca and . . . everything."

George smiled at him and slipped his arm across Billy's chest, "If you do anything tonight, do it on your side of the bed and don't get any on me."

Billy laughed and elbowed him.

"What's your regret?"

Ashamed, George lowered his eyes and said, "I killed six men."

"But George, think about it. That first guy that came to our house. Jamie Graff said he was a paid killer and he was sent to kill all of us. If you wouldn't have killed him, he would have killed us. The FBI and Jamie Graff agreed it was self-defense. At the hotel in Missouri, that crazy asshole starts shooting at us. Randy could have been shot. Hell, all of us could have been shot. If you hadn't jumped through the window and killed him, who knows what would have happened. That psycho nut job, Fuentes, comes into our cabin in Arkansas, tapes us to chairs and hurts Danny and tries to kill me. If you hadn't killed him, we'd all be dead.

"And those three assholes who were out to kill you and dad in Arizona . . ." He stopped and shook his head.

George whispered, "Killing is not the way of *Dine'*. It is not the Navajo way."

"But you had to, George. Don't you see that?"

George said nothing.

"That morning Rebecca and I were laying there. The sun wasn't up yet and it was cold."

George smiled and said, "That happens when you don't have clothes on."

Ignoring him, Billy said, "When the shooting started, I just about lost my mind. God, George! I was so scared. I started crying. I couldn't help it. I kept thinking that I was with Rebecca doing . . . stuff and you and dad were up there with those men who were trying to kill you." He began to cry.

"It's over, Billy. Shhh, it's over."

"But I was so scared."

George hugged his brother and his friend and repeated, "It's over, Billy. It's over."

CHAPTER TWENTY-EIGHT

He didn't fall asleep right away because of his conversation with Billy. It troubled him and brought back horrific memories. The truth was however, that these memories were with him most of the time anyway. Billy, of course, fell asleep right away which wasn't surprising. Billy could sleep anywhere and sleep through most everything.

There were the series of dreams, but George didn't know if they were actually dreams. The traditional Navajo believed dreams were linked to the spirit world and were messages from beyond. George clung to this belief just as his grandfather had before his death and his belief in them had saved his life and the life of his family during the summer of death.

It was also true and believed to be true by Jeremy, Jamie Graff and certain members of law enforcement and the FBI, that George received visits from his deceased grandfather. Jeremy and Graff didn't understand it, but they did believe it.

George's grandfather was his greatest teacher, his greatest influence and his greatest mentor. Mostly these visits occurred while George was asleep, but at least on one or two occasions, they occurred while he was awake. Generally, these too, were warnings and George had listened. And like the dreams, these visits saved his life along with the lives of others.

But as George lay in bed next to Billy considering what he had just woken up from, he decided that these dreams didn't seem to be warnings of any kind. They weren't quite nightmares, but rather a series of unsettling images stitched together haphazardly with no real beginning and no real end.

Yet, he would think about them some more and if they appeared to be anything at all, he would tell his father and Jamie. That was the promise George had made to them. They would decide whether or not to pass this on to Pete Kelliher and Summer Storm at the FBI.

He got out of bed quietly, repositioning the covers so that Billy would stay warm. Jasmine lifted her head, but continued to lay on the rug on George's side of the bed. He tiptoed to the window that was open an inch, and the air coming from that opening was bone-chilling.

Just as George had predicted, it had snowed about six inches over the night. He gazed out over the backyard covered in snow, mostly pristine and perfect. The only interruption in the white carpet were tracks of a rabbit or two and what looked like deer. Whenever he took the horses out into the woods, he saw deer sign and once spotted a pregnant doe hiding in the tall brush. He smiled, picturing a young fawn following its mother and father after the spring thaw. He experienced a sense of déjà vu from the summer of death when he, the twins and Danny spied a buck, a doe and a fawn drinking from the stream near their rented cabin in Arkansas. The same cabin Fuentes had visited in order to kill them.

He sighed.

He dressed quickly and quietly, bracing himself for the cold of the predawn morning. Jasmine followed him down the hall to the room where Brett and Brian slept.

As was the case in any room where Brett slept, the door was left open to a four or five inch slit. This was his practice after being in captivity and forced isolation for nearly two years behind a locked door. Brett couldn't sleep in any room with the door completely shut. That is, if he slept at all. And he never slept alone. Ever.

Jasper lifted his head from where he lay on the rug on Brett's side, but put it back down content to sleep as long as Brett or Brian slept. George bent down, scratched him behind the ear and Jasper gave his hand a thank you lick.

Brian lay on his back with his head tilted back and towards Brett, who slept on his side with his arm across Brian's chest in much the same way George and Billy slept.

Brett quietly and carefully shifted to his back to look up at George through groggy, sleep filled eyes. He yawned, stretched and took a look at George's clothing.

He whispered, "You're not going running."

George smiled and shook his head. "I'm going to shovel."

"How much did we get?"

"About six inches."

"They won't cancel school Monday, will they?"

George shook his head and Brett made a face.

"Do you need help?"

George smiled, reached out and placed a hand on Brett's chest and said, "No, sleep."

Brett knew that it wouldn't pay to argue, so he rolled back onto his side, placed his arm over Brian's chest and shut his eyes. George gave his shoulder a gentle squeeze before leaving the room with Jasmine at his heels.

As was customary, George stopped at Jeremy's door, but the light wasn't on. He opened the door a crack, peered in, saw two lumps under the covers and heard two sets of deep breathing. Victoria, Brett's and Bobby's mom, must have gotten off work early and came to their house rather than heading back to an empty home.

George smiled, happy that Jeremy and Vicky were together. He walked down the hallway to the steps where Momma slept, keeping a watchful eye on everyone from the top of the landing.

He sat down on the step, gave Momma a hug and whispered, "No harm can come to our family, okay?"

Momma lifted her head from her paws, rested it on George's thigh so he could pet her. He bent down and kissed the top of her head, got up and tiptoed down the steps to the kitchen to the small entryway where his boots, scarf, stocking hat and gloves were. He dressed quickly, snatched the keys to the pickup off the hook on the wall beside the door and walked outside.

The early morning was bitter cold and still. A quarter moon hung in the sky with Venus hanging just below it like a large diamond stud on black velvet. Stars glittered above and the snow glittered below. His youngest brother, Robert, would sometimes wake up in the night needing to go to the outhouse and would wake George up to take him. Almost always, Robert would want to sit on George's lap on the porch and look at the stars. It was one of George's favorite memories of his life before Wisconsin, before the summer of death.

George shut his eyes until the memory faded into the background. He focused on the present, his current life, allowing the cold to bring him back.

He didn't mind the cold and he loved snow which was unusual for someone who grew up in the desert. The Navajo reservation did have dustings every so often with more snow at the higher elevations, but it wasn't until he moved to Wisconsin to live with Jeremy and the twins did he experience anything like real snow.

He smiled broadly, bent down to pet Jasmine who had come back from relieving herself at the edge of the woods and got to work.

He began shoveling off the stoop and steps and the sidewalk to the front driveway circle. He walked back to the garage. The pickup with the blade on the front sat on a little carport under an awning that kept most of the snow off the windows.

He had driven a pickup since he was ten. His grandfather owned an old blue on white Chevy truck that the family used around the small ranch. It kind of tilted to one side, had rust over the wheel wells and would be considered a beater by most anyone who saw it. But it ran and it worked and to a kid like George who didn't have much by way of possessions, he loved it. Whether he was a driver or passenger, he was comfortable and at home. After his family had been murdered, George gave the pickup to Rebecca and Charles.

With Jasmine as his co-pilot, George plowed the circle drive, the driveway out to the highway and the area in front of the mailboxes. When he had finished, he drove a tenth of a mile down the highway to Jeff's and Danny's house and plowed their driveway, the area in front of the stable and then got out and shoveled off their stoop and steps, drove home and parked the truck back on the carport.

And that was where he saw it.

An owl flew out from somewhere and landed on the hood of the truck and stared at George. Jasmine sat up, moved closer to George, but didn't growl. Fascinated, George didn't move.

The owl waddled up the hood to stand inches from the windshield. The owl had yellow eyes and a round head with no visible ears, a sharp beak and what looked like a black and white bow tie under its chin.

George had seen hawks and eagles, but had not seen many owls. In fact, he couldn't ever remember seeing one. This bird tilted its head, as if the bird was an inquisitive professor trying to understand a pupil's question.

Neither George nor Jasmine moved. Perhaps neither breathed. George certainly didn't.

There were Indian nations that believed in shape shifting, where man could become an animal and shift back to man. The Navajo didn't believe in shape shifting. But they did believe in portents and omens as clearly and as definitely as dreams and visions.

George knew he was witnessing more than just a bird, an owl. He was being given a message.

CHAPTER TWENTY-NINE

Almost dawn, but the sun wasn't quite up. Tat Boy was, however. He was ready.

He had tried to sleep, but sleep wouldn't come. Even digging into his own stash didn't bring him any relief. He was too keyed up.

He had called the man, told him what had happened, made the suggestion, something he had been keen on doing because he didn't want anything to come back on him and received the man's permission. Not that he needed it, but it didn't hurt to have his okay. To be safe, Tat Boy recorded the conversation. Just in case.

So he made the phone call, telling Fat Boy to meet him in the back of the North High School parking lot near the tennis courts. Fat Boy didn't even question it since the way Tat Boy put it, it was an order from the man. Tat Boy got there first and had waited with the engine off, even though it was freezing.

He saw the head lights and hoped it wasn't a cop making rounds because his presence on school grounds would be difficult to explain. As the car got closer, Tat Boy recognized Fat Boy's boat as both he and Fat Boy called it.

Fat Boy pulled up, nose to nose and Tat Boy hopped out and climbed in on the passenger side.

"Your car is warmer than mine."

"Why didn't you have the engine running?" Fat Boy asked.

"Didn't want to draw any attention. Too risky."

"So what's this idea you have?"

Tat Boy sat forward slowly, staring out through the driver's side window.

"Is someone out there by the school? Look!"

Fat boy turned away from Tat Boy, squinted into the dark of the parking lot towards school and said, "I don't see . . ."

Which was as far as he got.

Tat Boy pushed Fat Boy's head against the window, brought the knife out of his pocket and slit his throat. Fearing that he didn't cut deep enough, he plunged the knife into Fat Boy's ribs, his stomach and his chest so many times his arm got weak and tired.

Either his knife was that sharp or Fat Boy's neck was that soft or both. He marveled at how easily the knife sank into Fat Boy's body.

Tat Boy watched Fat Boy die.

Fat Boy clutched his neck trying to stem the flow of blood that pulsed between his fingers and down his hand and onto his BoDeans' t-shirt and down-feathered jacket. No way to treat Sammy Llanas or Kurt Neumann, but it couldn't be helped. Fat Boy's mouth worked, and gurgling sounds came out and his eyes bugged wide open. Then he was dead.

Yessiree, Fat Boy was dead, and Tat Boy had done it. Piece of cake. As easily as it was getting a blow job not once, but twice in one night from his girlfriend. Not actually his girlfriend, but it was a girl and it was two blow jobs and that was all that mattered. His dick was a little sore and his balls hurt, but he'd take that any day of the week for two blow jobs in one night.

As Tat Boy got back into his car and drove away, something popped into the back of his mind. It began as a spark and grew into a raging fire that had him sweating and nervous.

If the man gave Tat Boy permission to kill Fat Boy, might he also give someone permission to kill him?

CHAPTER THIRTY

When George got done in the shower and before he dried off, he leaned against the counter and did a quick Google search about owls and matched the owl he saw to the Great Grey owl. What was disconcerting to him was the fact that the Great Grey was not common to Wisconsin. He saw it, a rare sighting at that, in Southeastern Wisconsin in a suburban area and it confirmed what he had suspected- that it was an omen.

He wanted to tell Jeremy about it, but decided to wait until after church and after their Sunday meal. Maybe sometime in the early evening. He would also tell him about being followed when they went to from the movie to the pizza place and about his dreams, though he still wasn't convinced the dreams he had meant anything in particular. In fact, he could barely remember them, and he usually remembered his dreams.

He dried off, wrapped a towel around his waist and walked across the hall to the room he shared with Billy. He dressed quickly, walked back across the hall, brushed his teeth, lifted up his shirt and smeared deodorant under his arms, brushed his long damp hair and walked downstairs just in time to slip on his scarf and jacket and hop into the Expedition for the ride to church.

"How come you're so quiet?" Brian asked.

George said, "Just tired."

Jeremy parked towards the back of the church parking lot and his guys, as he called them, got out. Randy opened the door for Vicky and helped her out and was rewarded with a kiss on the cheek.

George was only beginning to understand what the Catholic mass was about. He and the twins, along with Brett, Bobby and Brian were enrolled in catechism classes. His brothers had all been baptized and were progressing towards confirmation, while George was deciding whether or not he wanted to be baptized. He wasn't sure, mostly because he saw a little bit more being chipped away from being a Navajo and his Navajo tradition. More than that, he wondered if his grandfather would have approved of him becoming a Catholic. Jeremy had left it up to George to decide what he wanted to do. He and Jeremy talked about it from time to time. Mostly, George would ask questions and Jeremy did his best to answer them.

One night Brett shared in a private moment that he didn't know if he believed in God. He used to, sort of, as much as a twelve-year-old believed in God. But when he was abducted, he prayed, he confessed, he promised, he bargained and nothing, nothing ever came of it except for one pervert after another in a steady river of filth using him and his body any way they had wanted. One after another for twenty-two months.

Billy was pretty ambivalent about religion. He was born and raised a Catholic, practiced it because Jeremy and Billy's father and mother before him, practiced it with regularity. Bobby, like he did with most everything in life, went with the flow and did what was expected of him with a smile and a laugh, but mostly because he loved and respected Jeremy. George wasn't sure about Victoria. She went to church on Sundays with them unless she was working and prayed with them before supper when they ate together, but other than that, he didn't know.

Randy was the most religious of his brothers, with Brian not far behind. Randy, like Jeremy, prayed, read the bible and knew certain verses by heart. Randy seemed earnest about being spiritual, but even more than that, was a good person. George thought of Randy as being one of the kindest, most loving and most sincere people he knew. In fact, George saw him as being so much like Jeremy that they were virtually one and the same person, one older, one younger.

George thought it was amusing that each Sunday, not only did they attend the same service, they sat in the virtually the same pew and pretty much sat in the same order. Bobby sat on the end with the aisle on one side and Jeremy on the other, who sat next to Vicky, who sat next to Brett. Next came Brian, George, Billy and Randy. Each Sunday.

And after mass, there were parishioners who would greet Jeremy and Vicky, while their children would visit with the boys. After they would pile back into the car and either go out to a family restaurant for an early lunch or more often, head back home for a large family meal.

The boys grabbed their coats and scarves from the back lobby. Jeremy helped Vicky into her coat and was given a kiss and a smile for his effort and all trooped out to Jeremy's red Expedition to head back to their home for a big lunch of a baked casserole dish made with ziti macaroni and a sauce that included meat, sausage, mushrooms, peppers and onions. It was already put together and just waiting for Vicky to bake it. There would be homemade garlic bread and a freshly tossed salad and for dessert, homemade cannelloni. Jeff and Danny Limbach would join them for the big meal.

"Dad, what's that on the windshield?" Billy asked.

Jeremy crossed the street, slipped on a patch of ice and almost fell, but caught himself. He picked up the large yellow mailing envelope with his name written across the front. Not only was it sealed with the envelope's adhesive, but it was also taped shut.

He frowned, not knowing what to make of it.

"Okay guys, let's roll."

As the boys got themselves situated, Jeremy held the door open for Vicky, who thanked him with another kiss. He handed her the envelope before he shut the door and crossed in front of the large SUV to get in behind the wheel.

"Do you want me to open it?" Vicky asked.

Jeremy shook his head and said, "Let's wait until after we eat. I don't want to spoil my appetite."

"You think it's that bad?"

Jeremy made a face and said, "If it was good, it would have been handed to me in person."

Before driving home, they dropped Brian off at his house. Jeremy walked him up to the front door of a modest ranch, gave his shoulder a squeeze and Brian surprised him with an embrace. More than an embrace, Brian clung to him.

Jeremy hugged him back, kissed the top of his head and said, "Are you going to be okay?"

Brian didn't have an opportunity to answer before Nancy Kazmarick opened the door.

"Hi, Jeremy. David and I were just talking about you. Thank you so much for all you do for Brian. We really appreciate it and I know Brian appreciates it too."

Jeremy shook her hand, smiled and said, "I told Bri that as long as you and David are okay with it, he's welcome at our house whenever he wants. Anytime."

She placed both of her arms around Brian from behind and said, "That means a lot to us, Jeremy. Thank you."

Jeremy waved and said goodbye and Nancy went back into the house, while Brian turned back towards Jeremy, smiled weakly, waved and went in, shutting the door behind him.

"He didn't look all that happy, did he?" Vicky asked.

Jeremy shook his head.

"He said that his parents were making his favorite meal. Steak, steamed asparagus, baked potatoes and apple pie for desert," Bobby offered.

"When did he tell you this?" Brett asked.

"Just before church. He and I didn't have much time to talk this weekend," Bobby said.

"Sounds like they're trying," Vicky suggested.

Jeremy only hoped so.

George however, had a funny feeling. A tickle, his grandfather called it, in the back of his mind.

CHAPTER THIRTY-ONE

"An early morning jogger, Wilson Meadows, found him. He runs this way five out of seven days a week. I admire his consistency, but running sucks."

Jamie knew from looking at Tom Skeer's belly, that running never entered the patrolman's mind.

Jamie peered into the driver's side window which was smeared with blood. The driver, an overweight kid with a round head and thick, full lips and dark brown or black hair, had been butchered by someone not too skilled with a knife. The slice across the kid's neck was jagged and didn't run from ear to ear the way a professional would have done it. The wounds in the kid's torso showed panic and disorganization. While the murder might have been planned, the method wasn't well-thought out, but rather more in a frenzy. His first thought was that it was a drug deal gone horribly wrong and he had the notion to call O'Connor, but he didn't. The fat kid looked to be about sixteen or seventeen-years-old.

Jamie was pissed off because he was yanked out of bed two early mornings in a row. This was supposed to be his weekend off and neither morning did he get to sleep in.

Ike showed up and he stooped a bit more than usual and was a little grumpier because it was yet another dead kid on yet another freezing morning. He was tired of working on dead kids and even more tired of Wisconsin winters. Probably more so the dead kids, but Jamie knew Ike had wanted to retire to someplace warmer, a lot warmer like Florida or Arizona. The trouble was Ike had talked about it for five or six years, but had done nothing except talk about it.

"What do you think, Ike?"

He mumbled something Jamie didn't get and shook his head. "I'll know more when I get him back to the lab."

The crime techs finished up. Buddy Winslow, the on-call driver from Suburban Towing, waited impatiently for the fat kid's body to be moved from the car so he could get the car towed to the police impound. From there he didn't know what would happen to the car and frankly he didn't care. It was cold, the Packers were playing Atlanta at noon at Lambeau and all he wanted to do was get home, grill some brats, eat some potato salad, drink some Bud Light and sit in front of the big screen and watch Aaron Rodgers teach Matt Ryan a thing or two about playing quarterback in the NFL.

The kid was pulled as gently as possible out of the car, carefully even for a dead body. Before he was placed in a black body bag, Jamie slipped on a latex glove, took the wallet from the kid's back pocket and read the driver's license. He recognized the name and knew the family, and not in a good way. Finally, the body was stuffed into the back of the ME's truck for transport to Waukesha Memorial Hospital.

Jamie had directed the techs to take pictures of the footprints to and from the kid's car, as well as the tire tracks. At least the ones that weren't obliterated by the patrol cops and other vehicles that had arrived on the scene.

When most everyone had left, Jamie sat in his car with the lights off and engine running, sipping now lukewarm coffee from his travel mug. The question he kept coming back to was how this kid's death might be related to the other kids' deaths. There was no obvious linkage. Perhaps they might find something when the techs examined the kid's car more extensively, but at the moment, there was nothing. Only a hunch and Jamie was big on hunches.

CHAPTER THIRTY-TWO

Angel Benevides didn't know what was being planned, but he knew something was going to happen. MS-13 was pissed about someone trying to cut into their business and they wanted payback. They were armed and ready and just needed to be pointed in the right direction.

Beyond that however, he knew that the skinny dude, Fuentes, had it in for George but didn't know why. Most everyone liked George. In fact, he couldn't think of anyone who didn't.

In a roundabout way Angel asked Manuel about Fuentes, but his older brother didn't say anything. Angel knew Manuel was as leery of Fuentes as he was. Perhaps actually afraid, like having a pet tiger and not being able to control it. Angel knew Fuentes wasn't anyone's pet, but he was also every bit a tiger that there was.

"We have some deliveries to make."

Angel was about to refuse, but Manuel said, "Don't give me shit, Ass Wipe. I need backup just in case."

"I'm not into that shit, Manny. No!"

Manny swung on Angel, connecting with Angel's eye. Angel was knocked off his feet. He landed on his ass and his head and shoulder hit the wall, leaving a smudge on the faded cheap lilac paint. Stunned, he shook his head. His eye was already swelling and his vision was blurred.

Pissed, he got up and charged at his older brother, who wasn't expecting Angel's reaction. They both ended up rolling around on the floor swinging and cursing. Manny ended up on top and got in two quick punches to Angel's stomach. Angel answered with a knee to Manny's balls, not once but twice.

Still on top, Manny took a handful of Angel's hair and slammed the back of his head on the floor and punched him in the mouth loosening a tooth.

Carmen, their mother, took a frying pan to Manny's back swinging it like

Bryce Harper swinging on a fastball.

"Goddam, you crazy bitch!"

That only brought another swing that connected with Manny's shoulder.

Manny stood up wobbly and pushed his mother to the floor as she was getting ready to swing again. He turned around and kicked Angel in the stomach.

"You're gonna pay for this you little shit!"

"Get out!" his mother cried. "Get out and don't come back!"

"Fuck off, Bitch!"

Angel tried to tackle his brother, but Manny threw him off and he crashed into a little curio cabinet shattering the glass and some figurines and other trinkets his mother loved. She had so few prized possessions, it infuriated Angel.

"I'm calling the police," his mother cried, pushing herself off the floor.

He slapped her, knocking her back down to the floor and said, "If you do, I'll come back for both of you!"

Before he left the little house, he turned around, stared at Angel and said, "You're going to pay, Bendejo! You can bet on that!"

CHAPTER THIRTY-THREE

Dinner was eaten and bellies were full and there was nothing left but a few pieces of garlic bread, but Vicky was sure they'd disappear before anyone went to bed. She also doubted that the two or three cannelloni would last. As was the usual case, there was plenty of laughter and conversation. It was Randy's and Brett's turn to clean up the kitchen and they did it quickly with laughter, a snapping of a towel and a flick of dishwater. The other guys lounged around the family room in front of the TV watching the NFL Pregame Show with Howie and Terry and the guys. Jasmine laid next to George with her head on his thigh and Jasper curled himself around Bobby's stocking feet.

Momma laid on the floor in front of the fireplace in the study. She'd lift her head to check on Jeremy and Vicky who sat on the couch in almost the same position as Jeremy and Brian had the evening before. Jeff sat in the leather lounger with his feet up. The cold weather bothered his hip and leg and having them up helped as did the heat from the fire.

Vicky had her feet and legs curled under her and used Jeremy's shoulder as a pillow. Her long dark brown hair hung loosely on her shoulders and her chestnut eyes focused on the papers Jeremy handed to her as he finished reading them. As she finished she would lean over and hand them to Jeff, who read so quickly that more often than not, he was waiting patiently for her to finish.

Jeremy finished with the last one, sighed and took a sip from his glass of wine. Without looking at him and continuing to read the final page, Vicky held her hand out until Jeremy handed her his glass so she could take a sip and she handed the glass back for Jeremy to finish.

She passed the final sheet to Jeff who read it and stacked it with the others neatly and handed them all back to Vicky, who handed them to Jeremy. He placed them into the envelope that had been placed under his windshield wiper earlier that morning.

"What now?" Jeff asked.

Jeff was a prolific and best-selling writer and each of his last six books debuted in the top five on the New York Times Best Seller List and each had climbed to the top spot. Four of his books had been made into movies and Jeff had written the screen adaptation for two of them and in one, had a bit part. His name in horror fiction ranked up there with King and Straub.

He got the limp as an unwelcome present back when he was eighteen. As he was riding his motorcycle home from a football game late one Friday night, a drunk driver or someone who the police had assumed was a drunk driver pulled up alongside of Jeff and squeezed him into the guard rail dragging him and the cycle for thirty yards before throwing him off the bike and into a field, where a farmer had found him early the following morning. It was the helmet he had worn, the moist, muddy earth he had landed in and the grace of God that had saved his life.

As it was, Jeff had spent several weeks in the hospital, suffering agonizing surgery after surgery. Equally painful rehabilitation followed up each surgery. He had to relearn to walk and his football playing days were over which was a tough way to end his senior year in high school. As a lasting remembrance of the accident and of the many surgeries he had suffered through since that accident, Jeff had an ugly scar and a permanent limp. He used a fancy cane made of dark wood with a pearl handle to help him get around.

The only good that came from all of those long stretches in the hospital confined to a bed was that Jeff developed a love for books and writing. It led him first to a career teaching English at North where he met Jeremy, who taught social studies and coached basketball, and where he met Jamie Graff who was the School Resource Officer. The three of them, known by their colleagues as *The Three J's*, became lasting friends.

"Someone gave this to you for a reason," Vicky said. "Any idea who it might be?"

Jeremy shook his head and said, "Not a clue. I mean, it could have been anyone."

"The amount of information in this," Jeff said shaking his head. "Someone has firsthand knowledge. He or she detailed names, places and dates. Whoever did this wants you to do something with it."

"I think I need to call Jamie," Jeremy said.

"Excuse me," George said from the doorway. None of them had noticed him standing there or for how long. George's nickname, given to him at the age of twelve at his coming of age ceremony by his grandfather was Shadow and it fit.

"What's up, George?"

Looking unsure of himself which was rare in itself because George was one of the most confident young men Jeremy knew, he said, "Father, I have something to tell you."

Vicky and Jeff looked at one another and Vicky said, "Would you like us to leave?"

"No, please. I think you and Uncle Jeff need to hear this."

Jeremy had an uneasy feeling and he could sense Vicky did too just based how her body tensed up. He knew Jeff so well that he imagined that Jeff felt the same way. He took her hand in his.

"Okay," Jeremy said.

"Father, last night we were followed."

George told them the whole story finishing with, "I did not think much of it until this morning."

"What happened this morning?" Vicky asked sitting up.

"I went out to plow the driveway with the truck and an owl flew out from somewhere and landed on the hood and stared at me."

"Huh?" Jeremy asked.

"It . . . stared at me. It walked up to the windshield and stared at me. It was not bothered by Jasmine, and Jasmine did not bark or scare it off."

Jeremy glanced at Jeff and at Vicky, but didn't know what to say.

Jeff cleared his throat and said, "We live out in the country, George. We're surrounded by woods so it isn't uncommon for an owl to be near us."

George nodded, reached into his back pocket, fired up his phone, walked over to the couch where Jeremy and Vicky sat and showed them the picture.

"This is the owl I saw."

Jeremy wrinkled his brow and shrugged and glanced at Vicky, who shrugged her shoulders. George walked over to Jeff to show him.

"It's an owl," Jeff said.

George nodded and said, "It is a Great Grey Owl."

"Okay," Jeremy said.

"Great Grey Owls are rare in Wisconsin. They do not live here."

Jeremy, Vicky and Jeff exchanged looks and waited for George to continue.

"The *Dine'* believe sometimes spirits are sent to us in the form of animals. *Biligaana* call them omens. They are like the spirit world speaking to us in our dreams. Father, I believe this was a warning . . . an omen."

"Of what?" Jeff asked. It wasn't a question of doubt and it wasn't a question of disbelief.

"I am not sure, but I also had a series of dreams last night. I cannot remember them, but they disturbed me."

"Did your grandfather . . .?" Jeremy asked.

"No, Father. Grandfather was not with me last night. They were just . . ." he shook his head not sure how to explain them. "They bothered me."

There was silence and Jeremy felt Vicky stiffen.

"Who knows about this?" Jeremy asked.

"Billy and Brett know about us being followed. Billy looked up the kind of car and he thinks it was a black or dark blue Camaro. Only you and Mother and Uncle Jeff and I know about the owl and my dream."

Jeremy sighed and said, "We have to call Jamie."

CHAPTER THIRTY-FOUR

Brian got to school a little later than usual and even though the guys had texted him wondering where he was, he stopped in the guidance area looking for Jeremy.

"Hey Kaz! What's up?"

Kristi Johnson, the guidance administrative assistant always had a smile and a sunny disposition even on the darkest of days. It was one of the things the staff and particularly the students liked about her. She was considered to be a *friendly*: a safe harbor and refuge, a place where kids could go when they needed to escape an angry teacher or one that was unreasonable. It didn't hurt that with her blond hair and blue eyes, she was young and attractive.

Brian blushed and smiled and said, "Is Mr. Evans around?"

"He is, but he's in a meeting. Do you need me to get him?"

Brian hesitated, shook his head and said, "Would you just tell him I stopped in to say hi?"

Kristi looked at him doubtfully. She knew Brian's backstory and knew Jeremy was looking after him.

"Kaz, I can go get him if you need him."

Brian smiled shyly and said, "No, it's okay. I have to go find the guys. If you could just let him know I stopped by to say hi, I would appreciate it."

"When he's done with his meeting, do you want him to call you down or have him find you?"

"No, it's okay. Really. Thanks," he answered already turning around and heading for the door.

Kristi watched him leave and head down the hallway to the cafeteria where she knew most of the students were waiting until the five minute warning bell that would cause the mass exodus to first period. She took out her phone and texted the twins to let them know he was on his way and she pulled a yellow sticky note from the dispenser and wrote a note to Jeremy. She got up from behind her desk and stuck it to his computer monitor.

The meeting was a big one. It was held behind the closed door of the small conference room in the main office. Chuck Gobel, the principal, Bob Farner and Liz Champion, the assistant principals, a skinny long-haired dude wearing jeans, a sweatshirt and tennis shoes and who wore a badge on his belt, along with a short stocky red-haired guy with freckles who was dressed in khaki slacks, a blue button-down shirt and a tan sport coat. Jamie Graff was in there and of course, Jeremy.

It had begun just as she had arrived and from the somber mood of the participants, who knew how long it would last. She deflected questions from office staff, from the teachers and from the few students who had wandered into the guidance office looking for Jeremy. That was easy to do, actually, because the only thing she knew for sure was that it was serious.

Some had speculated it had something to do with the early Sunday morning murder of Kevin Longwood, found in his car in the school parking lot. The stories varied. One was that he was shot in the face. One was that his throat was slashed. One was that it was yet another overdose added to the growing list of kids who had died experimenting with needles and drugs.

She doubted that Jeremy or anyone else would share anything that they didn't want anyone to know. But if someone were to hear anything it would be Kristi.

CHAPTER THIRTY-FIVE

Brian's mom and dad had weirded him out. He loved the steak. His dad had grilled it just right. He had stuffed himself. But the conversation was weird. Really strange.

"*Brian, your dad and I need to do some planning. We'd like to know if something were to happen to either of us . . . well, both of us, where would you like to live?*" his mom had asked.

It was like someone had sucked all the air out of the kitchen. He gaped at his mom, then his dad and back to his mom.

"*This is only a precaution. Your mom and I don't have a will and we don't want anything left to chance and we both feel you're old enough to decide for yourself,*" his dad said.

Brian lost his appetite and stopped eating. He put his fork down and put his hands in his lap on his paper napkin.

"*You have your Uncle Bart and Aunt Sue. You like them. You have your Uncle Alex and Aunt Hannah. Either of them would take you because they love you,*" his mom suggested.

"*Or if you wanted to, maybe you could live with Sean and his family. Or Jeremy and the guys. They aren't family, but they might take you in,*" his dad said. "*We'd have to discuss this with them of course.*"

"*Anyone you choose, we'd have to ask, especially if you choose someone who isn't family,*" his mom said.

In the end he didn't hesitate. He picked Jeremy. His Uncle Bart and Aunt Sue lived in Des Moines, Iowa, and he didn't want to move that far away. His Uncle Alex and Aunt Hannah lived in Waunakee, near Madison, but while that was closer, it wasn't close enough. He liked Sean and his parents, but it was too quiet there.

At Jeremy's, there was always something to do and someone to do it with.

There was noise and laughter and always someone around. Jeremy's house with the guys was the opposite of his house with his parents.

Maybe the worst part of the day was going through Brad's things, picking out what he wanted to keep and what he didn't. Everything else was placed in cardboard boxes with Brad's name written with black magic marker and sealed with clear packing tape.

In the end, Brian had chosen a picture of the four of them, Brad's arm slung across Brian's shoulders laughing at something or someone like he always did. Brian was laughing too. Brad always made him laugh. He made everyone laugh. Brian smiled even though he had tears in his eyes. He took a leather bracelet that Brad liked to wear, a couple pairs of shorts and that was it. Brian had outgrown the rest of Brad's clothes, which dismayed him. Brian had always thought of Brad as bigger than he was. Larger, somehow.

Brian had thought about calling Jeremy a couple of times that night, but didn't. He texted Bobby. Mostly about basketball and Bobby's songs, but nothing about his feelings. He wanted to talk to Jeremy face to face which was why he had stopped in guidance.

He almost walked into the restroom to gather himself together, but didn't not wanting to run into any of the dirt bags who might be in there. Instead he bent down to get a drink of water even though he wasn't all that thirsty.

He wiped his mouth and chin off with his hand, stood up and came face to face with Doug Sweeney and two of his shit-for-brains friends.

"So, Ass Wipe, you think you're going to take my place on the team? You really think you can take my place?"

Brian said nothing, his eyes searching the hallway for a friendly face and coming up empty.

Sweeney bounced a finger off Brian's chest and said, "I asked you a question, Ass Wipe."

Though Brian quivered on the inside, he thought he disguised it pretty well. At least well enough to not show any of the panic he felt.

Sweeney, who stood a good head and then some taller than Brian, bent down so that their noses almost touched.

"Too bad your weenie brother died and not you. I would have kicked his ass too, but you're nothing compared to him."

He pushed Brian's forehead back and said, "You're nothing."

"Get your hands off of him!" Caitlyn said wedging herself in between the two of them. Sean stood behind him and off to the side, his fingers rapid fire over the keys of his cell.

Sweeney laughed showing off to the rest of the crowd in the hallway who had gathered around to watch hoping for a fight.

"What, a girl has to talk for you, Ass Wipe?" he spread his arms and laughed looking at all who had gathered to watch the little show. "Seriously? Your shitty brother is probably rolling around in his grave embarrassed as shit."

"Why don't you crawl back in your hole, Sweeney?" Caitlyn said.

Brian knew she meant well, but he wished she wasn't around and mostly wished she wouldn't say anything.

"And you're the one Harrison picked to take my place? What a joke!" he laughed again.

"Whatcha doin', Doug?" Brett asked pushing himself into the little circle followed by George, Billy and Randy. "You waiting for George to kick your ass some more? You didn't get enough Friday night?"

Sweeney's composure faltered a hair, but it was noticed by everyone.

"Why don't you tell everyone how George wiped your face all over the brick wall, huh?"

Sweeney licked his lips, his eyes darting at George and the twins.

"Oh wait. You probably told your douche' bag friends how you tripped and fell or something." Brett laughed and turned to the crowd in the hallway and said, "No, Sweeney got his ass kicked by a freshman half his size. Bet you never told that to anyone, did ya, huh, Doug?"

"What's going on here?" Gordon Huggins had come out of the front office and was on his way to his classroom when saw the crowd and pushed his way in.

"Sweeney was acting all tough," Brett said, "trying to push Brian around."

"Everyone get to class."

No one moved so Huggins said, "I said get to class or do I need to call security?"

The crowd mumbled, but moved on.

"Sweeney, I want to see you in my classroom right now!"

"I might be late for class."

"In my room *now!*"

His two friends left him to fend for himself and moved along towards their classrooms with the rest of the crowd.

When Brett and the twins, Brian, Caitlyn and Sean didn't move, Huggins said, "Get to class."

Before Brian left, Huggins said, "Brian, are you okay?"

"I didn't do anything to you did I, Brian?" Sweeney suggested.

Huggins turned on Sweeney and snarled, "In my classroom!"

He followed Sweeney inside and shut the door behind him.

"Are you okay, Kaz?" Billy asked.

Brian didn't answer, but took off for his Algebra class on the other side of the building. Caitlyn left with him taking hold of his hand as they walked.

George watched them and sighed.

Randy said, "I'll let Dad know," taking out his phone. He began the text message barely after it left his pocket.

"I have Advanced Algebra near Bri, so I'll meet up with him after first," Billy said.

"He and I have English together second period," Sean said. "And Randy and Brian have World History together."

"Okay, we take turns watching Brian until Dad can get to him," Brett said. "I don't have anything with him except lunch. Hopefully Dad will get to him before that."

The bell chimed three times letting them know they were all tardy to first period. That meant after school detention.

Sweeney left Huggins' classroom, glanced at them but kept walking.

"Guys, let me give you a pass to class," Huggins said coming out of this classroom. As he was writing one after the other he said, "I'm not sure what happened or why, but I assume you'll tell your father. If he needs to talk to anyone, let him know I saw what happened."

"Thank you," Randy said. "We will."

Brett stopped them before they walked into Huggins' classroom. "Guys, we need to stay away from Sweeney," Brett said looking directly at George. "All of us." He paused and added, "Okay?"

George would have told Brett that he had no intention of doing anything to Sweeney unless he tried to start something with one of his brothers or his friends. But he was too busy watching Brian and Caitlyn holding hands as they walked to class.

At the other end of the hallway, Angel Benevides had watched everything. He didn't like Sweeney or any of his friends and he didn't actually know George or the others except for their reputation. Because of that reputation, he believed he had nothing in common with them. He only had a wish and a hope and sometimes that was enough.

CHAPTER THIRTY-SIX

Jamie turned off his cell, looked up and said, "We can't get the dogs in here before Thursday."

"Friday's a better day anyway according to these notes," O'Connor suggested putting his copy of the notes back in the envelope and sliding it on the table in front of him. "It says that most of the deals take place on Wednesday or Friday."

"We've set up surveillance on the three outside locations where kids are buying," Eiselmann said. "I'm a little surprised about the McDonald's parking lot and the Roller Rink. Both are pretty public."

"Hiding in plain sight," O'Connor said. "Makes plenty of sense at least for pot, pills or tabs of LSD. Even heroin."

"What about the kids named in this?" Jeremy asked. He turned to Farner and Champion. "Are you going to search them?"

"That wouldn't be a good idea just yet," Jamie said.

"And there's too many. If you or we begin searching them and if none have anything on them, they will be more discreet and we might never catch them," Eiselmann said.

"It might be best to use the school security system to watch them." O'Connor pursed his lips, shook his head and said, "Like Paul said, we can't take the chance that they won't have anything on them. It would be best to wait until we bring in the dogs. That will give us reasonable suspicion. But if we use the security system, we can gather evidence against them. Someone would have to monitor the system and specifically look for each of the players. But the thing is, the more we bring into this circle, the bigger the possibility that word will leak. And if word leaks and if the kids find out, we lose any chance of catching them."

"So what do you propose we do?" Farner asked. Bob Farner was the most senior of the two assistant principals. He was heavy and bald with a great sense of humor and a ready laugh, though he wasn't laughing now. "I don't like not doing anything. It's dangerous for the kids who use."

"Your security staff knows the camera system the best." O'Connor leaned forward and said, "But if you give an order for one of them to collect tape on these kids, they'll know something's up."

"How long does the system run before data is erased?" Eiselmann asked.

"The capacity for keeping data stored on the system is set for a maximum of sixty days unless the data is shifted to a DVD. After sixty days, the system erases any data that has been stored," Champion said. "It's the makeup of the digital system the district paid for."

"That's a serious upgrade from when I worked here," Jamie said.

"Sixty days is plenty of time," Eiselmann said.

"It should be. If it takes us sixty days to find answers, there will be a whole pile of bodies around here," O'Connor said.

"I think we should chunk the film on DVDs to make it easier to go through. It will make cataloging it easier for us," Eiselmann suggested.

"If we start stockpiling film on DVDs, that will guarantee some questions," Farner said.

"And as you said, if there are questions, there will be leaks," added Champion.

"How much do you trust your security?" Eiselmann asked.

"I think we can bring in Bud Foster," Gobel said after some thought. "He knows the system and I think he'll be fine. We'll need to make sure he doesn't tell Parker or Kruchinski. We tell them we're shifting assignments. We give Bud overtime every other day to do the recording and he delivers the DVDs to my office."

"Chuck, it might be better if he delivers them to me. I oversee security, so it might be less suspicious that way," Champion said. She was young and aggressive and smart. Definitely on the fast track for a principal's office either in Waukesha or in one of the surrounding districts.

He nodded and said, "Good point. We'll do that."

"You realize that there will be talk just because we're meeting in here," Farner said. "Jeremy, you're likely to be asked some questions."

Jeremy shrugged and said, "I'm a counselor. Counselors live with confidentiality."

"What are the chances of Pat and me talking to George?" Jamie asked.

"Shouldn't be a problem, but that could raise some eyebrows."

"Well, not necessarily," Eiselmann said. "I'm doing a follow up on his altercation with Sweeney."

Jamie nodded. "And as his father, you could be present."

"That might work." Jeremy showed them the text from Randy. "I need to check on Brian at some point."

"How is Weenie involved in all of this?" Farner asked. He had unpleasant dealings with the Sweeney family before.

Jamie looked at Jeremy. Jeremy shrugged and Jamie said, "Don't know yet. Don't know that he is, but we don't know that he isn't." He looked over at O'Connor.

"I'm guessing fringe player. Drugs are too risky for him. He might smoke weed. He might pop a pill or two, but heroin?" O'Connor shook his head and said, "I doubt it."

Chuck Gobel scratched his head and said, "You know . . . everyone knows there are drugs in schools. All schools, not just North. I just didn't realize it was this bad."

"It's bad anywhere, Chuck," Jamie said. "North is no worse than any other school."

"Why doesn't that make me feel any better," Gobel answered with a humorless laugh.

"Jeremy, do you or your boys have any idea who might have given this to you?" Farner asked indicating the folder.

Jeremy shook his head. "The boys don't know what was in the envelope. Vicky, Jeff and I didn't show them and we didn't talk about it with them."

"They wouldn't know who is using or dealing anyway," Eiselmann said. "They don't hang with anyone like that."

"Just wondering," Champion said. She stopped and took a drink from her lukewarm mug of coffee. "Does any of this have anything to do with Kevin Longwood? I mean, he died in our parking lot."

The men looked at each other, but it was Jamie who spoke. "We believe there is a connection, yes. We just don't know what the connection is."

He wasn't about to reveal any of the evidence gathered from the abandoned building or Longwood's car. O'Connor and Eiselmann knew, of course. No one else needed to know. Not even Jeremy.

CHAPTER THIRTY-SEVEN

George was in a sour mood. His smile was noticeably absent, his dark eyes more intense, his jaw set. Danny met up with him in Spanish IV and couldn't pull him out of his funk. They stuck together because they were the only ninth graders in the class full of juniors and seniors, evenly split between boys and girls.

He smacked him on the upper arm and said, "What's up?"

George frowned and shook his head once and Danny backed off.

The first part of the lesson was on conjugating past tense verbs, followed by a short five minute video clip of a mother talking to her daughter about shopping for a dress for her to wear on Saturday night for dinner and a play. The students had to translate the Spanish dialogue to English. For George and Danny, it was as natural and easy as transcribing English to English which was why they were in Spanish IV. The other kids in the class struggled with it and asked George or Danny for help or in a couple of cases, just looked at their papers and copied their work.

After the transcription which was turned in as a benchmark test grade, the students had to come up with a Spanish dialogue discussing the Spanish version of *Don Quixote* that would be presented to the class the following day. Danny and George were paired together by their teacher, Don Lehmann with the instruction to work on the symbolism of the story.

George picked up his notebook and a copy of his book and sat down on the other side of the room at a desk facing Danny leaving his backpack at his desk. He and Danny talked about the book the entire time in Spanish. Both took notes, laughed a little- Danny more so than George, but were busy the entire time. Those who sat nearby stared at them in awe.

The bell rang which for them meant first lunch. For others, another class before lunch and still others who would go to class, lunch and back to the same class.

Danny gathered his things and waited patiently for George who stuffed his book, his notebook and pen back into his backpack. He slung his backpack over one shoulder and met Danny at the door and together walked down the hallway towards the cafeteria.

They didn't get halfway there when a girl, neither of them knew or saw before, handed George a note and said, "Some guy asked me to give this to you." She handed George a folded piece of paper and just as quickly disappeared into the crowd moving the other direction and vanished from sight.

"Who was that?" Danny asked.

Bewildered, George stared off hoping to catch a glimpse of her, but failed to.

"What's the note say?"

The two boys leaned against the lockers out of the way and read the note together.

George didn't get scared easily, but he felt himself grow pale and sweat broke out on his upper lip.

"Jesus, George! You have to show this to your dad! Now!"

Rooted to the spot, he didn't move.

"Did you hear me? Now! Go now!"

George took off, quick-walking to the guidance office dodging huddles of kids dotting the hallways before the bell rang for the next class.

CHAPTER THIRTY-EIGHT

"There have been so many kids who've overdosed. What's being done about that?" Katrina Brady asked.

"The police are doing their best, Katrina," Jeremy said.

"What does that mean, 'doing their best'?" Gordon Huggins asked. "I mean, I know the police are doing their best, but kids are dying."

"I know, Gordon. I don't have any answers."

"Is there anything we can do? Maybe have a school assembly about drugs to at least warn the kids? There's bound to be one or two who might listen."

Jeremy knew they both meant well. They were leaders among the teachers and popular with the kids and their hearts were in the right place. He found it frustrating that he couldn't share anything with them because of all the members of the faculty, these two could possibly provide help.

"Guys, that's out of my control, but that isn't a bad idea. You might want to talk to Chuck or Liz about putting something like that together."

Their little talk wasn't going anywhere and wanting to end it, Jeremy stood up, reached out a hand to Katrina and said, "Thanks for caring for the kids. I really mean that."

He shook her hand and the hand of Gordon Huggins and said, "Thank you both."

Huggins opened the door, let Katrina out and said, "Jeremy, what was that all about between the Kazmarick kid and Sweeney? And what happened between George and Sweeney Friday night?"

Katrina hung in the background listening. Jeremy knew Huggins had witnessed what took place between Sweeney and Brian that morning, but he was surprised he had already found out what took place between Sweeney and George Friday night after the movie. Yet he shouldn't have been surprised, because Huggins had a way of knowing who was doing what to whom and when it was taking place.

"Nothing, really. One kid shooting his mouth off and another kid standing up to him."

"Well, I admire George. Most of the teachers do. He's quite a young man. In fact, all your kids are. They take after their father," he said with a smile, shaking Jeremy's hand. Brady nodded in agreement.

"Thank you, but I don't think I had much to do with it."

Jeremy really did believe that. All he had done for George, the twins, for Brian and the McGovern boys was to open his door and his heart and give them an opportunity to grow. Whatever the boys had accomplished, they did it on their own.

"Well, speak of the devil," Huggins said with a smile.

George stood near Kristi Johnson's desk, lost in thought as he texted someone on his phone.

Before Huggins and Brady walked out, they said hello and George politely smiled and nodded, though he didn't feel like doing either.

Phil Keneally, an older and quiet social studies teacher had wandered in from the mailroom and spoke quietly with Gloria Beatleman, one of the other counselors in front of her office door.

"Aren't you supposed to be at lunch?" Jeremy asked with a smile.

"Father, may I speak with you?"

Jeremy recognized the look. Huggins smiled and nodded at Jeremy, at George, and he and Katrina Brady left the office.

"What's wrong?" Jeremy said quietly. He spoke quietly because there was one senior working on a career interest inventory at a computer on a desk against the wall and a boy and a girl sat in chairs holding hands while waiting to speak to Beatleman or Gary Floyd. Jeremy didn't know.

George didn't answer right away, but walked into Jeremy's office. When Jeremy followed him in, George shut the door behind them and stood with his back against it.

"George?"

George handed him the note. Jeremy read it once, looked up at George and read it again.

"Where did you get this?"

"A girl. Danny and I never saw her before." He went on to explain what she said and how she disappeared after giving it to him.

Jeremy read the note again, ran a hand through his hair and over his face and sat down in his desk chair.

"I texted Agent Pete and Detective Jamie," George said. "Maybe they know who he is."

Jeremy sighed.

He had thought it was all over. All of it. Everyone safe. No more shooting. No more killing. All done and over.

The boys trooped in led by Brett and Randy. Sean and Caitlyn stayed outside Jeremy's office in the guidance lobby.

"Danny told us," Billy said.

"Mr. Farner said I could I bring you a chicken sandwich," Brian said. "Mr. Farner said I could," he repeated to Jeremy because everyone knew that no food was supposed to leave the cafeteria.

George didn't have an appetite, but he took it from him and said, "Thanks."

"So is this Fuentes guy . . . is he related to the one who tried to kill everybody at that cottage?" Brett asked.

"I do not know," George answered.

"Dad, I think we need to tell Jamie and maybe Kelliher," Randy said. "They might know."

"I already texted them," George said.

"Could he have been the guy who followed you guys Friday night?" Randy asked.

"Billy told us," Brian said.

"Guys, let's not get ahead of ourselves," Jeremy said. "We don't know if this note has any validity. We don't know who gave it to George. And we don't really know who this Fuentes is."

"So what do we do now?" Brett asked.

"You guys need to get to class in about four minutes," Jeremy said. "If Jamie or Pete call, I'll talk with them and we'll decide what to do."

None of the boys moved towards the door and it was clear by their expressions that they weren't too happy with that plan.

"Guys, really. The bell is going to ring-"

George's cell buzzed. It was Kelliher.

CHAPTER THIRTY-NINE

It was a busy day and they had planned for it. David Kazmarick was a list maker, always in priority order and he would go about checking each task off his list as he accomplished it. He almost always completed his list and today was no different.

He and Brian were similar like that. Serious, though David more so than Brian. Both tended to be quiet and thoughtful and both planned and calculated the risks and weighed the options and left nothing to chance. Brad was more like his mother. Outgoing and friendly and who went through life with a smile and a laugh and with the attitude that whatever happened, happened and that all was good in the world. The summer of death however, tested that theory and that theory failed the test. Neither boy looked like either parent, but one could tell the boys belonged to them. Both were handsome with dark wavy hair and greenish-hazel eyes and soft features.

He and Nancy began shortly after David dropped Brian off at school. They stopped at the insurance agency and made sure their beneficiary designation was in order. It wasn't, as it still listed a fifty-fifty split between Brad and Brian and it listed David's younger brother, Bart Kazmarick as being the designated guardian and administrator of the policy. They removed Brad altogether and changed Brian's designated guardian. Their agent, Mike Strazinski answered their questions and he asked some questions of his own and received satisfactory answers complete with smiles and reassurances from both David and Nancy. David and Nancy placed a rush on the paperwork, three copies, and Strazinski promised to have it ready for them by early afternoon.

Their second stop was to a notary public. Their document, five copies, were all signed and notarized and placed in separate ten by eleven inch yellow envelopes with appropriate names indicating whose copy was whose.

They stopped at their bank and spoke to the assistant manager. After the brief conversation, Brad's account was closed with all the money placed into Brian's and a signatory was added to David's and Nancy's joint checking and savings and to Brian's account. They withdrew one thousand dollars from their savings in fifty and one hundred dollar increments, placing five hundred dollars each in two of the yellow envelopes. They left after thanking the assistant manager.

They ate a light lunch, picked up the updated paperwork from Strazinski and headed home. There, they sorted clothes and pictures and placed them in carefully labeled boxes. They went through knickknacks, taking some of the more memorable and expensive ones and placed them on one box, while placing others in different boxes. Those that they wanted to keep, they marked *Keep*. The other boxes were marked *Goodwill*.

When the last box was packed, taped up and labeled, together they carried the Goodwill boxes to the minivan and dropped them off.

They sat in the parking lot with the engine off.

David reached for Nancy's hand and entwined his fingers with hers, though he kept his eyes forward.

"You know I love you."

He nodded, swallowed though his mouth was dry and said, "And I love you."

They sat for another moment or two and then drove home.

CHAPTER FORTY

Just as students poured out of the building seconds after the bell signaling the end of the school day, Jamie, Pat O'Connor and Paul Eiselmann muscled their way into the school like salmon swimming upstream. They found Jeremy in the guidance area, walked into his office and shut the door. George sat in a chair at the side of Jeremy's desk.

"Hey, George. Where's everyone else?" Jamie asked.

"The twins, Brett and Brian are at basketball practice and Danny is in the band room," Jeremy answered.

"Bobby is at Butler's basketball practice with Stephen and Mikey," Eiselmann said. "I'm picking Stephen and Mikey up at five."

O'Connor leaned against the door, while Jamie and Eiselmann sat down facing Jeremy and George.

"Kelliher called me," Jamie said. "It was nice talking to him again. I just wish it was under different circumstances. I gave him all the information we had, including the evidence we collected in the building and what we found with the dead kids."

"Did he have any theories?" Jeremy asked.

Jamie flashed him a look and said nonchalantly, "He said he'd look into it."

George caught Jamie's look and knew there was more to it than that.

"Um . . . George." O'Connor stopped, thought for a bit and began again. "George, the girl who gave you the note. Was she Latino . . . Hispanic?"

George shook his head and said, "No, Sir."

O'Connor stared at the floor.

"Why?" Jeremy asked.

"Fuentes is MS-13. You already met his cousin, Jorge, or as he liked to be called, 'The Blade,'" Jamie said.

"So they are related," Jeremy said. It wasn't a question, more like a statement of resignation.

"Related, but different," O'Connor said.

"Ricardo Fuentes is a member of MS-13. Jorge wasn't." Jamie said. "At least he wasn't at the end of his career."

"Jorge was a hired assassin. We think and Kelliher agrees, that Ricardo is nowhere near as lethal," O'Connor said. Jeremy and George heard the same thing from Kelliher himself when he had called earlier that afternoon.

"We don't have much paper on him," Eiselmann said. "All we know is that he's based out of Chicago. He's upper level gang, but not at the top. We think he was sent here to find out who's trying to move in on the drug trafficking and stop them."

"The kids who OD'd," Jeremy said.

Jamie nodded. "Someone's experimenting with a heroin, fentanyl bundle and they don't have the right combination yet."

"Yet," O'Connor said.

"Why is Fuentes after me?" George said.

"Don't know," Jamie said. "Best guess is revenge for killing his cousin."

"Are my brothers and father and mother in danger?"

"Possibly. MS-13 is dangerous. Probably the most dangerous of the gangs in the country," Eiselmann said. "Certainly the most violent."

"They're dangerous, but predictable. It's their predictability that makes them vulnerable," O'Connor said.

"What does that mean?" Jeremy asked.

"MS-13 is interested in making money. Prostitution and drugs are their primary sources, but they also run weapons," O'Connor said.

"Because they're predictable, they will find out who's trying to cut into their drug trade and teach them a lesson. We have to find out who that is before they do or it's going to get messy quickly," Eiselmann said.

"We think Fuentes came up here from Chicago to find out who it is and to stop them," O'Connor said. "We think you're a side trip."

"Wait, wait!" Jeremy said waving his arms. "We never knew this Fuentes existed until now. Kelliher didn't say anything about him to us. So if he wanted George, why didn't he come up here sooner? Why now? He could have come up here at any point in the last two years."

"We don't have that answer, but Pete is looking for it. We are too," Jamie said. "What we do know is that kids are overdosing on heroin and fentanyl and we have MS-13 pissed that someone is trying to cut into their drug business. That's what we know for sure."

"But we also have something that Fuentes and MS-13 don't have," Eiselmann said.

"What?" Jeremy said.

O'Connor pointed at the note on Jeremy's desk and said, "Somebody sent George a message . . . a warning. Somebody has George's back and Fuentes doesn't know it."

CHAPTER FORTY-ONE

There were times when Jamie wondered if he was tripping down the bramble path scraping up the palms of his hands and tearing holes in his knees as he crawled along blindly. There were other times he felt like he was speeding along the autobahn in a shiny red convertible with the top down on a sunny day at a hundred and twenty miles an hour. Police work was like that. As John Denver used to sing, *Somedays are diamonds, somedays are stones.* And Jamie understood the thing about police work was that he never knew from day to day or from moment to moment if he was on the bramble path or the autobahn. At this point in the investigation, he had the sick feeling he was on the bramble path and didn't know how to get off.

He had worked this case for what- two or three days? And he still didn't know what he had or where he was going. Shit, it felt like two or three years. When kids died ugly deaths, it always felt like years, not days.

The three cops didn't say a word. The closest thing to a word was a grunt from O'Connor. He'd read something, run a hand through his long hair and grunt. More like a "huh" or an "um." Something like that. The first couple of times he did that, Jamie would look up expecting a comment or an insight. Instead he got nothing, so after the fourth or fifth time, Jamie didn't look up at all.

Jamie rubbed his eyes. He was tired of reading and frustrated from not finding much to work with. He just wanted to get home to Kelly and Garrett, eat a nice dinner and drink a beer.

"Okay, what do we have? Tell me one of you found something useful."

Eiselmann said, "I don't see anything here you don't see. I mean, we have Kevin Longwood's prints and DNA in the building. Hell, they were easy enough to match, since his prints and DNA were all over his car. So one thing we know for sure is that he was involved in at least two deaths, probably more."

"And," O'Connor started and stopped. "And my gut tells me that whoever killed him is the other set of prints in the building and in the car. Whoever it is, I'm guessing it's a boy, not a girl and probably the same age as Longwood. I'm betting they were friends. He has prints on the syringe and on the rubber thingy and prints all over Longwood's car."

"Tourniquet. The rubber thingy is called a tourniquet," Eiselmann said.

Ignoring their banter, Jamie asked, "But we don't know who it is?"

"Yet," Eiselmann said pointing a pen in his direction. "If we run the school security tapes back, we find who hangs with Longwood, find a way to get his prints and we get him. We watch the places in the notes given to Jeremy and I'm willing to bet our guy shows up. It's only a matter of time."

Speaking to Eiselmann, O'Connor said, "You don't believe just one kid and Longwood were behind all of this, do you?"

Eiselmann shook his head and said, "Nope. But if we find the kid who killed Longwood, he'll lead us to whoever is behind it all."

"And we know it isn't MS-13."

"No, you have me convinced on that."

Jamie nodded, reminding himself just how good Eiselmann and O'Connor were. Not just good cops. Great cops.

"I agree with you. It's not MS-13. And that's not a bad idea, Paul. We could run the security tapes back to the time the first kid or two showed up dead and go forward from there. Chances are Longwood and the perp hung out. We run the faces of the kids through Jeremy, Farner or Champion."

"We'll cross-check them with the list of names somebody gave Jeremy," Eiselmann said.

"Ah."

"What?" Eiselmann and Jamie said in unison.

"The two APs . . ."

"Farner and Champion," Jamie said.

"Yeah, Farner and Champion," O'Connor said. "Do you really want them to ID Longwood's killer? Seems risky."

"Why?" Jamie asked. He knew both of them. Jamie had worked with Farner when he was the SRO and had worked with Champion when she was still a math teacher. Both were top notch, good people. And they pretty much knew as much about the case as they did. Almost as much as they did.

"Not sure. Fewer people, maybe. Jeremy knows the kids as well as anyone," O'Connor explained. "Maybe just run them by Jeremy." He glanced at the two detectives and repeated, "Maybe."

Both Eiselmann and Graff stared at O'Connor and finally Eiselmann asked, "What is it you don't trust about them?"

O'Connor frowned, ran a hand through his hair and avoided eye contact. He shook his head and said, "Not sure."

"Is it a lack of trust or is it the fact that you don't know them?" Jamie asked.

O'Connor shrugged and said, "Not sure."

CHAPTER FORTY-TWO

"Dad, I think I'm going to play tomorrow night," Brian said as he hopped into front seat of his dad's black 4Runner. He shut the door to the dark and cold late afternoon.

He had skipped showering after practice, because his dad was already in the parking lot waiting for him. Brett disapproved stating, "It's unhealthy leaving the locker room sweating and gross without showering." Brian had smiled and said, "I gotta go. Dad's waiting," and out the door he ran, slipping a little on some ice formed from snow melt during the day that refroze after the sun and temp went down. He caught himself before he fell using the door handle for support.

"That right?"

Brian beamed. He had a good practice. Coach Harrison said so. He wasn't a starter, but he and Randy were the first subs.

"Coach Harrison said he wants me to shoot."

"That right?" his dad said again.

"Yeah. He said when I'm open I'm supposed to let it fly. That's what he said. He said he wants me to let it fly. Pretty cool, huh?"

"Okay, Bri."

Brian glanced at his dad questioningly. He could tell from his dad's voice and from his expression that his dad wasn't excited. Brian didn't think he had heard a word he said.

"I think I bombed a math test this morning," Brian said without passion, almost in a monotone.

A lie. Maybe the first lie he had ever told his parents. He turned his head, his breath frosting the inside of the window making it difficult to see anything. Or maybe it was a tear or two. He wiped them away angrily.

"Sounds good, Brian."

All the joy, all the life was sucked out of Brian in that one moment. It was something he had thought about ever since the summer of death. It was something he had suspected. But in that moment, he understood that he had stumbled unwilling onto the truth. No matter what he did, no matter what he said, his parents had only cared about Brad.

He didn't matter anymore. Maybe he never did.

CHAPTER FORTY-THREE

"Boys, can we talk for a minute?"

The three of them sat at the kitchen table. She drank coffee while Brett peeled an orange. Bobby had a glass of orange juice.

Victoria McGovern. Olive skin that tanned evenly in the summer sun, long dark hair and dark eyes. Trim, fit, and smart. She knew her boys got their looks and their athleticism from her side of the family. Both Brett and Bobby had chestnut eyes and brown hair. And even though they were a little over a year apart, they could have passed as twins. Tom's side gave them their soft features, but also their intelligence and inquisitive nature, though she was no slouch in those departments either.

Vicky had grown up wanting to be a nurse and had gravitated to the surgical side when the opportunity presented itself. When it did, she seized it and never second-guessed herself.

The relationship side of her life was the opposite of her professional life.

As forthright and as confident as she was directing traffic in surgery, she was tentative, hesitant and insecure. She questioned herself when it came to men. All men, and Jeremy was a man. She loved him. They had discussed marriage and she knew that her boys and Jeremy's boys had wanted them to get married. And she and Jeremy wanted to get married, but they had decided to move slowly.

It wasn't yet a year that her divorce from Tom had been finalized. So she and Jeremy needed time. Not much, but a little more. Maybe it was she who had needed more time.

It was her former husband, Thomas and his string of affairs that caused her to question her fitness for marriage. Was it something she had done? Not done? Was she pretty enough? Smart enough? Was there a flaw in her personality? Was she interesting enough? Maybe she just wasn't good enough?

So maybe it was Vicky who had tapped on the marriage brakes more so than Jeremy.

She loved Jeremy. She was certain of that. He was gentle; a listener and a thinker. She saw how her boys interacted with him and how he had accepted them without any expectation or hesitation on his part. She loved to watch Bobby reading a book while he rested his head on Jeremy. Jeremy would read or watch TV with his arm around him, finger comb his hair or lean over and kiss the top of his head. She loved listening to Brett and Jeremy tease one another, laugh about it and end up in an embrace with both kissing each other's cheek. He would sit and talk quietly with Brett, sometimes with his arm slung around his shoulders, other times Brett would stretch out on the couch with his head on Jeremy's thigh.

He made time for them just as he made time for the twins and George. And he made time for Brian.

Brian.

He seemed so lost, so confused, so lonely. Even worse, he seemed alone.

"Mom, what's wrong?"

Brett had stopped peeling his orange, his hands frozen in place, his expression one of concern. Bobby held onto his glass of orange juice with both hands as if it were about to lift off and fly around the room.

She was lost in reverie and had no idea how long she had been gone.

"Hmmm . . . what?"

"What's wrong?" Brett asked again. "What did you want to talk to us about?"

"Did you and Dad have a fight or something? Is everything okay?" Bobby asked.

She shook her head and said, "No, Jeremy and I didn't have a fight and yes, everything is fine."

Brett frowned at her and she said, "Really. Everything's fine."

Without taking his eyes off of her, Brett slipped a slice of his orange into his mouth.

"I'm worried about Brian."

Bobby relaxed a little as did Brett, but only a little.

"You know, Bobby . . . I look at Brian and it's like I'm looking at you when Brett was gone. Your father and I treated you the same way Brian's parents are treating him. The thing is, they don't realize it, just like your dad and I didn't realize it. And to find out what my brother . . . your uncle did to you . . . to both of you." She shook her head willing herself to keep her emotions in check. "I think Tom and I were just as much to blame for what had happened to you because we weren't there for you."

"It's okay, Mom," Bobby said blushing. "Really. It's okay."

Bobby didn't like thinking about it and he didn't like talking about it. The occasional nightmares brought it all back: the pain, the humiliation, the anger. There were times he hated shutting his eyes because all of it sat a click away, tucked inside the jack-in-the-box in his mind waiting for the fateful crank that would spring it back to life.

He caught Brett's eye, who nodded slightly. Brett knew, perhaps as well as anyone, probably better than anyone that nightmares were the flip side of dreams.

Vicky shook her head and smiled, "That's kind of you to say, but we both know it's not okay. Your dad . . . Tom and I weren't there for you and that's not okay."

Bobby blushed and shrugged and wished he was invisible.

"I look at Brian and I see you. The same expression. The same loneliness." She shook her head and said, "We were so worried about Brett, we forgot about you."

She turned towards Brett and said, "And what did I do the first time I saw you after two years and all the hell you'd been through? I slap you because I didn't like you talking about my brother like that."

She shook her head, angry with herself and said almost in a whisper, "Despite what Agent Kelliher and Detective Graff had shown us, I just couldn't bring myself to believe what my brother had done."

"That was a long time ago, Mom. We're good. You and I are good."

"God, you must have hated me," Vicky said.

"No, Mom. I didn't hate you. I could never hate you."

It was a true statement. Brett didn't hate her. He had never hated her. Ever. He might have been hurt and disappointed, but he never hated her.

"Guys, will you ever forgive me? Tom?"

"Already have, Mom," Bobby said.

Brett smiled and said, "Yup, except that Tom is just some guy I used to know. Jeremy is dad."

"What he said," Bobby said with a smile.

"But he is your father."

Brett shook his head, his thoughts dark and his expression darker.

Vicky frowned at Brett and said, "You never talk to him . . . to Tom. When Bobby goes to visit, you never go. He never asks about you. Why? What happened?"

Brett shook his head once and set his jaw. There was only one person who knew what had happened and he had never intended for him to know. He just happened to have overheard Brett's side of the conversation and put the rest together. Brett swore him to secrecy. A secret he had kept.

CHAPTER FORTY-FOUR

The eight by ten glossy prints were spread out over the conference table at the police station and Graff, Eiselmann and O'Connor hunched over them examining each and tallying the number of times other kids showed up with the deceased Kevin Longwood.

In some respects, police work was calculated guess work, but more times than not, that was what happened in any open case. A cop looked at the evidence and based judgments upon human response and in almost all cases, the science in the evidence. Then the cop made plausible, logical guesses. Most times the guesses panned out. Other times not so much.

Graff picked up the ME's report on the Longwood murder and scanned it.

"We've pretty much ruled out a girl, right?"

"Pretty much," Eiselmann said as he tapped information into an Excel spreadsheet using his department issued laptop.

"Logic," O'Connor started. "Logic tells me that the frenzy of the attack isn't congruent to the murders of the kids who OD'd. In the OD's, there is planning and calculation. In the Longwood murder, there isn't much planning other than to get Longwood to the school. The murder itself is haphazard. The wounds, particularly the neck wound, weren't professional. I don't think it was even planned."

"What you're saying is that the stab wounds weren't working, so whoever killed Longwood went for his neck," Eiselmann said, looking up from his laptop.

"That's . . . that's what I think."

"The ME said that the stab wounds had a degree of force behind them," Graff said. "There was bruising at each of the wounds. That tells me there was strength. So I think we're right that the killer is a guy. That is unless the girl is unusually strong."

"Okay we have seven guys and one girl who show up on film regularly with Longwood. Of the seven guys, five of them are with him in just about every shot. Two of them are in and out, but with him," Eiselmann said.

"What we need to do is show these pictures to Jeremy and see if any match the names of dealers on the list he was given," Graff said.

"How soon?" O'Connor asked.

Graff checked his watch, thought about calling Jeremy, but it was getting late. He knew it was a school night and that Jeremy was an early to bed, early to rise kind of guy.

"First thing tomorrow morning, I'll stop at the school, bring him the pictures and the list and we'll go through it together."

"Would it be possible for us to match any of these kids with pictures of kids who show up at the sites we're watching?" Eiselmann asked.

"Those are local hangouts any kid goes to. There's bound to be some crossover. Our only bet would be to catch them making a deal," O'Connor said.

"It would be way too convenient to catch one of these kids," Graff waved his hand over the security camera still shots, "making a deal at one of those hangouts."

"Way too convenient," O'Connor said.

"Way too convenient isn't about to happen in this case," Eiselmann said.

He thought for a minute, closed out his Excel file and powered down his laptop. He pushed it away and rubbed his eyes.

"Pat, did you find anything on Fuentes? Any idea where he might be holed up?"

O'Connor shook his head, his long hair dancing listlessly.

"Just possibilities. Either he's staying with a member of MS-13 or he's tucked away in a smallish hotel. My guess is that he's with MS-13."

Graff asked, "Any idea who he would be with?"

O'Connor shook his head and bit the inside of his lip. "Not really. I have a couple of ideas. He'd be with upper level MS-13, at least upper level for Milwaukee or Waukesha. I'm guessing he's in Waukesha. There aren't that many upper level members out here. I have three under light surveillance. My guess is that one of them will lead us to him one way or the other."

"Can I ask a question?" Eiselmann asked. "Why George? There has to be more to it than revenge."

Jamie set his elbows on the table, folded his hands and rested his chin on them. He sighed and said, "Nate Kaupert's report was sealed. So were Tom Albrecht's, Earl Coffey's and Brooke Beranger's reports. Captain O'Brien and Agent Pete Kelliher went to a federal judge and had them sealed. They said it was because George was a minor, but Pete said the FBI had a special interest in him and that had to have come from above Pete and his partner, Summer Storm. I'm guessing it came from Deputy Director Davenport."

Eiselmann frowned and said, "I don't understand. What does that mean . . . special interest?"

Graff didn't want to disclose anything, but he felt he owed it to both Eiselmann and O'Connor who worked so closely with him.

"What I'm about to tell you is classified. I could lose my job and be in a shitload of hot water."

He waited for their response which was a simple head nod from both sheriff deputies.

"Both of you know, to some extent, that George has special abilities. He can shoot. He can track. He can handle a knife and as near as anyone can tell, he's ambidextrous."

O'Connor and Eiselmann nodded.

"There are times George has dreams and visions. Sometimes, his grandfather visits him."

"His grandfather is dead, right?" Eiselmann asked.

Graff nodded. O'Connor wore no expression.

"George is responsible for killing six men. Seven if you count a shithead FBI agent in Chicago, but technically, the asshole shot himself. In each case, George acted in self-defense. There was an attempted hit on Jeremy and the twins and George, and George fought him off with his knife. Killed him at the side of Jeremy's house. He had just come to Wisconsin and he was fourteen and the guy he killed had a long, long list of hits. He also happened to be Victor Bosch's nephew."

"The guy who ran the trafficking ring?" Eiselmann asked.

Graff nodded and continued.

"In Missouri, one of the guys who had gotten away showed up at the hotel where Jeremy, Jeff and the boys were staying and shot into the boys' room.

God, I don't know how many rounds he shot and I don't know how any of the boys didn't get hit. The only person who did get shot was some guy staying in a room next to the boys. He survived, but even he said that George had saved his life.

"George jumped through a window and killed the shooter. The shooter was a veteran cop, just like the three guys George killed in Arizona up on that mesa. Again, it was ruled self-defense just like the three cops in Arizona. Jeremy was with him up on that mesa, but basically it was George armed with his knife and a 30.06 against three ex-cops with machine guns."

"What does that have to do with Fuentes?" Eiselmann asked.

"Nothing really, other than to point out that George is very skilled and that he isn't afraid to put his life on the line when it comes to protecting Jeremy and the twins, Danny and Jeff, but he only acts in self-defense."

"So . . ."

"One morning while George was out running and saying his morning prayers, Jorge Fuentes showed up at the cottage. He used duct tape to bind the twins, Danny, Jeremy and Jeff to their chairs and tape their mouths shut. That way, they couldn't call out for help or warn George. From what the boys and Jeremy said, Fuentes toyed with them and pinched Billy's nose shut. With his mouth taped, he couldn't breathe and he passed out. Luckily *only* passed out. At some point, George had entered the cottage from the backdoor, saw what was happening, and challenged Fuentes.

"Fuentes was known as *The Blade.* His thing was to use two knives, one in each hand. George had only his knife. The fight didn't take long, but it was bloody . . . brutal and ugly. George basically cut off his fingers and parts of each hand. He cut off Fuentes' balls and most of his dick and sliced open his belly and all his shit fell out. But all that was *after* he offered Fuentes the opportunity to leave. Fuentes didn't and George killed him."

"So, his cousin, our Fuentes, somehow found out what George did to him and wants payback," Eiselmann said. "But if the reports were sealed, how did he find out about George and what was done to his cousin?"

"Your guess is as good as mind. You know George wouldn't say anything. By all reports, he was ashamed and embarrassed at what he had done. He still is. You know the twins and Danny wouldn't say anything. They're protective of each other. And you know for certain that Jeremy and Jeff didn't say anything."

"Well, if they didn't and if the reports are sealed, who?" Eiselmann asked.

Graff shrugged and said, "Small town cops maybe. State police maybe. Folks at the resort. The county medical examiner. Could be any of them. Could be all of them."

"So how do we protect George," O'Connor asked, "and keep that family safe?"

"We find Fuentes before he has a chance to move on George. I have to think that Fuentes, MS-13, Longwood and the kids who OD'd are all part of the same puzzle."

CHAPTER FORTY-FIVE

Brian spied the boxes as soon as he and his dad walked into the house. Brian stood wide-eyed, his feet stuck to the rug in the foyer.

"We're downsizing, that's all, Brian. We took a lot of stuff to Goodwill earlier today."

"Are we moving?"

His dad put his arm around Brian's shoulder, gave it a squeeze and said, "No, Brian. We're not moving."

"No matter what, your dad and I will always be with you. That's a promise," his mom said and that sent a chill up Brian's spine. He didn't know what that meant and a part of him didn't want to know. *Were they just going to up and leave him?* He was suddenly afraid.

Dinner was awkward and uncomfortable.

The three of them sat at the kitchen table pretending to enjoy the meal. His parents chit-chatted about this and that, mostly small talk and Brian smiled at appropriate times, but otherwise stayed quiet.

"Honey, do you like your fried chicken? Do you want more shrimp?"

"Sure, I mean, yeah, it's fine. No, thank you, I'm good," Brian answered without looking at her.

It wasn't fine. It was all wrong. The fried chicken and broiled shrimp, the mashed potatoes and the green beans with cherry crisp for desert, it was all wrong. This was Brad's favorite meal.

"Brian, I've always believed that you and Brad had a special bond. I've watched you and Brad grow up and it was like you had the same mind. You were brothers, but you were more than that."

Brian said nothing, the fried chicken tasting like two day old road kill.

"Do you ever, I don't know, *feel* him? Do you ever *feel* his presence?" She glanced at the empty chair and smiled.

Brian didn't know what to say. He could lie and say that he didn't, but the truth was that there were times especially at night when Brian felt Brad's presence. There were other times, moments when he was alone when he caught a glimpse, a shadow and somehow knew it was Brad.

In the end, Brian said nothing, only shrugged, but he glanced at the empty chair between bites.

"This is Brad's favorite meal," Nancy said smiling at the empty chair.

They ate the rest of the meal in silence.

His dad had his eyes fixed on his plate. He didn't eat, but rather pushed his potatoes and green beans around his plate like a snow plow pushing around snow in the school parking lot.

After dessert, Brian walked back to his room, stripped off his clothes and left them in a pile on the floor. He covered himself with the t-shirt and boxers he wore as pajamas and walked into the bathroom across the hall. Standing naked in front of his sink, he brushed his teeth and rinsed his mouth with cold water.

He stared at himself in the mirror. His arms and chest weren't as muscled as Brett's, Billy's or Randy's. He didn't have a six pack like them, but he wasn't chubby or doughy either. His legs were thick, though. He decided he looked more like George than he did the others. Even Bobby had more muscles than he did, except Brian's legs had more muscle.

He stepped into the bathtub, pulled the curtain shut and stood under the shower. He washed his hair and used the *Old Spice* Shower Gel to lather up. His soapy hands lingering longer on his dick and balls liking the slick feel and almost giving in, but he stopped himself in time and finished washing up.

His parents had never been the same since Brad was shot and killed. If he was honest with himself, he would say that he hadn't been the same either. But tonight was different. Way different. Spooky, weird different.

He placed both hands on the wall and let the water run over his head and shoulders, soap cascading off him with the power of the spray.

Suddenly and without warning, a thought occurred to him.

What if his parents were waiting for him in the hallway?

He heart raced and it was hard for him to breathe. He was one hundred percent petrified that his mom or dad or both had something planned. With the water running, he moved the shower curtain just enough to peek out to see if they were in the bathroom waiting for him.

No one.

He turned off the water and whisked water from his eyes and face. He listened. Nothing. No sound. Not the TV. No voices speaking quietly. Nothing.

He slid the shower curtain slowly and softly to the side, reached for a towel and dried himself off half-assed, because his back, his butt and his balls were still damp, if not wet. It was good enough.

Brian slid into his boxers. He smeared some Old Spice deodorant under his arms and pulled on the t-shirt.

Before he opened the door, he put his ear to it and listened.

Nothing.

He opened the door a crack and peered out, first left and then right. He couldn't see much, so he opened the door a little wider, took a deep breath, and stuck his head out.

Neither his mom nor his dad was in the hallway.

He let his breath out slowly and tiptoed to his room. The door was closed and he panicked, not remembering whether or not he had shut it.

What if they were in there waiting for him?

Goosebumps popped out on his arms, legs and chest. The little hairs on the back of his neck stood at attention.

Brian placed his hand on the doorknob, but didn't turn it. Couldn't turn it.

He grit his teeth and held his breath and in one quick move, he turned the knob and pushed the door wide open.

They weren't there.

Unless, they were on either side of the door.

Brian took one step back and glanced at either end of the hallway. No one was there. In his bare feet, his boxers and a t-shirt, he could get to a door and get outside, but he wouldn't be able to run very far before he froze to death. If he stayed and fought them, he would be able to take his mom. She was smaller and lighter than he was. But his dad was taller, bigger. Brian knew he was faster than his dad, but again, his bare feet couldn't compete with his dad who was probably still dressed.

"Brian? Is something wrong?"

Brian jumped and gasped. One moment no one stood in the hallway and the next minute, there she was. He didn't know how long his mother had been standing there.

"No, I'm good. It's all good."

"Are you sure?" His mother frowned at him, her head tilted to the side like mothers sometimes do when they are scrutinizing one of their children. "Are you feeling okay? Are you sick?"

"No . . . no, I'm good. Just thinking about the game tomorrow night," Brian lied. "I'm tired, so I'm going to bed. Goodnight."

He forgot about his dad, walked into his room, didn't see anyone and shut the door behind him.

There was a knock on the door.

"Brian, can we come in and say goodnight?"

He didn't answer right away, hoping they would go away. Quietly, he pulled the covers up to his neck.

"Brian?"

"Sure."

His mom opened the door and walked in, followed by his dad. She sat on the side of his bed while his dad stood slightly behind her.

"Is everything okay, Bri? School, friends, girls?"

"Yes, everything's fine."

"Do you have any homework for tomorrow?" his dad asked.

Brian shook his head. He had finished it in the team study hall before practice.

His mom smiled and pushed his bangs off his forehead and brushed his cheek with the back of her hand. He flinched at the touch.

"Are you guys coming to my game tomorrow night?" Brian asked already knowing the answer.

"We'll try, Honey. Promise," his mother said with a smile.

He looked up at his dad.

"We'll see."

Brian knew that 'We'll try' and 'We'll see' were code words for 'No, we're not coming.'

"Brian, your father and I will always be with you. Always."

"What . . . what does that mean? Are you going somewhere?"

Nancy smiled, opened her mouth to speak, but before she could, David placed a hand on her shoulder and said, "It means just that as your parents, we love you, Bri. We always will. Always."

His mom added, "As long as we keep each other in our heart, we'll always be together. Always." She gave him a hug and a kiss on his lips and said, "Remember that, okay?"

Brian thought he nodded, but he wasn't sure.

She hugged him again and got up and out of the way so David could hug and kiss his son. His embrace was long and tight. He kissed Brian once, twice and a third time on the side of his head. He let go and stepped away.

Brian was certain that his father brushed tears from his eyes. He was the first to leave Brian's room. His mother stood at the door, smiled and pulled the door closed behind her.

It was creepy.

Brian's mouth was dry. He blinked at the door and sat up.

Yes, his parents had acted strangely ever since Brad had died, so he was used to it. But this was a whole new level of weird. He didn't understand what his parents were trying to tell him. Or more importantly, what they weren't telling him.

He picked up his cell. He wanted to tell Jeremy or Brett, but he knew both of them would be in bed and Brett would be pissed that Brian was still awake. George would probably be in bed and Randy too.

He texted Bobby with a simple, *"r u awake?"*

Seconds later he received an answer, *"what's up?"*

CHAPTER FORTY-SIX

George did what he always did when he woke up from one of his dreams. He kept his eyes shut and tried to remember as much of the dream as he could, reaching for the images, the words, the people, including animals and birds. There were times when the animal or bird meant more than anything else besides the feeling generated from the dream. The *Dine'* believed that dreams were not only connected to the spirit world, but that animals and birds were sent as warnings. Sometimes they conveyed the message in the dream.

George never moved. His breathing, deep and slow, never changed.

He was both disciplined and focused.

When he felt he remembered as much as he could, he rolled slowly onto his back and away from Billy who was up against him in a spoon position. George had his arm across Billy's chest as was usual for them and when George moved, Billy changed position to his stomach, snuggling deeper into his covers. George placed his hand gently on Billy's back.

He frowned.

Like the dream from the other night, there wasn't anything to grab hold of. There wasn't anything of substance George could explain to Jeremy or anyone else. It was more of the *feeling* and the *look* of the dream.

He needed his grandfather to help him understand what he was dreaming and why he was dreaming it. But what frustrated him more than anything was that his grandfather had not visited him in more than a year, ever since the summer of death. Once so present, not only in his dreams but also in visions when he was awake, now so very . . . gone. Absent. Nonexistent.

Seldom, if ever, emotional, George brushed a tear from his eye, angry that he had given in to this weakness. It wasn't the Navajo way, the way of the *Dine'*.

He glanced at the clock on the nightstand. It was too early for him to get up, but he did so anyway. Slowly, carefully, he slipped out from the warmth of the sheet and blanket and tucked the covers around Billy so he wouldn't get cold. Jasmine opened first one eye, but didn't raise her head from the rug she slept on. He bent down and scratched her behind her ear, but still Jasmine didn't move.

He retrieved a sweatshirt from the chair in his corner of the bedroom and pulled his head and arms into it. He pushed his bare feet into his moccasins, grabbed his knife and leather sheath from the nightstand and bent down one more time and gave Jasmine a scratch behind the ear.

With a simple gesture using one hand, he signaled her to stay with Billy. She sighed, but did as she was told.

He slipped out of the room and into the darkened hallway and stood just in the doorway. Facing him was the bathroom he and Billy used. Looking at one end towards his father's room, and Randy's room across the hallway it was dark and still. At the other end were another bathroom and the two spare rooms, the ones where Bobby and Brett stayed unless they bunked with one of the other guys. At the top of the stairs on the top landing lay Momma, ever protective. No one unexpected would get past her. Ever.

He sat down next to her and with both arms and hugged her head. He was rewarded with a doggie kiss. She set her head back on her paws and continued her sentry duty.

George quietly walked down the carpeted steps and stood at the front door. He was still in awe of his new home, though he had lived with Jeremy and his brothers for the past year and a half. This home, however, was nothing like his little ranch home in *Diné Bikéyah*.

There, his hogan was tiny. A four room ranch house with an outhouse and a barn, a small stable and sheep pen. A room and the bed he had shared with his two brothers. No TV or electricity. Cooking over a fire outside in good weather or the hearth inside in bad. Cozy and happy. It was home to him. In many respects, it would always be home. His heart and his soul would forever belong to *Diné Bikéyah*. And to his first love, Rebecca.

He turned to his right and tiptoed to the living room. It was a formal room, seldom used except by Bobby and Randy. They would sometimes go in after school before dinner and play the electric piano or their guitars.

George walked down the hall and into the kitchen and stood just inside the doorway. Quiet. The only sound he heard was the hum of the refrigerator. The only light he saw was the soft glow from LED lights on the microwave and double stove.

On his way to the small entry way, the mud room as Jeremy called it, he ran his hand over the smooth granite counter, dark and beautiful. He saw the red light on the security system telling him it was armed and ready to warn the family should any intruder enter through any window or door unexpectedly.

He walked out of the kitchen and across to the family room. A beautiful room with dark wood flooring and a couple of throw rugs, leather furniture and a stone fireplace. Framed pictures on the mantle of each of the boys, including Brett and Bobby. The only one missing was Brian.

George stood in front of the fireplace gazing at each of the pictures. He sighed. The metal gun cabinet stood in the corner, secured with a combination lock much like a safe. A sliding door led out to a stone patio and matching stone barbecue pit and the hot tub. The furniture had been taken in and stored for safe keeping in the small shed around the side of the house.

This was a happy room where he and his brothers often sat and watched TV or played video games or just sat and talked about this or that. Sometimes wrestling with each other and laughing. He found himself smiling.

He turned around and walked down the hall to the study, his father's favorite room. Another fireplace with a comfortable couch and matching chairs. A dark wooden desk with a matching two-drawer file cabinet off to the side facing the sliding glass door and the woods beyond. A computer monitor sat on the desk.

A magnificent house. Big and beautiful, but friendly. Happy. His home.

George tiptoed to the slider and peered out into the darkness. Still. Cold. A bit of frost on the glass. The sky black, the moon and stars covered by clouds. He guessed it might snow.

An owl, a Great Gray Owl like the one he had seen as he plowed the driveway, flew down from somewhere and landed on the small stone porch outside the slider. It spread its wings and blinked at him.

George took a step back. Slowly, perhaps instinct taking over but not exactly sure why, he pulled the knife out of its sheath and gripped it tightly. The owl waddled up to the slider, spread its wings, blinked at him and vanished.

Vanished.

It didn't fly off. *It. Just. Vanished.*

George took another step back and the back of his legs touched the side of the couch and he jumped, turned and crouched into a fighting stance.

No one was there.

He pivoted quickly and smoothly towards the sliding glass door, half-expecting to see someone or something.

Nothing. No one.

He pivoted around again, expecting someone behind him, but the room was empty.

Moving sideways, glancing first at the slider, then back to the family room, George tip-toed out of the room. As he reached the hallway, he moved quickly, catlike, taking the stairs two at a time.

Alarmed, Momma raised her head, stood, head bent low, tail pointed down, weight on her back legs ready to pounce.

George reached for her and hugged her, but she never relaxed, her eyes focused on the steps and the front door.

"It's okay, Momma," he whispered. "It's okay."

But he didn't feel okay at all.

CHAPTER FORTY-SEVEN

He was creeped out and the little sleep he had managed to get didn't help. Even texting back and forth with Bobby late into the night didn't assuage his fears. The anxiety he felt the night before hadn't abated.

So Brian rolled out of bed a little earlier than he normally did. Because he had showered the night before, he just knelt down, stuck his head under the bathtub faucet and washed his hair. He brushed his teeth, smeared on some deodorant and added just a touch of cologne just in case. In case of what he didn't know, but he figured it wouldn't hurt.

He went back to his room and dressed in a light blue button down shirt, khaki slacks and Sperry's. He took a blue and tan tie he thought would match and folded it neatly in his basketball bag. Lastly, he gathered together the books and notebooks he'd need for the day and stuffed them into his black backpack in the order he would need them.

He thought he had beaten his parents to the kitchen, but he hadn't. He could smell the eggs and bacon from the hallway. They were already sitting at the table, dressed casually and not for work. That was unusual, since his father seldom took time off from work and this was the second day in a row he had done so.

His mom served him his breakfast with toast and some orange juice to wash it down. Brian didn't feel like eating, but did anyway.

He received a text from Sean that they were on the way, so he got up to leave. He gathered up his dirty dishes to take them to the sink, something he had done on his own and without being asked to do so ever since he was little.

"Just leave them, Brian. I'll take care of it," his mom said.

Flustered, out of his normal routine and rhythm, he hesitated.

"It's okay, Bri. Your mom and I will clean up," his dad said.

His mom kissed his forehead and hugged him tightly. His dad held his face in both hands. He seemed to want to say something other than what he said, "Have a great day, Bri and good luck tonight." In the end his dad embraced him holding him uncomfortably long.

Brian grabbed the water bottle he had placed in the refrigerator the night before and said goodbye. With his jacket barely on and zipped up, he ran out the door and down the driveway to join Sean, Caitlyn and Brett. Mrs. Drummond was behind the wheel. Brian had hoped to see Bobby, but knew that he would be catching a ride to the middle school with his mom, Gavin and Garrett.

"Where's your tie?" Brett asked.

"In my bag. I'm going to ask your dad to tie it for me."

Brett nodded.

Caitlyn sat between Brett and him in the middle of the backseat. Whether it was real or his imagination, he felt heat coming from her. She smelled of soap and lotion and she looked so pretty. Her blue eyes danced and she smiled at him. Brian smiled back and blushed, feeling a little guilty because he knew George liked her.

"I understand you've been moved up to varsity," Lydia Drummond said.

She was much shorter than her husband. Short cut blond hair, a smattering of freckles across her nose and under her blue eyes. Pretty. Sean looked a lot like her and so did Caitlyn.

"Yes."

"Are you nervous?" Brett asked.

Brian shook his head and said, "I don't get nervous before games."

"Not even a little?" Sean asked.

Brian shook his head again. "Nope."

Brett believed him and smiled. "Good."

Mrs. Drummond joined the que for parent drop off and the four of them got out and joined the throng of students entering the school before she even had a chance to drive off. They met up with a couple of friends who talked about the game or homework, but Brian wasn't paying attention.

"Are you okay?" Caitlyn asked.

Brian nodded.

"I'll go with you to guidance if you like?" When Brian hesitated, she added, "I can wait in the lobby."

"That's fine, but you don't have to."

She did anyway, taking hold of his hand as they walked down Central hallway.

They entered guidance and Kristi said, "Hey, Bri. Hi, Cat!"

"Hi, Ms. Johnson. Is Jer . . . Mr. Evans in his office?"

Brian was never sure what to call him. In fact, even when he was at their house, he never referred to him as Mister or Jeremy. Instead, Brian would ask a direct question by looking right at him so Jeremy would know he was being spoken to. When he was with the guys, he would just say, *your dad.*

Jeremy was seated at his desk, his chin resting on the heel of his hand as he read something on the computer screen.

Brian knocked lightly on the door, but didn't say anything.

Jeremy turned around, smiled and said, "Hi, Bri. What's up?"

"Can you help me with my tie?"

Jeremy had helped him the morning of each game, first during the soccer season and now in basketball, trying to teach him as he did so. He knew that Brian probably knew how to do it, but it was Brian's way of saying hello and checking in.

Brian held out the tie and Jeremy took it. There was a little mirror in Jeremy's office and Brian turned around and faced it.

As Jeremy fixed his tie, he walked Brian through the steps patiently, finishing with, "The tip or point of the tie should come to the top of your belt buckle."

Brian turned around and noticed that his tie did just that and he raised his head, looking somber.

"Bobby texted me this morning and said you were bothered by something last night. He didn't say what."

Brian blushed and asked, "My parents were acting really weird. They had stuff in boxes." He shrugged and said, "It was . . . weird." He wanted to say creepy.

"Did you ask them about it?"

"All Dad said was that they were down-sizing."

Jeremy nodded thoughtfully and said, "Perhaps that's a good sign. You know, moving on."

Brian shook his head.

"What's bothering you, Brian?"

Brian shook his head again and said, "Will you be at the game tonight?" already knowing the answer.

"Absolutely. Vicki and I will be there cheering you and Randy, Brett and Billy. I think Jeff and Jamie Graff are coming too."

Brian nodded, his chin quivering slightly. His eyes filling with tears. He turned to leave, but Jeremy placed a hand gently on his shoulder.

"I will be there supporting you, Brian. No matter how much or how little you play. I mean that."

Brian nodded, tried to smile and wiped a tear from his eye. He and Jeremy embraced and Jeremy kissed the side of Brian's head and his forehead.

"I mean that."

Brian nodded and turned around to leave. As he got to the door, he stopped, turned around and said, "My mom and dad won't be there."

"Are you sure?"

Brian wiped another tear from his eye and said, "They said they would try, but they won't."

"Would you like me to call them?"

"No, please don't." For emphasis, Brian added, "*Please.*"

"Got it. I won't."

Brian opened his mouth to say something else, but shut it without saying anything.

"You know I love you, right?" Jeremy asked.

Brian nodded, turned around and took a step, turned back around and walked back into the office and hugged Jeremy fiercely.

CHAPTER FORTY-EIGHT

"That accounts for all seven boys and the girl," Eiselmann said looking up from his laptop. Jeremy was able to name all the kids who had appeared in the pictures with Kevin Longwood. "Can you get us their class schedules? I want to interview them as soon as we can."

Jeremy scanned the list and shook his head. "We can try. Some of these kids are chronically absent. Out of these eight kids, we'll be lucky if we get three or four."

Eiselmann turned to Graff and said, "That explains why some of these kids are spotted at the watch locations during the day." To Jeremy, he said, "I would like to know who the author of this document you received is. For an anonymous tip, this is proving to be incredibly accurate."

Graff nodded thoughtfully.

"I can get Kristi to print the schedules off for us," Jeremy said picking up the list of names. He glanced out of his office window and saw Phil Keneally, Gordon Huggins and Katrina Brady chatting quietly with Gloria Beatleman and Kristi Johnson. Rather than ask in front of them, he called her using one of the speed dial buttons on his phone. She picked up after one ring.

"Kristi, can you step into my office please?"

"Be right there." Kristi laughed at something Huggins had said as she stepped away from her desk still smiling and knocked once on Jeremy's door before opening it.

"Can you run off the class schedules for these students please and bring them to us? And also, can you check their attendance for today?"

She glanced at the list and saw some of the eight by ten photos lying on Jeremy's desk. She looked at Jeremy, the unspoken question and his answer hung in silence between them. She nodded and left his office shutting the door behind her.

She tried to shield the list from the three teachers and the counselor near her desk as she sat down at her computer.

"Are they any closer to finding out who murdered Kevin Longwood?" Katrina Brady asked almost in a whisper glancing towards Jeremy's door.

"No idea," Johnson said quietly.

"They're working on it, though right?' Keneally said.

"I'm sure they are," Beatleman answered. "I think this is their third or fourth visit to the school," she said nodding at Jeremy's office. "It's terrible to think that one of the students might be his killer."

"How do you know that?" Keneally asked. "I mean, that it could be one of the students."

She fumbled for an adequate answer and said, "Who else would it be? That's what the rumor is anyway. I'm sure you heard it."

"But how reliable are rumors?" Huggins said. "I think it's gangs."

None of them had an answer for that. They watched Johnson work at her computer.

Finally Brady said, "Gotta run. I have hallway duty."

"Better than working attendance," Huggins said as he left the office with her. Keneally followed behind them and Beatleman walked off to the mailroom.

Kristi finished running off the schedules and as she brought them into Jeremy's office, Graff's cell went off.

He did a lot of listening and grimaced once or twice. He glanced at Jeremy and at Eiselmann. He turned his back to both of them and listened some more.

"Any ID?"

He nodded, picked up the list of names from Jeremy's desk and shook his head. Finally he said, "I'll get back to you."

Jamie sat down in the chair facing Jeremy and next to Eiselmann, sighed and said, "That was O'Connor. Seems like you can cross Ronald Terzinski off the list. A squad found him at that abandoned building."

Eiselmann glanced furtively at Jeremy, wondering just how much Graff was going to share in front of him.

In answer to that unasked question, Graff said, "Jeremy, describe for me again how Fuentes bound you at the cottage that summer."

Jeremy blinked, first at Jamie and then at Paul, but regained his focus and said to both of them, "With duct tape. He used duct tape on our ankles and wound it a couple of times around the chair legs. He did the same with our hands to the arms of the chair. He put a piece of duct tape over our mouths." He paused and said, "Why?"

"Because that's how they found Terzinski, except that Terzinski was nude. Two of his fingers had been cut off along with two of his toes." He didn't mention that his balls and his dick had also been cut off.

"Jesus!" Jeremy said.

"They . . . Fuentes tortured him for information. He's trying to find out who is behind the heroin and fentanyl mix on the street," Eiselmann said matter-of-factly. "This is becoming a turf thing."

"I'm guessing they got what they wanted," Graff said. "And that means that one or more of these kids and possibly whoever is the brains behind this operation is in danger."

"What do you mean by the brains behind this?" Jeremy asked.

"You don't think this is run by kids, do you?" Graff shook his head. "Someone has connections and that takes brains and money, especially when it comes to Fentanyl. That's medical according to O'Connor. Unless they're buying it off the Internet, there has to be some sort of medical connection, more than likely veterinarian that is somehow linked to all this."

"He and I already put together a list of all veterinarians in a fifty mile radius and cross-checked them with the names on this list," Eiselmann said. "We've come up empty."

"What if the medical link, as you call it, is linked to whoever is in charge of this operation?" Jeremy asked.

Jamie and Eiselmann both nodded.

"Good idea, Jeremy. I'll have O'Connor dig into that angle, at least into the backgrounds of the vets in that radius."

"Do we have a time or cause of death?" Eiselmann asked. "For Terzinski I mean."

"Blood loss. The ME thinks it was the severed carotid artery. He, or someone, slit his throat. Sometime last night."

"Jamie, if this is Fuentes, this is a lot more than just kids peddling substance," Jeremy said.

"I have to call O'Connor," Graff said. "He needs to find this asshole."

Kristi Johnson walked back into the office, saw their expressions and said quietly, "Here you go. Do you want me to send for them?"

"Not yet, please," Jeremy said. "I think we need to let Chuck Gobel know about this latest bit of information and what we're doing. It's his building."

Graff nodded and said, "Good idea."

"Just let me know when you want to start," Kristi said as she left the office shutting the door behind her.

"Can you run through George's dream for us again?" Eiselmann asked.

Jeremy sighed and shrugged.

"I found him on the top of the stairs. He had his knife in one hand and his other arm around Momma."

"He must have made his rounds and came back upstairs," Graff said.

Jeremy nodded. "When I woke him up, he said that he had one of his dreams and went downstairs to check doors and windows. When he was in the study, the owl . . ."

"A Great Gray Owl not common to Wisconsin," Eiselmann said.

"Right, not common in Wisconsin. George said that he saw the owl or that the owl flew and landed on the patio, walked towards him and vanished."

"It didn't fly away," Eiselmann stated.

Jeremy shook his head and said, "George said it vanished."

"And the Navajo believe . . ." Graff asked.

"That animals . . . birds, deer, any animal, I guess, are sometimes messengers."

"How do they know what kind of message they're bringing?" Eiselmann asked.

Jeremy shrugged and said, "That's what frustrates, George. When he was younger, his grandfather would have helped him understand it. With his grandfather deceased, there isn't anyone local who can help him with that."

"So, he's left to figure it out himself," Eiselmann said. "And with no clear direction or interpretation, it could mean anything."

"There is one thing we do know for sure," Graff said. "It isn't likely to be good news."

"Is Terzinski's death the start of it?" Jeremy asked.

Eiselmann said to Jeremy, "O'Connor is working the gang angle, trying to locate Fuentes. That's why Jamie and I are doing the interviews."

As if reading Jeremy's mind, Graff said, "We're going to do all we can to protect George and your boys, Jeremy. No one is going to come close to them without going through us first."

CHAPTER FORTY-NINE

"Where are you?"

Tat Boy hated these phone calls. He resented them and was tired of taking orders from him. The only good thing was that when he saw who the caller was, he remembered to push the record button. A convenient contraption he and a buddy hooked up for his phone.

"Why?" he asked with a touch of defiance.

"Because the cops are at school and from the looks of it, they're about ready to haul in some students to interview. I'm guessing the topic of discussion is Kevin Longwood. Your name is on the list."

"That will be tough to do if I'm not at school."

The Man couldn't believe how simple-minded kids could be.

"Well that's true. But it won't stop them from stopping by your house. They probably have your make and model of vehicle and will be looking for that too, now won't they?"

Tat Boy hadn't thought of that. He wiped some sweat off his upper lip and ran a hand through his longish hair.

His fingerprints in Longwood's car can be explained away, because they hung out sometimes. But there were matching fingerprints on the syringe and rubber tube and possibly all over the basement of the building. That would be harder to explain. He was screwed unless he made a deal.

"Are you there?" The Man asked impatiently.

"Yeah . . . I'm here."

"So, where are you?"

"At a friend's house."

"We have to think of something. We need to have a plan."

"What kind of plan?"

The Man thought for a minute and said, "Stay invisible. Stay away from your house. If you drive anywhere use someone else's car. If you drive your own take back streets. Stay away from the police. There's a wayside on Genesee Road about two miles out of the city on the right side of the road. I will meet you there at four. Park towards the back and if you can, out of sight. I'll try to come up with a plan."

Tat Boy hung up before The Man. He hadn't done that before and it felt good.

He sat up and swung his bare legs over the side of the bed.

His mom was at work. His dad lived in Milwaukee and he seldom saw or visited him. Maybe he could hide there. No. The cops would look for him there too.

He hung his head and thought.

"Who was that?" she asked reaching around his bare stomach dipping her hand between his legs holding him gently.

"Nobody."

He laid back down, her hand exciting him again.

"I want to do you," she said as she took him into her mouth.

Tat Boy knew he needed to plan for his meeting with The Man, but it could wait until later.

CHAPTER FIFTY

"Who is this?" The Man asked through clenched teeth. This had been the sixth or seventh call. All he had heard was the faint sound of someone breathing. There were two calls the night before and they hadn't stopped since and it wasn't even noon. "I'm warning you, prank calls are against the law."

Just breathing, slow and steady. No other noise.

And then a click and the call ended. Same thing each time.

The Man stared at his cell. He didn't recognize the number. Back in the old days before cell phones, he could do a *Star 68* and find out who the caller was. Cell phones however, were anonymous by nature. Unless he knew the caller's program provider and got a lawyer to seek a warrant, he couldn't demand to know the identity of the person who had called. He didn't want a lawyer because they asked too many questions. Privacy and confidentiality be damned.

So that left him with two choices. He could either get a new cell and number or he could suck it up.

It was probably some kid who had gotten his number somehow and eventually, the kid would tire of the game.

The Man put his cell back in his pocket. His class was about to begin.

CHAPTER FIFTY-ONE

"Shit!"

Eiselmann looked up at Graff and said, "What?"

Graff shook his head and said, "I should have thought of this sooner." To Jeremy he said, "You and I need to go find Liz Champion. We need to have that security guy look at some film for us."

"Bud Foster?" Jeremy asked. "Why?"

"Because I want to know who gave that note to George. Whoever that was knows where Fuentes is."

"What do you want me to do?" Eiselmann asked.

"Begin the interviews with the kids on this list. We need to find out who killed Longwood. Whoever did that is also responsible for killing those kids. Start at the top and see how far you get. Remember, we're not accusing them of anything. We're just collecting information. But follow your gut. You know how to do it. O'Connor says your one of the best."

Eiselmann blushed, smiled and said, "I'll see what I can do."

"Let's find Champion," Graff said to Jeremy as he walked out of the office.

CHAPTER FIFTY-TWO

The kitchen was clean, spotless. The morning dishes were in the dishwasher that purred quietly. A bit of steam rose from the vent in the front of it. The house had been dusted and vacuumed and smelled of Pledge and Carpet Fresh. It was the way she liked it. The envelopes were on the table addressed to their owners. David even had the foresight to pay all of the December and January bills. The envelopes with checks stuffed in them were in the mailbox with the little red flag up stamped and ready for pick up.

She was ready. She couldn't wait.

She wasn't so sure about David.

Quietly, Nancy tiptoed down the stairs to the basement and soundlessly opened the gun cabinet and took out the rifle. She loaded it with three cartridges, took a deep breath and tiptoed back upstairs.

Nancy knew that their neighbors on either side of them were at work. So was their neighbor behind them and their neighbor across the street. She knew this, because she took the time to learn the comings and goings of her neighborhood.

David was working on something in the spare room that served as his office away from his office. He sat with his back to the door and in front of his computer. He wasn't typing, however. His elbow rested on the desk and his chin rested on the palm of his hand. The boys often sat just like that when they studied or read. Just like their father in so many ways, especially Brad.

She smiled.

She didn't have any fear. She didn't have any reservations about what she was going to do. It had been her idea, but David hadn't tried to dissuade her. Both of them knew this is what they would do.

Still smiling, she took aim at David's back, just at the base of his neck and pulled the trigger.

David pitched forward and didn't move. This was good, because she didn't want him to suffer.

Moving quickly, she set the rifle against the wall and holding onto her husband's limp and lifeless body, pulled him on the chair out of the room, down the hall and into Brad's room. Struggling a bit, she pulled and rolled David onto Brad's bed, taking the time to fold his hands over his chest that had a crimson blossom of blood soaking the front of his shirt that had an ugly, jagged hole just above where his heart might be.

Next, she pushed the chair back into David's office and placed it neatly at his desk.

She thought briefly about cleaning up the blood and tissue on David's computer and desk, but didn't want to take the time in case by chance some neighbor had heard the gunshot.

Moving quickly now, she picked up the rifle and went back into Brad's room and shut the door.

She laid down next to her husband and whispered, "Dad and are coming, Brad."

Still smiling, she put the barrel of the rifle under her chin and pulled the trigger.

CHAPTER FIFTY-THREE

"Okay, there's George and Danny leaving their Spanish class," Jamie said pointing at the screen.

None of them were overly big. Foster had quite the belly developing and with them all huddled around the computer desk, the office seemed tiny. He was seated at the desk running the video and Jeremy, Jamie, and Liz Champion crammed in and around him. The smallish office had a bear's den feel to it and it smelled like that to Jeremy.

"Slow it down," Champion said. "Just a little."

"The hallway is really crowded," Jeremy said.

"Go split screen using this camera angle and camera seven from the other side and see if we can get a better look from that one," Champion said.

Foster fiddled with the computer and in seconds a second picture appeared on the screen showing George and Danny in a profile, but more clearly than the first camera angle.

"There! It looked like that girl just gave George a piece of paper!" Jeremy said a bit too loudly.

"Freeze it!" Champion said.

"That's Katherine Turner. A junior," Jeremy said. "I didn't think she knew George."

Foster turned slightly around and said over his shoulder, "Mr. Evans, everyone knows George. Danny too. For that matter, everyone knows the twins and Brett too."

Jeremy shrugged wondering if that was a good thing or not.

"Okay, we need to backtrack the Turner girl. We need to see where she came from and find out who gave her the note," Champion said.

Foster ran the tape backwards at slow motion and it didn't take long. Even with the crowded hallway, they followed Turner as she walked backwards into the English and world language hallway. A boy stood to the side of the hallway, gently touched her arm, had a brief conversation with her and handed her the folded note.

"Keep it moving backward. I want to see what classroom that boy and Turner came from."

Foster continued the film in reverse slowly. Turner came out of one English classroom and from one door down, the boy did too.

"Okay, both came out of English classrooms. George came out of Spanish. The classrooms are in the same hallway just doors down from one another," Champion said. "Run it forward slowly."

Kids exited classrooms so obviously the bell had rung. The boy was the first to appear and waited just outside the Turner girl's classroom. George and Danny had already exited their classroom and were in the herd of kids moving slowly towards the cafeteria.

They watched the Turner girl step out of the classroom, where the boy stood. He greeted her, touched her arm and had a brief conversation with her. They watched Turner shrug, smile, nod and walk away from him quickly, but not at a run. The boy looked up at the camera in the hallway.

"Freeze it!" Champion said.

"That's Angel Benevides," Foster said. "His brother, Manny is bad news."

"Manny was expelled for dealing and hasn't been back," Champion said. "Angel isn't a bad kid though."

"We know his brother," Jamie said. "We have nothing on Angel."

"So now what?" Jeremy said.

Jamie gave him 'the look' but only said, "Let's head back to your office." As he and Jeremy moved out of the security office, Jamie turned around and said, "Thanks for your help. I ask that this remain confidential please."

"Of course," Champion said. "Let me know if you need anything else."

The two men walked back to guidance in silence, preferring to discuss particulars in private. Kristi was at her desk and on the phone, but she smiled at them and gave a little wave. Eiselmann was camped out in Jeremy's office behind the closed door.

Jamie peeked in and saw he was with one of the boys, who sat on the edge of one of Jeremy's chairs fidgeting, hands restless and his left leg bouncing nervously.

"Paul has a live one," Jamie muttered with a smile as he turned around towards Jeremy. "Any place we can talk privately?"

Jeremy led him to a small unoccupied conference room and shut the door behind them.

"Okay, now what?"

Jamie leaned against the wall with his arms folded on his chest, brow wrinkled in thought.

"If we go directly at this kid, it's likely he'll shut down and we won't get anywhere."

"Even if I ask him for his help?" Jeremy asked. He was good with kids and trusted his ability to work with them.

"Look at it this way. He might be an innocent. The note would indicate that right? But you're authority and George's dad. Those two facts are working against you. And the way he looked up at the camera . . . it seems to me that one, he knew he would be watched or seen and he didn't care."

"I think he wants to help. At least that's what I read into it."

"Maybe, maybe not. Could be defiance. It's obvious he knows Fuentes. It's obvious he cares about George and what might happen to him. The note indicates that. If he didn't, he wouldn't have taken the time to pass it to him right?"

Jeremy nodded, suspecting where Jamie was headed.

"Here is what I propose. It's up to you, but I think it's our best course of action."

"You want George to talk to him," Jeremy said.

Jamie smiled and said, "Yes. It's safer that way. Watching Benevides give the note to the Turner girl, it looked to me like they know each other or at the least know of each other. But we leave the girl out of it. You bring George in or better yet get him out of his class and speak to him in the hallway."

"How much do I tell him?"

"We need to know where Fuentes is and Benevides knows where he might be. George thanks him for the warning. He appeals to him about being able to protect you and his brothers. Something like that."

"If this Fuentes is a piece of shit like I suspect he is, wouldn't Angel be in danger? For ratting him out, I mean," Jeremy asked.

"He's already in danger because of the note. I think he knows that. It could be that his brother, who is a true piece of shit, is involved somehow. We know his brother has gang connections. Either Angel will help us or he won't. If he does, piece of cake. Easy shmeazy. If he doesn't, we put a tail on him and his brother and maybe one or the other will lead us to him. Would take time though, and I don't know how much more time we have."

Jeremy thought it over. He trusted Jamie and loved him like a brother. Finally he nodded.

"Okay, I'll talk with him. I'll have Kristi print out a picture of Angel and take it with me to show George in case he doesn't know him. He's in Spanish now and we know Angel is in English a couple of doors down. Bell rings, George waits for Angel and has a conversation with him."

"In Spanish. I'm guessing Angel knows Spanish. That way none of the other kids would know what they're talking about."

"Good point. They have a conversation in Spanish."

"He doesn't push him though. Kind of feels him out. Asks for help on behalf of you and his brothers. To protect you and them," Jamie suggested.

Jeremy nodded. Of his sons, George and Brett were the two most street smart and could pull it off. Randy, Billy and Bobby, maybe but probably not.

"Jamie, I wanted all of this behind us. I thought after that summer all of it was. When is this shit going to end?"

Jamie shook his head and said, "Soon I hope, Big Guy. Soon."

CHAPTER FIFTY-FOUR

Ricardo Fuentes liked to sleep in, especially if a girl was handy and in bed with him. And a thirteen-year-old girl, young, skinny and hung over and on the downslope of an ecstasy high lay under him panting and moaning. Up until the night before she was a virgin.

He finished, but didn't roll off. He and she were sweaty and sticky having been at it all night.

"How was your first time?" he asked.

She kissed his neck and whispered, "Like a dream."

He eased himself out of her and lowered his face to her small breasts, taking a nipple into his mouth.

"You don't learn this in school," he said between licks.

"I would if you were the teacher."

He wanted one more go at her, but he had to get going. People to meet, people to see and someone to kill. Several to kill, actually.

Fuentes sat up, but stayed between her legs staring down at her.

She was a white girl with brown straight hair. Her skin had a sheen of sweat. Her thin lips were parted and her brown eyes partially closed. Her left hand clutched his thigh, while her right played with him.

"You want more?" he asked with a smile.

"Oh, yes! Yes!"

He positioned himself closer to her head and said, "Use your mouth."

She obeyed, though she grimaced at the taste.

When he was ready he pulled out and said, "Get on your hands and knees."

Again without a word, she obeyed.

"Spread your legs a little. Yes, that's it. Here I come," he said as he took her from behind.

He shut his eyes as he worked on her, liking the picture in his mind.

White girls needed to be fucked from behind. They were no better than dogs. Their mouths needed to be filled until their lips were chapped and their bellies were full. White girls were less than animals, less than dogs. Black girls were better than white girls. More experienced, their skin dark as mahogany and molasses. But nothing beat a hot Latino girl.

He was almost ready. He picked her up by her waist to get a better angle and quickened his pace. She responded in similar fashion.

With one hand, he reached for the knife on the chipped, compressed wood table on the side of the bed and just as he released inside of her, he grabbed her by the back of her hair, lifted her head back and slit her throat from ear to ear.

She clutched her neck, did a little dance on her knees, her feet spastically pounding the bed next to him, sometimes kicking him. He pushed her head into her pillow and that was how she died.

He had done this before and never tired of it.

Fuentes pulled out of her still dripping a little, slapped her ass once and then once more for good measure. He stepped into the bathroom and urinated. He ran hot water, stepped into the tub, shut the curtain and let the shower cascade over him. He picked up the soap and lathered up. He had to get the stink of the white girl off of him.

When he was finished, he toweled off and stepped into the bedroom.

The girl hadn't moved and he didn't expect her to. She was dead. Deader than dead.

"Manny!" he yelled from the bathroom doorway.

Manny Benevides stepped into the room and froze when he saw the girl, the blood in the bed and on the headboard. He glanced at Fuentes standing naked with his hands on his hips.

He wanted to ask, *why the fuck did you kill her?* But instead asked, "You want me to get rid of her?"

"No, Puta, let's keep her right there. What the fuck do you think I want done with her?"

Not paying any attention to Manny as he struggled wrapping the dead girl in the sheets and thin blankets from the bed, Fuentes went to the dresser, picked up his cell phone and dialed the number. He let it ring and ring, but

The Man never answered. He ended the call before it went to voicemail.

"Looks like a motherfucking burrito," he said with a laugh as Manny hoisted the girl wrapped in sheets and a blanket over his shoulder. "Like a big fucking joint," he said with another laugh.

Manny wasn't laughing as he left the room.

Fuentes didn't bother to dress, but sat spread-legged on the couch facing the stripped bed. He lit a joint and sucked in the sweet smoke, holding his breath as long as he could before he exhaled. He had at least three visits to make and hopefully, a dead body would be at each stop when he left. More, if someone got in his way.

CHAPTER FIFTY-FIVE

George waited outside his classroom. Danny wanted to wait with him, but George sent him on his way to the cafeteria. He didn't tell Danny why, but Danny accepted that George had a reason and that was good enough.

He caught Angel's eye and there was a moment when George thought Angel might turn around and walk in the other direction. There was a moment when both boys stood still, eyeing one another and judging the degree of danger. It was Angel's head nod that assured George that Angel wasn't someone to be feared.

George waited for Angel to walk near him and George fell into step alongside of him.

In Spanish George said, "Thank you for the note. I appreciate it."

Angel said nothing. He didn't deny giving him the note, but he didn't acknowledge it either.

George continued in Spanish, "I am worried for my father and my brothers."

Angel's eyes darted towards him, but otherwise remained forward.

"Two years ago, I lost my whole family. They were murdered because I tried to help. My father took me in when he didn't have to. My brothers accepted me when they didn't have to. I cannot let anything happen to them."

Angel slowed his pace, but kept his eyes straight ahead.

"If I knew where Fuentes was, I can help protect my father and my brothers."

Angel stepped to the side to let other students pass by. He leaned against a bank of lockers and George stood next to him.

"Why is Fuentes after you?"

Calmly, matter-of-factly and without any boast, George said, "Because I killed his cousin."

Angel studied him, looking for any sign of dishonesty. Not finding any he said, "Why?"

"We were on vacation and he broke into our cabin. He taped my family and my friend, Danny and his dad to chairs. He hurt Danny. He hurt Billy and I was afraid he was going to kill all of them."

"Where were you?"

"I was out running."

"How did you kill him?"

George studied the floor and sighed. He started once, twice and sighed again before he said, "With my knife."

Angel squinted at him expecting more.

George repeated, "He had my father and my brothers all lined up. He almost killed by brother, Billy. I was afraid that I would lose my family once again." He turned towards Angel and said, "I do not want to lose my family, Angel. I want to protect them."

Angel nodded, but remained silent.

"If you know where he is, I would like to know so I can protect my family."

Angel shook his head and said, "You won't be able to do that by yourself, mi amigo."

"I know that. There are others who want to help me, but they can't if we don't know where he is. If we don't know where he is, my father and my brothers are in danger."

It was Angel's turn. He had a decision to make and he knew that his life and perhaps the life of his mother were on the line. The decision George wanted him to make might and probably would, cost him his life and the life of the only person who mattered to him, the only person he truly cared about.

The silence lingered, weighed heavy and George felt he had lost.

"Do you have a cell phone?" Angel said.

"Yes."

"Give me your number. When I know where Fuentes is, I will let you know. And when I do, you'll have to act quickly because there won't be a second chance. You will die. Your father will die. Your brothers will die. And my mother and I will die."

He paused, stared at George and said, "Do you understand, mi amigo?"

George nodded. Yes, he understood. He understood all too well what was at stake.

Tat Boy came up with a plan. He wasn't sure how good it was, but it was a plan. He needed someone to help him and his girlfriend conveniently agreed. She didn't actually know what Tat Boy was involved in, because Tat Boy had never told her. All she knew was that some guy was going to meet her boyfriend at Brookfield Square in the food court. Tat Boy explained that he was supposed to meet the guy in a rest area, but there was no way he was going to meet the man there. Not in some private place. No, he explained, he wanted to meet with him in public.

Tat Boy and his girlfriend arrived one hour earlier than he was expected. They took her car, not his. Just to be safe, they entered the mall from different entrances at different times and found tables kitty-corner from each other. Close but not too close. Tat Boy was very clear with her. No eye contact. No talking. When the man showed up, he and Tat Boy would talk. He didn't know how long it might take, but when it ended, Tat Boy would leave first. She would wait five minutes and leave and they'd meet at her car.

Tat Boy knew she was nervous. No, she was scared. Surprisingly, he wasn't. Nervous maybe, but not scared.

Tat Boy saw the man right away, but the man didn't see him or if he did, he didn't show it. Instead, he strolled the perimeter of the food court like any other customer might trying to decide what he might want to eat. He settled for a chicken sandwich, fries and a soda from McDonald's. He carried his tray over to Tat Boy's table and sat opposite him.

With three weeks to Christmas and it being a week night, the mall wasn't very busy. Not like it would be on a weekend and closer to Christmas. Still plenty of people, but Tat Boy saw many more than this on weekends.

"Good idea to meet here," the man said. "I should have thought of it."

Tat Boy smiled tentatively.

"I'm about to tell you some things that you may or may not know. Don't show any expression and don't panic," he said between French fries. "Okay?"

Tat Boy nodded, sipping a Coke.

"The cops were at school today interviewing four students. They found Ron Terzinski dead."

Tat Boy blinked. "When? How?"

"Quiet down. Remember what I said, don't panic. Cool and calm."

Tat Boy nodded.

"I don't have any details, but Ron is definitely dead."

"It wasn't me," Tat Boy whispered.

"I know that," the man said with a smile. "I know that. But now Kevin is dead and Ron is dead."

It didn't take long for Tat Boy to link it together. Kevin and Ron. Next him.

His eyes grew wide and he could feel himself go pale. His eyes darted left and right. He wanted to run but didn't know where. His first instinct was to go to the cops. Confess and play them the recordings from his phone. The one that was on the table near his right hand, on and recording this conversation. He dare not look at it. Not even glance at it.

The man reached for his coat that was thrown over a chair. He brought out a fat envelope and pushed it across the table towards the boy. His eyes searching for anyone who might be watching.

"What's this?" Tat Boy asked.

"My plan," the man said. "Hear me out."

He took a sip from his soda, ate another French fry. He hadn't touched his chicken sandwich.

"In this envelope is five thousand dollars. It's enough to get you out of here for a while. Go to California where it's warm. Maybe Florida. Find a cheap hotel near the beach. Stay hidden until this blows over."

"What do I tell my mom? I can't just leave," Tat Boy whispered leaning forward towards the man.

"You have to. It's not safe. First Kevin and now Ron. The cops interviewed kids today and some of them you've sold to. The cops could be at your house right now waiting for you."

Tat Boy held his head in both hands, his mind racing. He had to think.

"Pick a place. Florida or California. Which one?"

Tat Boy had never been to California and the only things he knew were from TV and movies. When he was younger, he had traveled to Disney World and Ft. Myers with his parents. He had always wanted to see Miami.

"Florida, I guess. Miami," he said. He didn't sound all that excited about it, though.

"When I leave here, I'll drive to the airport and get you an open ticket. Do you have some place you can stay tonight? Some place safe?"

Tat Boy nodded and said, "Yeah, I think so." He almost broke his own rule and glanced over at his girlfriend.

"Good. When I buy your ticket, I'll text you the airline along with your flight information."

Tat Boy felt like crying. He was scared. He knew he had lost. Yes, he had his cell and he had the recordings, but would the cops listen to him.

"Don't think about it too much," the man said gently. "You can't think about it or you'll freeze up and you'll be caught. Neither you nor I can afford for that to happen."

Tat Boy nodded unenthusiastically.

"When things die down, I'll text you and you can come home."

"What do I tell my mom?" Tat Boy said wiping a tear from his eye.

The man sighed. He didn't think he liked the kid all that much, but he had to admit his heart broke a little.

"Tell your mom that you love her, but you have an opportunity to travel to California for a little while. Tell her you'll be back soon."

"California? I thought . . ."

The man smiled and nodded and said, "Tell her California. That way, if the cops ask her, that's what she'll tell them. Don't tell her Florida, because if they decide to look for you . . ." he finished with a shrug.

Tat Boy nodded and said, "Okay. I can do that."

"When you get to Miami and you settle in somewhere, text me. If you need anything, text me. I'll do what I can for you."

Tat Boy nodded again.

"I'm going to leave now. Wait five or ten minutes before you leave. Remember, look for my text tonight. I'll have your airline and flight information. Stay safe and stay out of sight."

Tat Boy nodded and tried to smile, his lips trembling.

"It will be okay. It will work out. I'll let you know when everything blows over. Stay safe and out of sight. Stay under the radar. Don't do or say anything that will get you noticed."

The man slid his chair back and stood up. He gathered up his trash and uneaten chicken sandwich and pitched them in a nearby receptacle. He picked up his coat, smiled at Tat Boy, turned around and left the food court at a leisurely pace.

CHAPTER FIFTY-SEVEN

"Rob Kirlie never showed up for school and neither did his girlfriend, Hannah Milton," Eiselmann said. "Kirlie's mother and Milton's parents both said that they left for school at the usual time. Neither seemed particularly worried. My guess is that this isn't the first time they skipped school with each other."

They had agreed to debrief at the end of each day so they could keep themselves on the same page. Graff also believed that three sets of eyes looking at a puzzle piece might help them place it properly in the puzzle. So the three of them sat around a conference table at the police station. Pictures had been spread out in front of them and pertinent portions of reports read out loud even though each of them had copies. Eiselmann assumed the role of recorder and sat in front of his laptop.

"Any idea where they are?" Graff asked.

Eiselmann shook his head and said, "Not a clue. I took a run at a couple of the kids, but they didn't know either."

"What are we doing right now?" O'Connor asked. He had spent the morning and all afternoon chasing down one lead after another on Fuentes, but came up empty each time.

"We have a watch on Kirlie house and on the Milton house," Eiselmann answered.

"We're seeking warrants to tap their phone lines and separate warrants for their cell phones," Jamie said.

"What led you to Kirlie?" O'Connor asked.

"Four kids fingered him as a dealer. One or two bought from him and said that he asked them if they might be interested in something heavier. They asked what and he said, a special bundle," Eiselmann shook his head. "The kids said that Kirlie didn't elaborate, only that it was new stuff."

"Have you been able to do anything with the information George got from Angel Benevides?" Graff asked.

"Not much. We're watching the Benevides house, but Manny doesn't live there. Maybe he'll swing by or something. We're looking for his car. We have a last known address on him, but he moves around a lot. We have eyes on a couple of his friends," O'Connor said, He added, "All of them are MS-13."

"Is the little brother?" Eiselmann asked.

O'Connor shook his head, "Nah. He's actually pretty straight. Not a bad kid. Lives with his mother. His dad split five or six years back. That's when Manny started dealing. He got jumped in shortly after that and climbed up to lieutenant."

"How does Fuentes fit in?" Graff asked.

"Chicago sent him up when one of our Waukesha MS-13, probably Manny, informed them that someone was trying to move into their drug trade."

"How do you know this?" Graff asked.

"Street talk mostly. The feds have someone undercover in Chicago. Buried deep from what I understand."

"Shit!" Eiselmann said pushing away from the table. "I can't do undercover stuff like you or that fed guy. Couldn't pay me enough for that."

"Did you get anything significant off the Terzinski boy's body? Anything where you found him?" Jamie asked.

O'Connor shook his head. "Too early to tell. Ike might have something in the morning. We're checking his prints against those found in Longwood's car and against the ones on the rubber tourniquet and syringe. Terzinski was found in the same building where we think the other murders took place."

Eiselmann stood up and stretched.

"A date tonight?" O'Connor asked smiling.

"Going to the North game with Sarah."

Jamie checked his watch and said, "I think I'm heading there too."

All three men stood up and replaced the pictures and reports into their manila folders. Jamie was the last to leave, shutting off the lights and closing the door behind him.

"Guys, if something happens, if you hear anything, we let each other know, right?"

O'Connor and Eiselmann nodded.

The three of them walked out of the building together into the late afternoon. It was already dark and the temps had dropped at least ten degrees. What had melted had turned back into ice and crunched under their feet.

Graff would head home to Kelly for a quick dinner before she and Garrett and he would head to the game, unless Kelly got a babysitter for Garrett. Jeremy and Vicky would be there and so would Jeff Limbach. In any case, it should be a relaxing night.

"God bless it! I hate this shitty cold weather," Eiselmann said. "I wanna go someplace warmer."

"You'll have to convince Sarah to go with you. She might jump at it, but Stephen might be a tougher sell," Graff said with a laugh. "All his friends are here and I don't see him moving."

"Ah, shit! You're right," Eiselmann said with a cough. "I hate cold weather. See you guys at the game," he said jogging off towards his car.

"What are you going to do tonight?" Graff ask O'Connor.

O'Connor hunched his narrow shoulders and said, "Probably go to the game. Brett wanted me to see them play. And I want to keep an eye on George."

"I'll see you there," Graff said patting the tall, skinny sheriff deputy on the back.

O'Connor nodded and walked away.

CHAPTER FIFTY-EIGHT

Kirlie strolled out of the mall, hood up, head down and hands in his jacket pockets. He felt numb, but not from the cold. As hard as he tried, he couldn't figure out how it got this far.

He had a great mom. He saw his dad whenever, and that was just about how he felt about him. He had a wonderful girlfriend who really liked him, maybe even loved him.

He wasn't stupid, at least he didn't think so. But he had done some really dumb things. The worst was listening to the man, but now the man was trying to help him. Confusing.

The thing he kept coming back to was that even if he went to Miami for however long, he would still come back and the cops would find him and he'd be screwed. Really screwed. He watched enough cop shows to know that he probably would be tried as an adult and even though Wisconsin didn't have the death penalty, he'd get life.

Life in prison.

It was somewhere between the door he walked out of and Hannah's car that he found himself weeping.

Rob reached Hannah's car, an older white Chevy Impala with a dented side panel on the passenger side and because he had the keys, he unlocked it and opened the passenger door. Without thinking, he did something he had never done before.

Maybe out of disgust. Maybe out of despair. Maybe because he wasn't thinking at all, he tossed his phone on the driver's side seat.

He didn't get in right away. Instead, he placed both hands on top of the car to think and that's when it happened.

A pair of hands slammed his head on the door frame twice.

He felt his knees buckle and the world spun around him. His head hurt.

Blood poured from a nasty gash on his forehead and another on the bridge of his flattened nose.

At least two sets of hands dragged him towards the back of a car and just before they threw him in the trunk, they pummeled him in the back, his stomach, his head and his balls.

He never saw who they were. He didn't see what kind of car they threw him into.

He rolled himself into a ball and fell asleep, not knowing if he would wake up. And he wasn't sure if he wanted to.

CHAPTER FIFTY-NINE

Coach Harrison made sure Brian and Randy were sitting next to him on the bench, although Harrison didn't sit much. North was down by seven to a tough, quick and senior-heavy Racine Case team. Still because of Brett, Billy and Troy Rivera, North was in it.

"Brett's getting pissed," Brian said.

"I know," Randy answered.

Jimmy Holcomb, a junior started at the shooting guard position, but he wasn't shooting. He wasn't playing much defense either. What he was doing was committing fouls and turning the ball over. Deke Tilke wasn't doing much better at the power forward spot.

Harrison sat down next to Brian and said, "What do you see?"

Brian didn't know Coach all that well, but he was asked a direct question so Brian answered, "Jimmy isn't anticipating. He's thinking too much. Brett can't read him."

"Mr. Evans gave you boys some advice before the game, right?"

It had begun quite by accident beginning with the first scrimmage of the season. Jeremy had stood at the corner of the court watching warmups when Billy came over and stood in front of him.

Jeremy had said, "Play hard. Basketball is a game of mistakes, so mistakes will happen. The team who makes the least amount of mistakes wins. So you have to relax and play. Try not to think. Just go out there and have fun, regardless of how much you get to play."

When Billy had left, Brett had come over. The message was similar, but Jeremy had added, "Brett, you have to be the coach on the field. You're a tough competitor, but you need to know when to put the pedal to the floor and when to ease off. Same way with handling your teammates. You have to read them just as you read the other team."

And from that point on, Billy and Brett would get a little pep talk before each game. Randy and Brian had received a similar pep talk before their JV game. In each case, it was followed by a hug and a kiss on the cheek.

With all four on varsity, the order didn't change much.

To Randy, Jeremy had said, "Randy, you can't afford to be nervous and you can't afford to think too much. Just play. It's different from playing quarterback. Basketball is a game of reaction as much as it is forcing the action. Anticipate. Make a decision and go with it, mistake or not."

"He said that I need to read Brett as much as I need to read whomever I'm guarding or whomever is guarding me. He said I need to listen to you. He said I have to shoot to take pressure off Billy and Troy. He said most of all, anticipate and play at full speed for as long as I play, long or short."

Harrison nodded and said, "That about sums it up." He looked at Randy and said, "And you?"

"He said I shouldn't think too much. Anticipate, react, play hard."

Harrison nodded and said, "Good advice." He waited a beat and said, "Kaz, you better go in for Jimmy before Brett kills him. Randy, go in for Deke. And guys, do just as your dad told you."

Both jumped up, reported in at the scorer's table and knelt down in front of it. It wasn't long before Kevin made another turnover allowing both boys to substitute in.

Brett and Brian slapped hands and Brett and Randy did the same.

"Kaz, I want to press. Keep your man to the outside, but if you can jump the lane, do it."

Brett went after Case's senior captain, Dujour Lorge, shading his right hand, forcing him to dribble to his left towards Brian. Brian anticipated the pass, stepped in front to intercept it and took off for an easy uncontested layup.

"Again," Brett said taking off to defend the inbound play.

Brian went for a steal, missed, but recovered nicely. Case took a shot, missed and Troy snagged the rebound, passed it to Randy, who fed Brian setting up on the wing beyond the three point line. He shot, missed and a Case defender got the rebound. That player passed to his outlet on Brian's side. Brian got trucked big time when the offensive player didn't stop in time and ran him over.

"Kaz, you okay?" Harrison called from the sideline.

"Fine," Brian said picking himself up slowly.

"Good. Keep shooting," Harrison said. He added with a laugh, "but make 'em."

And so it went. By halftime North was down by two. Brian had eight points, six on two three-pointers. Billy led the scoring with nine, followed by Brett with eight. Randy and Troy had four apiece. Brian and Randy had entered the game with three minutes left in the first quarter and played the rest of the half.

Going into the locker room the Case coach screamed at his team, "You're getting your butts handed to you by *freshmen* and two of them weren't even on varsity until tonight! *Freshmen!*"

Brett laughed, turned to Randy and Brian and said, "He's talking about you."

"Somebody's going to get their butts chewed," Brian laughed.

CHAPTER SIXTY

Puzzled, Hannah came out of the mall at the prescribed time expecting Rob to be waiting in her car.

He wasn't.

She stopped walking and did a slow one-eighty scanning the parking lot looking for him.

Nothing.

The lights in the lot weren't that bright, but they were still plenty bright enough. She spied her car and as she drew near her puzzlement turned to fear. The passenger door was slightly open and there was something spilled on the passenger window.

Blood looks like chocolate syrup in the dark. When she opened the door, the car's overhead light came on and it was clear that it wasn't chocolate syrup.

She screamed and cried and called his name.

A few shoppers heading into or out of the mall stopped momentarily, frozen at Hannah's scream. Of the few, only one, an off-duty cop went to see if he could be of any help.

And she had yet to spot Rob's cell phone.

CHAPTER SIXTY-ONE

He woke up slowly like a swimmer breaking the surface. Everything blurry and out of focus. Pain in his back, his head, his stomach. His balls. He was unable to move his arms and legs.

He was freezing and he shivered uncontrollably. Goosebumps covered every inch of his skin. He looked down at himself and he was naked. He was duct taped to a chair. His arms were bound behind his back and legs spread open. Tentatively, he tested the tape on his wrists, but there was no give. He did the same with his ankles, but again no slack and no chance to break away from his bounds.

"Ah, you're awake, Puta." It wasn't a question and the speaker didn't care if there was an answer.

He shook his head slightly trying to clear it, but his head hurt too much.

He opened his eyes fully and recognized where he was. He and Kevin Longwood and Ron Terzinski had visited it frequently. He turned his head to the corner to see if the syringe was still there, but it wasn't. He had guessed the cops had it. But that was the least of his worries at the moment. In fact, he hoped that some cop, any cop, would come busting down the stairs right now to save him.

He turned back to the front. A wiry Hispanic stood in front of him smiling.

Rob chose to say nothing.

"We have your friend too," he said stepping to the side and sweeping his arm like Vanna White towards the naked and bound man directly across from him only a yard or two away.

Gordon Huggins bled from a wound above his right ear and from a cut above his left eye. His right eye was swollen shut and his left blinked rapidly.

Rob didn't like looking at the naked man, but couldn't take his eyes off of him. Obviously, there wouldn't be plane tickets waiting for him.

"We followed him to the mall and that's where we saw you. Taking both of you in the parking lot saved me time. Convenient, no?"

The wiry Hispanic stepped lightly, but slowly to a table and picked up an instrument. Kirlie didn't recognize what it was. It looked like a pliers, but saw that it was some sort of cutting tool.

"I'm wondering who will talk first."

He stood between them smiling like a fox about to eat a chicken. He pointed the instrument at Huggins and then at Rob.

"Here is what I need to know," he said moving slowly towards Huggins. "You're a fucking teacher. Where would someone like you get heroin and fentanyl, hmmm?"

He stepped over to Rob waving the instrument slowly in front of his face.

"And you, you're nothing, Puta," he said patting Rob's cheek with the metal object. "But I wonder how much you might know?"

The Hispanic stepped back between them and making a show of it said, "Oops, I forgot. I need my gloves. I don't like touching anyone unless it is a beautiful girl."

He went back over to the table and pulled on latex gloves. He smiled at both Rob and at Huggins and said, "This could get messy. Painful too."

CHAPTER SIXTY-TWO

She had been practicing her story.

"We were shopping," Hannah sobbed. "We went to the food court to get something to eat and Rob saw one of his teachers and he wanted to talk to him. I know him, but I don't have him as a teacher. It was something about a test or something. Rob didn't tell me. We were going to leave, but I had to go to the bathroom. I told him I would meet him at my car. I even gave him the keys."

She alternately hugged herself and flapped her arms. One of the patrol cops and two mall security personnel checked around the car while the other patrol cop took her statement. The off-duty cop stood with her.

"Did Rob have any enemies? Was there anyone who didn't like him?"

Hannah shook her head, cried and said, "No. No. There was no one."

"Is there anyone who might have taken him somewhere? Anywhere he might have gone?"

"No. No. He was with me." She pointed at the top of the passenger door and on the window. "Who would have done this? Who? Why would someone hurt him?"

"Excuse me," said an older mall security cop. His white mustache had frozen over and it was either snot covered or iced over from his breathing. "Whose cell phone is that on the front seat?"

Hannah and the sheriff deputy bent down to look and Hannah said, "Oh my God! That's Rob's! He never goes anywhere without it! Oh my God!"

The sheriff deputy said, "Don't touch it. We'll bag it for evidence."

"What? Why? You can't take his phone," Hannah protested. "That's Rob's phone. He didn't do anything wrong."

"It's evidence and there might be a clue as to his whereabouts," the deputy said cutting off any further argument.

The tall patrol cop was on a radio to someone, caught the eye of the shorter cop who had interviewed Hannah and the two of them strolled away from the little group.

"They're being looked for. There isn't as much interest in Hannah as there is with Rob."

"So her story is bullshit?" Phil Bunch said.

The tall cop who had been on the radio, Alex Jorgenson shook his head and said, "Not necessarily. Not totally, anyway."

Jorgenson stood six foot five. He had short-cropped red hair and was a new member of the Waukesha County Sheriff Department, but had already earned the respect of higher ranking deputies with his quiet nature, quick wit and the ability to laugh at himself. He was a former all-state football player who earned a division two scholarship to Winona State University, while majoring in criminal justice. He gave up playing football after his freshman year because he was tired of it, burnt out. He still had the physique of an athlete and that served him well in the academy.

"What are you thinking?"

Jorgenson thought for a minute, looked up and pointed, "I think we should see what the cameras picked up."

He pulled out his little notebook that he kept in his breast pocket. He thumbed through it rechecking his notes from the briefing before he had left on patrol and found what he was looking for. He pursed his lips, nodded and said, "I am going to call Detective Pat O'Connor."

Only down three with less than a minute and a half to go. Neither Brett nor Billy had come out of the game at any point other than a timeout or quarter change, while Troy had a two minute rest at the end of the third and Brian and Randy hadn't come out since they had entered the game.

Brian kept himself focused. Like Brett and Billy, Brian operated on remote due to pure athleticism. He knew he hadn't missed from the free throw line, but he couldn't actually remember how many trips he made. He knew he had more steals than assists and more assists than turnovers, but again he didn't know how many of each. And that was pretty typical because he had never been one to follow stats. His brother could report every stat after every game, but Brian wasn't interested in stats. He just liked to play.

Harrison called a time out and the boys hustled over with Brett, Brian and Billy looking up at the scoreboard.

"Balls to the wall, guys!" Billy muttered. Both Brett and Brian nodded. All three along with Randy and Troy were dripping sweat. None of them were huffing or puffing though. Randy and Billy had a habit of biting on the top of their jersey, sweaty or not and the identical twins did just that, not realizing it and standing side by side. If the situation wasn't so serious, Harrison would have laughed out loud.

"We're in this game, boys, but here's what I need."

He had long ago shed his sport coat, loosened his tie and opened the top button on his white shirt. He wasn't a very formal guy anyway.

He grabbed the small whiteboard and drew up a play, explaining that Brian was to use a double pick set up by Randy and Troy and position himself on the wing for a three point shot. The alternate was Billy breaking the other direction off the same double pick for a shot from the baseline.

"If there's a miss, get the rebound," Harrison said to Randy and Troy.

"Brett, don't let them get anything long. We need to press, but be smart about it. Trap when you can, if you can. If you see two teammates going for a two-time, you have to cover up. Near man first, others fill in behind," he said drawing it up.

The buzzer blew and the guys huddled up with one hand each to the center and on top of Brett's left hand.

"Balls to the wall," Brett said. "Leave it on the court. Don't take anything with you to the locker room." He paused eyeing each of them, actually glaring at them. "One, two, three, *North!*" they yelled together.

They left the huddle.

Troy inbounded the ball passing to Brett who broke off of a double pick. North set up their half-court offense in a double low post, Brian stacked behind Troy on one side with Billy behind Randy on the other. Brett dribbled to the top of the key and Billy and Brian broke, first out and then across the lane with Brian circling high, Billy low. Brian couldn't shake his man, so Brett passed to Billy. He shot a ten footer that bounced off the back of the rim, but Troy snagged it in and kicked to Brian who had burst free beyond the three point arc at the baseline. He reared up and swished it, tying the game with less than a minute left.

Harrison couldn't afford for Case to set up in a half-court game because of their size, so he called for a soft press, just enough to harass. Brett and Brian put pressure in the backcourt while Randy and Billy roamed with their men at half court. Case passed it up the side neatly and caught Randy over-playing. His man caught a lob over the top for a layup putting Case ahead by two points with less than twenty seconds.

"Shake it off," Harrison yelled from the sideline. "We need two to tie. No turnovers."

North set up in their familiar double low post. However this time, Brian broke across the lane, while Billy broke up the lane to set up a high pick. Brett shook his head just once and North reset.

Less than fifteen seconds and counting.

Brett never rattled or fussed. Never. Not when he played football. Not when he ran track or played basketball. If he was nervous no one could tell. He had the same demeanor and carried the same expression whether he was ahead or behind, facing a friend or a man with a gun, and in his short life he had faced both.

"Again," Brett yelled with eleven seconds set to play.

That was all he said, yet they knew what he meant.

The crowd had been standing since the fourth quarter began and had worked themselves into a frenzy. Shouting, screaming, stomping the bleachers. It seemed the only people who weren't going nuts were the players on both sides of the court.

North realigned in the double low post and Brian and Billy repeated what they had done only moments ago. Using Billy's pick, Brett feinted left and drove hard right towards the basket. Case defenders closed off his path.

Brian had drifted low towards the baseline losing his defender in the process. Brett kicked it to Brian in the corner who caught it, reared up and shot, but missing.

Randy grabbed the rebound, but was unable to shoot it, so he kicked it back out to Brian, who reset himself up line but beyond the arc. He took the three pointer and swished it putting North up by one with less than two seconds remaining.

The Case coach called time out. In the process, he threw a squirt bottle down and water splashed up on his assistant's pant leg and black leather shoe. For good measure he kicked the front of their bleachers. He stood glaring at the North players jumping up and down with fists and arms raised on their way to the North bench.

"It's not over yet," Harrison reminded them. "They have two seconds."

Instead of sitting, they stood in a circle around him, arms across each other's shoulders.

"Press hard, but don't foul. Call out picks. Support one another. We can't afford to trap, because that leaves someone open and it puts too much pressure on our front line. We can't afford anything deep. Randy, watch the backdoor lob. Troy, own the lane. You'll have to fight around the set, but you can't foul. Billy, Brian and Brett, apply pressure, but be smart about it. No fouls. Nothing easy."

"Two seconds! We can do this." Brett remained calm, but the guys recognized his intensity. "On three: one, two, three, *North!*"

Case had the length of the court to go. Billy took the in-bound man under the basket. He did his best to disrupt any passing lane. Two Case guards lined up one behind the other at the free throw line with Brett on the left and Brian on the right. Randy and Troy guarded their men lined up on either side of the half-court line.

Brian's man set a side pick on Brett's man and broke to the corner, but Brian got there first and intercepted the throw in. He dribbled out the clock and the buzzer sounded.

Pandemonium.

The crowd of students poured onto the court disregarding security and administrators who had set up to prevent that very thing. The players on the bench charged the court from the other side, all surrounding Troy, the twins, Brett and Brian. Everyone screamed and hugged each other.

Harrison breathed a sigh of relief, took a squirt of water from a water bottle, turned around and caught Jeremy's eye. Jeremy pointed at him and gave him a thumb's up.

Brett regrouped the players so they could line up and congratulate the Case players, some of whom sat on the bench with heads hung. More than one or two leaned back and stared at the scoreboard in disbelief before they got into line.

As the boys went through the line slapping hands and saying "Good game!" the crowd chanted, "North! North! North!"

After shaking hands with the Case players, the crowd gathered around the boys. Big Gavin, Mikey, Stephen, Danny and Sean pushed their way to the center and found their five friends. George waited patiently for his turn.

Brian turned around to look up into the stands, but didn't see who he had wanted to see.

"Hey!"

Brian turned to his right and found Caitlyn Watkins smiling at him.

She took him by his sweaty shoulders and kissed him on the lips. It was longer than a peck, but without much passion.

Brian smiled and Cat smiled back and she kissed him again. Long and with her mouth slightly open.

It took Brian's breath away and his heart thumped widely.

When they broke it off, he wanted more. He held her tightly and they kissed again, longer and deeper. There might have been shouting and congratulations all around them, maybe a pat or two on his back, but as far as they were concerned, he and Cat were alone and in their own little world.

Again they broke it off and backed away, still holding hands and smiling at one another. Cat turned to congratulate Brett, Billy and Randy.

Brian turned around smiling, but his smile faded when he saw George. George smiled sadly, nodded and was lost in the crowd of bodies moving towards the exit.

Brian knew the look of pain every time he gazed in the mirror. He knew the feeling of pain because it was with him each and every day.

He started to follow wanting to apologize, but was stopped by Jeremy and Vicky. He accepted their congratulations and a hug from both. By the time he had finished with them, he had no idea where George, the twins or Caitlyn were.

CHAPTER SIXTY-FOUR

Rob was no stranger to death having been a party to killing middle and high school kids. He wasn't numb to death, but he didn't really feel much remorse either. Truth was he didn't know what he felt.

But he had watched helplessly as the Mexican snipped two toes off Huggins' left foot laughing each time he did. Rob watched the Mexican cut off the pinky and ring finger off Huggins' left hand.

And it didn't matter that Huggins answered the Mexican's questions after the first toe was snipped off. Huggins told him everything. He didn't hold anything back.

Rob never knew who was actually in charge. He never knew who had supplied the fentanyl or where the heroin came from. But hearing it as Huggins screamed and cried it out, it made sense, at least in some sick way.

Huggins cried and screamed himself hoarse. He fought against his restraints and failed. He had pissed and shit himself; mocked by the Mexican when he did. Each time something was snipped off he had passed out, but they revived him by throwing cold water in his face.

Rob was forced to watch, having been threatened with having his eyelids cut off to keep his eyes open.

"We're almost done, my friend," Fuentes said.

His hands and arms up to his elbows were covered in Huggins' blood. He walked over to the table and picked up a box cutter. With a sinister smile, he waved it in front of Huggins' face.

"We're almost done," he said patting Huggins' cheek. "We need to do a little more cutting."

Huggins shook his head, his eyes wide in terror.

Fuentes reached between Huggins' legs and pulled his sack forward and cut it off with one swipe. He tossed it on the floor in front of him. Blood ran freely down his legs, pooling on the floor between his feet.

Huggins screamed. He shook his head from side to side and Rob thought for a moment that Huggins' head might fly off.

"One more cut," and Fuentes reached down, stretched out Huggins' dick and sliced it off slowly, taking his time, wanting Huggins to feel maximum pain.

When he was done, he held it up, blood dripping out of it and said, "This is a little boy's dick. You won't miss it anyway."

Fuentes turned around and smiled sickly at Rob.

"As soon as I'm done here, you and I will have a little fun, right, Bendejo?"

Fuentes turned back around, walked slowly behind Huggins and slit his throat from ear to ear. Blood sprayed out like a leaky garden hose. Strapped to the chair, his bare feet danced and jerked. He went still.

Dead.

CHAPTER SIXTY-FIVE

Jamie left Kelly and Garrett with the car so they could get home from the North game. He caught a ride with O'Connor and Eiselmann, who like Graff left his car with Sarah so she and Stephen could get home.

They huddled in the mall security office and watched video from the parking lot. They recognized Manny Benevides, but the two other guys were only vaguely familiar to O'Connor. Fuentes wasn't present. At least not on camera.

Eiselmann winced at the beating Kirlie took and mumbled, "Jesus!"

"The plate isn't visible, but the car is a dark Charger," O'Connor said. "That's Manny's car."

"Can we back it up to see who Kirlie was talking to in the food court?" Graff asked.

The security guy fiddled with the computer and a split screen popped up. He ran it backward until they saw Kirlie sitting at a table with a taller, middle-aged man.

"That's Gordon Huggins," Graff said quietly.

"Wasn't he hanging around the guidance office?" Eiselmann asked.

Graff nodded, frowning, his mind working in hyper-drive.

"What's the envelope he's handing him?" Eiselmann asked.

O'Connor checked the notes from the interview and the initial search of the car. There was nothing mentioned about any envelope.

They watched Huggins and Kirlie talk. From Kirlie's expression, it didn't look like he was happy and it looked like Huggins was pleading with him. They watched until Huggins got up and threw his food in the trash.

"Wasn't very hungry was he?" Eiselmann said.

"Did you catch that?" O'Connor asked, pointing at the screen. "Back it up slowly, a frame at a time if you can."

The security did as he was asked.

Stunned, Graff took a step back and said, "Kirlie recorded the conversation."

"Are you sure?" Eiselmann asked.

"That's what I think," O'Connor said. "He didn't check for any calls. He didn't check for any texts. He didn't even look at it. He pushed a button on the screen, but hardly even glanced at it."

"We need to look at his phone," Graff said. "Where is it?"

"At the station," O'Connor said reading the report. "Jorgenson brought it with him."

"Paul, call the station and tell them that no one, and I mean no one, fucks with the phone," Graff said.

Eiselmann took out his cell, called dispatch and was transferred three or four times until he got routed to where he needed to go. He reiterated the urgency that no one touches the Kirlie cell phone using Graff's choice of words.

"I want to check something out," O'Connor said. "Can you run it backwards?"

"You're looking for Benevides and the other two guys?" Eiselmann asked.

"Maybe Fuentes," Graff said, nodding at O'Connor's intuition.

The security man ran it backward and both Graff and Eiselmann hunched over the computer, eyes not looking at Kirlie, but scanning beyond and at the perimeter.

"Wait!" O'Connor looked through the notes of the interview with Kirlie's girlfriend and he frowned.

"What?" Graff asked.

O'Connor scratched his head and said, "The girl . . . Hannah Milton said she and Kirlie went to the food court together. When he saw his teacher, he went to go talk to him." He pointed to the screen and said, "They didn't even go the food court together and they aren't sitting at the table together."

"You're right," Graff said. "He's waiting." He looked at the two deputies and asked, "Why?"

They ran the film backward and sure enough, Milton sat down at one table and Kirlie at another. They didn't talk to one another nor did they even look at each other.

"It's a meeting," Graff said. "About what?"

O'Connor stared at the detective and said, "You know the answer."

Graff stared back at him, eyes narrowing.

"Huggins is involved in this."

O'Connor's expression never changed.

"We need to go back to the parking lot and find Huggins. I want to see what happened to him," Eiselmann said.

The security guy began at the point where Kirlie was beaten up and stuffed in a trunk, and ran it backward. They watched Kirlie walking out of the mall.

"Okay, there!" Eiselmann said. "That's Fuentes and Benevides, and Fuentes has a gun." They watched Huggins start to raise his hands, but Benevides punched him in the ribs. They bum-rushed Huggins to the backseat of a dark BMW four door. The backdoor was opened by a heavyset Hispanic wearing a red bandana, who punched Huggins in the stomach and followed Huggins into the backseat.

"Those aren't Wisconsin plates," Graff said.

"Illinois," Eiselmann said. "That's Fuentes' ride."

The three detectives were lost in their own thoughts. O'Connor searched for magic in the notes. Eiselmann stared at his laptop willing it to give him answers. Graff frowned at the wall.

"Okay, we have two missing persons, Kirlie and Huggins, but we need to confirm that Huggins is actually missing," Graff said though he had no doubt about it.

He pulled out his cell, had dispatch run the plates on Huggins' car along with an address and requested that a patrol car run by his house to see if he or his car was there.

"Okay let's go," Graff said.

"Where are we going?" Eiselmann asked.

"We need to interview the girl to see what else she knows, because I think she knows more than she let on. And we need to find Kirlie and Huggins."

CHAPTER SIXTY-SIX

George had one of his feelings.

It had begun when he saw the owl the second time, but it grew stronger and steadily as the day progressed. At the game the feeling he had grown urgent and he found himself watching the crowd as much as he watched the game. Sean and Cat had asked him several times if everything was okay and each time he had nodded all the while watching the game and the crowd. He had visited the concession stand, once for a pack of gum and once for a bottle of water, though he had wanted neither. Rather, he wanted to scan the gym lobby and restroom for anyone who didn't fit.

No one appeared out of the ordinary.

Still . . .

Cat blamed herself and tried speaking with him about her feelings, about wanting to be friends, about her feelings for Kaz. It was hard to do because her cousin Sean was there along with several hundred students and fans. George said that he understood, but Cat wasn't so sure, especially since he had hardly spoken to her before, during or after the game.

To be honest, George wasn't so sure either, though he didn't blame Cat and he didn't blame Brian. While he believed what his grandfather had told him so many years ago and what he, himself, repeated to Brett more recently, he wasn't sure that he had understood it.

After the team had held their postgame meeting and after they had showered and dressed, the twins, Brett and Brian walked out of the locker room to more cheers and congratulations from students and parents who had hung around waiting for them.

"George," Brian said softly. He was nervous though the two boys had counted each other as best friends.

They walked a few steps away from everyone, but the gym offered no real privacy.

"About Caitlyn and me . . . I don't know what happened. I never meant for this to happen. I mean, I like her and all, but I know you like her. It . . . just sort of . . . happened."

George nodded and said without any expression Brian could read, "Sometimes one's head does not catch up to one's heart."

Brian blinked at him. George speaking formally didn't bode well.

"It is okay," George said.

"I really am sorry." Though it was a sincere apology, it came out as a plea.

George smiled and said, "You played well tonight."

Brian exhaled.

"Yeah, I guess."

George turned away to talk to his friends Chris and Troy leaving Brian standing by himself until Cat found him.

Their group ended up at Jimmy's Grotto, kids at one large round table, parents at another a short distance away. Sean, Cat and Danny Limbach joined the twins, George, Brett and Bobby. George sat between Billy and Brett. Brian sat between Brett and Cat.

They rehashed the game, talked about the game coming up, relived various shots and rebounds and steals and assists and through all the laughter, taunts and teasing, they stuffed themselves with pizza and garlic flavored breadsticks.

George didn't feel like eating, but instead, like at the game, studied the other occupants of the restaurant and the parking lot beyond or at least as much as he could see of it.

"You got fucking lucky tonight."

Doug Sweeney stood behind their table and between Brett and Brian. Sweeney's girlfriend and one other friend stood behind him smirking.

"My give-a-damn isn't working," Brett answered.

"I could take any of you one on one and kick your ass."

"Whatever."

From their table, Jeremy and Vicky along with Jeff Limbach and Sean's dad, Dr. Dave Drummond talked and laughed and never saw what was happening at the kids' table.

"If I had played, we would have won big."

"I'm sure of it."

"You're a smart ass, McGovern."

Brett sighed and said, "You know Doug, you're probably right, but I don't care."

"What do you mean you don't care?"

Brett rolled his eyes and said, "Look I don't have the crayons or the time to explain it to you. I just don't care. Don't you have somewhere to go and get drunk?"

Sweeney glared at him and said, "Are you making fun of me, Smart Ass?"

Brett worked hard to keep from laughing and said, "I just wish you were more of a visual learner."

Billy couldn't help it and laughed out loud.

Sweeney glared at him and shoved Brett.

"Hey!" Brian said. "Just leave!"

The parent table overheard the comment and turned in that direction.

Sweeney gave Brian's head a shove and said, "What the fuck are you going to do about it? Everyone thinks you're a fucking hero or something, but you played like shit."

"Yeah, well at least he played and didn't quit," Randy said. "So leave."

Jeremy and Dave Drummond started in their direction.

Sweeney laughed. "It's a free country. I don't have to."

"Yeah, it's a free country, but you can exercise your freedom somewhere else," Cat said.

Sweeney laughed.

"So, you put out for Indian Boy, now you're putting out for Spaz?" He gripped her shoulder and inched his fingers towards her breast. "When's my turn?"

Cat dug her fingers into the back of Sweeney's hand and he jerked it away, swearing. Drops of blood blossomed from two long scratches.

"You bitch!"

George and Brett stood up together.

"Oh what? Seriously? You two? I've been looking forward to this," Sweeney said.

"Doug, you need to leave. Now," Jeremy said. He had moved quickly, but quietly and stood directly behind him.

Sweeney spun around, hands balled into fists, but stopped himself from swinging when he saw who it was.

"Leave now and I won't have you thrown out. Stay and cause any trouble including laying a hand on one of my kids and I'll have you arrested. Enough is enough."

Sweeney took a step back and licked his lips, unsure of what to do or how to respond.

"Leave now and from now on, leave my family alone."

Sweeney regained his swagger and said, "I don't have to listen to you. I'm not in school and you're only a stupid counselor. You don't know shit."

Both George and Brett took a step towards Sweeney, but Jeremy waved them back.

"Maybe, maybe not. In any case, I'm warning you to leave my family alone. Do you understand me?"

Sweeney laughed and said, "Is that a threat?"

"Technically it's only a warning. A threat is an intimation of harm. I didn't hear any intimation of harm, so it was only a warning."

When Sweeney turned around to see who was talking, Sheriff Deputy Brooke Beranger flashed him her badge and a smile that had nothing to do with love or sweetness.

"I think Mr. Evans asked you to leave."

Sweeney glanced at his friends and back at Jeremy. To his friends he said, "Let's go."

He stalked off without looking back and his friends followed him in similar fashion.

After he was gone Jeremy said, "Did Jamie send you?"

Brooke smiled at him and said, "Tom Albrecht and I have been watching you since yesterday." She smiled and added, "Seems like old times," referring to the summer of death and their trip to Arizona.

Jeremy nodded grimly wishing they didn't have to have someone to watch over them. To the boys he said, "Everyone about finished?"

The boys and Caitlyn answered that they were, so Jeremy asked for the check, boxed up what was left and headed back out to the cold.

He walked Vicki, Brett and Bobby to their car, kissed Vicki lightly and did it again.

"What's your schedule like tomorrow?"

Vicki smiled and said, "I have surgery at eight and two."

"Dinner at my house?"

She kissed him and they held each other tightly and she said, "We'd love that."

"It's a date," Jeremy said with a smile helping her into her car, a newer dark brown Toyota 4runner.

Bobby stood in front of him and said, "Butterflies," and Jeremy put his right eye to Bobby's left and they blinked rapidly. They did the same with their other eye and Bobby said, "Eskimo," and they rubbed noses. "Regular," and they kissed and smiled at each other.

"There is nothing very regular about you," Jeremy said to the boy.

"That's what makes me special," Bobby said with a laugh hugging Jeremy before getting into the backseat.

Jeremy turned to Brett and said, "You had an outstanding game tonight, little man."

Brett smiled at the compliment and said, "Thanks."

They hugged each other and kissed each other's cheek.

"Love you, Dad."

"Love you too, Brett."

Brett hopped into the front passenger side and Vicki drove slowly away, waving as she went.

Jeremy walked to his car hunched over from the cold. George waited on the sidewalk scanning the street.

Worried, Jeremy said, "Everything okay?"

George didn't say anything right away, but finally said, "I am not sure. I think so. Maybe."

Jeremy stood next to him, the cold night air and a tingle of fear chasing away any warmth left from the restaurant.

"A feeling or is it more?"

George shook his head in answer and got into the back seat next to Brian and Randy. Billy had called shotgun.

Jeremy got in and as they drove towards Brian's house, he studied the streets carefully.

"Did you know Brooke and Tom were watching us?" Jeremy asked

George.

He nodded and said, "Since after school."

"How do you do that?" Randy asked.

George shrugged.

"It's still okay if I sleep over, right?" Brian asked.

"As long as your parents give you permission," Jeremy answered.

"I tried calling them, but there wasn't any answer."

Jeremy smiled at him through the rearview mirror and said, "We'll stop and see what they say, okay?"

Brian nodded, wondering what kind of reception they'd get when he got home.

CHAPTER SIXTY-SEVEN

He rolled past the house once, turned around at the corner and passed the house again. One light was on in the kitchen, another in one of the other rooms. Light flickered in still a different room and Fuentes decided a TV was on.

After turning around at the end of the block, he made one more pass and parked down the street and waited.

It wasn't long before Manny Benevides ran across the street from between two houses. He held up his chinos with one hand and held his jacket closed with the other. One dog barked and from further down the block, another dog barked in an answer to the first.

Fuentes watched the fat boy run towards the car. Disgusting! Maybe he'd cap his ass along with the Indian boy before he drove back to Chicago.

Benevides jumped into the passenger seat huffing and puffing from the short run.

"Anyone else inside?" Fuentes asked.

"I think so, but I couldn't tell for sure," he answered between gulps of air. "I couldn't see through any of the windows because the curtains were closed. There's a dog. From the pile of shit I saw, I'd say it was big motherfucker."

"If you get any fucking dog shit in my car, I'll cap your ass!"

"I didn't get any dog shit in your ride."

Fuentes sniffed the air to be certain. Satisfied that he didn't smell anything other than the fat boy's cheap cologne, Fuentes stared at the house and tapped his knuckle on his side window as he considered his next move.

"Where's your punk ass little brother?" Fuentes asked as he stared at the house.

Manny shrugged and said, "The faggot is probably at home. He don't come out much."

Fuentes shut his eyes, disgusted at the fat boy's poor grammar.

"Why isn't that asshole with us?"

Manny shrugged, unwilling to tell Fuentes that Angel wanted out of MS-13. Loyalty was one thing, but family was another.

Fuentes shook his head and pounded the steering wheel. "I thought when we picked up that dude and the punk we'd be done. But there's always one more to get rid of."

Manny remained silent. When Fuentes got angry, he was unpredictable and dangerous.

He pounded the steering wheel again and shouted, "*And I want that Indian Bendejo! I'm tired of waiting for him!*"

Manny had a hand on his .9 mm, but he managed a weak smile as he said, "I'm working on it."

CHAPTER SIXTY-EIGHT

She sat on the couch of her living room on the edge of the seat with her knees together and her white fingers laced. Her mother and her father sat stoic on either side of her.

For the better part of an hour, Jamie played bad cop and Paul Eiselmann played worse cop and through it all, Hannah didn't deviate from her story. The only thing she did allow was that the man, Huggins, called Rob every so often and told him stuff. That's what she had said, *'Told him stuff.'* More importantly, she gave them the password for Rob's cell and his mom gave Jamie permission to access it.

Once they got back to the station, it didn't take long before Eiselmann, second to none on the force when it came to tech skills, found the recorded incoming and outgoing calls. The three of them listened to the recordings and following strict chain of custody, Eiselmann made three CDs. Jamie got a judge out of his Barcalounger long enough to listen to some of the recordings from the CD and to sign a warrant to search both Huggins' and Kirlie's houses.

The three men left the judge's house together, but they decided they would split up. Graff and Eiselmann headed over to Kirlie's house to begin the searches, while O'Connor wanted to go off by himself to hunt the location where Fuentes might have taken Huggins and Kirlie.

"Do you have any ideas?" Jamie asked him.

O'Connor frowned and said, "I." He shook his head and said, "Some thoughts."

"Don't do anything stupid. Fuentes is about ten miles past crazy."

O'Connor smiled and said, "Traveled there myself. At times."

"No hero shit, Pat," Eiselmann said. "I mean that. The *Thirteen* don't play games."

O'Connor smiled and said, "I won't." He smiled slyly at his partner and best friend and said, "I don't either."

CHAPTER SIXTY-NINE

The air had changed subtly. Most would not have noticed, but George was a rancher who was taught by his grandfather to notice and read the differences in the wind, the temperature and the feel against his skin. Farmers and ranchers depended on knowing. At least, the good ones did.

It had gotten warmer, the breeze had all but ended and the air felt damp.

George craned his neck to stare up at the sky and sure enough, the first few flakes were drifting down from the heavens. He smiled.

Instead of parking in the driveway, Jeremy parked along the curb in front of the house. Jeremy debated about keeping the vehicle running, but decided that he and Brian wouldn't take that long. Ozone layer and all that.

"Brian and I should only be a minute. If it takes longer or if you get cold, turn the car back on and warm yourselves up." He placed the key fob on the front console and got out shutting the door behind him.

George let Brian out, who quickly caught up to Jeremy, who was standing at the foot of the driveway. Jeremy slid his arm around the boy's shoulders as they walked up to the house.

'You need to go with you father and brother, Shadow. They cannot go in by themselves.'

George blinked and stared from Billy to Randy to see if they had heard it. Both boys were enmeshed with their cells, Randy on Instagram and Billy on Twitter. He hadn't heard that voice in months, but there was only one person who had ever called him Shadow. After all these months, George had in fact thought that his grandfather had abandoned him. At the deepest unspoken level, George thought that his grandfather was disappointed in him.

'Now, Shadow. Go now.'

It wasn't a command, but it was urgent. Gentle, but firm.

Jeremy and Brian had slowed as they reached the backdoor. Brian fumbled in his backpack for his key.

"Randy, call Mother and Brett and Bobby and tell them to come here quickly," George said as he got out of the car.

"George?" Billy said.

Before shutting the door, he bent down and said, "Stay here and lock the doors. Do not let anyone go into the house." When he saw the twins not moving and staring at him in fear he said, "Please." Confident that the twins would do as he had asked, he shut the door and quick-walked to the back stoop.

Just as Brian opened the door, George jogged up to them.

Jeremy cocked his head and squinted at him and said, "I thought you guys were going to wait in the car."

George didn't say anything, but when Brian pushed open the door he held them both back and said, "We need to be careful."

He squeezed past them and stood in the kitchen on a small burnt orange braded rug. He slipped off his boots and held the door open to them.

"Please, take off your shoes and don't touch anything."

"George?" Jeremy asked.

"What's happening?" Brian asked.

George flicked a switch at the side of the door and the kitchen flooded with light. He noticed a slight odor underneath the disinfectant. It was faint, but present nonetheless. And George knew that smell.

The three of them crowded together on the little rug.

"Mom? Dad?" Brian called.

No answer. No echo.

"Maybe they're in bed," he offered though he questioned his own words.

George turned to him and said, "Brian, we're friends. Do you trust me?"

"Yeah, but what's going on?"

"Please stay here with father. I need to go take a look."

"George?" Jeremy said again.

George pulled a chair from the table and said, "Brian, please sit here and wait until I get back."

"George . . ."

George guided him to the chair and sat him in it. He squatted down in front of him, smiled and said, "Stay with father. I'll be right back."

Brian searched George's face, his eyes, and finally, a tear ran down Brian's cheek and he asked, "Mom and dad . . . are they?"

George brushed the tear away with his thumb and hugged him. He pressed his lips softly on Brian's forehead and whispered, "Stay with father."

Jeremy gripped his shoulder before he left and George turned to him and in a quiet voice, said, "Grandfather spoke to me."

CHAPTER SEVENTY

O'Connor drove slowly around Waukesha searching. He started with one broken down and abandoned building and moved on to others, all the while knowing where he would end up. He had even checked out an abandoned house or two, but leaving bodies in houses didn't feel right. That was something he would never have done and the only way he had succeeded and lived as long as he had was because he thought like a criminal.

With each strike out, the thought solidified that perhaps Fuentes and Manny Benevides hadn't strayed too far from their killing ground.

He drove past the YMCA slowly dreading what he might find. His eyes darting from side mirror to rearview mirror and back out the windshield. Streets were pretty empty. Nothing looked out of place or out of the ordinary.

He turned onto another, darker street and it too was empty. Nothing moved. Snow gathered unimpeded in the street, on the parked cars and on sidewalks like a sparkling white blanket. His car making the only tracks.

O'Connor loved freshly fallen snow. He loved the purity of it. In his world it was the only thing that could be classified as pure.

He parked down the street from the building and sat in his car with the engine off.

Across the street sat the crumbling apartment building. Only a few lights were on behind the curtains. The rest were dark.

Out on the street nothing moved. All was still. That didn't bring him any comfort though. He knew what he was going to find. He just didn't know how gruesome it might be. He shook his head considering the irony of the purity and the whiteness of freshly falling snow and the ugliness of what he knew he'd find down in that basement.

He had stalled long enough so at last he opened the door of his car, unfolded his lanky body and shut the door with barely an audible thud. He pulled the .357 mag out of his shoulder holster and held it tightly to his leg, his index finger at first positive position.

O'Connor moved with purpose, his head on a swivel. By the time he reached the familiar doorway, his long hair and his shoulders were covered with big, wet snowflakes.

First thing O'Connor noticed was that the yellow police tape had been torn away as was the sticker warning away any intruders that the building was a crime scene and therefore anyone entering would be trespassing. Fitting, he supposed, that they would disregard a simple warning that would have been effective for most right-thinking individuals. But Fuentes and MS-13 were not right-thinking. No, they were twisted and somewhere around the corner and down the street from right-thinking.

He slipped on a pair of latex surgical gloves and gingerly and carefully tested the door latch on the handle and found it unlocked.

O'Connor took a deep breath, swung his gun up at the ready, opened the door and stepped quickly in and to the side, crouching down and blinking rapidly allowing his eyes to adjust to the darkness.

CHAPTER SEVENTY-ONE

Graff let Eiselmann take the lead in questioning Kirlie's mother. She was plump and plain and worn out with streaks of gray in her hair. She gave off the general air of desperation and of having given up on life a long time ago. Mostly, she seemed to Jamie as being tired. A box of Kleenex sat in her lap. She had one tissue, well-worn and damp, twisted in her hands.

Jamie felt sorry for her. She knew nothing about her son that would give either detective a clue as to what he might have done to get him on the wrong side of MS-13. In fact, it occurred to Graff as he listened to her answers that she had no clue about her son. None. She might have given birth to him. She might have raised him. But she didn't know him. Not his activities or anything that might have interested him beyond sixth grade. She didn't know any of his friends and was surprised that he had a girlfriend, though she had suspected it because when she put away his laundry, she came across an open box of Trojans.

"Can you find my Robbie?" she whispered.

"Ma'am, we're doing our best," Paul reassured her. "Can we take a look at his bedroom?'

She nodded, her face crumpled in pain, dabbing at her eyes with the twisted Kleenex.

Graff thought that Kirlie's bedroom looked like just about every other teenage kid's room. Not that he had been in all that many.

It was messy. The bed was unmade. There were clothes, mostly socks and shirts, distributed in piles on the floor and around the half-filled laundry basket. There was a laptop on his cluttered desk and Eiselmann went to work on it.

Graff stood at the foot of the bed with his hands on his hips and did a slow turn around the room. They already determined that Kirlie was a dealer and because of that, he had to have a stash hidden somewhere. It would be somewhere where his mother wouldn't find it on accident.

The first place he looked was the closet. He didn't bother looking into the pockets of any clothes, but rather ran his hands under and among the sweaters and sweatshirts on the shelf. Nothing.

Next, he got down on his knees and searched the floor, especially the corners. Nothing.

He stood back up and grunted.

Next he searched under the bed, including between the mattresses. Nothing.

With Eiselmann tapping away at the laptop, Jamie went through the drawers, even pulling them out and running his hands along the track. Again, nothing.

"No luck?" Eiselmann asked.

"Nothing."

"Maybe he keeps it in his car."

Graff shook his head. Maybe, not likely.

He left the bedroom and walked across the hall to the bathroom. The medicine cabinet had the normal stuff. Oxy pads. Toothpaste. A container of floss. Deodorant. Nothing much.

Graff checked the back of the toilet and inside the tank. Nothing. He searched inside the linen closet. Towels. Wash cloths. Extra soap, shampoo, and toilet paper. He ran his hands along the inside of the shelves. Nothing.

He considered the top of the medicine cabinet. He stood six one, six two, so he didn't have any trouble reaching the top. He also checked the back of it, but it was secured to the wall with no room to stash anything there.

Graff was about to leave the bathroom but stopped and considered the top of the linen cabinet. It was high enough that he couldn't reach it without standing on the edge of the bathtub.

He stood on the tub and placed one hand on the wall for balance. With the other, he ran his hand on top of the cabinet.

Bingo.

"Paul, can you come in here?"

Reluctantly, Eiselmann pushed away from the desk and walked across the hall.

"I need you to record this and list it as evidence."

Eiselmann pulled out his cell and began filming and recorded a narrative to go along with it describing the location, date and time and each baggie. Rough cut marijuana. Rolled joints. White powder. Pills. Several bundles. Five baggies in all.

"What do we tell his mom?" Eiselmann asked.

"The truth." Graff said stepping off the tub and onto the linoleum floor. "Most of it anyway."

CHAPTER SEVENTY-TWO

It was difficult, but O'Connor managed to move down the steps crouched and off to the side knowing that if anyone was waiting, they'd be more inclined to look straight ahead. Being off to the side would give him an advantage, even if it was only momentary. In a gun battle moments mattered.

He reached the second to last step and listened for any sound. There was nothing that would indicate anyone waiting for him, but he couldn't take any chance. He glanced back over his shoulder up the stairs. Nothing. No one cutting off his retreat. He took a deep breath, let it out slowly and still crouched, crab-walked the last step and fully into the basement.

He took in the bodies and gasped.

O'Connor knew he had to clear the basement, but he had trouble taking his eyes off of the two nude victims duct taped to their chairs facing each other. He would glance to the corners, but his eyes came right back to them.

There was no one in the basement but the three of them and he was the only one alive.

Each had toes and fingers laying haphazardly on the cement floor in puddles of blood. Each had their genitalia cut off, nothing left but bloody holes.

O'Connor had seen a lot in his life, but as much of the veteran and professional as he was, he turned away, bent over, put the back of his hand to his mouth and dry heaved.

When he was certain he wasn't going to lose his lunch or dinner or whatever the hell it was he had eaten, he straightened back up, but kept his back to the bodies. He shook his head wondering when he had last eaten. It wasn't unusual for him to miss meals or miss sleep, but more and more it had begun to wear on him.

"Fuck," he whispered to no one, echoing softly in the emptiness. He wiped his mouth with the back of his hand and ran his hands over his face.

He pulled out his cell, speed-dialed Graff and said, "I found Huggins and Kirlie."

CHAPTER SEVENTY-THREE

George smiled at Brian, nodded at Jeremy and walked quietly out of the kitchen and down the hallway, careful to walk to the side and not down the center where one would normally walk so as not to disturb any evidence.

George had been in Brian's house many times in the past year and had even spent the night on occasion. So while he knew the house and walked it from memory, his motivation on this night was different.

Just out of sight from the kitchen, George squatted down and like any of the traditional *Dine'*, he asked any *chindi* for forgiveness and for permission to walk the house for the purpose of trying to find out what had happened. It wasn't that the Navajo people were afraid of ghosts. It was their long tradition passed down from one generation to another that if a person died violently or even if the person died accidentally or from natural causes, the spirit might not leave but rather seek justice of its own. And rarely did the Navajo speak the name of the deceased. George, however, never held this particular tradition.

At the start of the hallway, George flicked on a light. He took two more steps and saw dark spots on the carpet. He knew what they were before he bent down to look closely at them. Careful not to touch, he got down on one knee to examine them and with his cell took a picture of whatever he saw.

George stood back up and sighed. He decided to follow them and the further he went, the larger they got. He stopped every so often to snap a picture. They ended in front of a dark room George knew to be Brian's father's home office.

He took a tentative step in and turned on the light. There was no mistaking the blood on the computer monitor, but it wasn't just blood. George had seen the effects of a high caliber gunshot before. Several came from his own hand.

He took pictures from multiple angles and sent them via text messages. He followed that up with hitting speed dial.

"Graff!"

"Detective Graff, this is George Tokay."

Impatient because he and Eiselmann were speeding over to the abandoned building after receiving O'Connor's call.

"Yes, George, what is it?"

"You need to come to Brian Kazmarick's house. I think there has been a murder. I sent you pictures of what I found."

Graff took the cell away from his ear and stared at it. Eiselmann, who was driving at racecar speed in spite of the snowy streets, did a double-take.

"What did you say?"

"I think there has been a murder. I sent you pictures. Please check your messages."

"Hold on a minute," Graff said as he checked his messages. He saw the pictures and paled. He normally didn't get shook up, but he was this time. He said, "Who's been murdered?"

"I am not certain. There is blood in the hallway and in the office. Blood and tissue on the computer keyboard and monitor."

Graff felt sick to his stomach. He turned to Eiselmann and said, "Turn around. Now."

"What the hell! Why?"

"George, you can't touch anything. Who's with you?"

"Father and Brian. My brothers are waiting in the car. Mother, Brett and Bobby are on their way over."

Eiselmann, who only heard one side of the conversation said, "What's going on? Is Pat okay?"

Graff waved him off.

"George, listen to me. I want that house sealed. No one touches anything. No one goes into that house."

"What about Father and Brian?"

Graff took the phone away from his mouth, held it against his jacket and shouted, "Fuck! Goddammit!"

He put the phone to his ear again and said, "Where are Jeremy and Brian right now?"

"In the kitchen. I have already told them not to touch anything. Brian is sitting at the table and Father is standing near Brian. There are envelopes on the kitchen table. They are addressed, but without stamps."

Graff breathed a sigh of relief and said, "Go to the kitchen and wait for us. Don't touch the envelopes. We're about fifteen minutes away. I'm calling dispatch to have a squad car sent to you."

"Yes, Sir."

"Wait! Brooke Beranger or Tom Albrecht should already on site or at least nearby. Why didn't you find them?"

George hesitated. He had actually thought of letting Brooke know, but decided not to blow her cover in case they were being watched. He told this to Jamie.

Graff nodded and said, "Good thinking, George. We'll be there but a squad should be there sooner."

"Yes, Sir." George smiled to himself as Graff ended the call.

Before he walked back to the kitchen, he decided to follow the blood trail. The further he went, the more blood there was. He found himself standing in front of Brian's brother's room. He wanted to open it, but didn't want to disturb any prints on the doorknob.

George wanted to make absolutely certain, though there was no doubt in his mind at all. He continued on down the hallway and pushed open Brian's door, saw the unmade bed, a shirt and a pair of jeans on the end of the bed. His room was otherwise clean and tidy. He tiptoed to the remaining door and quietly, carefully, opened it to a darkened master bedroom. It was empty, just as he thought it would be. Reluctantly, he walked back to the kitchen.

Brian sat with his chin on his chest and his hands in his lap. Jeremy stood behind Brian with both hands on his shoulders. George squatted down in front of Brian and took his hands in his.

"My mom and dad . . ."

Brian never finished the question. Knowing what he was going to ask, George gently squeezed Brian's hands in answer.

CHAPTER SEVENTY-FOUR

O'Connor studied the boy and the man, or at least what was left of them. The scene mirrored how they had found Terzinski. Fingers, toes, dick and balls cut off and throats slashed. O'Connor guessed their throats were slashed after everything else was cut off since the ME hadn't shown up yet. He shook his head in disgust.

He began at the center of the room, standing between the two seated bodies and spiraled out looking for anything on the floor that could be used as evidence. The dead boy and the dead man served as a silent audience as he worked.

O'Connor wasn't sure if he if he imagined their screams or actually heard them. He wasn't sure if he heard their chairs rattling as fingers or toes hit the ground. He winced and hunched over at the thought of their male organs being sliced off.

Even though it was an impossibility, O'Connor found himself glancing over his shoulder to be certain that neither had loosened the tape securing their arms and legs to the chairs they sat on. Their eyes were half-hooded. Their heads were tilted to the side. There was anguish, pain and terror evident on their faces. Blood everywhere.

O'Connor shivered and it wasn't from the cold.

He found nothing of any importance on the floor or on the walls. He found nothing that could be bagged or tagged. Except, of course, for assorted fingers, toes, a penis or two and four balls nearly falling out of their sacks.

He turned to the wall and dry-heaved once more as his cell buzzed.

He breathed in slowly and deeply to calm himself before he answered, "O'Connor."

"Pat, this is Paul." O'Connor knew who it was from the caller ID. "I dropped Graff off at the Kazmarick home. We're guessing it's a murder-suicide."

"Is Brian okay?"

"I don't know. I don't have any details. The ME is coming your way along with a squad or two. Graff wants us to run the scene."

"Who's running the Kazmarick house?"

"Graff, but I think Mr. Clean is on the way over."

Mr. Clean was Captain Jack O'Brien. Built like a brick shithouse and bald, he scared people when he smiled because his smile looked more like a sneer. And no one had ever called him Mr. Clean to his face and lived to brag about it.

"How is Brian?" O'Connor asked.

Eiselmann didn't know how to answer that. Those boys, all of them, had been through so much. Stuff that kids never should have lived through or witnessed.

"Messed up. Wouldn't you be?"

Yeah, O'Connor thought. He be messed up. But there was a toughness in Brian that not many people saw. Maybe he wasn't as tough as Brett or George. But maybe he was, at least in his own way.

O'Connor and Graff had taken Brian, George and Brett hunting in the fall and fishing in the spring and summer. Even though George was born shooting a rifle, Brian matched him shot for shot. Brett was better with handguns than either George or Brian, but all three could shoot and shoot well. The three of them liked fishing, but Brian was good at it. Probably better than Graff who lived for a lake, a rod and reel and a cooler of beer.

"Pat, you there?"

"I'll see you when you get here."

O'Connor ended the call, turned around and stared at the dead boy and the dead man. It was true that those two were responsible for dead kids. One of them, he guessed the boy, had murdered Kevin Longwood. But neither deserved to die this way.

O'Connor discovered that he was angry. Mostly, he was frustrated that the good guys were always one step behind Fuentes and that pissed him off.

A finger of fear ran up his spine as he realized that there was at least one more person on Fuentes' list.

George.

CHAPTER SEVENTY-FIVE

George spoke barely above a whisper as he walked O'Brien and Jamie through the house pointing at the spots on the floor and at the blood and tissue on the computer monitor and keyboard. He pointed at the computer chair and the marks left in the carpet in the hallway leading to Brad's room.

"Used the chair to move his body to Brad's room," O'Brien said.

They stood in front of Brad's door and Graff hesitated. The ME and his assistant had been through the house. The crime scene techs had dusted for prints, though there wasn't any doubt that it was a murder-suicide. While Ike drove to the building where O'Connor and Eiselmann were, his assistant waited patiently to bag and tag the bodies and transport them back to the basement of the hospital where the ME's office and examining rooms were.

"George, you've been a big help, but I don't think you should come in here," Jamie said.

George nodded and walked back to the kitchen to wait with Brian and Jeremy.

The doorknob had already been checked for prints, but Jamie snapped on a pair of latex gloves and opened the door slowly and flicked on the light.

On the bed side by side were Nancy and David Kazmarick. Jamie wasn't sure how David's head had remained on his shoulders. The hole that blew out of his neck and upper chest was huge. That said, there wasn't much left of Nancy's head. The ME and his assistant assumed it was her. There was no way anyone would ask Brian to identify her.

Ike told them, and his assistant agreed with him, that she must have used the rifle to shoot her husband in the back, put him on the bed, laid down next to him and shot herself. End of story. Neither Graff nor O'Brien couldn't find any fault with that theory.

Graff turned to the assistant ME and said, "I know you want to get the bodies out of here, but I need to ask Brian a couple of questions first."

The assistant nodded with a sigh.

Graff pulled up a chair and sat down in front of Brian. He leaned over with his elbows on his knees. Brian barely glanced at him. He had been weeping on and off, wiping his nose and eyes with tissue Jeremy found on the counter near the sink. O'Brien stood on the other side of the kitchen table, next to George.

"Kaz, how are you doing?"

Brian shrugged, but didn't make eye contact. Jeremy stood behind the boy.

"I think we can talk all about this in the morning, but I do want to ask a couple of questions before you leave, okay?"

Brian nodded, still not making eye contact.

"When you last saw your parents, where were you and what were you doing?"

Brian dried his eyes on a tissue and said, "Eating breakfast. Right here. I sat where George is standing. Dad sat there," pointing to the head of the table to his right. "Mom sat there," pointing to the seat to his left.

"Did you always eat breakfast together?"

Brian shrugged and said, "Sometimes. Not really."

"Did they act any differently this morning or last night?"

Brian didn't want to go into all of it, at least, not right away. His eyes flicked up at Jamie, and back to his hands.

"Sort of."

Jamie glanced up at Jeremy who nodded at him.

"Okay, one last question and we're done for now, okay?"

Brian nodded.

"This isn't an easy one, Kaz, and I'm sorry I have to ask it." Jamie paused knowing that there wasn't a delicate way to ask it. "Your mom used a rifle. Where would she have gotten it and whose would it have been?"

Brian looked squarely at Jamie and said, "From the gun cabinet in the basement and it's probably Brad's."

"Why do you think it's Brad's rifle?"

Brian sighed and said, "They're in Brad's room, right? Mom always liked Brad better than . . ." he didn't finish and he didn't have to.

"Could you show me where the gun cabinet is?"

Brian got up and without waiting for Jamie, headed to the door to the basement, opened it and started down the stairs. Jamie had to hustle to keep up. George decided to follow them, but O'Brien and Jeremy stayed upstairs.

They reached the basement and Brian said, "The cabinet is open. It shouldn't be. Dad always told us to keep it locked." He pointed to the drawer there the ammunition was kept. "The drawer is open and so is the box of bullets. Dad would have been really pissed if we left it like this."

Jamie nodded and said, "So just to be sure, whose rifle is missing?"

Brian opened the cabinet wider and said, "Brad's." He pointed to the one on the left and said, "That's Dad's. This is mine. Brad kept his in the middle."

"Do you mind if I look at yours?"

Brian shrugged.

Jamie picked up the Remington 30.06, looked it over and sighted it against a wall away from Brian and George.

"You're sure this is yours?"

Brian nodded and held out his hands for it. Jamie gave it to him after checking to see if it was loaded. Brian saw what he did and shook his head, his face registering anger.

"We never keep them loaded. Not in the house. And, I always keep the safety on. See?"

He took it from Jamie, showed him that the safety was indeed on, placed it back in the cabinet and shut the door. He closed the carton of shells, placed them back in the drawer and shut it.

Without asking or waiting for the others, he pushed past George and went back upstairs to the kitchen. He went to the cupboard next to the sink, opened it and reached for a glass and went to the refrigerator and used the water dispenser to fill it. He drank half in one chug and finished with a second. He rinsed out the glass and placed it in the sink because the dishwasher was full of clean dishes.

"Bri, are you okay?" Jeremy asked.

He whirled around and said, "Oh, sure! Everything's just great! I heard what the cops said! My mom shot my dad and she shot herself. I'm alone and I have no place to go. So yeah, everything is just great!"

He kicked a chair against the table, pounded the counter with both hands and burst into tears.

Jeremy moved quickly to hug him and at first, Brian fought him. Jeremy hung on and wouldn't let go and slowly, Brian melted in Jeremy's arms, sobbing against his chest.

Jeremy let him cry a little longer. He said, "Let's go get some clothes, pack up a bag and head home."

He felt Brian nod his head and Jeremy gently held Brian's face.

"You're going to come home with us. You have a home as long as you want it. And that's a promise." He kissed Brian's forehead and said, "Okay?"

Brian looked up at him through teary eyes searching Jeremy's face for any falsehood, any doubt, but didn't see any. He finally nodded.

"Let's go pack up some things, okay?"

Brian nodded and led him out of the kitchen and down the hall.

George stayed rooted to the kitchen floor. He experienced a strong sense of Déjà Vu in that it was only a year or so earlier when Jeremy had opened up his home to him. George had felt much like Brian did. Alone. Lonely. Scared. A lot of questions that might never be completely answered, at least to his satisfaction.

He moved to the sink and from the same cupboard Brian had used, found another glass and got himself a drink of water, though he sipped it slowly instead of chugging it like Brian had.

Brett, Bobby, Randy and Billy had long since left for home with Vicki. Brett had texted that they would be staying there all together for the next few days, maybe longer, and that he'd wait up for them. He said Billy was in pretty bad shape because it reminded him of coming home after school and finding his dad lying on the hallway floor. Bobby wasn't doing too well either, because the scene at Brian's reminded him of the night his uncle had come to kill them.

Jamie stood in the living room just off the kitchen and was on the phone with O'Connor and Eiselmann. He had used the speaker so O'Brien and a policeman whom George had never met could listen in.

"Does Ike have a time of death?"

George recognized O'Connor's voice. "Not yet. It was recent though. Blood wasn't quite dry."

"Any similarities to the other one, to Terzinski?" Jamie asked.

"Everything was similar. I'm not sure why, though."

George walked quietly into the living room. When he was noticed, the patrol cop said, "You shouldn't be here, son."

Jamie took his eyes away from the phone and caught George's eye.

"Wait, Pat. George, what's wrong?"

George stared at Jamie and said, "Describe it to me, please."

"You shouldn't be here," the patrol cop repeated. He turned to Mr. Clean and said, "He's a kid. He shouldn't be here."

O'Brien squinted at George and said, "Do you know something?"

George repeated, "Describe the scene to me, please."

Jamie nodded and said, "Pat, George is here. I want you and Paul to describe what you see in that basement. No names, please. Just the description."

"Okay," O'Connor said tentatively. "Both the boy and the man are nude. They're taped to their chairs."

"With duct tape?" George asked.

"Yes, duct tape."

"Tape over their mouths?"

"Yes."

"It's Fuentes, isn't it?"

It was Jamie who spoke. "Yes, we think it was Fuentes."

George nodded.

"Keep going, Pat."

"Gees, Jamie. Really?" Paul asked.

"Yes, describe what you see."

"Shit, okay," Eiselmann answered. "The boy and the man had toes and fingers cut off."

George waved a hand and asked, "The same number? How many on the boy and how many on the man?"

He heard them moving around the room and said, "The boy had two fingers cut off. The pinky and ring finger."

"So does the man," George heard O'Connor say.

"They both had two toes cut off. The little one and the one next to it."

George waved again and placed a hand to his forehead.

"Wait, Pat," Jamie said.

With a vacant stare George asked, "Which hand on the boy?"

"The boy's right hand," O'Connor said.

"The man's left hand," Eiselmann said.

"It was the boy's right foot and the man's left foot," George said.

"Yes, that's correct," Eiselmann said.

George stared at Jamie and said, "The boy and man were facing each other like in a mirror."

"Yes, they are facing each other about three or four steps away from each other," Eiselmann said.

"There is a table between them, but off to the side," George said.

"How the fuck . . . yes, there's a table between them. On the boy's right and the man's left. How did you know?"

"Because that's where Fuentes kept his knife and whatever he used to cut off their fingers and toes."

"Why wouldn't he have just kept his knife on him?" Eiselmann asked.

"By having it out in the open, it would have scared them. He would want them scared."

He heard O'Connor say, "Hey," and he heard what sounded like snapping fingers. "Dust this table for prints. Check for any blood."

"What else?" George asked.

"They had their . . . male parts cut off," Eiselmann said.

George stared at Jamie.

"How did they die?" George asked.

"Their throats were cut. Ceratoid artery," Eiselmann answered.

George nodded.

"We think he . . . Fuentes, just got off on torturing them. Just to prove a point."

George shook his head and said, "No, he was seeking information."

"What? How do you know?" O'Brien asked.

"Did the man and the boy know each other?" George asked.

There was silence and no one spoke. Jamie was trying to decide just how much he wanted to share and O'Connor and Eiselmann weren't going to say anything without permission.

Finally Jamie said, "George, this is confidential. We don't want this out there."

The patrol cop said, "He's. Just. A. *Kid!*"

O'Brien's expression said nothing.

Jamie said, "George, do you understand me? This is confidential."

George nodded and said, "Yes, Sir."

"The man is a teacher at North. The boy is a student at North. We think they knew each other, yes."

George nodded and said, "Fuentes was seeking information. He was interrogating them."

Jamie opened and closed his mouth.

O'Brien, who had remained quiet, but interested said, "Son, explain that."

George said, "This is about the drugs, right? The kids who are overdosing?"

Jamie nodded and said, "We think so."

"The man would know more than the boy, but he is a teacher. He would not know much about drugs. The boy would know less than the man, but he is a dealer. That is what he knows."

"So, what are you saying?" O'Connor said.

"Fuentes would torture the man to find out who gave him the drugs. He would already know the boy sold them. Fuentes would want to know who is in charge."

"Why wouldn't Hug . . . the man be in charge?" O'Brien asked.

"Mister Huggins is the man?" George asked.

"George, this is confidential. We've already told you more than you should know," Jamie said though he recognized that George actually told them more than they knew.

"Mister Huggins would not know about drugs, Detective Jamie. He teaches business, not science. What kind of drugs?"

"Pat, tell George," Jamie said.

"Heroin with Fentanyl mixed with it."

George shook his head and said, "Mister Huggins would not know about that. I was born and raised on a ranch. Sometimes fentanyl was given to our horses when they needed it. Uncle Jeff calls a veterinarian for our horses at home. It is a dangerous drug and only veterinarians use it. But not all veterinarians. Only veterinarians who work with large animals like horses or cows. A veterinarian who works on dogs or cats would not use something like that."

No one spoke. Jeremy and Brian had come out with two suitcases and two duffle bags, along with Brian's backpack. They set them down in the kitchen and waited, listening to the conversation.

"Fuentes would seek information from the man, from Mister Huggins. When he got all he could, he killed Mr. Huggins and got whatever information he could from the boy."

"Wait, what?" Eiselmann said.

"Why the man, Huggins, and then the boy? Why not the other way around?" O'Connor asked.

George sighed and said, "Because if Fuentes worked on the boy first and killed him, Mister Huggins would know he was going to be killed anyway. He might not tell Fuentes anything. So Fuentes had to start on Mister Huggins and get all the information he could. The boy would not know as much as Mister Huggins anyway, so it would not matter if the boy saw Mister Huggins get killed."

Again, silence. Each of the cops processed what George had said so succinctly.

"Jesus!" Eiselmann said. "If this is true . . . if what George said is accurate, there is someone else involved who provided Huggins and Kirlie with not only the heroin, but with the fentanyl." He knew he slipped using Kirlie by name and hoped that George didn't catch it.

"Or if not the heroin, at least the fentanyl," Jamie said.

"George, you're suggesting that it would be a large animal veterinarian who would have access to this drug." O'Brien stated it as if to clarify it for himself and the others. "It's possible that whoever it was could get it off the internet."

"Yes, Sir, I suppose that could be right."

"So let's assume that Huggins gave Fuentes the name of the person who is in charge," O'Connor said.

"And I think we need to assume the name of the person who provided the fentanyl," Jamie said, "if that's not the same person."

"And he's already hunting," Eiselmann said.

"Fuck!" Jamie said what the other cops were thinking.

"It's not over," O'Connor said. "He's just getting started."

CHAPTER SEVENTY-SIX

The ride from Brian's house to the Evan's house was silent and uncomfortable. George stared out his side window and Brian stared out his. Jeremy didn't attempt any conversation because there wasn't anything to say and even if he said anything, he was certain it wouldn't have been heard. The only positive was that Brian seemed all cried out. For now.

Jeremy allowed Jamie and Jack O'Brien to read the contents of his envelope. It was written in layman's legalese like any well-meaning parent might have done. But essentially, the three of them knew what was in the envelope before it was opened. Brian had refused to open his and Jeremy cautioned him to keep it safe because there was money in it.

When they arrived home, the boys were seated around the kitchen table pretending to do homework or fiddling with their cell phones. Vicki sipped a hot mug of coffee as she leaned against the counter watching them, Billy in particular. The boys stood as Brian and Jeremy pushed through the doorway carrying suitcases and the backpack. George was the last to enter carrying both duffels.

Brett and Randy rushed over to take the suitcase and backpack from Brian, but they weren't sure where to take them.

"Guys, why don't you take them upstairs." It sounded like a question, but it was a statement. Jeremy turned to Brian and asked, "Did you want to sleep in your normal room tonight?"

Brian slipped out of his shoes and kicked them to the rug in front of the door and his face registered disgust as he stepped into a bit of melted snow.

Sitting in the kitchen while the police crawled all over the house, *his* house, but especially in the basement after Detective Graff checked the rifles in the gun cabinet, he had made a decision. He rehearsed what he felt he needed to say on the ride from his house to . . . here.

He mustered up what courage he had, angrily brushed a couple of tears off his face and said, "I'm not a charity case. I don't want to be called Kaz anymore. I don't want to talk about it or anything. I'm going to bed and I want to be left alone."

He grabbed the two duffels from George and walked between Randy and Brett and out of the kitchen. It was either step aside or get run over, so Brett and Randy hopped out of his path.

After he had left, no one moved. All eyes ended up on Jeremy, then on Vicki and finally among each other.

"Billy, what's wrong?" Bobby asked.

Billy shook his head, dried his eyes on the front of his shirt, packed up his math homework, got up and left the room without answering.

"Did I say something wrong?" Bobby asked looking from Jeremy to Vicki.

Randy came to his rescue by saying, "He freaked when the cop cars and the ambulance showed up at Brian's house. It reminded him of the day he found his dad."

"Sorry," Bobby said.

"You didn't do anything wrong, little man," Jeremy said gently. "Guys, it's late. Everyone is tired."

Vicki walked over to Bobby and slipped her arms around him and kissed the top of his head.

"Do we say anything to him?" Brett asked.

Jeremy shook his head and said, "Give him space. Brian will mull it over and he'll seek out one or two of us to talk to. Don't push him. Let him know you're open to him. In time, he'll be willing to talk." He thought it over and said, "Probably the same with Billy. He'll be a little more reticent to talk because he likes to keep things in, so give him a little space too."

CHAPTER SEVENTY-SEVEN

His door was shut tight, but unlocked. That was the way he had always slept. Always. He checked the clock one more time.

1:12 a.m.

Each of them had come in to say goodnight. Brett and George came in together, neither speaking much and after a hug from both, they left. Randy came in and counseled and comforted, while Billy stood in the doorway with his head down, scratching his side and his belly. Brian felt awful for him, wanted to say something to him, but didn't because he didn't know what to say.

Bobby came in and stayed the longest. He sat on the end of the bed and talked about the game, his own team at Butler Middle School, classes, teachers and homework. Basically everything except Brian's parents and what had happened. Brian listened and nodded, but didn't say much. He had the feeling that Bobby was stalling because he didn't want to sleep in a room by himself. Finally he left and shut the door behind him.

It wasn't that Brian didn't want Bobby to sleep with him. On any other night, it would have been fine. Not this night, however. At least he didn't think so at the time.

After the boys took their turns, Jeremy and Vicki knocked on the door and asked if they could come in. Vicki sat on the edge of the bed and Jeremy stood behind her. They talked and Brian listened without comment. A head nod here, a head nod there. A tear or two, maybe more. A hug and a kiss on his forehead from Vicki. A hug and a kiss on the side of his head and his cheek from Jeremy. He finger-combed his hair, something he had done to him a million times. It was soothing, something Brian had watched Jeremy do to all of the guys. He had wanted Jeremy to hold him, maybe until he fell asleep, but he didn't want to sound like a baby, so he didn't ask.

They had left and he was alone. And he didn't know if he wanted to be alone after all.

His cell had blown up.

It started out about the game and the win and how he had played and how he had made the winning shot. Then the texts changed. He read each, but didn't bother to answer them.

Texts from Sean, from Cat, from Mikey and Stephen and Big Gav. There were texts from his travel soccer coach and a couple of guys on the team, Mario Denali and Cem Girici, both eighth graders at Butler. There were calls from Coach Harrison and some of the guys on the team and a call from Jamie Graff. There were texts from Sean's parents, Dr. Drummond and his wife, and from Ellie Hemauer, who was Gavin's mom, offering him a place to live.

He received calls from his Uncle Bart and Aunt Sue, and from his Uncle Alex and Aunt Hannah with the same offer. Jeremy had told him while they had packed up clothes that he and Vicki would call to let them know. He didn't answer his relatives directly. He didn't want to be anyone's charity case.

His aunts and uncles would be arriving sometime late morning and he was sure that they would repeat their offers. He was nervous about them meeting Jeremy and Vicki. They could be stubborn. They were family and Jeremy and Vicki weren't. At least to them they weren't. But Brian felt the most at home here and there was no doubt in his mind that he loved them.

Brian checked the clock again.

1:57 a.m.

He wasn't tired and too much ran through his mind on a never ending loop. He tried turning it off, but couldn't. The button in his head was stuck on play.

He didn't hear anyone, suspecting that everyone was asleep. The only thing he heard was the furnace that would kick in and off or the gust of wind and snow that would blow against his window. All else was still.

Jasper lay on the rug next to his bed and sensing Brian was awake, he would stand up and rest his chin on the bed. Brian would reward him with a scratch behind the ear. He'd lay back down, only to get up so Brian would scratch him again.

Like he had most every time he slept over, he chose the bedroom next to George. Billy had shared that room with George, but on this night, he slept in

Randy's room. That meant that Brett would be with George and that Bobby would be in the room across the hall by himself. That made Brian feel guilty because he knew Bobby and Brett didn't like sleeping by themselves.

He had toyed with the idea of going into Brett's and George's room, not so much to talk, but just to be with them. Anyone. Even though he had professed that he had wanted to be left alone, he really didn't. At the same time, he did. It was confusing.

Brian lay in bed with the covers pulled up under his chin with a million emotions running through his head and heart. He was angry. He was sad. He was confused. He wept until his sheet was damp and then he'd begin again.

He wanted to know why. He wanted to know why his parents didn't like him as much as they did Brad. He wanted to know why he wasn't good enough for them. That was mostly it. He wanted to know what he had done to them and more importantly, what he could have done for them. He felt like he had failed them.

Deep down, he knew some of the answers to all of the whys that ran around in his heart.

It was because of Brad and Brad's death. His murder. He loved Brad and in fact, he missed Brad more than anyone.

But why did his mom and dad . . . why would his mom and dad . . .?

He would never know. Not ever. And that was the most frustrating thing about it. Any answer he had hoped to receive died with his parents.

The door opened a crack and an eye peeked in. It opened a bit wider. Jasper stood and his tail wagged a hundred miles an hour.

"Bri, can I come in . . . please?"

"Yeah, sure."

"You don't mind?"

"Come in."

Bobby, dressed only in boxers, tiptoed into the room carrying his cell, two heavy blankets and his pillow. He set them on the floor near the closet and sat on the bed. He licked his lips and had trouble making eye contact with him.

Whispering so quietly that Brian had to raise his head off the pillow in order to hear him clearly, Bobby said, "I know you want to be left alone, but I was wondering if I could sleep on the floor over there by the closet. Ever since my uncle . . . did stuff, I don't like to be by myself. I can't."

"You can sleep with me."

"I'm not a baby."

"I know you're not."

"I can sleep on the floor. Honest."

Brian shook his head and whispered, "No, sleep with me." He added, "Please."

Bobby hesitated and said, "You sure?"

Brian nodded.

Bobby tiptoed to the other side of the bed and crawled in, but stayed on the far edge away from Brian.

"Why are you way over there?"

"I was giving you space."

"Sleep like you always do. Sleep normal."

Bobby slid closer, but stayed more to the middle.

Annoyed, Brian whispered, "Sleep normal."

"Well, if I sleep normal, I'll be naked, because that's how I sleep sometimes," Bobby said with a smile.

Brett did the same from time to time and Brian didn't mind.

"Well, not tonight, but sleep like you always do."

"I have a boner. I can't help it. I always get one at night."

Exasperated, Brian said, "I've slept with you before. And with Brett. And with Billy and George."

So Bobby rolled over and up against Brian with an arm across Brian's chest, his thumb brushing Brian's cheek.

"Your feet are cold. So are your hands."

Bobby smiled and said, "They'll warm up."

"I kinda have one, too. A boner, I mean."

"Seriously?" Bobby asked skeptically. He slipped a hand inside Brian's shorts and gripped him. "It's kinda hard."

"You're hands are cold and it's getting harder the longer you're holding it."

"Oh, yeah, sorry. God! Sometimes I'm so stupid," he said as he pulled his hand out of Brian's shorts.

"It's no big deal.

Embarrassed, Bobby said nothing.

"It's okay. Really."

Bobby replaced his arm across Brian's chest and ran his thumb gently across Brian's cheek.

"I saw you kissing Cat."

Brian shrugged.

"You like her?"

Brian nestled his head closer to Bobby's and said, "Yeah, I do. I feel bad for George because he likes her."

"George is okay with it."

"How do you know?"

Bobby gently gave Brian an Eskimo kiss and said, "Because I talked with him. So did Brett."

"What did he say?"

"That he likes her, but she likes you. He's good with that."

"Really?"

"Promise."

They lay content with their feet and arms tangled. The furnace kicked in and out.

"My aunt and uncle want me to live with them. Both of them do. So does Sean and Gavin."

Bobby gave Brian a kiss on the cheek and said, "I can maybe see living with Sean or Big Gav. You guys are friends and I guess that wouldn't be so bad. We'd be close and we'd see you. But you can't live with your aunts and uncles. They live too far away and we'd never see you."

"I know."

"You belong here. With us."

Brian turned his head so he could look Bobby in the eye.

"You do," Bobby continued. "Seriously, where are you the happiest? With Sean? With Gav? With us?"

Brian shrugged.

"Do you even think you'd be happy with them . . . I mean, your aunts and uncles?"

Brian made a face.

"See, so you've already ruled them out which means you're not totally retarded or anything."

Brian smiled, his first smile since the game.

"Which leaves Sean, Gav or us."

Brian shrugged.

Bobby placed the palm of his hand on Brian's forehead and said, "Demon of stupidity, come out!" as he shoved Brian's head into his pillow. "I said, demon of stupidity, come out!" and he shoved Brian's head into his pillow again.

"Will you stop?" Brian said with a laugh.

"Well?"

Brian slipped his arm around Bobby's shoulders, hugged him and held him close.

"I know it's hard, Bri."

A few new tears sprung from Brian's eyes. "I don't want to be a charity case and I'm scared."

"We're family. It's not charity if we're family. And you don't have to be scared. You have Brett and me. You have George and Billy and Randy. You have mom and dad."

Brian said nothing.

"You know the movie, *Rudolf, The Red-Nosed Reindeer*?"

Brian nodded. He and Brad and his parents used to watch all the Christmas movies together. Every year.

"Remember the part about the island of misfit toys?"

Brian nodded.

"That pretty much describes us. I mean . . . you have Brett and me. Our parents are divorced and our pervert dickhead uncle did shit to us. You have Randy, whose parents . . . before Jeremy, I mean, beat the shit out of him for no reason, and then he runs away and gets picked up by two pervert assholes who rape the shit out of him. You have Billy, who found his dad in the hallway dead from a heart attack. You have George, who had his whole family murdered and his house burnt to the ground."

Brian didn't respond.

"But the thing is, when we're all together with dad and mom, we aren't misfits any more. None of us are. We have each other."

Brian nodded.

"I don't know how this is going to sound, but I'm going to say two things to you."

Brian turned his head towards him and Bobby took a deep breath and said, "Bri, you haven't been happy ever since Brad died. The first day Brett and I met you, you were sad."

"Brad died the night before," Brian explained.

"I know, but listen. You're parents haven't been happy since Brad died. I didn't know them all that well, but they weren't happy. Now you have a chance to be happy again. I know it's going to take some time, but we can help. We're family and that's what a family does."

Brian nodded.

"The second thing I want to say is, I'm not weird or anything, but I love you. I know mom and dad love you. I know the guys love you, but I love you and I want you to live with us."

Bobby kissed his cheek again and Brian wiped his eyes on the sheet and took a deep breath.

"What's that thing you do with your dad, Jeremy . . . that butterfly, Eskimo and regular thing?"

Bobby smiled and said, "Butterflies," and he leaned closer, faces touching, eyes touching and fluttered his eyelashes. "Other eye," and he did the same thing. "Eskimo," and he rubbed Brian's nose with his. "Regular," and he kissed Brian lightly on the lips.

He smiled down at him.

"There's nothing regular about you," Brian said with a smile, unknowingly repeating what Jeremy had said earlier that evening.

Bobby smiled, gave Brian an Eskimo and another light kiss on his cheek and said, "And that's what makes me special."

Paul Eiselmann loved being a cop. He also loved computers and computer work, though he had no formal training. When he was given the opportunity to combine both and the Waukesha Sheriff Department asked him to do that more and more, he had the best job in the world. The department sent him for training, but mostly, he learned by doing and by making mistakes. His view was that they weren't mistakes at all. They were only steps to a goal and eventual success. In his brief association with FBI Agent Chet Walker, he had learned by watching, listening and asking him questions and a friendship had been born. Unfortunately, Walker died on the same soccer field where Brad Kazmarick and others had died during the summer of death.

Eiselmann couldn't write code and he couldn't build one from scratch, but he knew software and he was pretty good at snooping- legally and otherwise-without getting caught. One of the many tricks Walker had taught him, though he wasn't as good as Walker was. In fact, he doubted that he'd ever be as good as Walker was.

Armed with two warrants, he and O'Connor performed a search of Gordon Huggins' apartment that included any electronics.

Eiselmann used a combination of his work laptop, Huggins' home system and Huggins' laptop. He used a system CD to boot up Huggins' computer and access the file system on the hard drive. He booted up the computer using his "special" system CD and made an exact image of the hard drive to an external USB drive so it could be used as forensic evidence. He opened the original hard drive in the computer and went right to the Documents and Settings folder to look at the various user names on the personal folders within. Using Ophcrack Live CD, Paul was able decipher the passwords. He repeated the process on Huggins' laptop.

O'Connor laughed and said, "Guess what I found?" He tossed a small spiral notebook at his red-haired and freckled partner.

Curious, Eiselmann opened it up and said, "Are you shitting me?"

"I shit you not," O'Connor said with a laugh. "How long were you working on getting into those computers?"

"Well, my way was more fun," Eiselmann said though he was not at all amused. Huggins had written in tiny, neat handwritten script the name of the folder or program with the corresponding password. "Fuck," he muttered under his breath.

"I heard that," O'Connor laughed again.

"How stupid is this guy? He has a notebook with all of his passwords for everything except for turning on his computer."

Eiselmann went to work exploring files and folders and documents. Nothing jumped out at him until he came to a folder labeled, 'H-F'. In it were word docs and an Excel spreadsheet that detailed dates, amounts and payments. There weren't any names, per se, but initials.

"Hey Sherlock, you find anything yet?"

"Hmmm, maybe."

Eiselmann's tone caught his attention and he walked in from the hallway to look over his shoulder.

"H-F," Eiselmann said. "It can't be that simple, can it?"

"You said yourself he wasn't that bright."

"No, I said he was stupid. Not bright and stupid are kinda different."

Eiselmann ran his finger down the list. "We have RK."

"Could be Rob Kirlie."

"We have KL."

"Could be Kevin Longwood."

"We have RT."

"Ron Terzinski."

"GH."

"Gordon I-Am-Not-Very-Bright Huggins."

"Hmmm . . ."

"Who is EF?"

"Could be the guy who gave the information to Jeremy, but I don't think so. EF is making more money than Huggins, but not much more."

"And I don't think he'd rat himself out. Or herself," O'Connor corrected himself.

"Maybe the person at the top?" Eiselmann wondered.

"Judging by the dollar amounts, it could be. EF and Huggins have roughly the same amount of money. The kids considerably less."

Eiselmann leaned back and folded his arms over his chest. O'Connor straightened up, scratched his cheek and shut his eyes as he tried to recall all the names and links on the paper they had.

"Remember what George said about different veterinarians? One for large animals and one for smaller animals? We need to cross-reference these names . . . these initials with vets in a fifty or seventy-five mile radius. We need to find out who ordered fentanyl and in what quantities."

"Unless Huggins and EF are getting it off the internet," Eiselmann suggested.

O'Connor shook his head. "That . . . that doesn't . . . feel right."

He pointed to the screen and said, "This is a simple operation. Look at the spreadsheet. The initials, the payments. The lack of any serious password to get into his computer. A list of passwords for everything else."

Eiselmann nodded and said, "This lacks sophistication."

"Look at the dollar amounts. No one is making a great deal of money here. I mean . . . fifty bucks. A hundred bucks. If they wanted to make money, they would be dealing in coke or pot. But H cut with fentanyl?" He shook his head. "They'd make more money dealing in Oxy."

"What are you saying?" Eiselmann asked. "If they aren't into making money, what are they doing? What's their motive?"

O'Connor nodded and said, "That's one question. That, and who EF is."

"If we don't find out who EF is fast and I mean real fast, EF is dead because Fuentes already knows."

"There's one other thing to consider and it deals with the names on this spreadsheet and the lack of sophistication," O'Connor said. "And I don't know if Graff or Jeremy are going to want to go there."

CHAPTER SEVENTY-NINE

The wind howled and snow pelted against the window like fingernails tapping to get attention. George knew he'd have to work a little harder as he plowed and shoveled a little later that morning.

As much as he wanted to remain close to Brett and out of the chilly air in the house, he eased himself away from him.

"You want me to come with you?" Brett asked through a yawn.

George hugged him and said, "No, sleep."

And that's what Brett did. In fact, George wasn't sure if Brett even heard him.

He made sure Brett was tucked in. He slipped his feet into his moccasins, pulled a sweatshirt over his head and grabbed his knife off the nightstand. Jasmine wanted to come along with him, but George pointed to the floor and with a slight groan, Jasmine lay back down facing the door.

George stepped lightly out into the hallway, shut the door to an inch or two and listened. Nothing. Not a sound except the normal night sounds he had grown used to along with the wind.

Momma was in her normal nightly spot at the top of the stairs. George was sure she had heard him, but she gave no sign that she had.

George tiptoed down the hallway and opened Randy's and Billy's door. George smiled. Billy had taken over the bed leaving Randy to cling to the edge. He shook his head and touched Billy's shoulder once, twice and Billy rolled towards him, but remained asleep. Randy seized the opportunity to roll onto his back giving him more of the bed and more of the covers. Pleased, George smiled and tiptoed out of the room. He loved his twin brothers.

He walked up the hallway near Momma, bent down and stroked the big dog's back and scratched her belly. She rewarded him by licking his hand.

He peered into Bobby's room and saw the empty bed. He smiled.

He opened the bedroom door opposite and saw Brian and Bobby asleep in each other's arms. Bobby had his head tucked into Brian's neck and he slept with a little smile. Most of the time Bobby wore a smile. George loved his innocence, his playfulness and the joy he could find in anything.

George leaned against the doorway and sighed. Bobby had reminded him of his littlest brother of another time, of another place. Or rather, Bobby reminded him of who Robert might have grown up to be. Ironically they had shared the same name. Robert's eyes might have been darker than Bobby's brown, Robert's hair might have been darker and longer than Bobby's chestnut colored hair, but they shared the same spirit, the same curiosity, the same love for life and for others. Both were apt to say the wrong thing at the wrong time, but both were easily forgiven because of their innocence.

George wiped a tear from his eye.

Jasper raised his head. He lowered it back down and rested it on his front paws and watched George with interest.

He moved closer to the two boys, his youngest brother and his new brother. He knew the emotions that swirled in Brian's dreams because he had them once. Still had those dreams from time to time, though they had become less intrusive. Jeremy had told him that he wouldn't ever rid himself completely of those dreams because they were of his family, his mother, his two brothers and his little sister. And his grandfather. His family from another time and place.

He ran the back of his hand along Bobby's cheek. Still asleep, Bobby smiled and buried his face into Brian's neck.

Brian had a furrowed brow and George knew that look too. He had those kinds of dreams from time to time. That is, when he actually slept.

He gently finger-combed Brian's hair off his forehead. Brian didn't move, didn't respond. George repositioned the covers and quilt around the two of them and quietly left the room.

He tiptoed down the stairs and made sure the front door was locked. He moved silently through the kitchen to the backdoor and made sure the house alarm was set. He checked the lock on the backdoor. He stopped to look out the window and was amazed at just how much snow had fallen and how much more swirled in the wind. It was a frozen landscape and he loved it. He never tired of the snow or the cold which was so different from the heat and dryness of Navajoland, his beloved *Diné Bikéyah*.

George ran a hand through his long black hair and sighed. Deep down, he knew that Fuentes wouldn't come to the house. It was too big and unfamiliar and it was off a major well-traveled road for him to risk exposure. No, Fuentes would choose a spot in the city, probably near school to try to catch him off guard.

But George wouldn't be caught off guard. He would be waiting and he would be ready. He just had to make certain that his family would be safe.

He left the kitchen and moved across the hall to the family room. He checked the gun cabinet, though he knew it would be secure. He walked to the sliding glass door and checked the lock on that too.

He moved down the hallway to the study and walked slowly up to the slider. It too was locked, but he stood gazing out at the frozen night. Nothing moved except the snow propelled by the wind. He waited, wondering . . . maybe hoping to see the owl, but it didn't come. Nevertheless, George had been warned and knew that something was ahead.

He tiptoed back to the stairs leading to the bedrooms and found Brian sitting on the third step from the bottom wrapped in a blanket. His head hung, his elbows resting on his knees and his hands holding his head.

"You were asleep," George whispered.

Brian's response was a yawn and a weak smile.

George sat down next to him. Brian gave him part of the blanket and the two boys huddled together. George waited patiently for Brian to speak.

"Your grandfather told you that my parents were dead?"

George shook his head and said, "My grandfather only said that my father and my brother should not go in alone."

Brian raised his head and blinked. "He said that . . . he called me your brother?"

"Yes."

Brian mulled that over and said, "Do you ever see him when he talks to you?"

George sighed. Others have- Stephen and Mikey, Gavin, Brett and Tim.

"Only in my dreams."

"Sometimes I think I see my brother . . . Brad. Just a shadow and then he's gone. Sometimes I *feel* him, you know?"

George nodded.

"It's not creepy or anything. I miss him."

"I miss my grandfather too."

Brian looked away and asked, "How bad was it . . . my mom and dad, I mean?"

George didn't want to answer, but Brian had asked an honest question.

"I was not permitted to see them."

Brian said, "I saw a lot of blood. I saw my dad's computer."

George didn't respond.

"Why, George?"

George slipped an arm around Brian's shoulders and he kissed the side of his head.

"That's the thing that pisses me off the most."

George gave his shoulders a squeeze. And the silence grew to minutes.

"Why did you decide to live with Jeremy and the twins?"

"Because I love them. They love me. I could have lived with my cousin, Leonard . . . but," he stopped and shook his head.

Brian knew the story. Leonard had betrayed George to three killers for land, for sheep and for money. His own cousin.

"How did you feel after, you know, your family was killed?"

George shrugged and looked down at his feet, though his eyes were closed.

"Sad. Angry. Like you, I had questions. I felt it was my fault. They had come looking for me."

Brian couldn't argue with that. George wouldn't have accepted it if he had tried, so he said nothing, letting the silence envelope them like the blanket they were nestled in.

"Both of my uncles and aunts want me to live with them. And Sean and Gav."

George said nothing.

"If Jeremy didn't want me, I mean, if he felt that he couldn't, would he tell me?"

George said, "Father wants you with us. We want you with us. You are my brother. You are our brother. You are his son."

Brian rested his head on George's shoulder.

"We should go back to bed," George suggested.

Brian nodded and stood up gathering the blanket around him. They tiptoed back up the stairs and stopped to pet Momma.

Before Brian went back into his room, George stopped him by gently gripping his arm turning Brian towards him.

George placed his hands on Brian's shoulders and said, "You are my brother. Father is your father."

Brian nodded once, turned and went back into the room and climbed in next to Bobby. He wrapped Bobby in both arms and just like they had begun the night, Bobby threw a leg over Brian's, placed his arm across his chest and nestled his face in Brian's neck.

And Brian shut his eyes and fell asleep.

CHAPTER EIGHTY

"I would like to run this by Jeremy," Eiselmann suggested, "just to confirm our thinking."

It was only 5:00 a.m. and Jamie had been listening to Eiselmann and O'Connor for the better part of an hour already. They had mowed through a pan of scrambled eggs, a half a loaf of bread, a half a pound of bacon and an ocean of coffee. The huge breakfast was easier to digest than the theory that was laid out in front of him even though it made sense.

"What I don't get . . . what I'm having trouble with, is the motive. What is the motive?"

Eiselmann shook his head and said, "We haven't figured that out yet."

Eiselmann and O'Connor had been on the case all night. They had begun with Kirlie's room, his cell and his computer. They had not yielded much other than confirming what they had already known. They performed the search at Huggins' house and that led them down the path to the pot of gold. Or at least, the pot of gold was in reach if they could push and pull a little and bluff a lot.

"You have anything else that might . . . I don't know," he trailed off. He didn't disbelieve them, but he just couldn't swallow it.

"That's why I would like to talk to Jeremy. He would know who was close to Huggins," Eiselmann said.

"But more importantly, who he might take orders from," O'Connor said.

Jamie shook his head. "I just can't believe . . ."

CHAPTER EIGHTY-ONE

He got up shortly after George. He had offered to help shovel, but George hugged him and said that he had it. Brett laid in bed tossing, turning, shutting his eyes only to open them again and stare at the ceiling. He leaned up to look out the window but couldn't see out very well because it had frosted over and was snow and ice crusted.

Brett pushed the covers away, stood and stretched. He slept nude every so often. George didn't mind. He slipped on a pair of Billy's shorts that sat atop a pile on the side of the bed, went across the hall, used the bathroom, flushed and washed his hands and stared in the mirror.

He had grown, but not as quickly as he would have liked. His muscle definition had returned. He couldn't see his ribs like when he was first rescued and his six-pack was back. And his dark complexion had taken over the pasty whiteness of his captivity. Yet, he wondered for the millionth time how much taller and how much bigger he might be had he not spent twenty-two months locked in a room where he was forced to have sex with perverts. He shook his head and chased the thought back to a dark corner, but he knew that he could shake his head until his head fell off and that thought would never fly completely away.

Brett walked back into the bedroom and shut the door behind him. Normally, he would do a super set of forty to fifty pushups ten times. But on this morning, he dropped to the floor and did one hundred and twenty-five military-style pushups without stopping. He flipped over and did two hundred crunches, alternating right elbow to left knee and vice versa. By the time he was finished, Brett had a fine sheen of sweat covering his chest and face and his stomach and arms were a little tired. But only a little tired. He had been pushing himself every day since he had been rescued. Still, he lay on his back with his knees up and breathing deeply with both arms over his eyes.

Finally, he stretched out his legs and his arms reaching as far as he could. He sat up, took hold of his left foot with both hands and placed his nose on his knee. He did the same with his right leg. Finally, he put his legs together, took hold of both feet and placed his face flat on his legs. Stretching felt good and he knew it was necessary to keep himself flexible.

Brett jumped up off the floor, grabbed a towel off the same pile where he had found Billy's shorts, sniffed it and decided it didn't smell too badly, so he used it to wipe off his face, his chest and stomach and his under arms. He slipped his feet into a pair of Nike slides, threw on a Badger t-shirt from the same pile and headed downstairs to the kitchen to make breakfast.

He liked to cook when he was upset or when he had to think. Sometimes when he was bored.

He flipped on the lights and took sausage, bacon and eggs out of the refrigerator. He heated up two pans, one for the sausage and one for the bacon. He went back to the refrigerator and grabbed three medium-sized ripe tomatoes and one good-sized red pepper and one green pepper and diced them on a cutting board using a sharp knife. His hands moved deftly and his cuts were fast and small without wasting movement. To prevent them from burning, he'd turn over the bacon or stir up the sausage.

Brian tiptoed into the kitchen, silently watched Brett and said, "Do you need any help?"

Knowing he was there before he had spoken and without looking up from the bowl he was using to scramble the eggs he said, "You can get the Colby-Jack cheese and the tortillas out of the refrigerator."

Brian did as he was told and picked up the fork and turned the bacon.

"Can you give the sausage a stir?"

Brian picked up the spoon and stirred the sausage and said, "I think it's done. I don't see any red."

Brett leaned over to take a look and nodded. He poured the eggs into the pan with the sausage, turned down the heat and said, "Can you check the bacon?"

Brian lifted six bacon strips out of the pan and placed them on the plate with a paper towel to soak up the grease. He put in six more strips.

Brett went to the cabinet where the seasoning was kept and took out Mrs. Dash, Southwest Seasoning and pepper. He sprinkled it on the eggs and sausage and stirred it in. Next he added the peppers and tomatoes.

"I think we'll use all the bacon," Brett said off-handedly. "Billy, Randy and Dad will eat whatever is left."

Billy, Randy and Vicki entered the kitchen. Randy put their backpacks off to a corner and said, "Who wants a water bottle?"

"I do. Bobby and George will want one," Brett said.

"I do," Billy said quietly.

Catching the sound in his voice, Brett and Brian turned around as saw Billy seated at the kitchen table head down and dabbing at his eyes with a napkin.

Vicki sat down next to him and slipped an arm around his shoulders and held him.

George came in from outside. He stamped off his boots, slid them off and took off his hat and scarf and threw them in the dryer. Not sure what was happening, he entered the kitchen but stayed at the far end and leaned against the counter to watch.

Bobby hustled into the kitchen, took three steps and froze.

"Bobby, can you stir the eggs and watch the bacon?"

He turned to Brian and said, "Come here. Billy, come here."

The two boys walked over to him and faced each other. Brett put an arm around each boy's shoulders.

"Look, I'm only going to say this once, so I want you to listen." He stopped and to make sure he said, "Okay?"

Both boys nodded.

"Billy, we went over this, but I'm going to say it again. You did not cause your dad's death and you didn't cause your parent's divorce." He gave his shoulder a squeeze and pulled his head closer to him and kissed him near the temple.

He turned to Brian and said, "Look, you need to live with us. We're all a little messed up. Bobby and me, well, you know our story. You've been friends with Randy and Billy longer than us, so you know their story. You know George's story. No one had a perfect life. None of us.

"But now, this life . . . living here all together . . . is just about as perfect as you can get. You know that. Deep down, you know that."

As he did with Billy, he pulled Brian closer and kissed him near the temple.

"We're family."

As George watched, any number of feelings bubbled to the surface and he wiped his eyes with his hand. Randy and Bobby did the same.

"It sucks for you right now. For both of you, but look around . . . it sucks for all of us. But we have each other's back and we're together, so it'll be okay." For emphasis, he squeezed them both a little and said, "It will."

Both boys nodded.

Jeremy walked into the kitchen, stopped in mid-stride, looked over at Vicki and said, "Everything okay?"

She smiled and nodded and wiped a tear or two from her own eyes.

Brett said, "Now everyone, eat or it's going to get cold. George and I have to shower. Bobby, can you make George and me two burritos? We'll eat them on the way to school."

He turned to Jeremy and said, "We'll shower in your room. It's bigger."

"Together?"

"Yeah."

"You don't have to. We have three bathrooms."

"Yeah, but not a lot of hot water."

"Don't you want privacy?"

Brett smiled and said, "We'd rather have hot water."

Breakfast was mostly eaten in silence. Brian would glance at Billy. Bobby would catch his eye and smile.

"Bri, I'll take the boys to school because I have to attend a quick faculty meeting before school. I'll come home and then you and Vicki and I will go to your house and we'll pack up whatever you have left and want to bring here. I told your two uncles that we'll either be there or here and we invited them for dinner tonight. I think Jamie Graff is meeting us at your house because he has to take your official statement. George, he's going to speak with you at school."

"Sarah Bailey and Ellie Hemauer are meeting us at Brian's house. They want to help," Vicki said.

"Mom, I thought you had some surgeries," Bobby asked.

"I have coverage and I took the next several days off."

Twelve minutes later Brett and George hustled into the kitchen. Brett loosened the button on his jeans and unzipped his fly and tucked in his shirt.

George's hair was still damp.

"I just took your burritos out of the microwave," Bobby said.

Brett went to the refrigerator and grabbed two oranges and stuffed them into his backpack.

"George, you want anything else?" Brett asked.

"No, thank you. I'm good." However, he went to the pantry and took a protein bar and stuffed it into his backpack.

Before they headed out the door, the boys lined up and hugged and kissed Vicki and then Brian. Brian waited at the backdoor wanting to get the last word in, so he waited for Bobby to say goodbye.

"Butterflies," he said with a smile.

Without hesitation, Brian gave him butterflies.

"Eskimo."

And Brian rubbed his nose with Bobby's.

"Regular."

Brian and Bobby exchanged a kiss on the cheek.

Brett smiled and shook his head. He walked over to Brian and said, "Just think about what I said, okay?"

Brian nodded and Brett gave him another hug and kissed his cheek. "We're family."

The drive into the city was fairly normal. There was talk about teachers and homework and upcoming tests. There was the game on Thursday and speculation as to whether or not Brian would be able to play after missing school and practice today. Jeremy was a cautious driver anyway, but the snow and ice slowed him down even more. Other drivers did the same.

George noticed a blue Impala following them at a distance. He hadn't seen the car before on any of their trips to school, so he was curious and a little concerned. He knew there would be at least one deputy tailing them, but the car was too far back for him to see who was driving and who was in the passenger seat.

Jeremy pulled up in front of Butler Middle and Bobby, sandwiched between George and Billy, started to get out on Billy's side.

"No, come out mine. I'll walk you to the doorway."

Jeremy and Brett turned around, but it was Randy in the backseat who asked, "What is it?"

George said, "Not sure." To Bobby he said, "Come on."

Bobby got out of the car, started to turn around, but George put his arm around his shoulders and whispered, "Don't do that. Just walk into school like nothing's wrong."

Bobby nodded.

The two boys walked carefully up the stone steps of the school entrance and were met by Mikey, Gavin and Stephen.

Before Bobby left with them, George gave Bobby a hug, a fist bump to Stephen and Gavin and a hug to Mikey.

As he walked down the steps, he tried to get a good look into the blue Impala, but it slowly drove away. A Latino boy he didn't recognize stared at him out the passenger window.

CHAPTER EIGHTY-TWO

"Vato, who was that little kid?"

The small, wiry passenger turned back around and said, "His little brother."

The interior of the car was filled with sweet-smelling smoke from the joint they had shared. Their eyes were a bit glassy and their speech a tad slurred, but they were coherent enough to function.

The driver smiled and said, "Let's find Manny and Fuentes."

"*Homes*, Fuentes is one cold dude. He's *ice*, man!"

The driver couldn't argue with that. Fuentes gave him the creeps. He wasn't as spooked about him as his friend, but, yeah, Fuentes was unpredictable and scary.

The sooner Fuentes had George Tokay delivered to him, the sooner he'd go back to Chicago and they'd be rid of him.

"Did you hear me, man? Fuentes is a hard dude."

The driver ignored him and drove off to find Manny and Fuentes.

He had an idea.

CHAPTER EIGHTY-THREE

It was Chuck Gobel's meeting, but the district superintendent and her assistant were present as observers, though Jeremy considered that there was more to it than that. Chuck asked Jamie to add some reassurance as well as bring them up to speed on what he could with the investigation. While Graff couldn't and didn't want to give any details to the stunned teachers and staff members, he did say that the police department was working on it, had persons of interest in mind and hoped to close it in the next couple of days.

While he spoke, Eiselmann and O'Connor searched the large group of men and women, some of whom were in shock, others in grief. They watched one person in particular who gave away nothing other than an expression of grief.

After, Jeremy followed the three detectives into a conference room and sat down around a table. Eiselmann fired up his laptop, Graff took out a yellow pad and O'Connor listened and quietly sipped his Diet Coke.

"After you went into the Kazmarick house, what did you do?"

Jeremy shrugged and said, "George told us to stay in the kitchen and not to touch anything. Brian sat down and I stood near him."

"Did you suspect anything?"

Jeremy shook his head and said, "Not until George met us at the backdoor."

"What did George say?"

"That his grandfather told him not to let Brian and me into the house alone."

"Okay, what happened next?"

"George took off his shoes and tiptoed down the hallway. He came back a little later and said that he had called you. You know the rest."

Graff put his pencil down, looked at Eiselmann and O'Connor and said, "You guys have any questions?"

Eiselmann nodded and said, "Just a couple." He turned to Jeremy and said, "Can you think of anyone on the staff who didn't like Huggins?"

"You mean, someone who didn't like him enough to kill him? No, no one."

"Let's start out with anyone who might not have liked him or someone who maybe was angry with him."

Jeremy thought for a minute and said, "He is . . . or was a leader in the building. He was active in the union or association or whatever they call it. He was a Type-A kind of guy, so I'm sure he rubbed people the wrong way, but for someone to kill him?" He shook his head and said, "Not really."

"Anyone he had arguments with? Disagreements?"

Jeremy shrugged and said, "Hell, Paul, there are people who disagree with me. I'd like to think that my colleagues like me, but I'm sure there are some who don't. I'm sure there are some who might have had disagreements with him, but I can't think of anyone in particular."

Eiselmann nodded and said, "Okay, let's look at it from another direction. Who was close to him? Friends with him?"

Jeremy thought for a minute and said, "Sarah Bailey was probably his closest friend. His department mates."

Something passed over Jeremy's face, his eyes in particular, that Eiselmann picked up on.

"What? What are you thinking?"

Jeremy blushed and shook his head.

Graff jumped in and said, "Just now, what were you thinking, Jeremy?"

"Just some gossip, that's all."

"What?" Graff asked.

Jeremy shifted in his seat. "There were rumors that he was having an affair, that's all."

"He was single," Eiselmann said.

Jeremy made a face and said, "Yes, he was."

"Can you tell us who he was allegedly having an affair with?"

Jeremy shifted in his seat again, opened his mouth, closed it and said, "It's only rumor. I don't have any proof and it may just be rumor. You know how that goes."

The detectives waited.

"Liz. Liz Champion."

"Hmmm, okay," Graff said. "I wouldn't have guessed that. I mean, Liz?

Kind of a barracuda, if you know what I mean."

"Can you tell me who he might listen to? Anyone who gave him direction or advice?" Eiselmann asked.

Jeremy shrugged and said, "The administrators, but other than that, I don't know."

"Anything else you can think of that might help us?" Eiselmann asked.

Jeremy shook his head and said, "That's about all I have."

"Thanks, Jeremy," Graff said. "I know this is hard. I know you're worried about George and your family and now you have Brian to think of."

"It's all so sad. He's been through a lot already and now this. About Fuentes, are you any closer to finding him?"

Graff and Eiselmann looked at O'Connor who had been content with listening to the interview.

"We're on it. We have ideas and known associates. We have a tail on you and the boys so as best we can, you're covered."

Jeremy looked over at Graff and Jamie knew what Jeremy was thinking. *Was as best we can be good enough?*

Jeremy got up to leave, shook hands with the detectives and said, "I'll go home, pick up Vicki and Brian and head over to the house. It's okay to go inside?"

"Yes, should be," Graff said. "I'll meet you there in about an hour or so to talk to Brian."

Jeremy opened the door and saw George sitting in one of the lobby chairs. George stood up as he saw his father, but waited until Jamie called him in.

Jeremy walked over to him, gave him a fist bump and said, "They're just going to ask you a few questions, that's all. Shouldn't be more than a few minutes."

George nodded and went into the room and shut the door behind him.

"Have a seat, George. Are you doing okay?"

George nodded.

"How's Brian?"

"Sad. Being around us helps, I think."

"Probably right," Graff said. "I think the ice fishing might be on hold for a bit until we get things wrapped up, but we'll still go, okay?"

George nodded.

"We're going to ask you a few questions about last night," Graff said. He looked over at Eiselmann who he had decided would lead the interview.

"George, why did you go into the house with Jeremy and Brian?"

"Because my grandfather told me not to let Father and Brian go into the house alone."

"Did he tell you why?" Eiselmann asked. He had wanted to ask a million more questions, but settled on this one.

"No, Sir."

"You didn't have any idea why or what was in there?"

George was silent and when he spoke he said, "I knew it was not good."

"So you went into the house and what happened next?"

"I told Father and Brian to stay in the kitchen and not to touch anything. I went down the hall and saw blood on the carpet. I saw . . . more blood in the office. I checked his parent's bedroom and didn't see them. I called Detective Jamie and went back to the kitchen."

"Anything else you can add?"

George shook his head and said, "No, Sir."

He sat quietly while Jamie finished up his notes on the yellow pad and while Eiselmann finished typing into his computer.

"Can I ask you a couple more questions off the record?" Eiselmann asked.

George nodded.

"When you were at the house while Pat and I were at the murder site, you were specific on . . . what was down there. It almost seemed like you had been there with us."

George didn't say anything.

"How did you know about all of that?"

George frowned and said, "I do not know."

"We know you weren't there. We know you hadn't talked to anyone who was there," Eiselmann said nodding to Graff.

George looked at Eiselmann squarely and said, "I do not know how I knew. I just knew."

"A hunch? A guess?"

"I do not know. I just knew," he repeated.

The detectives waited and so did George.

Finally George said, "When I was little, my grandfather taught me to watch and to listen. He told me that if my heart and my mind were quiet, I would see." He shrugged but didn't blink when he added, "I do not know how I know things. Sometimes my grandfather speaks to me. Other times, I just know."

Graff cleared his throat and said, "Okay, George. We've kept you out of class long enough. Thanks for your help with this. I do ask that because this is an ongoing investigation that you do not talk about this with anyone. Fair enough?"

George nodded and said, "Yes, Sir."

He got up to leave, shook hands with each of the detectives and left the conference room. O'Connor shut the door, leaned against the wall and said, "Hmmm."

"What?" Eiselmann asked.

To Graff, O'Connor said, "That's why the FBI is interested in him, isn't it . . . because sometimes he just knows things."

Graff shrugged. Kelliher and Storm didn't go into much detail with him. They spoke about his physical abilities with a knife and rifle. They spoke about his tracking ability, his intuition. They told him more than once that he could walk a crime scene as well or better than some techs could and he had done so several times. But other than that, the agents said that George was a good kid who deserved a break and that the FBI was interested in providing him with one. If he wanted it.

"Does Jeremy know about the FBI's interest in him?" Eiselmann asked.

Graff nodded and said, "Kelliher and Jeremy spoke about it. Jeremy told him that he wanted George to be a kid as long as he could. He wants them to back off until after college."

"They can't do much until then anyway, can they?" Eiselmann asked.

"Not really."

"Okay, so now where do we go from here?"

Graff shook his head and said, "We keep an eye on our suspect and pull whatever information we can. We have to dig deeper because what we have is only circumstantial. Mostly, we have to find Fuentes. And soon."

CHAPTER EIGHTY-FOUR

Brian sat at the kitchen table. He rested his head on his left hand while he fiddled with the envelope, tapping first one edge on the table and then the other. Vicki sat across from him reading the newspaper and sipping hot coffee, a luxury she didn't have on many mornings. At various times she peered at him over the edge of the paper and whether Brian knew it or not, she didn't know.

Jeremy walked into the kitchen from the upstairs where he went to change into jeans and a black and red Under Armour sweatshirt over a maroon t-shirt. He went to the refrigerator, took out a can of Diet Coke and sat down at the end of the table and took the sports page from the pile Vicki had already finished.

Brian hadn't moved.

"Are you going to shower sometime this morning?" Jeremy said to him.

Brian set the envelope down and his eyes flicked from Jeremy to Vicki. "If I ask you a question, will you be honest?"

Jeremy set the sports page down and said, "You know I will."

"Promise me that you'll tell me the truth no matter what it is."

"Bri, you know our rule. We tell each other the truth. If we don't tell the truth, we don't have trust. If we don't have trust, we don't have a relationship."

"Just promise me," Brian said. To soften it, he added, "Please."

"Yes, I will tell you the truth."

Brian stared at Vicki until she said, "I will tell you the truth."

He nodded, took a deep breath and said, "Do you want me to live here or do you want me to live somewhere else?"

Jeremy opened his mouth, but Brian cut him off.

"I want to know if you really *want* me to live here. I don't want you to say yes just because you think you *have* to. Because I don't. I can go live with one of my aunts and uncles or I could live with Gavin or Sean. They all said I could." He paused and said, "So, do you really *want* me to live with you? Don't say yes because you think you *have* to."

Jeremy reached out and took hold of Brian's hand.

"Bri, I love you. I love you as much as I do the twins, George, Brett and Bobby, and I have for a long time. So yes, I want you to live with us."

Vicki reached across the table and took hold of Brian's other hand and said, "And I want you to live here. The boys want you to live here. I think they made that pretty clear this morning, don't you?"

Brian nodded. What surprised both Jeremy and Vicki was that there were no tears. Rather, there was a hardness or perhaps a determination that Jeremy saw on the basketball court and the soccer field.

"The question is, Brian, what do you want?" Jeremy asked.

Brian's eyes darted between the two adults and he fidgeted in his chair before he asked, "Are you going to get married?"

That surprised both Jeremy and Vicki. They looked at one another and both of them felt uncomfortable. It was Vicki who responded.

"We have talked about that. We love each other. Jeremy is my best friend."

"And Vicki is my best friend and yes, we've talked about it."

Brian said, "So you're going to get married."

Neither Jeremy nor Vicki answered. Jeremy wagged his head and Vicki took a sip of coffee.

Brian looked at Jeremy and asked, "When you get married, are you going to adopt Brett and Bobby?"

Jeremy blinked and glanced at Vicki before answering.

"I don't know. Do they want me to?" Jeremy asked.

Brian nodded and said, "They want to be Evans and not McGovern." To Vicki he said, "No offense."

Vicki shrugged and shook her head as if no offense was taken.

"That," he cleared his throat, "is something we haven't discussed. It is something I would consider." He looked at Vicki seeking support.

"I'm okay with that, but I think we'd have to run it by Brett's and Bobby's father," Vicki said. "He might feel otherwise."

"Okay. Because if I live here, I want to be Brian Evans. I don't want to be Brian Kazmarick. If I don't change my name, people will look at me and remember that I'm the kid whose parents killed themselves. I would like to be adopted and I want to be Brian Evans."

And there was that hardness again, that determination. Jeremy knew there was a stubborn streak to Brian and he knew that Brian wouldn't give in easily, if at all. And that made him smile.

"What?" Brian asked. "You don't want to adopt me?"

Jeremy laughed quietly, gripped Brian's hand firmly and said, "Yes, Brian, I'd be happy to adopt you. I'd like that very much. I'd like it if you were my son and I was your dad."

"You're telling the truth? You *want* to, not . . ."

"Shhh, Brian, listen to me, please. I already told you that I would tell you the truth, right?" When Brian didn't respond, he repeated, "Right?"

Brian nodded.

"Yes, I want you to live here with us. I want you to be a part of this family. And yes, I want to adopt you. I'm honored that you want me to be your dad."

Relief flooded over Brian. He tried on a smile and it seemed to fit so he wore it.

"Okay, so what do I call you? George calls you Father." He looked over at Vicki and said, "And he calls you Mom."

"Because I asked him not to call me, Mother," she said with a smile.

"How about if you call us what you feel comfortable calling us. It's up to you," Jeremy suggested.

Brian nodded and stared at the envelope in front of him.

"Are you going to read it?" Vicki asked. She was curious to read it, but she didn't know if Brian would share it with Jeremy or her or anyone for that matter, not even one of the boys.

"I haven't decided," Brian said.

"It might explain things a little," Jeremy said.

Brian was ready for that and his anger boiled to the surface like a volcano. "Like why they liked Brad more than me? Why living with me sucked? Why they decided to kill themselves and leave me alone?" He paused and said, "Those things?"

Jeremy and Vicki expected anger at some point. The fact that he flashed so quickly from happy to angry told Jeremy that it sat just below the surface like a shark waiting for an unsuspecting swimmer.

There weren't any tears, but Brian's face was red and his chin quivered, but his jaw was set.

"When you read it and if you want to talk, we'll be here, okay?"

Brian picked up the letter and pushed himself away from the table. Before he left the kitchen, Jeremy stood up and said, "Come here."

Brian and Jeremy embraced for a long time. Jeremy kissed the top of Brian's head.

"I do love you, Bri. You know that, right?"

He felt Brian nod.

"I love you, too."

Jeremy held Brian's face gently and gave him an Eskimo and said, "I love you and I want you to live with us. I want you to be a part of this family and I would like to be your dad."

As angry as he was, Brian smiled. It felt like a weight fell off his shoulders.

For the longest time, this is what he had wanted. He hadn't realized how much until just then. He had begun thinking about it half way through eighth grade when his parents hadn't paid any attention to him. At that point, it was only a dream, but it not only stayed with him, it grew each time he spent a weekend at the Evans' house and watched Jeremy interact with the twins, with George and with Brett and Bobby. It grew each time Jeremy interacted with him. It reached its peak the night he and Jeremy, just the two of them, stayed home to watch a movie and eat popcorn and talk.

On impulse, Brian gave Jeremy an Eskimo and said, "I love you."

And they embraced again, holding each other tightly.

CHAPTER EIGHTY-FIVE

They had been on the phone with the bank and the lawyer Jeremy had used when Billy was adopted. Jamie Graff hadn't shown up yet and neither had his aunts and uncles, though they had called to check on Brian. Currently, Jeremy and Vicki were in the kitchen talking to the life insurance guy. Brian was introduced to him, who expressed his condolences and Brian left the kitchen to go back to his room to finish packing. He didn't want sympathy eyes, as he called them.

He stood in the middle of the room, his eyes wandering over the walls that held his soccer posters, his dresser that held photos of him and Brad and one of his parents with him and his brother. He sighed.

Brad's room had been packed up by his parents, though some of the boxes weren't sealed shut. Ellie Hemauer and Sarah Bailey had cleaned the carpet in the hallway and the mess in the office. They were still in Brad's room cleaning what was left of Nancy Kazmarick's head off the wall and headboard.

He opened up the top drawer that held some of his treasures. He ran his fingers over some medals from tourneys his travel team had won. He picked up a couple of lucky coins, two of which were an Indian head penny and a buffalo nickel. He gently touched a couple of the sea shells he had collected on their family trip to the gulf coast. He picked up the four-leaf clover sealed in a small plastic covering. He found it while deer hunting.

Two navy suitcases were on his bed, but only one was partially filled. Brian had emptied the contents of two drawers, but he still had two to go, plus some things in his closet.

He walked away from his dresser and went to the closet. He reached up and took down the two photo albums his mom had put together for him. He pushed the two suitcases over to give him room to sit down and he opened up the most recent album. He sighed again.

"It doesn't look like you've done much packing," Vicki said with a smile.

He shrugged and said, "I don't have much to go."

She sat down on the bed next to him and he shared the photo album with her. She would ask about this one or that one and *ooo* and *aww* about a couple of others.

He liked the way she smelled. Like soap and her perfume was something light. He could see both Brett and Bobby in her face, especially around the eyes. She smiled like Bobby. Probably like Brett, too, though Brett didn't smile much.

Vicki said, "Are you going to have a bedroom by yourself or with Brett or George?"

Brian shook his head and said, "Bobby."

"Really? I'm surprised."

"I like Bobby."

"I do, too," Vicki said with a nudge to his ribs. "I just thought you'd be with Brett or George or Billy."

"Nah, Bobby. George and Billy will stay together and Brett wants to try having a bedroom by himself."

The shock registered on her face and she didn't bother to hide it.

That would be a first. Ever since he had been freed from captivity, Brett had never slept in a room by himself. He either slept with Bobby when they were home in their own house or with Billy or George when they were with Jeremy.

"As long as he has the door open, he'll be okay." Brian shrugged and said, "There will be times he'll end up with one of us."

He set the photo albums on the bed and went back to his dresser.

"Do you want any help?" Vicki asked.

Brian said, "No . . . thanks, I got it."

She watched him unload a drawer of t-shirts into a suitcase and begin on a drawer of socks. She picked up the two coins from his keepsake drawer and the sea shells.

"These are pretty."

"I haven't decided if I'm keeping them."

"Why?"

He shrugged and said, "I don't know."

"Brian, you need to take these with you. These are important."

He looked at her and said, "Why?"

"Because these are good memories. You need to hang onto them. They will remind you of all the good times you've had. And, even though you might not want to hear this right now, you need to hang onto the tough memories too."

"Why?"

"Because if you remember the tough ones, you'll remember that you beat them and that's always a good thing to remember."

"That's something Bobby or Randy or Jeremy would say."

"It's true though, don't you think?"

He shrugged and nodded.

"As tough as this is right now, Bri, you will look back on this and in time, you will remember that you beat it."

"I'd like to forget all this crap."

She nodded and said, "When Tom and I divorced it was tough. I was scared. I doubted myself. I didn't think I was good enough. I had two boys I had to raise by myself. Brett had just come back to us and I had to get to know him all over again. It was a tough, ugly time in our lives."

"Brett and Bobby don't talk about it much."

Vicki nodded and said, "I can understand that."

They packed together in silence, Vicki handing Brian clothes or things from the dresser and she sat down on the bed and said, "Sit with me a minute."

He sat down next to her.

"You asked if Jeremy and I are going to get married."

Afraid that she was going to tell him they weren't, he remained silent and sort of held his breath a little.

"We will. In time."

Relieved, he exhaled and said, "What are you waiting for?"

"I love Jeremy very much, Brian. Don't doubt that. I know he loves me. He's a good man. He's a terrific father and he'll be a wonderful husband."

Brian said nothing.

"Tom and I had our problems. I knew he was cheating on me, but I had the boys to think of. And even though he cheated, I knew he loved me. I know that sounds . . . wrong."

She smiled sadly.

"But I doubted myself. Was I good enough? Was there something wrong with me?"

Brian's eyes grew large.

She smiled again and said, "Some of the same questions you've been asking yourself, right?"

Brian nodded.

They sat side by side in silence for a beat or two and she said, "Like Jeremy said, if we're going to have a relationship, we have to trust one another and if we're going to trust one another, we have to be honest with each other."

Brian nodded again. This was the longest conversation he had had with Vicki. But at the same time, he wasn't uncomfortable with her.

"I guess what I'm trying to say and not very well, is that there will always be good memories and there will always be crappy memories. Hopefully, there will be more good ones than bad ones. But remember both. The good memories will make you smile, while the bad memories will remind you that you've survived, that you're tough."

Brian smiled.

She hugged him and kissed his cheek.

"I love you, Bri. I'm happy you're going to live with us and be a part of our family."

He smiled even wider and said, "Me, too."

CHAPTER EIGHTY-SIX

Bob Farner hated lunch supervision. The kids didn't have any restrictions other than to stay in the cafeteria until the bell rang. They could pretty much wander around, though most walked to and from the food lines with their trays and drinks and sat down and ate with their friends. Funny how the kids always sat at the same table in nearly the same spot each lunch.

Three lunches. Three supervisions. Five days a week.

He and Liz had duty together along with one of the security personnel and two teachers who were assigned this duty as part of their planning period. Other teachers ate lunch in the staff room.

Normally Farner would stroll down the rows, up one aisle, down the next. Sometimes he'd stand near the food lines to make sure kids weren't pocketing anything without paying for it. It didn't happen much if ever, but nonetheless.

He might have a conversation with Liz Champion or one of the teachers, but he'd rather keep moving to build up the number of steps he took during the day. His wife, Maryanne bought him a Fitbit after his last physical and ever since, he'd wear it and try to reach the ten thousand step goal. He seldom hit that mark, usually ending around six thousand steps.

Champion hovered near the table filled with Jeremy's kids and their friends. There wasn't the usual laughter or the loud animated conversation on this day. Mostly, the boys scrolled their cell phones while they ate.

Farner glanced at the clock again. Seven minutes left until the bell. He knew the old adage about watching water boil, but he couldn't help himself.

He watched Sweeney walk up to Brett McGovern and before Champion gave him that *better get down here* look, he started in that direction, casually.

"Where's Spazmarick?"

No one answered him.

"Oh yeah! His parents killed themselves because they couldn't stand his punk ass. Hell, I would've too rather than live with that piece of shit."

George could tell that Brett was hot and getting hotter. He could see it in his eyes. He had his hands balled into fists. His breathing had become shallow and rapid.

He put a hand on Brett's right forearm, gripped it and held on.

"Sweeney, leave us alone," Caitlyn said.

"Who asked you?"

George stood up slowly, placed a hand on Brett's shoulder to keep him seated and said, "Doug, leave us alone. I warned you."

"Ooo, Indian Boy speaks," Sweeney said with a false laugh as he took a step back.

Farner moved up behind Sweeney and said, "Doug, go to my office now before you do something you'll regret."

By now, kids had stopped eating. Some remained seated, while others stood up. There were whispers. Some pointed. Others had their cells out recording what was happening. One teacher moved to assist Farner, while the other used his radio to call security.

Sweeney spun around and said, "I didn't do anything, so I don't have to go to your office."

Farner clipped his radio to his belt behind his back and reached for Sweeney's arm.

"Let's go, Champ."

Sweeney batted the assistant principal's hand away and said, "I'm not going anywhere."

Farner reached out again and Sweeney pushed him backwards. Farner almost stumbled, but caught himself before he went to the floor.

"Do you want me to call the SRO and have you arrested? Because that's where this is heading!" He paused long enough to catch his breath and said, "Get to my office, now!"

Something snapped. George saw it in Sweeney's eyes, the twitch of his mouth. He watched Sweeney make a fist and pull back.

George reacted before Sweeney swung on the assistant principal. He hooked Sweeney's arm with his own and swept Sweeney's legs out from under him without letting go of Sweeney's arm. Sweeney landed flat on his back. George twisted Sweeney's arm in an improbable angle and placed the heel of his boot on Sweeney's throat.

"Do not disrespect Mr. Farner," George warned.

"Get off . . ." Sweeney's eyes bulged and he stopped talking as George stepped a little harder onto Sweeney's throat.

"You will stop now and do what Mr. Farner told you to do."

Two security personnel, Bud Foster and Linda Parker ran into the cafeteria followed by the SRO. Security first looked at Champion, who had done nothing to help Farner or stop Sweeney and finally at Farner.

The SRO walked up to George and told him to put his hands behind his back. Puzzled, George did as he was told.

"Not him!" Farner said. "He intervened when Sweeney pushed me and tried to hit me."

Sweeney scrambled to his feet and turned towards George. He swung, but George dipped his head and the punch sailed harmlessly over his head. He swung again and hit nothing but air, but this time, Foster and Farner jumped him and rode him back to the ground where the SRO handcuffed him. Foster and the SRO escorted him out of the cafeteria.

"George, thank you," Farner said, holding out his hand.

George smiled, shook it and said, "Yes, Sir."

Off to the side sitting at a round table with two of his friends, Angel Benevides had watched the Sweeney takedown and was impressed. For the first time since Fuentes rolled into town, maybe there was a way to get him out of town and out of his brother's life permanently. Now he just had to find him.

CHAPTER EIGHTY-SEVEN

Butler Middle School was the second oldest building in the Waukesha School District. It smelled like waxed floors and industrial strength disinfectant. The gym was a sweat box and no one knew if that's just the way it was heated or if it was because it was cold outside or if it was just because the building was old. In any case in any weather, the gym was a sweatbox.

Coach Diamonti put the boys through a grueling workout of sprints and shuttle runs mixed with three versus three drills and four versus four drills. Currently on a water break, Bobby stood among the sweaty boys breathing in great gulps of air with both hands resting on his head. He hadn't begun drinking his half-finished Gatorade. He just wanted to breathe.

He was shirtless and sweat dripped down his body just like the other guys. Mikey was seated with his knees up spilling as much water down his chin and down his chest as he did down his throat. Big Gav stood next to Bobby with one hand on his hip and one wrapped around a water bottle.

The team wasn't all that deep in talent. Mikey was the point guard and played a lot like Brett did for North. Bobby was the shooting guard and could double up as point if he was needed, and Big Gav roamed underneath the basket. Stephen and Garrett rounded out the starting five and did as best as they could. Stephen relied on his soccer skill and conditioning, while Garrett gutted it out like he did with everything. There were other guys who probably should have gone out for the team, but didn't because they didn't like the coach.

The boys finished up practice with a full court passing drill and free throws and headed to the locker to shower. The locker room and showers smelled of decades old sweat and dirty feet, but it was all they had and they were used to it. But they never walked anywhere barefoot just in case.

"Is Brian alright?" Mikey asked.

Bobby nodded and said, "About as well as he can be, I guess."

"It sucks losing your parents," Stephen said. Of anyone, he would know because his father was killed in a bomb blast during the summer of hell.

Mikey looked at him and whispered, "You okay?"

Stephen nodded, but didn't say anything.

The rest of the shower and changing clothes was accomplished mostly in silence. A couple of the guys talked about their homework and the middle school dance the following weekend. Others talked about the upcoming North game. The guys who knew about Brian's parents knew better than to talk about it.

They exited the locker by the side door. Some of the parents were already waiting, while others checked their cell phones to see how long their parents would be. Others just waited patiently knowing that sooner or later, their parents would get there.

Most of the guys had drifted off. Mikey, Stephen, Gav and Garrett had left, leaving Bobby and four others waiting.

None of them noticed the blue Impala parked a half a block away.

CHAPTER EIGHTY-EIGHT

"That's him. The one in the red hat and black North Face jacket," Suarez muttered. His lips were wrapped around a joint.

Fuentes stared him down, squinting to get a better look. Pretty good size, but still only an eighth grader. He'd be easy to drag into the car, especially since he had a backpack on his back and a duffle bag at his feet.

"Homes, how do you wanna play this?"

Fuentes glanced over his shoulder at Rico Rodriquez, who melted back into the seat unwilling to open his mouth again.

"We wait. I don't want too many eyes."

"We could just shoot 'em," Suarez suggested. "Five O wouldn't know."

Fuentes shut his eyes and shook his head. How stupid can they be?

A car pulled up and two of the boys waved goodbye, got in and left, leaving just Bobby and Rick Wilton standing in the doorway of the outside entrance to the locker room.

"Bendejo, get out and walk up the sidewalk." To the driver he said, "Pull up slowly, but not too slow. I don't want to be obvious." To the backseat he said, "When we get across from him, grab him and shove him into the backseat. You have to do it fast, Bendejo. You can do that, right, Puta?"

Rodriguez got out of the car mumbling. He turned up his collar and hunched his shoulders. He began walking up the sidewalk slowly with the blue Impala just behind him on the street.

Fifteen yards and closing.

Bobby stamped his feet with his head down intent on his cell.

An Expedition pulled up across the street and Jeremy beeped the horn. George, sitting in the backseat didn't wait until the car stopped before he opened the door and got out, slipping a little on the dirty frozen slush in the street.

He called, "Bobby! Let's go! Now!"

Bobby jumped at his name, picked up the duffle at his feet and jogged across the street, narrowly missing the slow moving Impala. He jumped in using the door George had opened.

George stared down the driver. He had already recognized the guy on the sidewalk. He could only guess who was on the passenger side.

The guy on the street jumped in the Impala even though it was still moving slowly and the car sped off.

But not before George got the license plate, a picture of the car and sent them both to Graff and Kelliher.

CHAPTER EIGHTY-NINE

Jeremy and Vicki worked with Brian's uncles and aunts to plan a small, private family service for his parents. Brian wanted Randy, Bobby and Danny to sing and provide the music and that was his only contribution. He didn't want to do a reading and he didn't want to say anything.

Jeremy told Brian and his aunts and uncles that the life insurance policy on Brian's father would be deposited into Brian's trust fund, minus expenses for the funeral and service. Because his mother committed suicide, her life insurance was declared null and void. No one was surprised at that. They were however, surprised at how big of a policy Brian's dad had on him.

He and Vicki contacted a realtor who agreed to put the house on the market. Anything over what was owed would be split between Brian's savings account and his trust fund. Jeff Limbach, Jeremy's best friend helped him set up the trust just as he had done for Randy and Billy and for George, Brett and Bobby. The cars were now Brian's to do with what he wanted. He sat down with Jeremy and Vicki and the three of them decided that both would be traded in for a new Suburban, something big enough that would be able to carry the whole family.

Brian wanted the photo albums, the three rifles and the fishing gear. He decided to keep his father's watch and his parents' wedding rings. All the other jewelry was given to his aunts after he had offered it first to Vicki, who politely declined with a kiss on his forehead. There were one or two other keepsakes that meant something either to Brad or to him, but other than that he wanted nothing else.

His aunts and uncles took what they wanted which wasn't much. They had planned to leave for home, but would be back for the service early Saturday afternoon.

Jeremy and Vicki dropped Brian off at school so he could attend afternoon classes. Normally, an athlete had to be in school for the entire day to participate in an athletic event that evening. However, Harrison, Jeremy and Chuck Gobel discussed it and given the unusual circumstances, it was decided that Brian would play and all agreed that it would do him good to get back to a normal routine.

'*I M fine!*'

That was Bobby's response to each and every text he received from George or Brett or Brian. Billy and Randy had called him and he had replied the same way, except he would add a laugh.

The night before as he was getting ready for bed George and Brett had spoken to him warning him to be more aware of his surroundings. Detective Eiselmann had called him and told him the same thing. He was embarrassed and he promised he'd do better next time. If there *was* a next time.

Bobby worked harder at practice than he ever had, probably since tryouts. He was more vocal and even though he was good on both ends of the court, he worked particularly hard on defense. But he found himself checking around the gym for anyone out of the ordinary.

Neither Brian nor Brett had any homework, so they spent a half an hour after school with Coach Harrison going over game film. Brett would stop it, run it backwards and forwards and point out defensive and offensive tendencies to Brian. Harrison would smile and shake his head, marveling at Brett's insight.

Randy and Danny spent after school in one of the band practice rooms going over a song they had written together. Billy and two other kids sat at a table in the library getting ready for an upcoming test.

George ran eight miles on the indoor track- four in one direction and four in the other. That way, his ankles wouldn't hurt too much because of the tight turns. After, he hit the weight room for upper body work. What struck the strength and body instructor, Rodney Delwig was that George wasn't even breathing hard when he finished. And it wasn't that he wasn't working or using heavy weights in his routine. Quite the opposite. For as slender as he was, for as flexible as he was, pound for pound George was one of the strongest, fittest kids in the school. And only a freshman at that. More than once, Delwig shook his head.

The whole time George worked out however, the only thing he thought about was Fuentes and what he might do next.

CHAPTER NINETY

After an early afternoon briefing, Graff had them all wired and on high alert.

Eiselmann would pick up Mike, Stephen, Gavin and Bobby and transport them to North for the game after they stopped to get something to eat. He would receive an undercover escort from Nate Kaupert and Sheriff Deputy Alex Jorgenson in separate unmarked cars. Once at North, Kaupert and Jorgenson would remain in the parking lot watching for a blue Impala or a BMW or the navy blue Camaro Manny Benevides drove. Eiselmann would be in the gym and Bobby was his sole responsibility.

O'Connor would blend into the crowd like he always did, but his whole focus would be on George.

Brooke Beranger and Tom Albrecht were to shadow Jeremy and Vicki in separate vehicles. They were good at it and Graff trusted them. Once they arrived at North, they would be in the gym with their eyes on the crowd looking and watching for Fuentes or Manny Benevides or anyone else who fit the look. Racial profiling or not, it didn't matter. Not on this night at least. A kid's life- make that several kids' lives- were at stake. They knew who to look for thanks to O'Connor and his gang and drug work.

Graff was at the gym early. He checked exits. He checked the locker room and the weight room. He checked back hallways and stairwells. He would repeat his steps several times before game time. He saw George, but other than a slight nod there wasn't any overt contact from either of them.

It was decided not to let the North administration know what was happening. At least not until it was over and only when necessary. Maybe not ever.

CHAPTER NINETY-ONE

The plan was simple because Fuentes believed things worked better the simpler they were.

The idea was to have two North High School students who were MS-13 members, low rung guys, lure him outside. If luring didn't work, they were to use a gun and force him. There, two other members would wait in a car and he'd be stuffed in the backseat and taken away.

A call would be made.

Simple. The way he liked it.

CHAPTER NINETY-TWO

George watched the crowd more than the game. He stood on the end next to the aisle about half way up the student section and next to Caitlyn and Sean. Over to his left in the next section of bleachers was the middle school group of Bobby, Mikey, Gavin, Garrett and several girls. He smiled. He wasn't sure who was flirting with who, but decided that middle school kids were pretty inept, not that he was one to talk.

Randy was on fire and playing possessed and Brett kept feeding him the ball. The second quarter had just begun and he had fourteen of the twenty-one points. Racine Park was bigger and more experienced, but North was ahead by six. For the second time, Park switched the defensive player on Randy and it was Brian who benefitted, sinking two three pointers and a layup in under a minute. The North crowd yelled, *"Bri-an! Bri-an! Bri-an!"*

"Time Out!" the Park coach yelled throwing down a clipboard and breaking it in half earning him a technical foul.

"What? Are you kidding me? Are you serious? What a joke!"

That earned him another technical and an ejection. He didn't go quietly, shouting and sweating and red-faced, arms flying as he unloaded on the official.

The North student section began singing, *"Nah nah nah nah, nah nah nah nah, hey hey hey, goodbye!"* and waving as they did so until he left the court.

Brian sunk all four technical shots, again to *"Bri-an! Bri-an! Bri-an!"*

All smiles, Jeremy said Vicki, "I think he's developing folk legend status."

North walked into the timeout with an eighteen point lead.

"George?"

George turned around to see who had called his name and it was a pretty dark-haired girl he recognized from his Spanish class. He smiled and said,

"Yes?"

"I was wondering . . . can you help me with my Spanish sometime after school? I can't get the preterit form," she said with a laugh.

"Sure, no problem," he said smiling broader.

She made a face and said, "No problem for you, maybe."

Embarrassed, he said, "I didn't mean it like that."

"I know," I was just teasing.

Caitlyn rolled her eyes. She wasn't sure why she was annoyed, but she was.

"We were wondering," Alexa Oshwieder said gesturing at her three friends, one of whom was Tricia Garland. He didn't know the other two other than that all four played for the North Girls Basketball team. "We have a game tomorrow night here against Tosa East. Would you and Randy and Billy and Brett want to go get something to eat after?"

"I think so," George said. "I can check with them tonight."

"Great!" Alexa said while the other girls were smiling and nodding. To Caitlyn she said, "You and Brian can come too, if you want."

"We'll see," she answered with a shrug of her shoulders.

Bobby climbed over the bleachers and snuck up behind George, who was caught by surprise- a rarity.

"Hi, Guys!"

Bobby eyed the girls behind George, smiled and said, "Who are you?"

Alexa smiled and said, "I'm Alexa. This is Tricia, Georgiana and Beth."

"Hi, I'm Bobby."

Tricia said, "You look just like Brett."

Bobby laughed and said, "I'm new and improved."

The girls laughed and Bobby seized the opening.

"Brett was born and God saw all the mistakes He made and eighteen months later, I was born. New and improved!"

"And full of shit," Sean said making the girls laugh.

To George, Bobby said, "I'm going to the concession stand. You want anything?"

"I can go with you."

Bobby hugged his neck and whispered, "Stay here with them. I'll be right back. Promise."

George hesitated not wanting Bobby to go alone.

"Really, I'll be right back. You want anything?"

"You have to be careful, Bobby."

On impulse Bobby hugged him and said, "I will."

At the same time Bobby walked behind the girls, Brian hit another three pointer and the whole student section jumped to their feet. Eiselmann lost sight of him.

"Pat, do you see Bobby?"

"No, lost him. He was just with George." Seconds later, "He's behind George about two rows up talking with a couple of students. His back is to us."

"You sure?" Eiselmann wasn't.

"I think so. Can't tell for sure."

That kid wasn't Bobby. During that conversation, Bobby had joined a pack of kids moving in mass down the stairs. Still in that group, he disappeared through the gym doors and into the lobby.

No one, not George or Eiselmann or O'Connor or anyone else noticed the two Latino boys following Bobby.

CHAPTER NINETY-THREE

Bobby took a look at the lines in front of the concession stand and decided he'd use the restroom first.

Tom Albrecht had his back to the restroom, his head craned watching the group at the concession stand. Brooke Beranger had overheard the conversation between O'Connor and Eiselmann, so she stood in the far doorway staring up at the student section.

Bobby was three long steps to the door to the restroom when someone snagged his right arm. Thinking it was a friend and with his guard down, he turned around to see who it was.

"I have a gun and it's aimed at your stomach," said a skinny Latino high school kid with his hand in his coat pocket. "We're going to walk out the door and you're going to get into a car. Don't pull away and don't try anything."

"Just in case you get any ideas, we have someone in the stands just behind your parents with a gun," the other boy lied. "He's crazy and not afraid to shoot."

Bobby froze, his eyes darting left and right.

"Don't think I won't pull the trigger, because I will. Let's move. Now," he hissed.

The other boy slung his arm around Bobby's shoulders like they were buddies and directed Bobby through the doors. A beat up Dodge Charger pulled up and a boy got out of the passenger seat and opened up the back door and slid in. The boy with his arm slung around Bobby's shoulders shoved Bobby into the back seat and got in after him slamming the door shut behind him. The boy with the gun got into the passenger seat. The two boys on either side of Bobby punched him. Bobby tried to cover up but couldn't effectively.

Deputy Alex Jorgenson had parked in the back of the student lot near the exit. He had listened to the radio transmission from inside the gym. When the dark Dodge Charger passed him, he noticed two boys throwing punches at another boy hunched over in the backseat.

Jorgenson sat up straighter. He looked through the photographs that were given to him during the briefing and he thought that the passenger riding shotgun bore a resemblance to one of them.

"O'Connor, Eiselmann, I need you to ID both Bobby McGovern and George Tokay right now! I mean *right now!*"

That created a jumble of radio traffic with people talking over one another.

"What's happening?" Graff jumped in.

"I'm looking right at George," O'Connor said.

"I still see the kid we think is Bobby. He hasn't moved," Eiselmann said.

"What do you see?" Graff asked.

"What do you mean, 'you think' is Bobby?" Albrecht asked.

"Oh, shit! The kid just turned around. That's not Bobby! We need to find him?" Eiselmann.

Jorgenson jumped in. "It might be nothin' or it might be somethin', but I'm going to follow an old Dodge Charger. It just left the lot and a kid was getting beat up in the backseat. One of the passengers looked like Enrique Suarez."

"I'm going into the stands now," Albrecht said taking off on a jog.

He took the stairs two at a time, pushing aside two kids taking their time to get to their seats.

"Hey, what the hell?" one of the called to Albrecht's back.

Albrecht reached George, pulled him into the aisle away from the other kids and said, "Where's Bobby?"

Filled with dread, George opened his mouth but froze. Albrecht shook him and repeated, "Where's Bobby?"

"Concession stand. He said he'd be right back."

"Brooke, Pat, check the lobby. Paul, check the restroom."

"What do you want me to do," Nathan Kaupert radioed in.

"Watch the parking lot!" Graff said. "Go up and down the rows. Look everywhere and report back." To Alex Jorgenson, he said, "Jorgy, stay with that Charger but don't get too close. Get a plate and run it. Keep us posted."

Albrecht started down the aisle, but stopped when George called to him. He held up his cell phone and said, "It's Angel!"

CHAPTER NINETY-FOUR

George texted Angel and told him he had to go to a quieter place because it was too noisy in the gym. He said he'd call as soon as he could.

Graff led him to the hallway in the back of the gym and Albrecht, Eiselmann, O'Connor and Beranger joined them. George was to call him, have him on speaker so they could listen, but say nothing that would give them away.

"Angel, this is George."

He spoke rapidly in broken sentences. Panicky, anxious, scared.

"George, I gotta pick you up, Man. Fuentes. He's crazy. He has your brother . . . Bobby, the little one, Brett's brother. Him and Manny and some other assholes, they have him and my mom. Unless I bring you to them, they're going to kill them. Please, George. I gotta pick you up, Man."

'Go with him, Shadow. I am there.'

"Where are they, Angel?"

"My house. Manny, my asshole brother brought them there."

"How many are there beside Fuentes and your brother?"

"Shit, George, maybe three, no four other assholes. I didn't want any of this gang shit, Man. None of it."

"I will wait for you outside in front of the gym."

Graff shook his head emphatically. O'Connor squinted at George wondering what he was thinking.

"I'll be there. Maybe fifteen minutes."

"I will be waiting, Angel. Do not worry."

"Fuck, George. My mom . . . I'm sorry . . . I don't know what else to do, Man."

'Tell him not to worry, Shadow.'

"Angel, it will be okay. Do not worry."

Benevides clicked off.

'I will be there, Shadow. A weapon will present itself to you. You will know when that happens.'

"George, I cannot and will not let you go. You will be walking to your death," Graff said. "Bobby's too."

George smiled at him and said, "I do not think so, Detective Jamie. My grandfather will be with me."

The men stared at him, mouths open, eyes blinking.

"He will be with me. I am not afraid."

Graff started to object, but O'Connor waved him quiet.

"Explain."

Without expression, George filled them in on what his grandfather told him.

Eiselmann glanced at his watch and said, "We're running out of time."

Graff turned his back on them, faced a wall and shouted, "Fuck!"

"Detective Jamie, I will go with Angel. I need to protect my brother and Angel's mother."

"That's one against six, George," Beranger said.

He turned to her and said, "My grandfather will be with me."

"No time, Graff," Eiselmann warned.

Jamie keyed his radio and said, "Jorgy, where are you?"

"A block down from them. They pulled up to a house. They have Bobby."

"Hold your position. We're coming."

As they moved to the front of the gym, Graff laid out their plan.

"George, Angel is not to know we know and he cannot know we're providing back up." To O'Connor he said, "Give George your radio. Stash it so they won't find it."

"Won't work, Jamie," Eiselmann warned. "First thing they're going to do is frisk him."

"You want me to send him in blind?" Graff answered. "Can't do that."

"George, once you're inside the house, you have to hold their attention. You have to make sure they're not suspecting anyone else. Just you and Angel," O'Connor said.

"We can give him ten minutes," Beranger said. "Tom and I will stroll up the sidewalk like we're taking a nighttime walk. If there are lookouts and I'm sure there will be, probably one or two, we take them out."

"We can do that," Albrecht said.

"Nate and Jorgy position themselves in the backyard to prevent any escape, but they stay hidden. You and Paul take the front door," O'Connor continued. "I'll go in the back."

"And if the doors are locked?" Eiselmann asked.

"George, can you make sure the back door stays unlocked?" O'Connor asked.

"I will try."

"If he can keep them occupied and if Brooke and Tom take out their lookouts, I'll pick the lock if I have to."

"Radio when you do and Eiselmann and I will crash the front door."

"Just don't catch any friendlies in a crossfire," Brooke warned.

They were near the front of the gym and Graff directed everyone to get to their cars. Fortunately, all of them were in their own vehicles, no cop cars, nothing marked or unmarked.

Brooke and Tom took off on a jog towards Albrecht's car. Nate sat in his car at the end of the parking lot in almost the same slot Jorgenson had parked in.

O'Connor and Eiselmann took off towards Eiselmann's car because it was the closest.

Graff turned to George, placed his hands on George's shoulders and said, "I don't want you to be a hero. Use your instincts. They're good. You're smart. But these guys don't give a shit and they will kill you and Bobby and everyone else if they need to. Do you understand?"

"Yes, Sir."

Time was short. Angel had to be right around the corner.

"George, you and the guys mean a lot to me. If anything happens to you . . ."

George smiled at him and said, "I will be okay, Detective Jamie. My grandfather will be with me."

"Car coming," Kaupert said.

Graff took off on a run.

"Show time, Guys. Pat, you and Paul know where they're headed. Get there but park far enough away so you won't be seen. Tom and Brooke, follow them, but not too close. George gets ten minutes max before we go in. Tom and Brooke, the lookouts need to be taken out before that."

"Got it," Brooke said.

"He's here," Kaupert said. "Driving a little fast. Kid must be scared."

"Fuck!" Graff mumbled. "Saddle up and get moving. Everyone comes home safe, especially George and Bobby."

CHAPTER NINETY-FIVE

"Please don't hurt us. Please don't hurt this boy," Lina Benevides pleaded. "Please."

"Momma, sit down and shut up," Manny shouted.

Bobby didn't know any of these people. He had never been to this part of town that he could remember. He sat naked in a kitchen chair that was dragged into the living room. His hands were duct taped behind his back and his legs were spread and duct taped to the chair legs. He was embarrassed being naked in front of them, especially someone's mother. He knew he had a black eye and fat lip and his stomach and balls hurt from the beating he took in the car.

'You're going to be okay, Bobby. I'll be with you.'

Bobby blinked. He was staring at Kaz, only it wasn't Kaz. He was a little smaller and he knew Brian was playing basketball. He tried to say something behind he duct tape across his mouth.

"Hey, Punk Ass, shut the fuck up!" Manny yelled.

'They can't see me and they can't hear me. You don't need to speak with words. Speak with your heart.'

'Who . . .'

'I'm Kaz, Brian's brother. Call me Brad. See this man? This is George's grandfather. We're here to help.'

Bobby blinked again and saw an old man with a wrinkled face and long gray hair tied back in a braid smiling at him. He stood directly in front of Bobby, kind of shielding him from Fuentes and Manny. Brad squatted down on one knee to Bobby's side and had a hand on Bobby's shoulder and one on his thigh.

'I need you to act scared. I need you to cry and act weak. We think that will help.'

Bobby glanced at him and up at George's grandfather who smiled at him and nodded.

He began to cry. It didn't take much, really. He was petrified. He didn't want to die. And he didn't want to die naked in a room full of people he didn't know.

'You're going to be okay, Bobby. Grandfather and I will do what we can. George is coming.'

'But they want to kill him!' Bobby cried even harder.

'Anything is possible, Bobby. Grandfather and I don't have any control over that. But I think you and George will be okay. But we'll be here with you. Promise.'

Bobby stared at the boy who had Brian's smile, his greenish-hazel eyes and dark wavy hair.

"What are you looking at, Punk Ass?" Fuentes asked. "Crying like a baby. No one here is going to help you."

Fuentes started in his direction, but Brad stood up and placed his arm around Bobby's shoulder and kind of hugged him. It didn't feel like a hug to Bobby, just a feeling of warmth and peace.

George's grandfather blocked Fuentes' path and waved his arms in a circle. He chanted something Bobby didn't understand.

But Fuentes stopped. He started forward again, but stopped again. He ran his hand over his face like something was in his eyes. He turned back around and waited for George and Angel to arrive.

"How long 'til they get here, Bendejo?" he asked.

"Should be quick now," Manny answered.

The boy, Brad squatted back down at Bobby's side with one hand on his shoulder and the other on his thigh and smiled at him.

'Keep crying and keep acting scared. It will help.'

Bobby nodded slightly and wept. A little snot ran from his nose and he was embarrassed by that.

'It's okay, Bobby. That'll help.'

One of the guys who pounded on him was outside with some other guy waiting in a car in front of the house. Fuentes and Manny and two others were crammed in the small living room glaring at Bobby and trying hard not to look at Manny's mother. Instead, they fiddled with their handguns. All four had one and Fuentes also had a big knife.

Bobby heard one car door and a second and he knew George had arrived.

'*Will George know you're here?*' Bobby asked Brad.

Brad smiled at Bobby and said, 'He already knows about his grandfather.'

Bobby was happy that George had come, but equally sad. He didn't want George to die because of him and that thought made Bobby cry a little harder.

CHAPTER NINETY-SIX

"Jorgy, you and Nate get to the back of the house. Stay hidden, but I want you ready. Brooke and Tom, get moving. Pat, get to the back door, but wait until you hear from me."

In situations like this, Graff acted on remote. Much of it, most of it, was his training, but a good share was gut instinct.

Brooke and Tom strolled up the sidewalk talking and laughing like any young couple might do. Graff admired how good they were and a second thought occurred that perhaps it wasn't an act.

"Huh," he muttered.

"What?" Eiselmann asked.

"Nothing."

Tom and Brooke reached the car when Brooke bent down to ostensibly tie her shoe. Instead, she pulled a gun from her back waistband and bull rushed the passenger side of the car as Tom ran around to the other side and rushed the driver. Car doors were pulled open and guns were shoved in the kids' faces giving them no opportunity to fight back.

They yanked the two boys out of the car and threw them onto the frozen earth. Brooke's fought back a little, so she clubbed him once on the forehead with the butt of her handgun. Stunned, she was able to throw him back down on the grass, cuff his hands and drag him away from the front of the house and down the street where Albrecht waited with his kid. They threw them in the back of their car after frisking them both. They found nothing except a couple of joints, a dime bag and rolling paper along with a couple of loaded clips for their Glock 17s. No other weapons.

"Pat, move into position, but wait for my signal." To Eiselmann, he said, "Let's go, but we move quietly and wait on George. No chances. Everyone, any shooting we move in fast."

CHAPTER NINETY-SEVEN

Angel walked in the door and was greeted with a fist to his face and one to his stomach. He was grabbed by his jacket and thrown onto the living room floor.

Lina Benevides shrieked.

George had shed his jacket in Angel's car before going into the house. Someone had waited to throw a punch at George, but he stepped out of the way and used the puncher's momentum to throw his face into the door frame. George grabbed him by the hair and slammed his face back into the door frame where he crumbled to the floor like a rag doll.

He heard a pistol cock and someone said, "Tough guy, I'll kill you right here."

George turned around slowly and stared into a strikingly familiar face, that of Fuentes. It wasn't that the cousins were identical, but the similarity between the two couldn't be dismissed.

"Why don't you join us in the living room, Puta?" he said with a sly smile.

George regained his focus, breathing slowly, deeply. He saw Bobby, naked, crying and scared. He flashed back to the summer of death when he had crept into the cottage and saw his father, his brothers, his uncle and Danny duct taped to chairs and Fuentes, the older cousin, hovering over them with two knives.

He saw his grandfather, who smiled at him and gave him a nod. George felt at peace. He saw Kaz or someone who looked like Kaz at Bobby's side. He smiled and George knew who it was. George nodded at him.

"So, Indian Boy. You murdered my cousin."

"We fought man to man. I gave him a chance to leave. He did not take it and he died."

Fuentes smiled, nodded and said, "That simple? How can I possibly believe you killed my cousin? He was a good man."

"He was a coward like you. He was dirt."

"You talk like a big man with a gun in your face," Manny said. "Don't disrespect my friend."

"You disrespect yourself by having him as a friend."

"Enough! Get your clothes off, Puta! Everything off!" Fuentes shouted.

"Please, no!" Lina Benevides cried.

George smiled at her and in Spanish said, "It is okay, Mother."

"I said get your clothes off!"

George shook his head and said softly, but firmly, "No."

Fuentes blinked at him, licked his lips and said, "No?"

George repeated, "No. You will kill me whether I have my clothes on or off."

'Shadow, a weapon will present itself to you. Be ready. Focus.'

"So, maybe I begin by cutting off parts of this piece of shit," Fuentes said pointing his Glock in Bobby's direction.

George took it all in. One gang member watched the exchange like a tennis match. Afraid that bullets would begin flying, he backed up into a corner. He had his 9mm at his side, but cocked and ready, his finger on the trigger. The other sat against the doorframe where George had slammed his face. He was able to register what was happening, but barely so. He had his gun in his lap. Clearly, he wasn't ready for any action.

"That would make you a coward like your cousin. Why not fight me man to man? Or are you afraid you might die like your cousin?"

Manny charged at him with his arm and handgun outstretched.

George reacted quickly and without thinking about it.

George grabbed the slide with his left hand preventing it from firing. He slammed Manny's arm with his right disarming the heavyset boy. The gun ended up in George's left hand, but he switched it to his right. His left hand grabbed Manny by the hair spinning him around and shoved the gun into his ear.

Rodriguez stood in the corner and raised his weapon instinctively. George shot him in the chest twice. The groggy kid sitting on the floor raised his weapon and George shot him in the face. Once was enough.

"Bendejo, you're using this puta as a shield?" Fuentes laughed. "What makes you think I care about him?"

He answered his own question by shooting Manny Benevides three times in the chest.

George stumbled as the large boy fell into and partially on top of him.

Fuentes stepped forward, his gun pointed at George's face.

CHAPTER NINETY-EIGHT

"Now! Now! Now!" Graff yelled.

Eiselmann kicked the door in. He scrambled in low and fast, while Graff went in high and fast after him. O'Connor kicked the backdoor in and ran through the small kitchen.

Their guns were pointed at the only one standing and all three fired at the same time. None of them knew exactly how many shots were fired, but they were pretty certain Fuentes was dead before he hit the floor.

It was deafening and the air smoky.

Lina Benevides screamed from underneath Angel who had jumped up and had laid on top of her.

Helpless and unable to move, Bobby had his eyes shut. His tears had stopped, but his fear, thick and ugly, was on him like a shirt.

On the floor, Fuentes twitched, raised an arm and George shot him once in the chest.

It was over.

CHAPTER NINETY-NINE

O'Connor, Eiselmann and Graff held their positions, their guns trained on Fuentes. Graff was the first to shift to Rodriquez crumpled in the corner. Blood dripped out of his mouth down his neck and onto his chest that had two holes clustered near his heart.

O'Connor spun around and pointed his weapon at the boy on the floor against the wall. He had a hole just above his right eye and most of his brains were splattered against the wall behind him.

"Is there anyone else in the house?" Graff asked.

There was no answer.

"Pat, clear the house," Graff said.

"There isn't anyone else here," Angel said. "There's two outside in the car in front of the house." He had his arms around his mother who held her face in both hands and cried in hysterical sobs.

Pat walked from room to room to be certain, but like Angel said, there was no one else. He came back and said, "All clear."

"George, are you okay? Did he hurt you?"

George rolled Manny off of him and stood up. "No, Sir. I am okay."

"Bobby, are you okay?"

George walked over to him and peeled the tape off of his mouth. He lifted his chin up and whispered, "Are you okay?"

Bobby nodded and whispered, "George, I want to get dressed. Please!"

"Angel, can I have a knife or scissors?"

Angel walked into the kitchen and George heard him opening a drawer and closing it. He came back and handed the scissors to him.

"Angel, can you help Bobby while I speak with George?" Graff asked.

George was torn between helping Bobby and talking to Jamie, but Angel said, "I will do this."

The living room was crowded with bodies living and dead. Lina stepped carefully over Manny's legs and helped Angel remove the tape from Bobby. Embarrassed, Bobby couldn't cover himself fast enough.

"George, whose weapon did you use?"

George pointed at Manny and said, "His."

"How did you get it?"

"I took it from him."

The three men didn't know how that was possible, so George asked Eiselmann to holster his weapon and in slow motion, he reenacted what he had done. The three men watched him and then looked at each other in disbelief.

"How . . . where . . ." Eiselmann said.

George shrugged and said, "Brett showed me when we went shooting. He said a handgun can't fire when you grab the slide."

"Wow!" was Eiselmann's response.

"Okay, walk us through who you shot and how many times you shot them," Graff said, "But do it quickly."

George didn't waste any time, using few words.

"Who shot Manny?" O'Connor asked.

"Fuentes," Angel answered.

O'Connor held up a hand and ran it through his long hair.

"What?" Eiselmann asked.

"We. We have an opportunity," he answered.

"George, can you help Bobby get dressed. Angel, can you and your mother go into the kitchen, please? Paul, stick your head out the backdoor and tell Nate and Jorgy to hold their positions."

That done, the three officers huddled.

"What are you thinking?" Graff asked.

"If MS-13 finds out George shot members of his gang, regardless of who killed Fuentes, they might want revenge. Possibly. Maybe."

Graff frowned at him and Eiselmann picked up Pat's train of thought.

"So George didn't shoot anyone. Manny had second thoughts and he not only defended his mother and brother, he protected George and Bobby."

"That way, George didn't shoot anyone," O'Connor added. "And we shot Fuentes."

Both officers waited for Graff to come around to their thinking.

Graff was as solid as granite. He didn't like to fudge on honesty because he believed that once you travel down that road, you can never get back.

"I want to call the Cap. I think he'll be okay with it, but I want to run it by him."

"You sure you want to do that?" Eiselmann asked.

"No, but I need to."

The longer he waited and thought about it, he might change his mind, so he stepped away and called Jack O'Brien, explained what had happened and what they had in mind and why. Graff listened. He added a "Yes, Sir" and "No, Sir" a couple of times, but mostly listened.

He dialed off, took a deep breath, faced the two other officers and nodded. "Let's get everyone back in here."

George and Bobby were in the bathroom.

"I need to pee, George," Bobby said, his voice shaking as much as his hands and legs.

He relieved himself as George steadied him. After, because he trembled so badly, George helped him lift his legs to get them into his boxers and jeans. He sat Bobby down on the toilet so he could put on Bobby's socks and shoes and finally, his shirt.

Still shaking, Bobby stayed seated. He was sweaty and pale and George thought he was going to be sick.

'Hey, Bobby, it's over.'

Bobby nodded.

'Look at me, Bobby.'

It took a little time, but eventually Bobby raised his head and stared at Brad through teary eyes.

'It's over and you and George lived. That's important.'

Bobby nodded.

Brad smiled at him and said, 'Bri loves you and I know why.' He smiled again and touched Bobby's chest.

To Bobby, he didn't feel a hand, but rather a warmth that a touch might bring.

'You're pure. You're honest. And there's no one like you.'

Bobby didn't know how to respond, maybe couldn't respond.

'Can you let Bri know I was here? And if he needs me, I'll be,' he touched Bobby's heart. 'Right here.'

Bobby and George were alone. Bobby looked up at George and blinked. George smiled at him and hugged his little brother and they held onto each other until Graff called to them to come out.

"George, don't tell anyone I was a baby, okay?"

George hugged him again, kissed his forehead and said, "You are not a baby. You were scared and there is nothing wrong with that."

It took a little convincing to get Lina Benevides to come around to it, but with Angel's help, she agreed. George remained stoic and Graff knew he wasn't happy. If Graff was honest, George was even more so.

O'Connor wiped Manny's handgun getting rid of George's fingerprints and placed it back in Manny's hand.

"I want to make sure everyone has the story straight," Graff said.

Each took part in the retelling except for Bobby who couldn't bring himself to look at anyone. He sat next to George on the couch with his head resting on George's shoulder. George had his arm around him.

George's grandfather stood quietly by the front door. George would look up at him and his grandfather would nod and smile approvingly.

'Grandfather, it is a lie.'

His grandfather nodded.

'You taught me to live in truth.'

His grandfather nodded again.

'You want me to speak a lie?'

'Shadow, there is one truth and there are shades of what is truth.'

'I don't understand.'

'Your brother, the one you hold. Would it serve him if you spoke the truth and he should die?'

George brushed Bobby's forehead with his lips.

'Would it serve your father and your brothers if you spoke the truth and they should die?'

George brushed Bobby's forehead with his lips again.

'There is only one truth. There are shades of truth, Shadow. The bigger truth is that you can save your father and your brothers.'

'But it is a lie.'

Grandfather smiled at him and said, 'It is good that you struggle with truth and untruth. It shows your goodness, Shadow. Your goodness is who you are. It grows in your heart and your heart grows stronger because of it.'

And Grandfather disappeared.

"George, what are you thinking?" O'Connor asked.

George looked at him squarely, at Eiselmann and finally at Jamie and said, "It is a lie. But it will save Father and my brothers. It will save Angel and his mother."

"Okay, it's settled," Graff said. "Mrs. Benevides?"

She nodded and said, "Si."

"Angel?"

He nodded and said, "Yes."

"Bobby?"

Bobby nodded, but kept his head on George's shoulder. In a tiny whisper he said, "Yes."

"Paul, run George and Bobby back to North. The game should just about be over by now and Jeremy and Vicki will be anxious."

"Pat, bring in Nate and Jorgy."

He took a deep breath and called Albrecht and Beranger.

"Take them to the station. Book them on first-degree intentional homicide, kidnapping, use or possession of a handgun and an armor-piercing bullet during crime, battery and if you want, throw in the pot. I'll touch base with you when I get there."

"Is everyone okay? George? Bobby?" Beranger asked.

"All's good. No collateral damage."

He hung up and thought, 'Except truth and honesty.'

By the time they got back, Brett, Brian and the twins had received a standing ovation as they were replaced with substitutes. They sat on the bench laughing and cheering and relaxed with a twenty-three point lead. George and Bobby were grilled by friends in the student section as to where they went and how Bobby got the black eye and split lip. Neither answered their questions other than to say they had taken a walk.

The final buzzer sounded and most of the crowd left. The four girls stayed behind, as did Cat and Sean. George and Bobby congratulated their brothers, even though neither were in the mood to do so. They had squinted at Bobby, at George and waited for an explanation.

"We'll tell you at home," George said quietly.

While the boys showered and changed, Jeremy and Vicki questioned them, but Bobby refused to say anything and George only repeated what he had told his brothers.

The ride home was silent. Jeremy and Vicki talked about the game, congratulated the boys and that was about it.

Jeremy dropped his family off in the circle drive and then parked the car in the garage. His cell buzzed. He pulled it out of his pocket and saw it was Jamie Graff. They had a long one-sided conversation. After, Jeremy walked up the back stoop and stamped his shoes before slipping them off on the little rug and in stocking feet, joined his family who had been seated at the kitchen table.

Vicki caught his look and knew something was on his mind, but waited.

Bobby sat between Brian and George, but closer to George. His chin was on his chest and his hands were folded in his lap.

Stoic and without much of a preamble, George said, "I have to tell you the truth."

He and Bobby had decided independently of one another, but it was the family rule about trust and honesty that moved them to the same conclusion.

As George told them what had happened, Bobby didn't say anything nor did he even look up from his hands. At various times during the telling, Brian reached over and held Bobby's hand. Vicki bit her lip and she felt cold despite the warmth of the house. What began for Brett as concern grew into worry and then anger the longer George spoke. Billy listened, his eyes darting from George to Bobby to Jeremy and to Vicki. Randy's expression, as it often did, mirrored Jeremy's. He even covered his mouth with one hand, just as Jeremy did.

At last he finished and no one said anything until Bobby said, "I'm sorry." His eyes were still downcast, his hands still in his lap.

"Why are you sorry?" Brett asked.

"Because I wasn't paying attention. Again. I'm sorry."

"Nothing to be sorry about, Bobby," Billy said. "You went to the concession stand and the restroom."

George and Jeremy locked eyes. Randy wasn't sure what was communicated, but he was pretty sure something was.

"So, it's over. I mean, really over?" Randy asked.

"Detective Jamie, Detective Pat and Detective Paul think so."

"But they don't know for sure," Brett said.

"Do you think Angel or his mom will say anything?" Brian asked.

George shook his head and said, "They are in as much danger as we are if they say anything."

Billy nodded thoughtfully and said, "It's over."

George didn't bother responding again.

Again, they sat in silence until Vicki said, "Does anyone have any homework?"

"I have to read," Billy answered pushing his chair back. He walked around the table, stood between Bobby and George, hugged them both and left the kitchen.

Randy did the same and said, "Thanks, George. Again," with an extra hug for George.

Brian and Brett stayed behind until Jeremy said, "Brett and Brian, can you excuse us, please?"

It was pretty clear to him that neither wanted to leave, but they slowly got up and left the kitchen to Jeremy and Vicki with Bobby and George."

When he was sure the four of them were alone, George said to Jeremy, "You already knew."

Jeremy nodded and said, "Jamie called me as I was putting the car in the garage. He and Jeff and I are best friends and he figured that you would tell the truth."

Bobby snuck a glance at Jeremy, at his mom and back down at his hands.

"He knew you had trouble with . . . the story, but that you agreed to keep us safe."

George said nothing.

"Is there something else you want to tell us?" Vicki said.

Bobby looked up at George and said, "Not yet. I want to talk to Brian first."

"Brian?" Vicki said.

"Then I can tell you and dad."

Vicki and Jeremy exchanged a worried look, but Jeremy said, "Okay. But he's still kind of fragile, so take it easy."

Bobby nodded and got up from the table to find him.

"I'm going to sit outside," George said.

"Would you like some company?" Vicki asked.

George smiled weakly and said, "No, Mom. I would like to be by myself."

As George headed out the door, Jeremy said, "It's cold out, George. Take a jacket."

But George didn't. He shut the door behind him and at first stood on the back stoop and leaned against the pillar. He sat down on the top step and stared off into the night.

Stars were brighter in the country. The moon, big and silvery, sparkled against the snow on the ground and the icy branches of the bushes and trees. George never tired of the snow and ice, so foreign to him coming from the dry southwest.

He wept silently.

He had killed two more and maybe a third on this night. In one and a half short years and at age fifteen, he had killed eight or nine men. The most difficult thing for him to justify was that as one of the *Dine'*, death was not their way. Their way was peace and life, not death.

He had even visited Father Donahue at St. Williams and while it technically wasn't a confession as much as it was a lengthy discussion, even he couldn't convince George that he had acted in self-defense and for the protection of his family and himself.

'*Can we look at the stars?*'

George knew the voice and recognized the question that had been posed to him so many times. He knew the little boy, barefoot and barebacked, before he sat down next to him.

'*Robert?*'

The little boy giggled, pointed up and said, 'That's the Big Dipper!' The little boy followed it and said, 'There's the North Star!' Proud of himself, he turned to George, smiled and kissed his cheek, although it didn't feel like a kiss so much as it did a feeling of warmth.

'*Robert?*'

'*You can tell direction from the North Star, right George?*'

George nodded, tears filling his eyes and spilling down his cheeks.

'*Why are you crying?*'

George shook his head.

'Are they happy tears or sad tears?'

'Both.'

'Why are you sad, George?'

George shook his head again and whispered, 'I miss you!'

The little boy giggled and said, 'Why?'

'Because I love you. I love you and I miss you. I love all of you and I miss all of you.'

The little boy laughed again and said, 'We are always with you, George. Mother, Grandmother, Grandfather, Mary and William. We're always with you.'

'You are?'

The little boy laughed. George loved his laugh. He had always loved his laugh. Perhaps he missed his laughter the most. Maybe not. He also loved looking at the stars with him, the brightness in his eyes, the sense of wonder in his face.

'William, too?'

He laughed again and said, 'All of us.'

George wiped tears off his face and said, 'You must be cold.'

He smiled and said, 'I'm never cold, George. You keep me warm.'

George shook his head, not knowing what the little boy meant.

'You keep me warm. You keep all of us warm.' He placed his hand on George's heart and said, 'We live in your heart, George. We have always lived in your heart.'

'My heart?'

'We will always live in your heart.'

The little boy kissed him on the cheek, smiled and vanished as quickly as he had arrived.

They had brushed their teeth side by side, took turns peeing and flushing and washing hands. Bobby stared at his face in the mirror, turning left and right. He gently pulled down his lip to take a better look. It had swollen and it bled weakly where it was cracked.

"Are your teeth loose?" Brian asked.

Bobby wiggled one or two and shook his head.

Brian took a tissue, wadded it and dabbed it on Bobby's lip. The tissue came up pink. Fortunately it was only weeping, but Bobby winced. Brian threw the tissue in the waste can.

Brian said, "Hurt?"

"Not much."

"I guess we won't be doing any butterflies, Eskimos or regulars for a while," Brian said with a smile.

Bobby smiled, reached out and held Brian's shoulder and said, "Butterflies."

The two boys did, but gently.

"Eskimo," Brian said, and the two boys rubbed noses.

"Regular," Bobby said.

Gently, the two boys kissed, smiled at one another and wrapped each other in a warm embrace, clinging to each other tightly.

"I lost one brother, Bobby. I don't want to lose any others, especially you."

Bobby kissed Brian's neck and said, "I was so scared."

"It's over now, Bobby," and kissed his cheek. "I love you."

"I love you."

The two boys stepped apart and Brian gently touched the bruises on Bobby's chest and stomach.

"These hurt?"

"A little."

There was a large bluish bruise that peeked out of his boxers, so Brian gently pulled Bobby's boxers down to get a better look. The bruise extended into his pubic hair and Brian traced it, probing it.

"How much do these hurt, Bobby? Tell the truth."

"They hurt."

Brian hesitated, but said, "I think we should go to bed." He helped Bobby pull up his boxers.

Both boys left the bathroom and walked across the hall into their room. Bobby shut the door behind them and they got into bed. Bobby had positioned himself away from Brian, more to the middle of the bed and on his side facing him. He knew he had to tell him but didn't know how.

"Why are you way over there?" Brian asked.

Bobby moved closer, his feet with Brian's and his hand on Brian's chest. Brian's heart thumped.

"Brian, I have to tell you something."

Brian rolled over onto his side to face Bobby. "What?"

Bobby licked his lips, took a deep breath and said, "You know how George sometimes sees and talks to his grandfather?"

Brian said, "Yeah. Brett saw him, too. In the hospital when the crazy psycho bitch tried to kill him and Tim. I think Stephen saw him. I can't remember if Mikey did."

"I saw him tonight. He stood in front of me when they had me taped to the chair. He did something to stop Fuentes when he came at me."

"Did you hear him talk? Did he say something to you?"

Bobby shook his head and said, "No, not to me. He spoke to George."

"What did he say?"

"Told him it would be okay. Focus. Watch for a weapon. Stuff like that."

Brian started to say something, but Bobby placed a finger on his lips.

"Brian, your brother was there. Brad."

Brian's eyes opened wide and he opened his mouth, but Bobby covered it and said, "Let me finish, okay?"

Brian nodded, so Bobby took his hand away.

"At first, I didn't know who it was, but he looked just like you, only smaller."

"Smaller?"

Bobby nodded. "He said he was there to help and it was like he knew who George's grandfather was. And he knew me."

"How could he know you?" Brian whispered.

"I asked George the same question. George thinks that because you know me, he came to me."

Brian shook his head. "But, why you? Why doesn't he come to me?"

"I knew you were going to ask that. George said this his grandfather comes whenever there is a need. That's what his grandfather told him. So George thinks that because I was so scared, Brad came to me."

Brian rolled over onto his back and put both hands on his chest and stared at the ceiling. He never considered whether or not Bobby was mistaken. He trusted him and he trusted George. He didn't understand it, but he didn't doubt it either.

And it wasn't that he was angry that Brad was with Bobby. It was just that he was sad Brad had never visited him, at least not directly.

Bobby placed a hand on Brian's chest and whispered, "Are you okay?"

"Yeah," Brian answered.

"Brad also said one more thing. I'm not sure what it means and neither does George."

Brian turned his head towards Bobby and asked, "What?"

Bobby patted Brian's chest and said, "Brad said that he will always be here . . . in your heart."

"My heart?"

Bobby patted his chest and said, "That's what he said."

He patted his chest again and said, "He said that you love me."

Brian nodded and said, "I do. When George told us what happened, I was worried. Pissed and worried. I don't need anybody else dying on me."

Bobby smiled at him, kissed him on the cheek and said, "I love you, too."

And he rolled up into his normal sleeping position with one leg over Brian's and his arm across his chest. Brian slipped an arm under Bobby and held him.

It was below zero, but George didn't feel the bite of the cold. He was far too elated, lighter than he had felt in a long time.

As the boys had been taught, George stamped his shoes on the stoop, pushed through the door and slipped them off and tidied up the pile of shoes on the little rug. He locked the door and went to the alarm and set it. At least on this night, he wasn't nearly as worried as he had been the past week or so. In fact, he smiled. A genuine smile, happier than he'd been since, well, for a long time.

The kitchen was lit by a lone light above the sink and Vicki sat at the kitchen table. Knowing she had waited up to speak to him, he sat down with her.

She smiled and said, "George, thank you for helping Bobby. For going to him."

"He is my brother."

Vicki reached over the grasped his hand. "You put yourself in danger. It was kind and brave of you."

George never did well with praise. He wasn't comfortable and never knew how to respond.

"Thank you."

Vicki stood up as did George and they embraced. She pushed his hair off his forehead, kissed him and said, "Thank you, George."

Blushing, George said, "You're welcome."

"Do you have any homework?"

George shook his head and said, "No, I finished it after school."

She rinsed her cup in the sink and placed it in the dishwasher and flicked off the light leaving the kitchen in darkness. George had waited for her and the two of them, followed by Jasmine and Momma walked up the stairs together.

"Goodnight, George. Good dreams."

"Goodnight. You, too."

He tiptoed into the bathroom, brushed his teeth, peed and washed his hands. He walked across the hall to his bedroom, but Billy wasn't there and Brett wasn't in his room. George stripped down to his boxers and went in search of his brothers and he found them in Brian's and Bobby's room. They were talking and laughing in hushed whispers. Brett and Randy made room for him on the bed. Billy was tucked in bed sandwiching Bobby between him and Brian.

Brian said, "Bobby told me about Brad."

George nodded.

"There were times I thought I saw Brad at my house. I would see him out of the corner of my eye, but I'd turn and no one was there. I swear I saw him. Sometimes I'd wake up and see him sitting on the edge of the bed. I'd sit up or blink and he'd be gone."

"Weren't you freaked out?" Billy asked.

Brian shook his head and said, "No, he's my brother. He wouldn't say anything to me, though. And if I looked too long, he'd like . . . vanish."

George said, "Your brother will always be with you, just as my family will always be with me. And if there is a need, he will be there, just like my grandfather has been for me."

"But why can't I see him just because I want to? What if I want to talk to him?" He began to weep and said, "I miss him so much. That's the hardest part of this . . . shit. I'm pissed at mom and dad. They didn't have to kill themselves. And I miss Brad."

George said softly, "I do not have all the answers, Brian. The *Dine'* believe there is a veil that separates the spirit world from the awake world. The spirit world comes to us in our dreams and if we listen with our heart, it speaks to us."

"So, you're saying if I dream about him . . ."

George smiled and nodded and said, "Perhaps. It is the spirit world that comes through the door of our dreams."

Brian didn't know what to make of that. Neither did Bobby or the others. But none of them had any reason to doubt him.

"I miss him, too," Randy said. "I've been thinking about him a lot lately. Sometimes I wonder if we'd all be friends."

"We were friends with Brad and Brian before he died," Billy said. To Brett, George and Bobby, he said, "You would have liked him. He was funny. He was always happy."

Brian turned to Bobby and said, "You and Billy remind me the most of him." To Bobby, he said, "You the most."

"I can see that," Randy said.

"Are you doing okay, Bri? I mean really okay?" Brett asked. Up until now, he had mostly been listening.

Brian shrugged and said, "I think so."

"It's never going to be the same," Billy said. "I mean, I think about my dad all the time. I miss him. As much as I love living here, there are times," he trailed off and wiped a tear from his eye.

"I know you miss your family," Brett said to George, who nodded but remained silent.

Randy slung an arm across George's shoulders and hugged him.

"It's hard for all of us. But this is our family now," Brett said. "We have mom and dad and us. We're family."

Billy added, "I said this before, but this is the best family. I'll always miss my dad, but I couldn't have picked a better family."

The boys all nodded.

"Is there anything we can do for you, Bri?" Randy asked.

Brian shook his head and said, "No, not really. I'll be okay."

"If you need anything, all you have to do is ask," Billy added.

"I know."

Bobby sat up straighter and said, "Has anyone told Brian about the Christmas present for mom and dad?"

Brian looked bewildered as each of the boys looked at one another.

Because it was Randy's idea, he laid it out for him, reminding everyone that they had to practice.

"I don't have a passport," Brian said. "I think I have the money in my account, though."

"Uncle Jeff is helping with the passports," Randy explained. "He's also making sure we get the tickets and stuff. He said you can always pay him back."

"And it's right after your soccer showcase . . . the, what?" Billy asked Brian.

"The Tri-State at the end of June," Brian answered.

"You get done on Saturday and we leave from Chicago on Sunday," Randy said.

"So, you had this planned before my parents . . ." Brian asked.

The boys smiled and Billy said, "Yes, that was the plan. We wanted you to come with us."

"Did my parents know?"

"Uncle Jeff and Randy talked to them," Billy said, "and they said it was fine."

Brian didn't know what to say.

"Bobby, how are you doing?" Randy asked.

Bobby said, "I was so scared. Brett, it was like the night Uncle Tony came. I couldn't stop shaking. I didn't want to die."

"It's over, Bobby. We don't have to worry about that anymore," Billy said.

"Sometimes I wonder if it will ever be over," Brett said. "Not tonight or tomorrow, but some shit at some point. It's like we're doomed or something. Always some dragon to slay."

"That's a cheery thought," Billy said, and all the boys laughed.

"Things will happen, good and bad," George said. "But there will always be a choice. The choice we make determines our future."

"Did your grandfather tell you that?" Randy asked.

George smiled and changed the subject. "We're going to the girl's game tomorrow night. After the game, we're going to get something to eat."

"We are?" Brett asked.

"It's a date. Brian, you and Cat are coming too. And Danny and Sean," George said.

"With who?" Randy asked.

"Have to wait and see," George said with a smile.

"Blind dates suck," Brett muttered.

"You suck, so it doesn't matter," Billy said putting him in a headlock.

"How badly do you want to get hurt?"

"Ooo," Randy said with a laugh.

"What about you? What are you going to do?" Brian asked Bobby.

"I'm going to Mikey's with Stephen, Gavin and Garrett."

"It's late and we have to get to bed. Bobby, if there is any pain, come wake me," George said.

George leaned across Brian and hugged Bobby, kissing him on the cheek. He did the same to Brian and all of the boys followed suit.

"This is the best family," Bobby said with a grin.

"Go to sleep," Brett told him. "You're delirious."

But all of the boys had to agree. They loved their family. Even Brian was coming around to that feeling, too.

Five days after the shootings at the Benevides house, they sat in the principal's conference room one more time and each of the participants could sense the tension. Graff had asked Chuck Gobel to host the meeting ostensibly to tie up loose ends and fill in the details of the heroin and fentanyl case. He had intended to do a lot more than that.

The three administrators, Principal Chuck Gobel and assistants Liz Champion and Bob Farner sat at one end of the table. Across from them sat Jamie Graff, Pat O'Connor and Paul Eiselmann. Paul had his laptop fired up. Jamie had a thick manila folder in from of him. Pat had nothing but a Diet Coke. Gobel and Farner had mugs of coffee, while Champion had a bottle of water.

Graff cleared his throat and opened his folder.

"Thanks for meeting with us. We wanted to bring you up to date on the deaths of the kids and Gordon Huggins."

Gobel nodded. As soon as he was finished here, he had a meeting with Superintendent Ellen Tompkins on the same topic.

"We've linked the deaths of the middle school kids and at least one high school student together with prints and DNA. We know Ricardo Fuentes and MS-13 wanted to put an end to someone cutting into their drug trade. Fuentes was sent up from Chicago specifically to do what was necessary. I don't want to go into details, but we have DNA that ties him to at least four murders, including Rob Kirlie, Doug Huggins, and Ron Terzinski."

"Who is the fourth?" Farner asked.

"A thirteen year old girl, Trina Mezy. She was found wrapped in a blanket and dumped out in the country."

He paused to see if they had questions. He pushed on.

"What bothered the three of us," Graff said, "is that we couldn't figure out how Huggins got his hands on fentanyl. I mean, he's a business teacher. He doesn't teach science and that might be the only way he'd have access to it, but that was unlikely."

As if it were rehearsed and the idea of it was, Eiselmann said, "So we began looking into his paperwork, his friends and a picture of Gordon Huggins came into focus."

"One thing Paul and Pat found was an electronic ledger. I guess that shouldn't have surprised us, since he was a business teacher," Graff said.

"We found payouts, amounts and initials of who they were made to. We found purchases of heroin, but nothing on fentanyl."

Through all this, O'Connor remained silent, but his eyes took in everything.

Graff said, "The initials EF kept coming up."

O'Connor watched a tic start. There was a shift of position in the chair. Eyes downcast for the briefest of moments, but downcast nonetheless.

"We couldn't find anyone in his life with the initials EF. He was a single guy, so we looked at anyone with whom he dated, man or woman," Eiselmann said.

"Man?" Farner asked. "Huggins was gay?"

"No, but we had to check it out," Eiselmann answered. "And the only person we could come up with was you."

The cops stared at Liz Champion.

"E stands for Elizabeth. F stands for Ford, your maiden name," Eiselmann said with a smile.

"That's ridiculous," Champion spit.

"We had been looking at veterinarians as far away as seventy-five miles. But your husband isn't a veterinarian, is he?"

"No, he is not," a smug Champion said.

"He is, however, in procurement at the Milwaukee Zoo. He would have access to fentanyl because he purchases it along with other drugs and food . . . all sorts of things for the zoo, doesn't he?"

"You're fishing and I don't like it. I'll sue your ass if this ruins my career."

"With the cooperation of the zoo administration and the Milwaukee County Sheriff Department, a warrant was issued and we have more than enough evidence that your husband, David, ordered fentanyl above what was requested or needed, but reported only the requested amounts," Eiselmann said waving his hand at his laptop.

"How am I supposed to know what my husband does at work?" Champion spat.

"Do you remember Rob Kirlie?" Graff asked. "It turns out he wasn't as dumb as we thought. He recorded several conversations with you, Liz." He turned to Farner and said, "With you, too, Bob."

"What conversations?" Farner asked.

Graff shook his head and said, "Nothing of any importance as far as you were concerned. You'd bring him into your office and talk about attendance, smoking in the restroom, things like that."

Farner shrugged and said, "He was in my alpha group."

"Right, he was in your alpha group," Graff said, "But he wasn't in your alpha group, was he Liz?"

"We deal with each other's discipline all the time. We overlap and we cover for each other."

"Except the conversations about his friends, Jerry Goldfarb and Doug Sweeney."

Champion laughed and said, "It's called trying to build a relationship, something you obviously don't know anything about."

"You also talked about drugs. What he used. How much. How often."

"So?"

"We interviewed the others on the list and asked them about their conversations with you. Same things you talked to Kirlie about. They remember one specific question you asked them. Each of them said that you asked if they had ever tried heroin and fentanyl."

"Again, so? You turn on the news and you see drug overdoses all the time. Heroin and fentanyl is the drug of choice."

Graff nodded and said, "That's true."

Eiselmann jumped in and said, "But it doesn't explain the journal entries. Huggins recorded money that was given to you."

"Even if what you say is true, do you think I would be stupid enough to put money into my account that would be tied to drugs?"

Eiselmann smiled and said, "No, you're smarter than that. But your husband, not so much. Do you know he had a separate savings account at a different bank that matched not only the amounts that were distributed to him, but were deposited within two days of each date in the ledger?"

Champion flushed. Her eyes darted around the room. Farner sat back in his chair. Gobel inched his chair further away from her.

"And, you were having an affair with Huggins," Graff added.

"That's bullshit!" Champion spat.

"We found his electronic diary. Times, dates, gifts. It's all there, Liz. Including that friendship ring you're wearing on your right pinky."

Reflexively, she covered the ring with her left hand.

He turned to Eiselmann and asked, "Isn't that silver bracelet also mentioned in his diary?"

"It looks just like the picture he posted next to the ring," Eiselmann said turning his laptop towards the three administrators so they could see them. "His diary had pictures."

"But the most convincing evidence came from the cell phone of Ricardo Fuentes. He has your name, address . . . all sorts of information." Graff looked up from his notes and said, "Why would a gang banger from Chicago have that information?"

"You forgot about the recording he made," Eiselmann said.

"I was getting to that, Paul." To Liz he said, "When he tortured Gordon Huggins, he made a recording. It's . . . pretty gruesome, so I'll spare you. But in it, after a toe or two had been snipped off, he named you as the one who organized this and your husband as the person who provided the fentanyl."

"Why, Liz?" Chuck Gobel asked. "Why?"

Champion laughed though there was no joy in it.

"You're so naïve, Chuck. These kids are pieces of trash. They're garbage. Bob and I spend ninety percent of our time on ten percent of the kids in this school. They don't care. Their parents don't care. And frankly, Chuck, you don't care. You spend all your time with the Student Council kids, the National Honor Society kids and the jocks. You never dirty yourself with the trash Bob and I deal with."

"They're kids, Liz," Farner said quietly.

"Fuck you, Bob. Just try to tell me how much you loved working with kids like Sweeney and Goldfarb. You couldn't stand them and you know it."

"But killing them?" Bob said shaking his head. "And what about the middle school kids? We didn't have any contact with them."

"Fuck you, Farner! I was doing everyone a favor. Those brats would have been a pain in somebody's ass eventually and you know it."

"So, what was the reason, Liz? To rid the school of troublemakers?" Gobel asked.

Champion stared at a spot on the wall above the door and remained silent.

Graff had enough. He stood and took out his handcuffs and said, "Elizabeth Champion, you are under arrest on accessory to commit murder, drug trafficking and anything else I can hang on you." He went on to Mirandize her.

Captain Jack O'Brien, Graff, Eiselmann and O'Connor discussed charges, but settled on these two for now. They felt others would be added as more evidence was brought forth through search warrants.

Graff had no reservations walking her out of the office past Gobel's administrative assistant or anyone else who happened to be around. In fact, he was proud to have her lead the parade.

It was two or so weeks since the shootings at the Benevides house. The morning was clear and cold. No wind, no clouds and the sky was a bright blue. George had started a fire in the fireplace with Billy's help, so the living room was toasty warm. A John Berry Christmas CD played softly in the background.

The boys sprawled around the floor in the living room littered with torn Christmas paper and tissue and opened boxes.

Hair disheveled and dressed in a t-shirt and dark-colored plaid pajama pants, Jeremy sat on the couch taking it all in. Vicki held a mug of hot coffee as she leaned against him. Both smiled.

They followed the family tradition of opening presents from youngest to oldest. The order was Bobby, George, Brian, Brett, Randy and finally Billy, followed by Vicki and last, Jeremy before Bobby would open again.

The presents had all been opened. The last gifts were from George who had made leather and turquoise bracelets for the boys.

Bobby, who had been sitting between Brian's legs and leaning against his chest said, "What does turquoise mean again?" He held his arm and bracelet out to Brett who tied it on his right wrist.

"The *Dine'* believe turquoise protects against evil."

"You gave a necklace like the one you wear to Pete Kelliher," Brett said.

George smiled, "Yes, when I first met him."

"Bobby, tie mine on," Brian said, holding his arm across Bobby's chest.

"Mom, there is one more present for you," George said. "It's from Brett and Bobby and me."

She smiled, sat up straighter and said, "You boys have given me too much already."

Brett handed her a thin square box wrapped in shiny silver paper. As he gave it to her, he kissed her.

She ran her finger under the edge lifting the paper away from the tape and tearing it where it wouldn't lift easily. She opened the box, lifted the cotton and gasped.

"This is beautiful!" She lifted up a silver necklace with sterling silver rectangles on a thin silver chain. There were bits of turquoise inlaid in the silver rectangles. "Where did you find this?"

"I asked Rebecca to ask Elizabeth Falling Water to make it for you," George answered.

"It's one of a kind, Mom," Bobby said.

"And matching earrings! Jeremy, can you clip this?" she asked, lifting up her long hair.

Jeremy did the honors and she asked, "How does it look?"

"Pretty, Mom!" Billy said and the boys nodded.

"Well, it so happens that we have one more gift or two for each of you," Jeremy said. He picked up some white envelopes off of the end table next to him and called out the boys' names, telling them they had to open them all at the same time.

"Okay, one, two, three," Billy said and the boys opened the envelopes.

Inside was a typed sheet of paper in a sort of certificate style announcing that each boy was headed to a summer athletic camp. Each boy, with the exception of George was going to a basketball camp and a football camp. George was going to a running and speed camp. Instead of going to a football camp, Brian was going to a soccer camp.

"This is so cool!" Brian exclaimed.

Randy cleared his throat and said, "Well we have a present for you, too."

"You have to wait here and you can't come looking for us?" Billy said laughing.

"Can I go into the kitchen and get another cup of coffee?" Vicki asked.

"And can I run to the bathroom?" Jeremy asked.

"Yes, but come back here and wait for us," Brett said.

The boys jumped up and ran up the stairs laughing all the way.

As Jeremy and Vicki walked into the kitchen, Vicki asked, "Any idea what they have in mind?"

"Not a clue," Jeremy said as he disappeared into the hallway bathroom.

About ten minutes later Billy yelled down the stairs, "Are you in the living room?"

"Yes," Jeremy yelled back.

"Okay, stay there," Brian said with a laugh. And Jeremy and Vicki heard him say a little quieter, "I feel so stupid."

They exchanged a questioning look, a smile and a shrug and heard footsteps and some more giggles and a 'Shhhhh'.

Randy and Bobby strummed their acoustic guitars and the boys sang, "Aruba, Jamaica, oh I want to take ya; Bermuda, Bahama, come on pretty mama; Key Largo, Montego; baby why don't we go; Jamaica . . ."

There was no mistaking the Beach Boys song, *Kokomo*. The boys danced their way into the living room wearing Hawaiian shirts, shorts, sandals or flip-flops and sun glasses. The harmony wasn't too bad either, aside from the giggles. The dancing, however, was pretty bad.

At the end of the song, George and Brian presented Jeremy and Vicki with a thick envelope each and when the song ended, the other boys landed on their knees with their arms spread out.

Jeremy and Vicki laughed and applauded.

"Pretty good, huh?" Billy said.

"It was something, all right," Jeremy laughed.

"Open them," Brett said.

"Okay, okay," Vicki said. She nudged Jeremy and said, "Together?"

"Yup. One, two, go."

They opened their envelopes and unfolded the paperwork.

"Read it!" Bobby urged.

Jeremy frowned and said, "Is this serious?"

"Read it! Read it! Read it!" Billy started the chant and the other boys joined him.

Vicki gasped and stared at Jeremy.

"We're going to the Bahamas!" Billy said excitedly because he couldn't contain himself any longer.

"For seven days," Bobby added.

"To an all-inclusive resort!" Billy said.

"We leave the day after Bri gets done at his soccer showcase," Brett said.

"How did . . .?" Jeremy asked.

"Uncle Jeff helped," Randy said.

"Oh my gosh!" Vicki said quietly. "This must have cost a fortune."

"We paid for all of it," Billy said. "All of us chipped in."

"Jeff let us use some of our trust money," Randy said.

"After all the crap that happened in the last year, we thought we could use a real vacation," Brett said.

"It was Randy's idea," Bobby said.

The boys exchanged high fives and gave Jeremy and Vicki hugs and kisses.

"This has to be one of the best Christmas' ever," Brian said. "*Ever!*"

"If I can have everyone's attention for a minute," Jeremy said, "I have one more present I'd like to give."

He put his hand into his pocket and said, "Guys, I can't tell you how happy you have made me. A couple of years ago, I wanted to adopt a son and Randy came along. Then Billy and George. That same summer, Brett and Bobby, though I haven't actually adopted you two. A couple of weeks ago, Brian, though I haven't adopted you yet either."

"In February," Brian said.

"Right, in February."

He turned towards Vicki and said, "But as happy as I am, I've been missing an important part. You came into my life. You are my best friend and I can't imagine not being with you."

Jeremy took his hand out of his pocket and in it was a small black velvet case. He knelt down in front of Vicki.

"Vicki McGovern, I would like very much if you would marry me."

Tears sprung to Bobby's and Brett's eyes. Brian slung an arm around Bobby's shoulders and Randy hugged Brett and George.

Vicki smiled at Jeremy and said, "Yes."

View other Black Rose Writing titles at and use promo code **PRINT** to receive a **20% discount** when purchasing.

BLACK✿ROSE
writing™

CPSIA information can be obtained
at www.ICGtesting.com
Printed in the USA
FSHW011105270421
80870FS